LIFEFORMED™

HEARTS AND MINDS

WRITTEN BY
MATT MAIR LOWERY

ART AND LETTERING BY
CASSIE ANDERSON

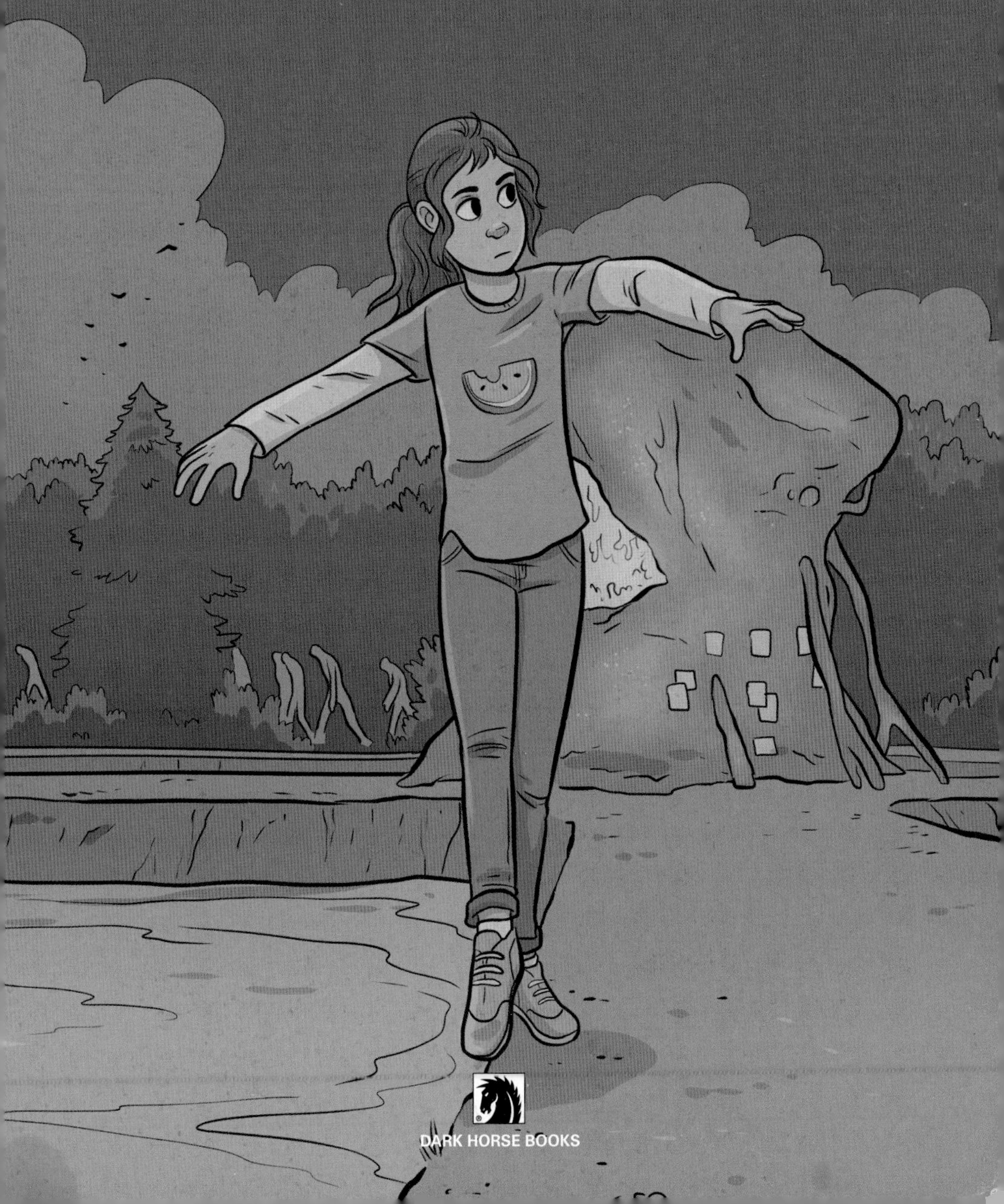

DARK HORSE BOOKS

For Mom and Dad. I love you more than all the
spaceships and books I drew. –CASSIE

For Addy and Eliza and their indomitable wills.
Always fight back. –DAD/MATT

PRESIDENT AND PUBLISHER **MIKE RICHARDSON**

EDITOR **RACHEL ROBERTS**   ASSISTANT EDITOR **JENNY BLENK**

DESIGNER **BRENNAN THOME**   DIGITAL ART TECHNICIAN **JOSIE CHRISTENSEN**

Neil Hankerson, Executive Vice President · Tom Weddle, Chief Financial Officer · Randy Stradley, Vice President of Publishing · Nick McWhorter, Chief Business Development Officer · Dale LaFountain, Chief Information Officer · Matt Parkinson, Vice President of Marketing · Cara Niece, Vice President of Production and Scheduling · Mark Bernardi, Vice President of Book Trade and Digital Sales · Ken Lizzi, General Counsel · Dave Marshall, Editor in Chief · Davey Estrada, Editorial Director · Chris Warner, Senior Books Editor · Cary Grazzini, Director of Specialty Projects · Lia Ribacchi, Art Director · Vanessa Todd-Holmes, Director of Print Purchasing · Matt Dryer, Director of Digital Art and Prepress · Michael Gombos, Senior Director of International Publishing and Licensing · Kari Yadro, Director of Custom Programs · Kari Torson, Director of International Licensing · Sean Brice, Director of Trade Sales

Sensitivity Review: Sabeeha Rehman, author of
Threading My Prayer Rug: One Woman's Journey from Pakistani Muslim to American Muslim.

Published by Dark Horse Books
A division of Dark Horse Comics LLC
10956 SE Main Street
Milwaukie, OR 97222

First edition: September 2019
ISBN 978-1-50670-937-6

10 9 8 7 6 5 4 3 2 1
Printed in China

Comic Shop Locator Service:
ComicShopLocator.com

Library of Congress Cataloging-in-Publication Data

Names: Mair Lowery, Matt, writer. | Anderson, Cassie, artist, letterer.
Title: Lifeformed : Hearts and minds / written by Matt Mair Lowery ; art and lettering by Cassie Anderson.
Other titles: Hearts and minds
Description: First edition. | Milwaukie, OR : Dark Horse Books, 2019. | Series: Lifeformed ; Volume 2 | Summary: "Cleo, orphaned in the wake of an alien invasion, left behind the life she knew to fight for the future of Earth. Now she and Alex, the shapeshifting rebel alien posing as her father, make a fearsome team in a guerrilla war against the invaders."-- Provided by publisher.
Identifiers: LCCN 2019016851 | ISBN 9781506709376 (paperback)
Subjects: LCSH: Graphic novels. | CYAC: Graphic novels. | Extraterrestrial beings--Fiction. | Survival--Fiction.
Classification: LCC PZ7.7.M3327 Lif 2019 | DDC 741.5/973--dc23
LC record available at https://lccn.loc.gov/2019016851

"Spectacular Views" by Jenny Lewis and Blake Sennett from Rilo Kiley's *The Execution of All Things* (Saddle Creek, 2002). Lyrics used by permission.

ONE

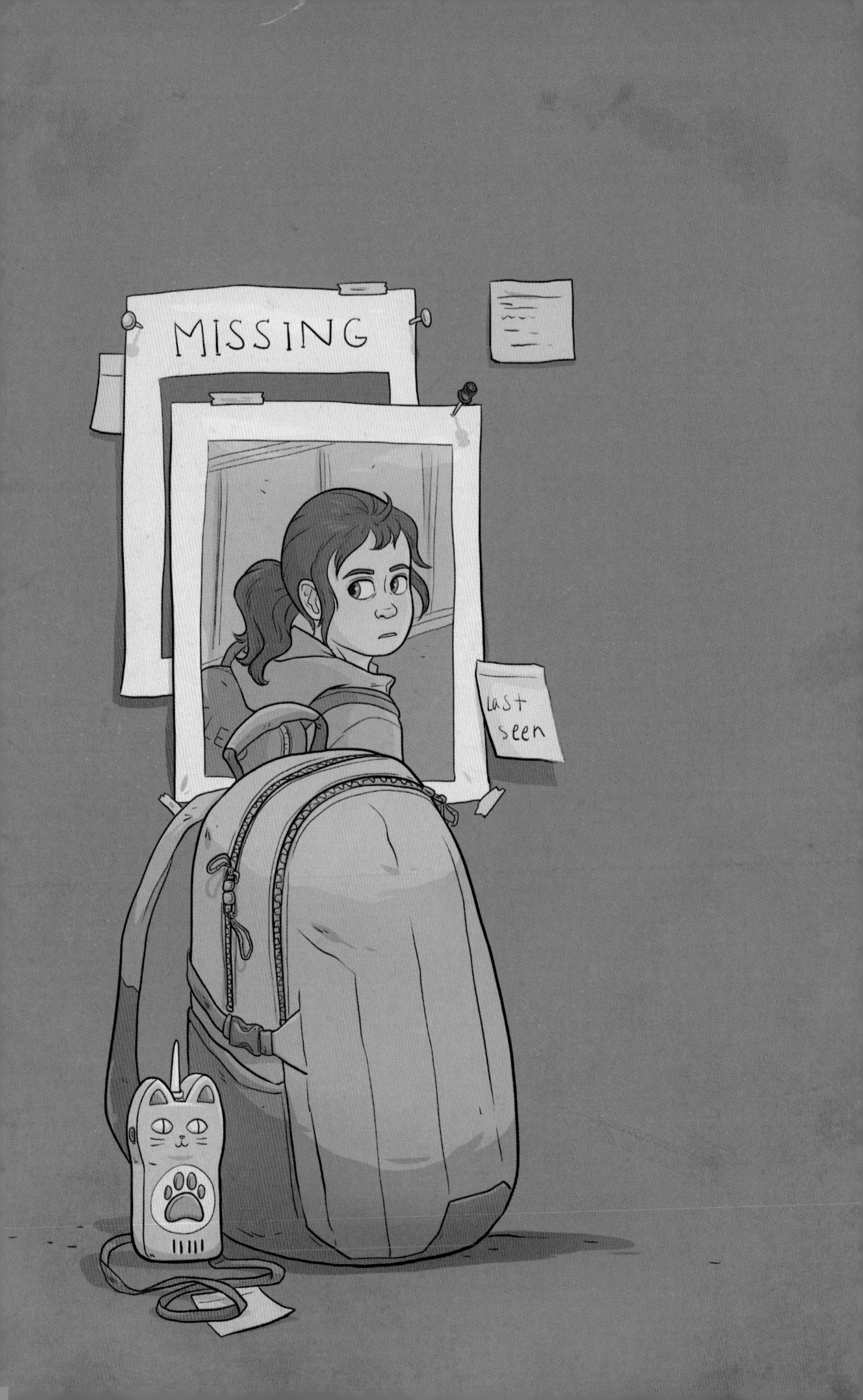
MISSING
last seen

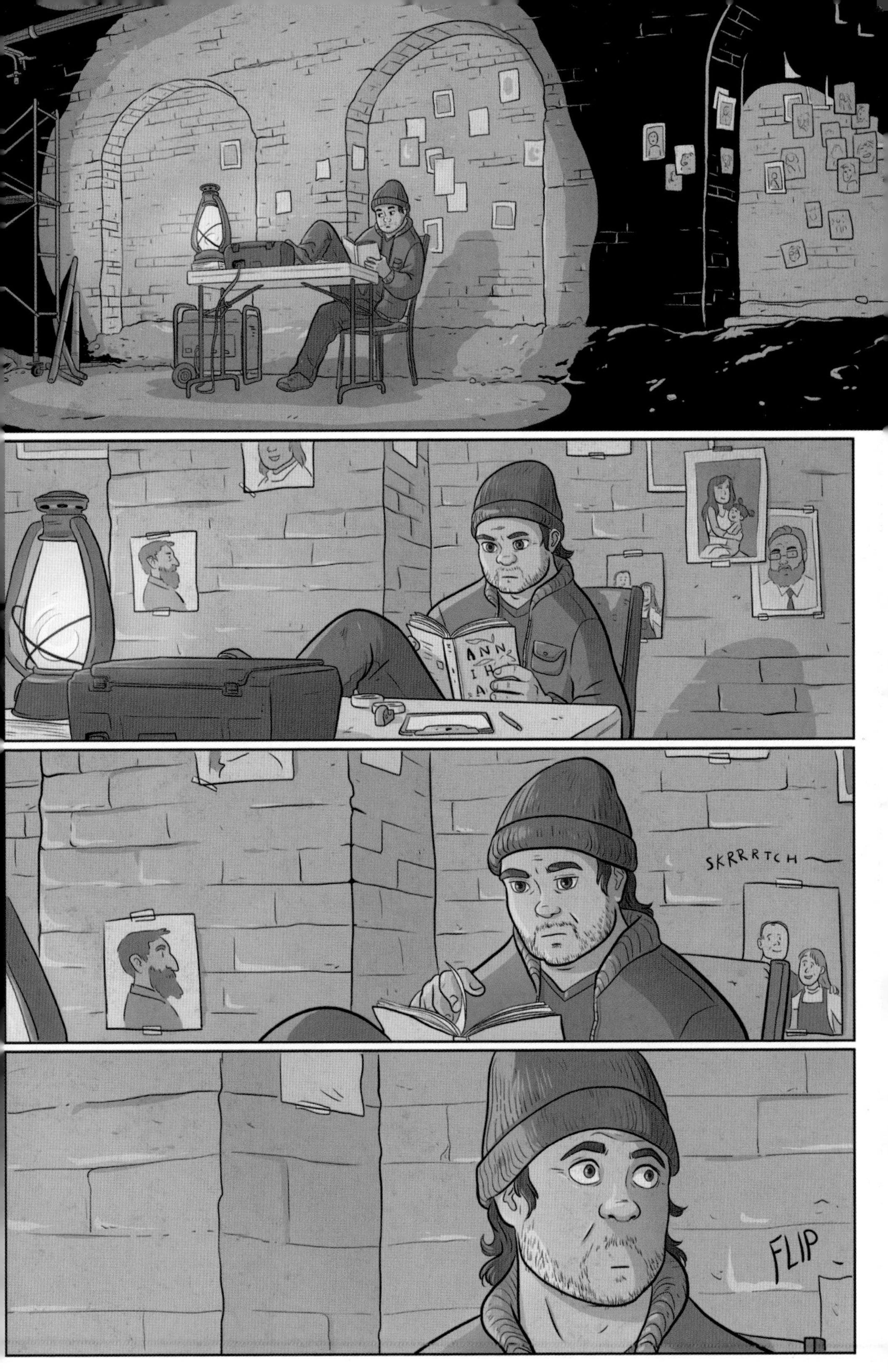

SKRRRTCH
FLIP

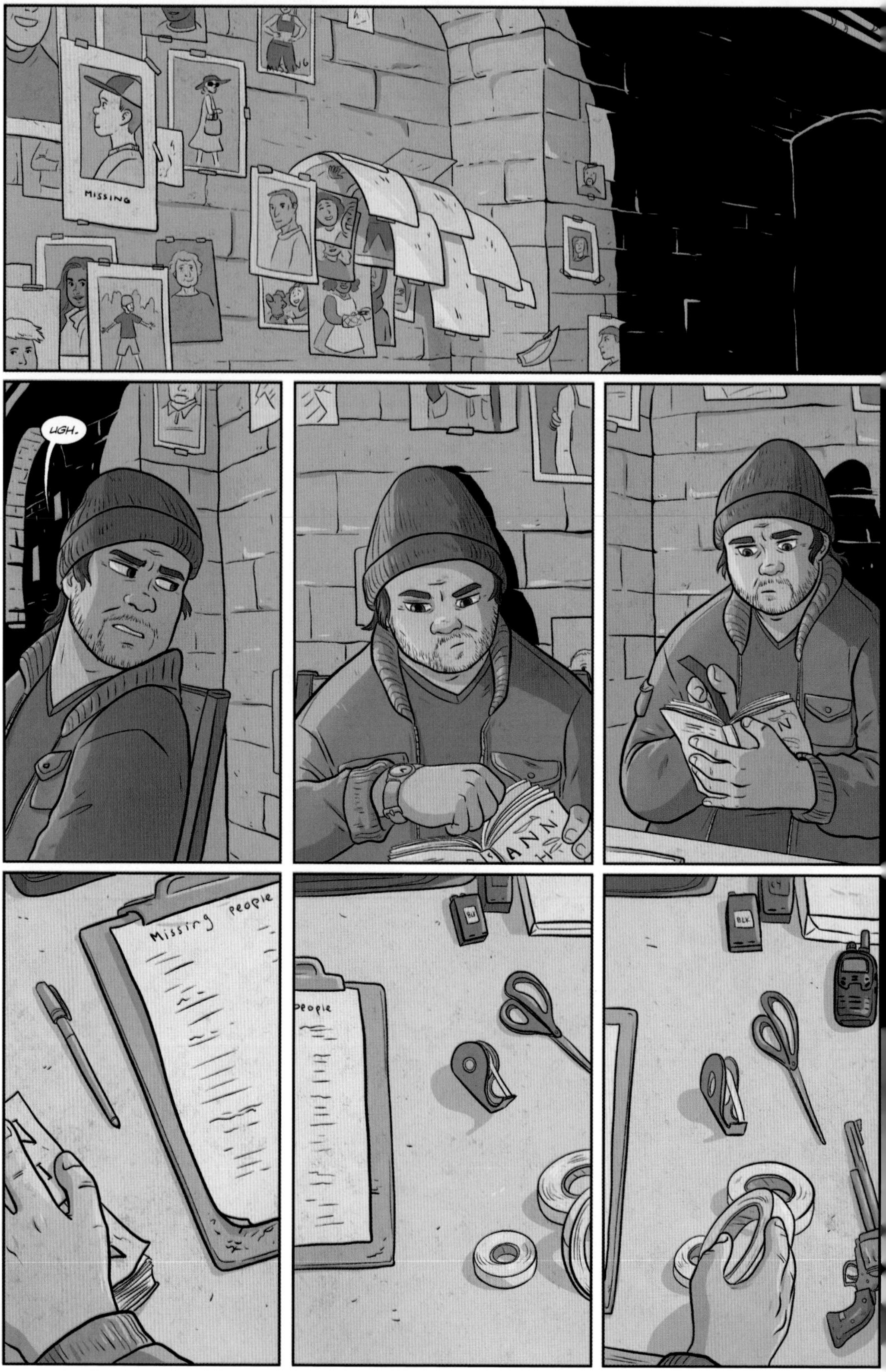
MISSING
UGH.
Missing people
people
BLK

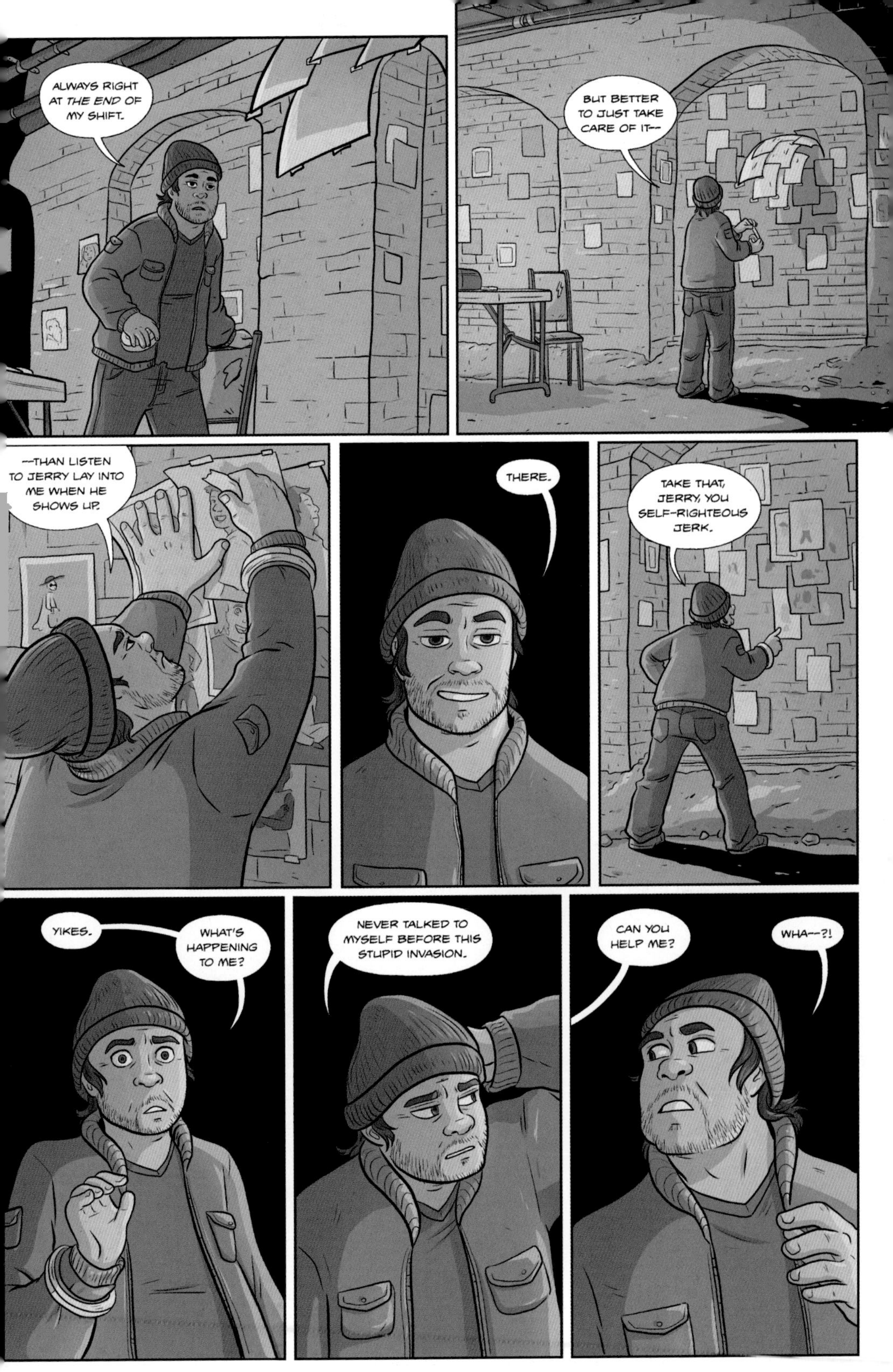
ALWAYS RIGHT AT *THE END* OF MY SHIFT.
BUT BETTER TO JUST TAKE CARE OF IT--
--THAN LISTEN TO JERRY LAY INTO ME WHEN HE SHOWS UP.
THERE.
TAKE THAT, JERRY, YOU SELF-RIGHTEOUS JERK.
YIKES.
WHAT'S HAPPENING TO ME?
NEVER TALKED TO MYSELF BEFORE THIS STUPID INVASION.
CAN YOU HELP ME?
WHA--?!

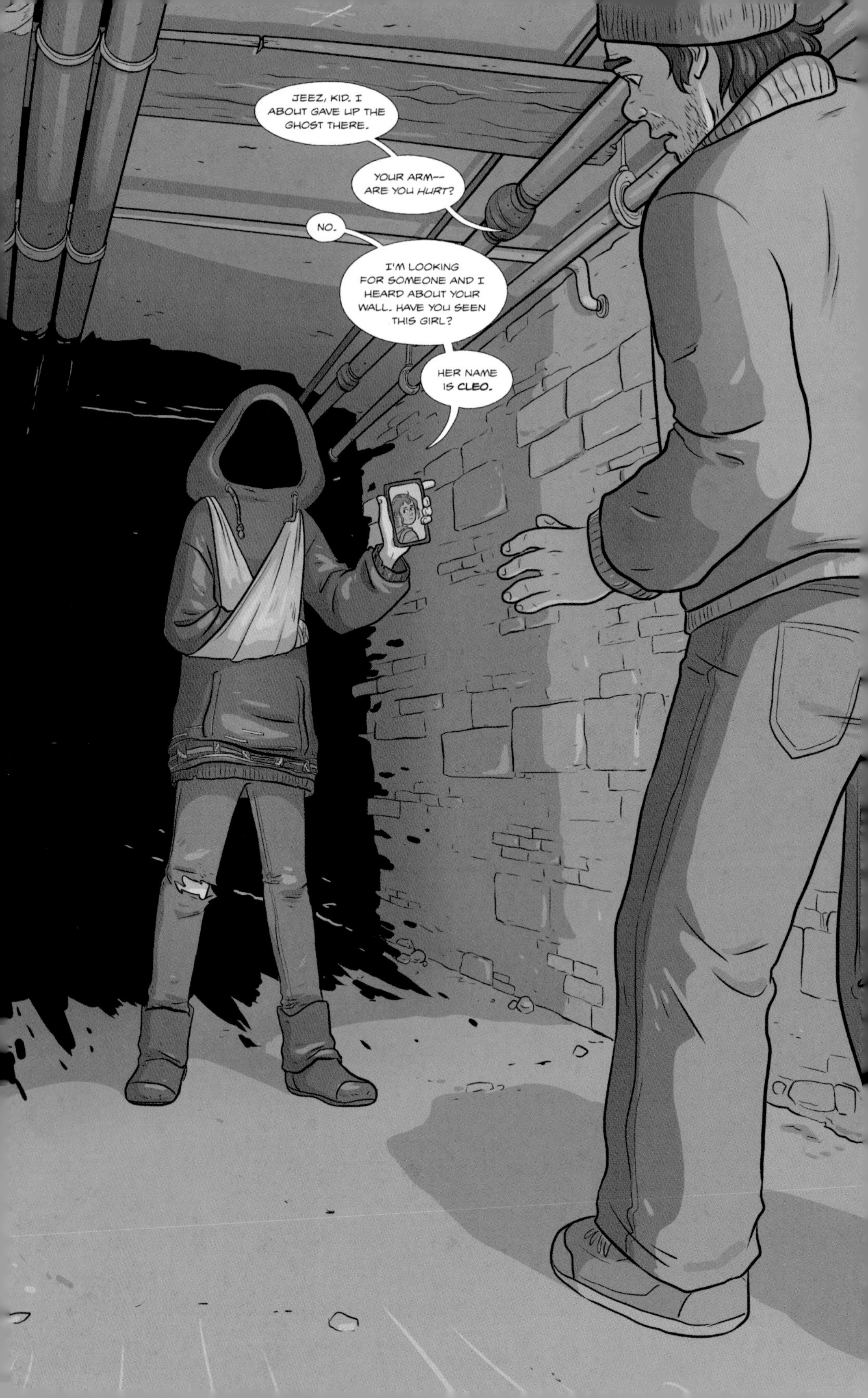
JEEZ, KID. I ABOUT GAVE UP THE GHOST THERE.
YOUR ARM--ARE YOU *HURT*?
NO.
I'M LOOKING FOR SOMEONE AND I HEARD ABOUT YOUR WALL. HAVE YOU SEEN THIS GIRL?
HER NAME IS **CLEO**.

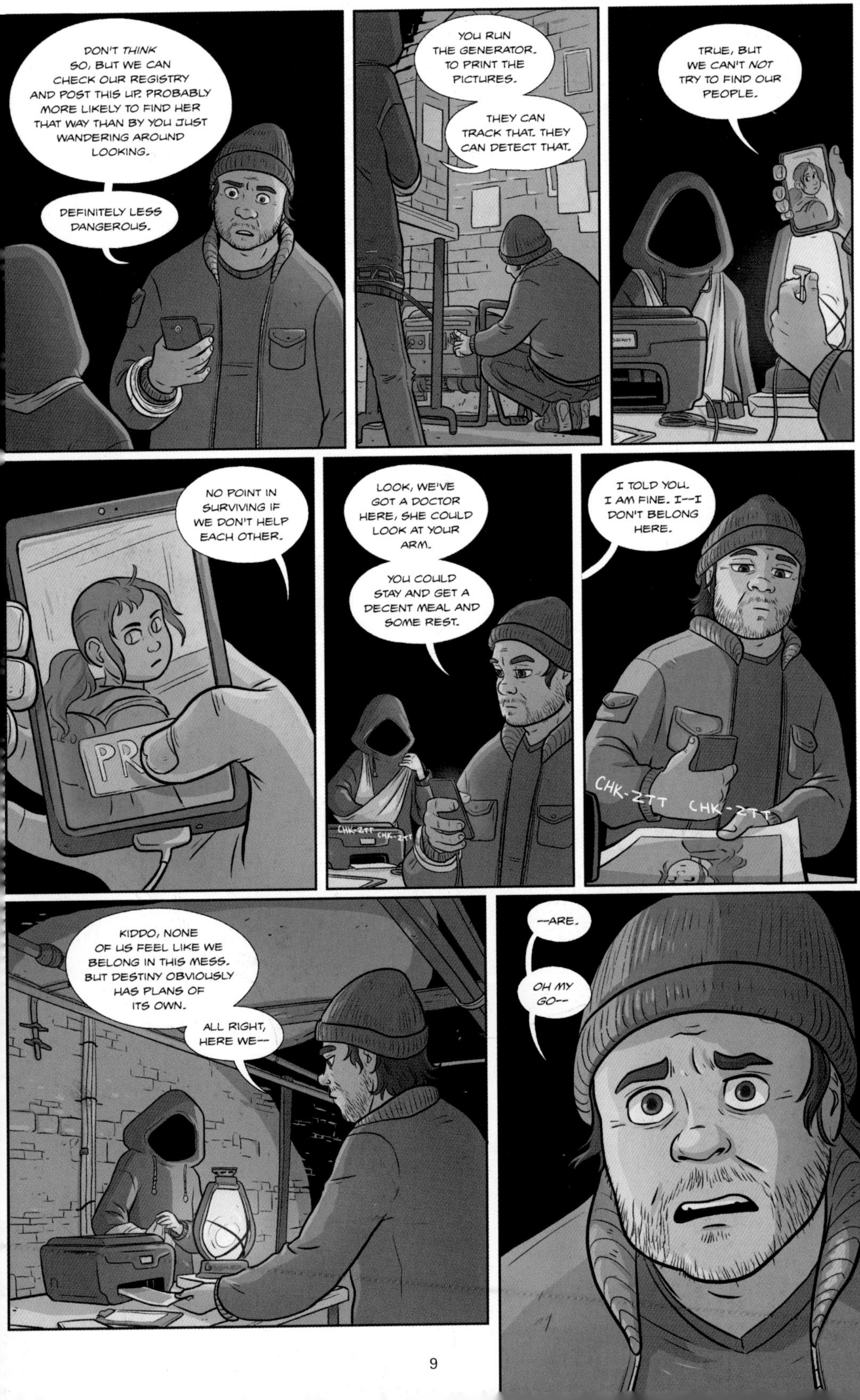
DON'T *THINK* SO, BUT WE CAN CHECK OUR REGISTRY AND POST THIS UP. PROBABLY MORE LIKELY TO FIND HER THAT WAY THAN BY YOU JUST WANDERING AROUND LOOKING.
DEFINITELY LESS DANGEROUS.
YOU RUN THE GENERATOR TO PRINT THE PICTURES.
THEY CAN TRACK THAT. THEY CAN DETECT THAT.
TRUE, BUT WE CAN'T *NOT* TRY TO FIND OUR PEOPLE.
NO POINT IN SURVIVING IF WE DON'T HELP EACH OTHER.
LOOK, WE'VE GOT A DOCTOR HERE, SHE COULD LOOK AT YOUR ARM.
YOU COULD STAY AND GET A DECENT MEAL AND SOME REST.
CHK-ZTT CHK-ZTT
I TOLD YOU. I AM FINE. I--I DON'T BELONG HERE.
CHK-ZTT CHK-ZTT
KIDDO, NONE OF US FEEL LIKE WE BELONG IN THIS MESS. BUT DESTINY OBVIOUSLY HAS PLANS OF ITS OWN.
ALL RIGHT, HERE WE--
--ARE.
OH MY GO--

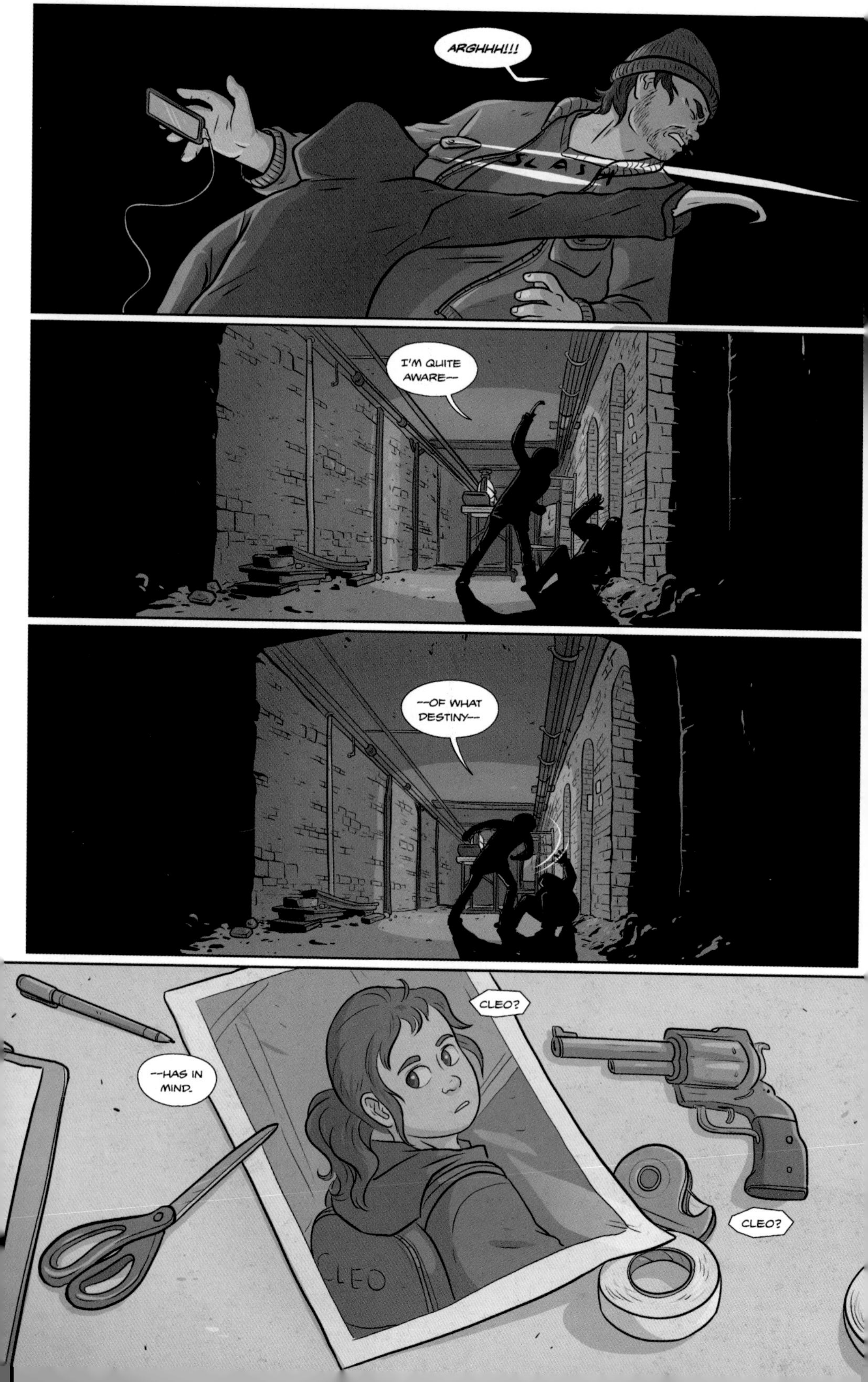
ARGHHH!!!
SLASH
I'M QUITE AWARE--
--OF WHAT DESTINY--
CLEO?
--HAS IN MIND.
CLEO?
CLEO

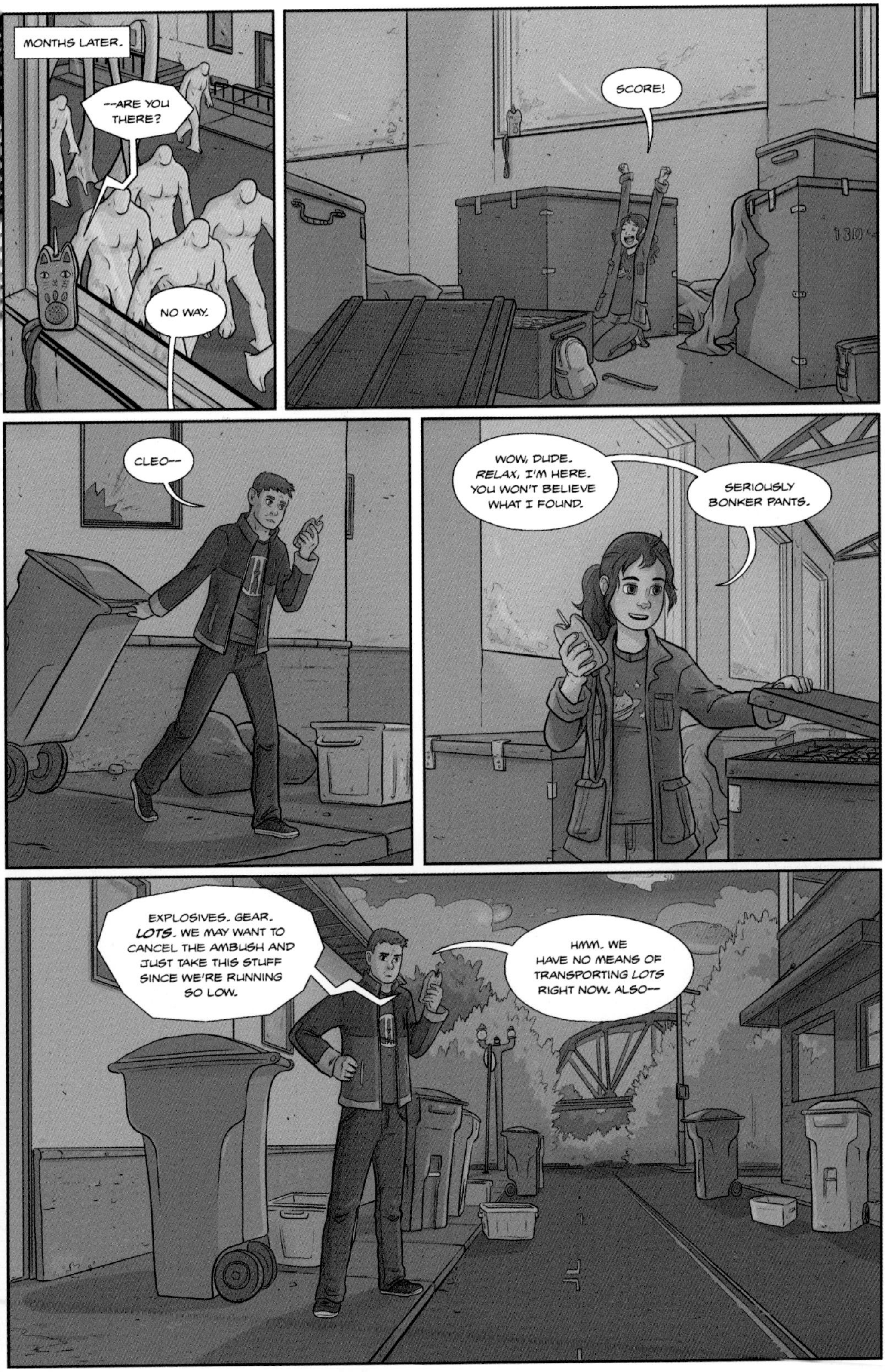
MONTHS LATER.
--ARE YOU THERE?
NO WAY.
SCORE!
CLEO--
WOW, DUDE. *RELAX*, I'M HERE. YOU WON'T BELIEVE WHAT I FOUND.
SERIOUSLY BONKER PANTS.
EXPLOSIVES. GEAR. ***LOTS***. WE MAY WANT TO CANCEL THE AMBUSH AND JUST TAKE THIS STUFF SINCE WE'RE RUNNING SO LOW.
HMM. WE HAVE NO MEANS OF TRANSPORTING *LOTS* RIGHT NOW. ALSO--

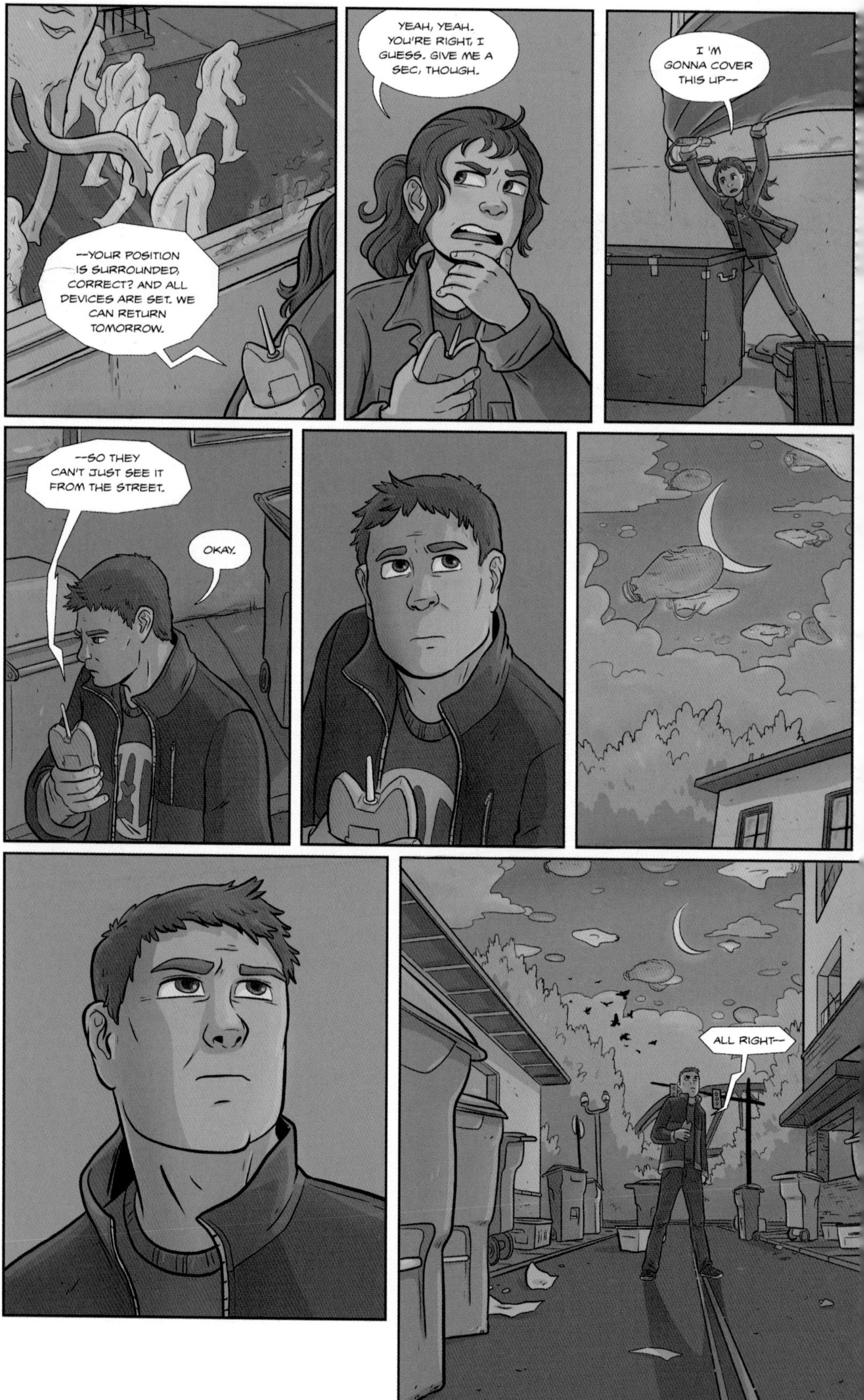
--YOUR POSITION IS SURROUNDED, CORRECT? AND ALL DEVICES ARE SET. WE CAN RETURN TOMORROW.
YEAH, YEAH. YOU'RE RIGHT, I GUESS. GIVE ME A SEC, THOUGH.
I'M GONNA COVER THIS UP--
--SO THEY CAN'T JUST SEE IT FROM THE STREET.
OKAY.
ALL RIGHT--

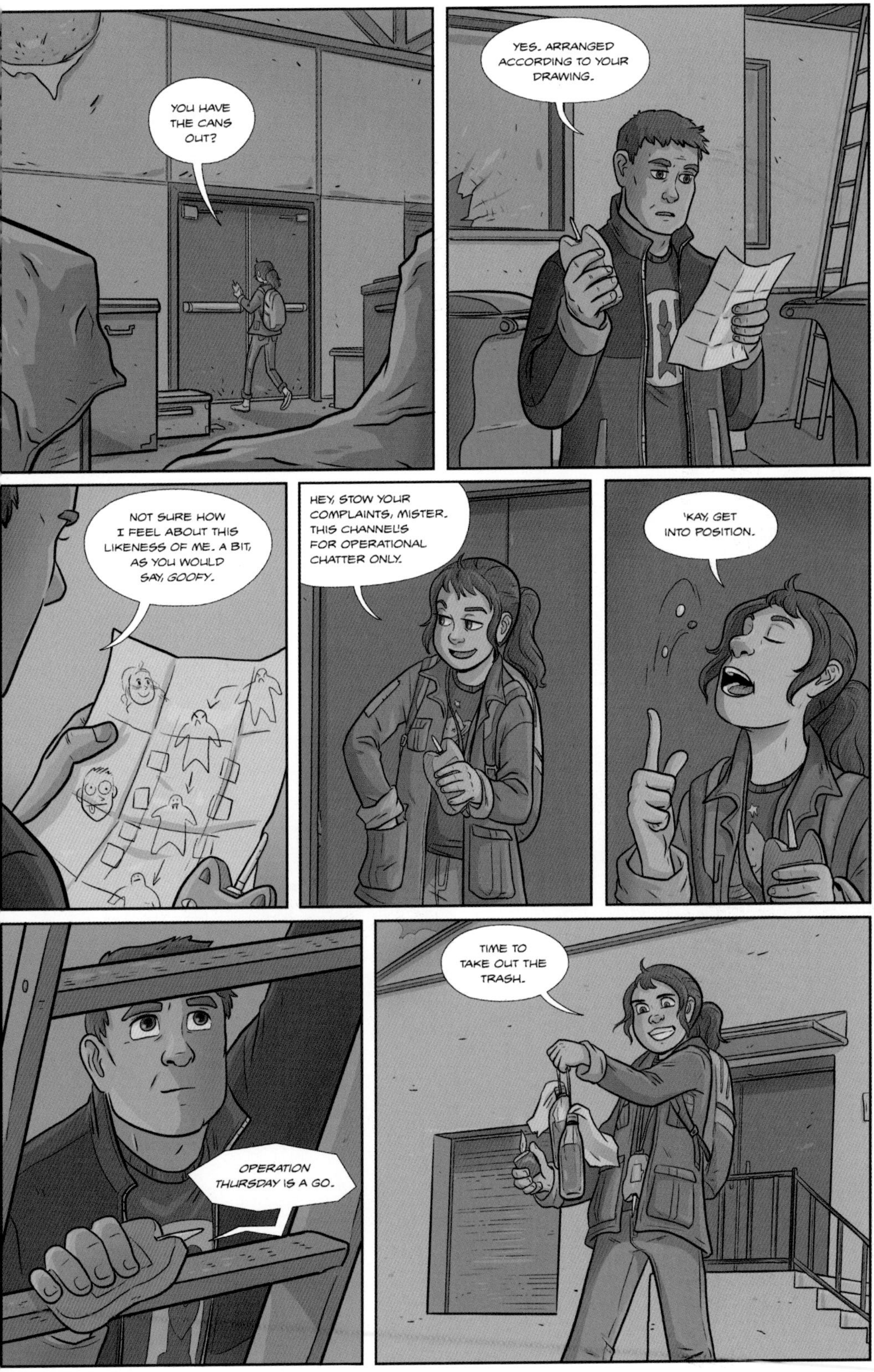
YOU HAVE THE CANS OUT?
YES. ARRANGED ACCORDING TO YOUR DRAWING.
NOT SURE HOW I FEEL ABOUT THIS LIKENESS OF ME. A BIT, AS YOU WOULD SAY, *GOOFY*.
HEY, STOW YOUR COMPLAINTS, MISTER. THIS CHANNEL'S FOR OPERATIONAL CHATTER ONLY.
'KAY, GET INTO POSITION.
OPERATION THURSDAY IS A GO.
TIME TO TAKE OUT THE TRASH.

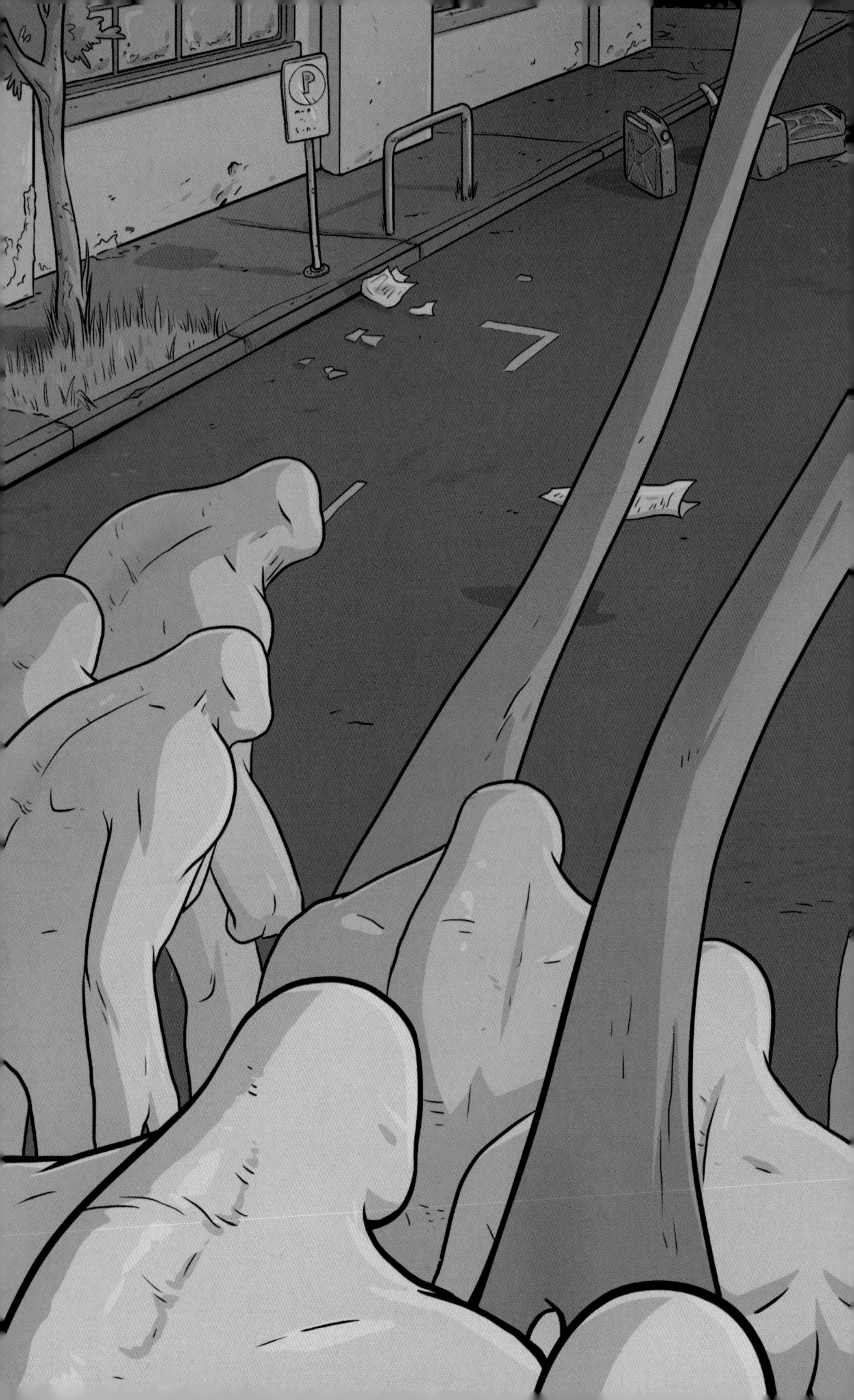

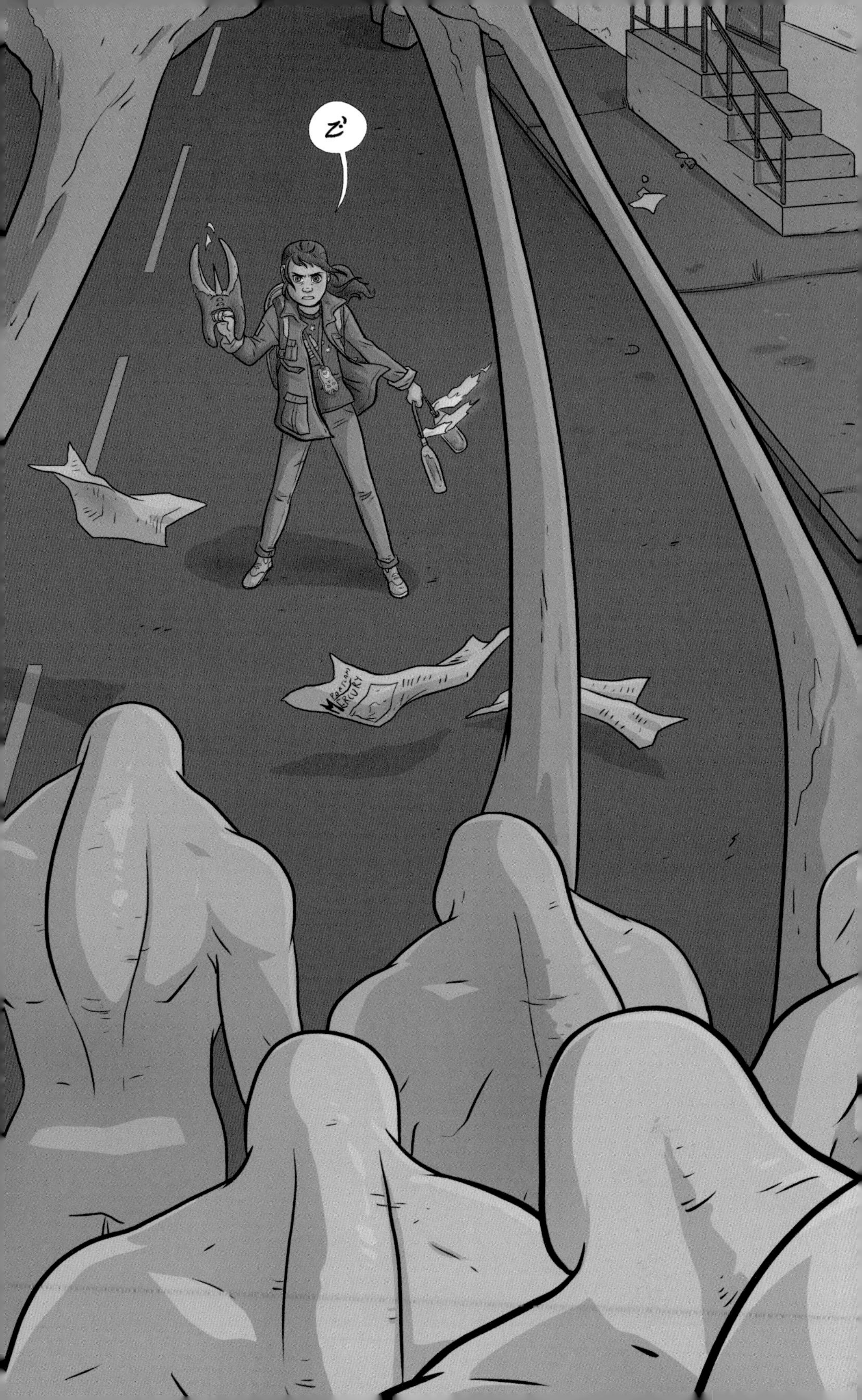
Portland Mercury

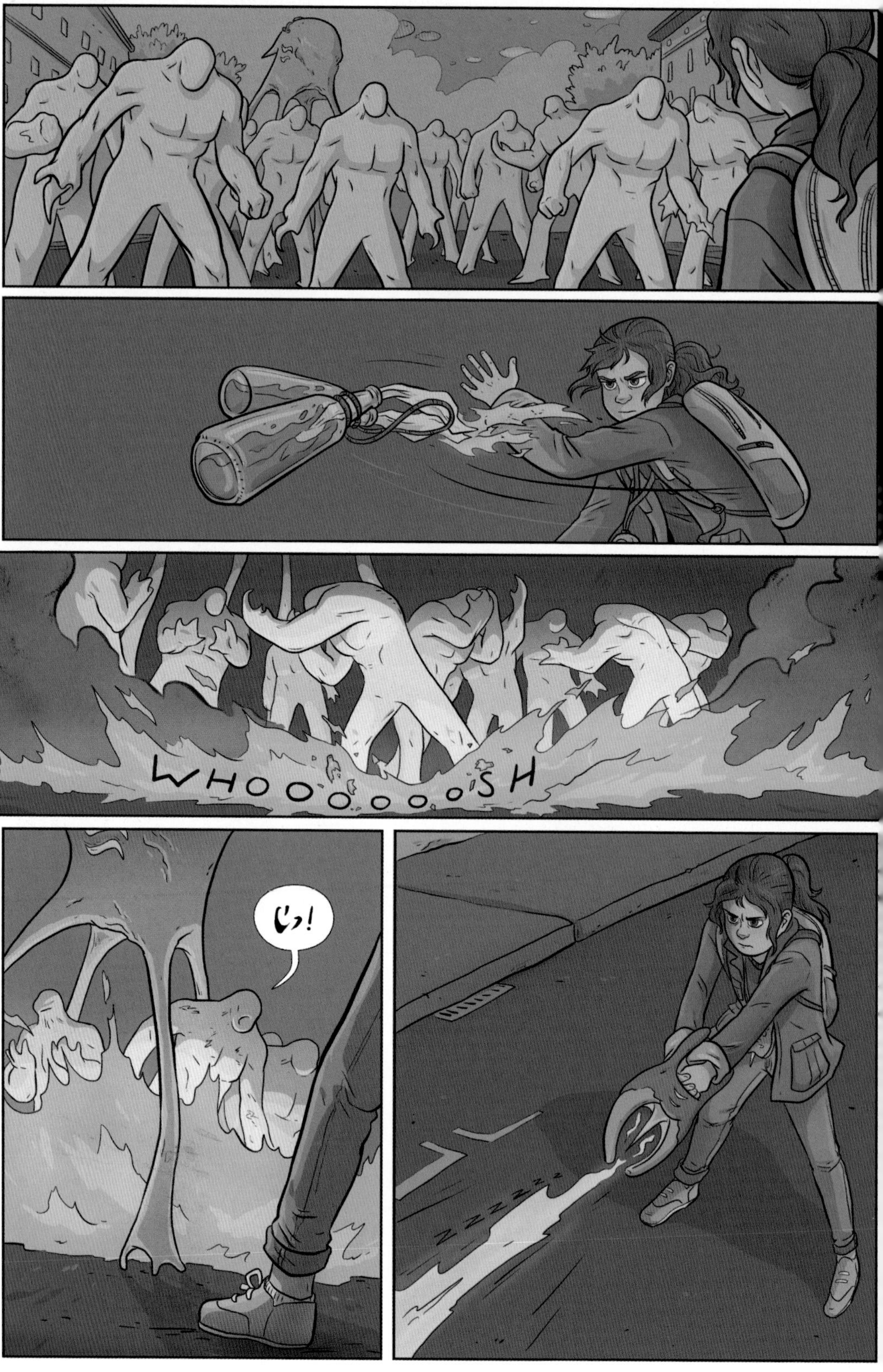
WHOOOOOOOSH

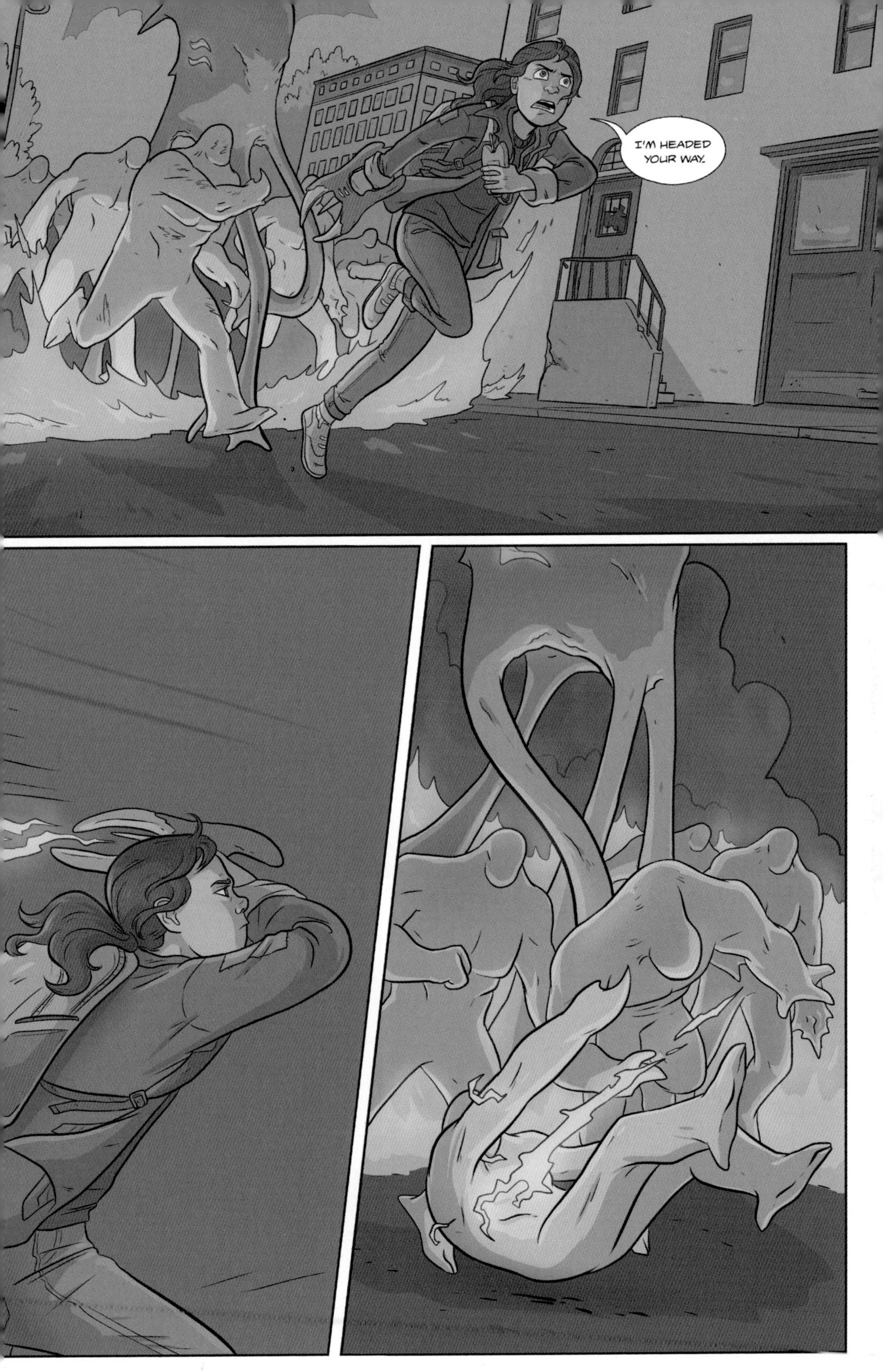
I'M HEADED YOUR WAY.

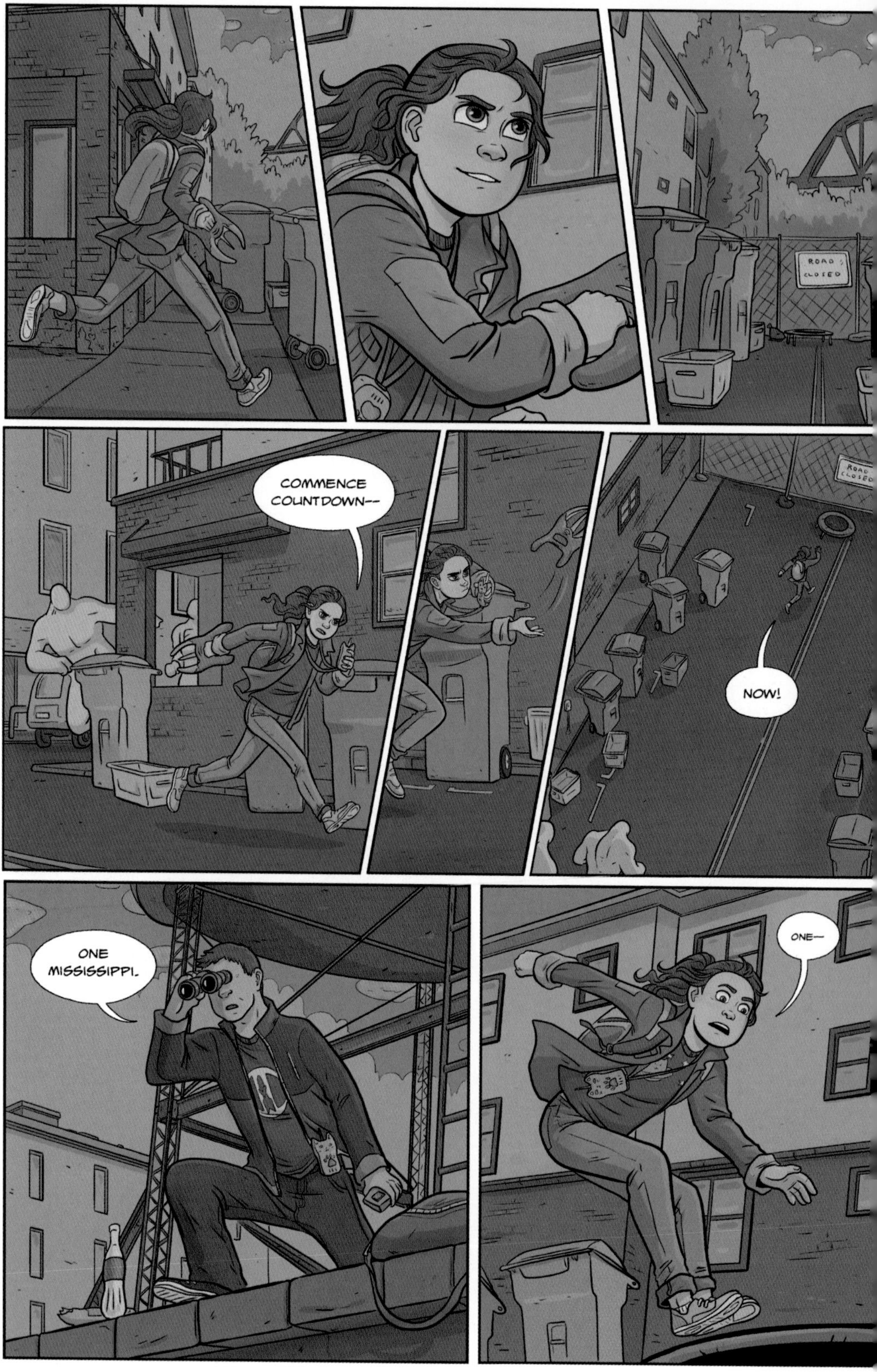
ROAD CLOSED
COMMENCE COUNTDOWN--
ROAD CLOSED
NOW!
ONE MISSISSIPPI.
ONE--

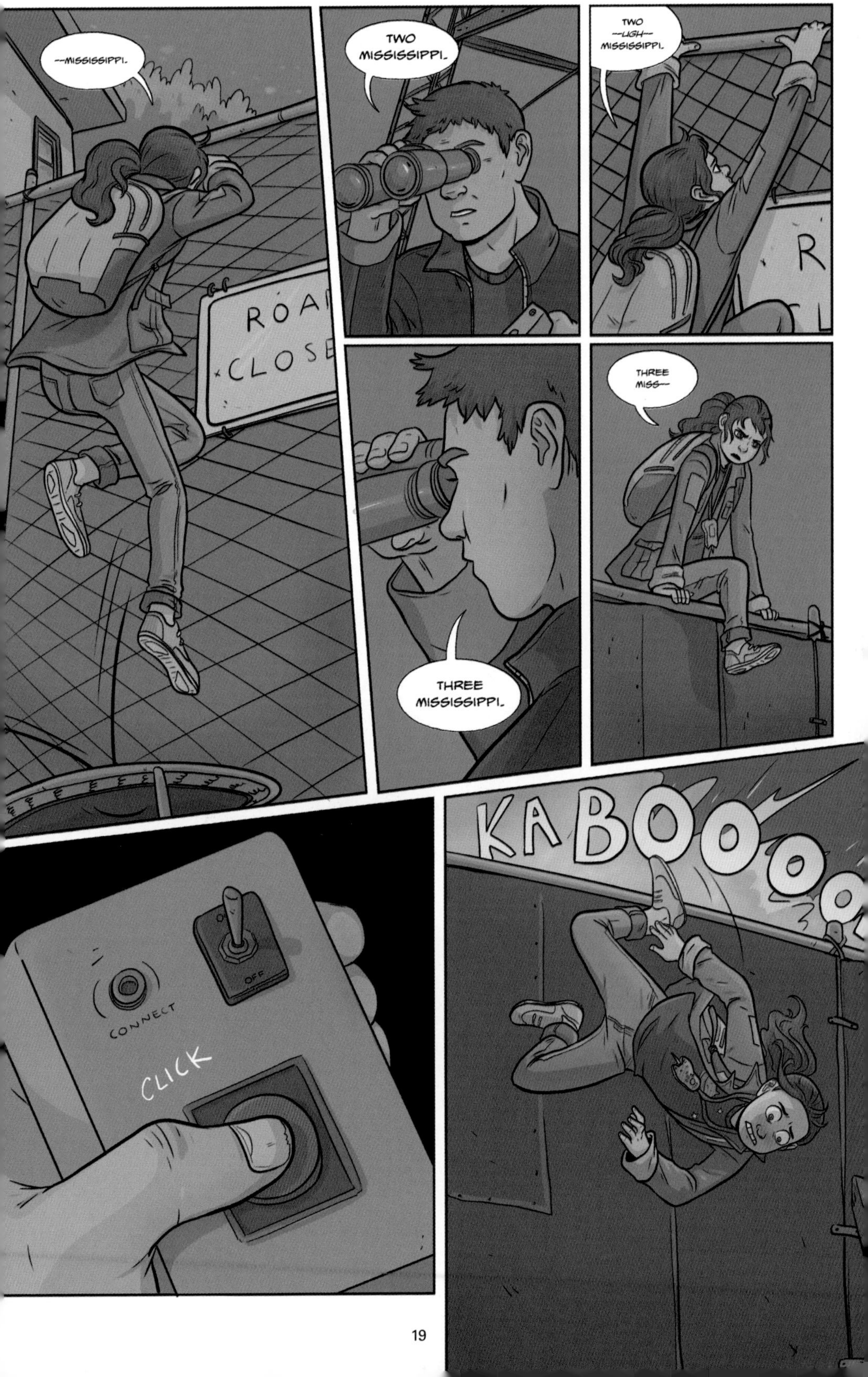
--MISSISSIPPI.
TWO MISSISSIPPI.
TWO --UGH-- MISSISSIPPI.
THREE MISSISSIPPI.
THREE MISS--
CONNECT
OFF
CLICK
KABOOOO

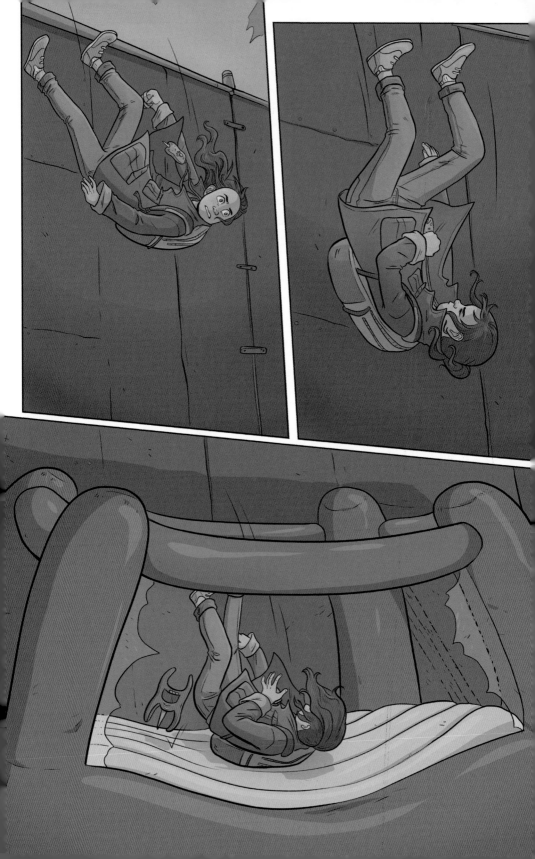

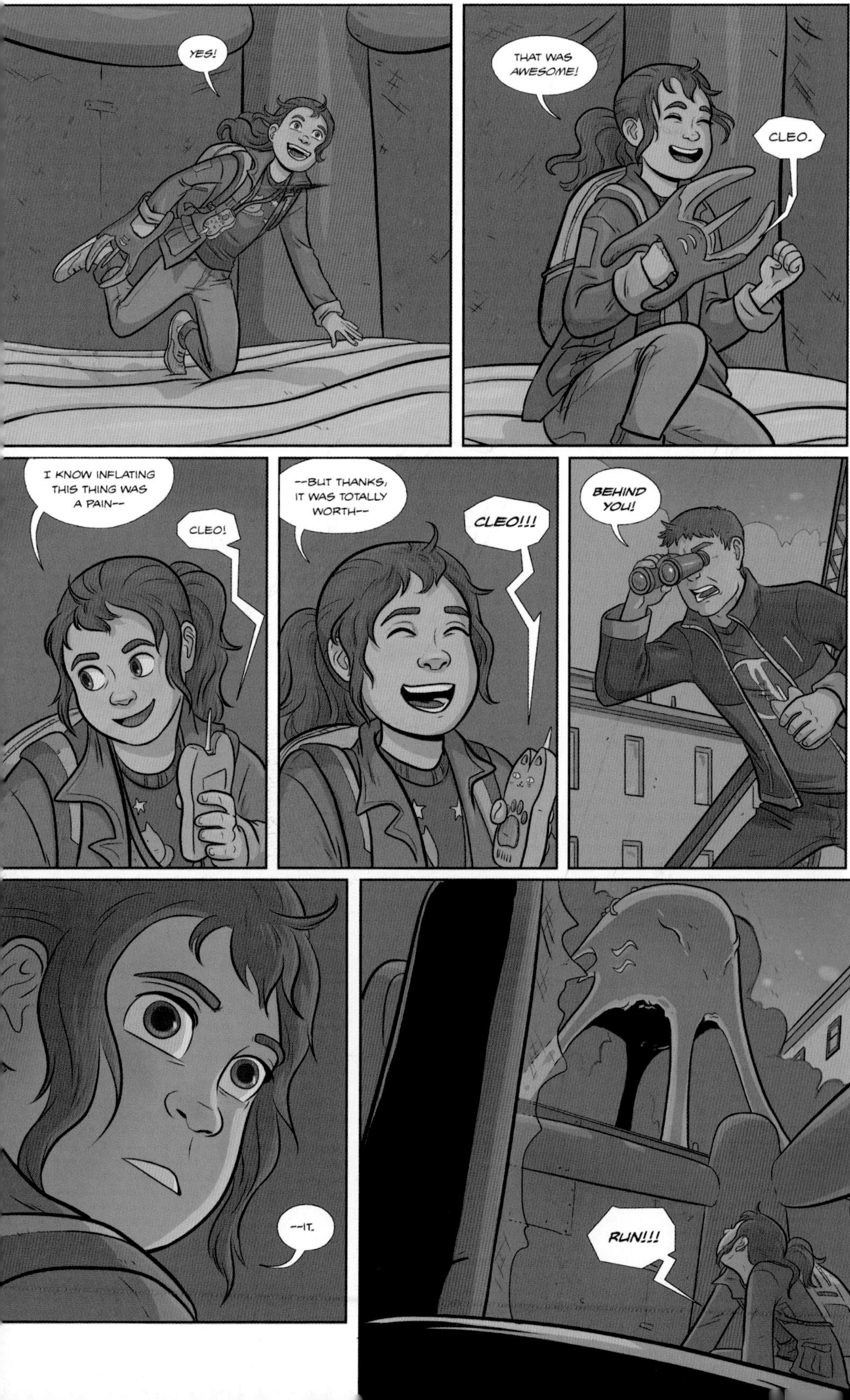
YES!
THAT WAS AWESOME!
CLEO.
I KNOW INFLATING THIS THING WAS A PAIN--
CLEO!
--BUT THANKS, IT WAS TOTALLY WORTH--
CLEO!!!
BEHIND YOU!
--IT.
RUN!!!

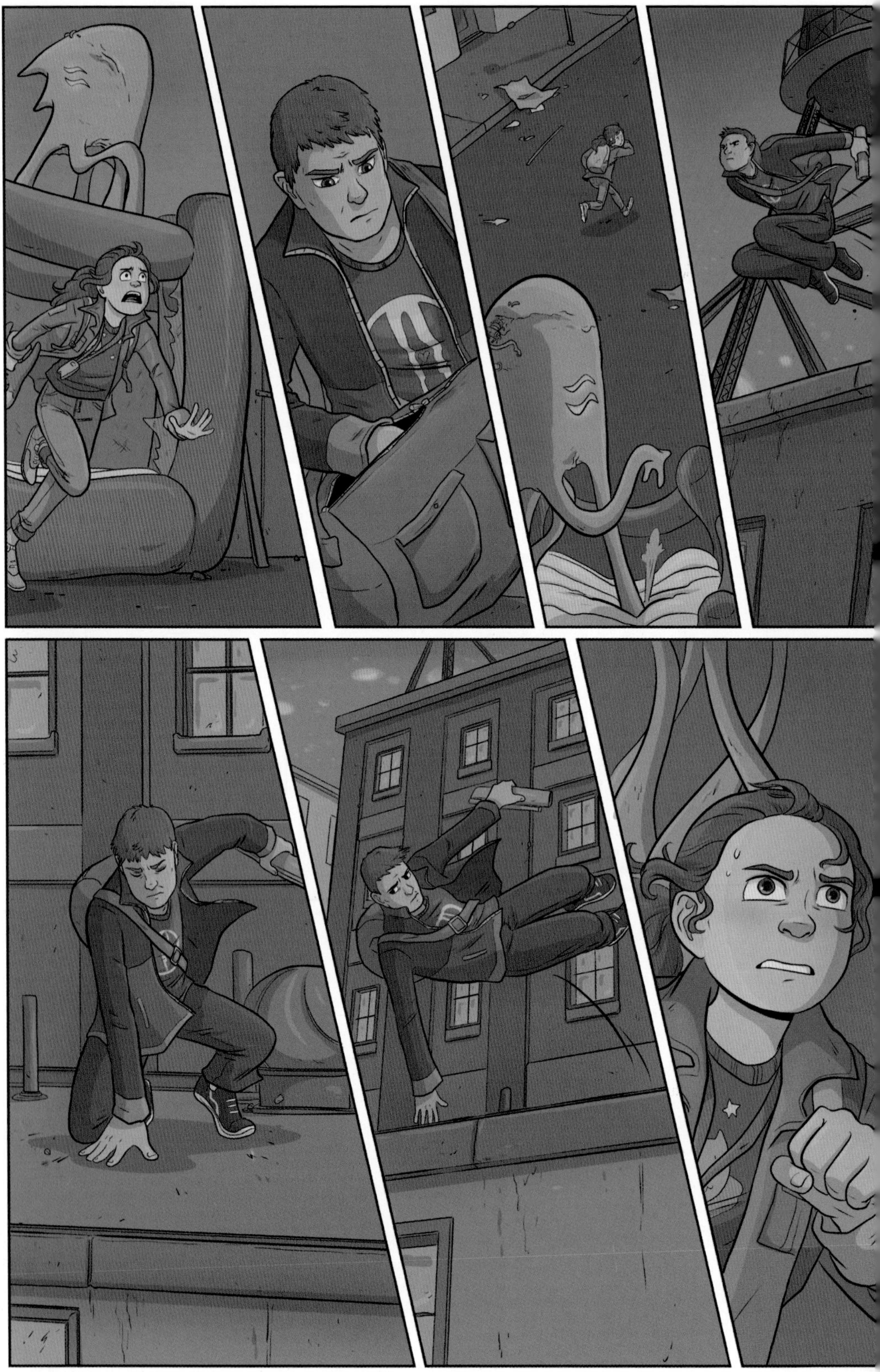

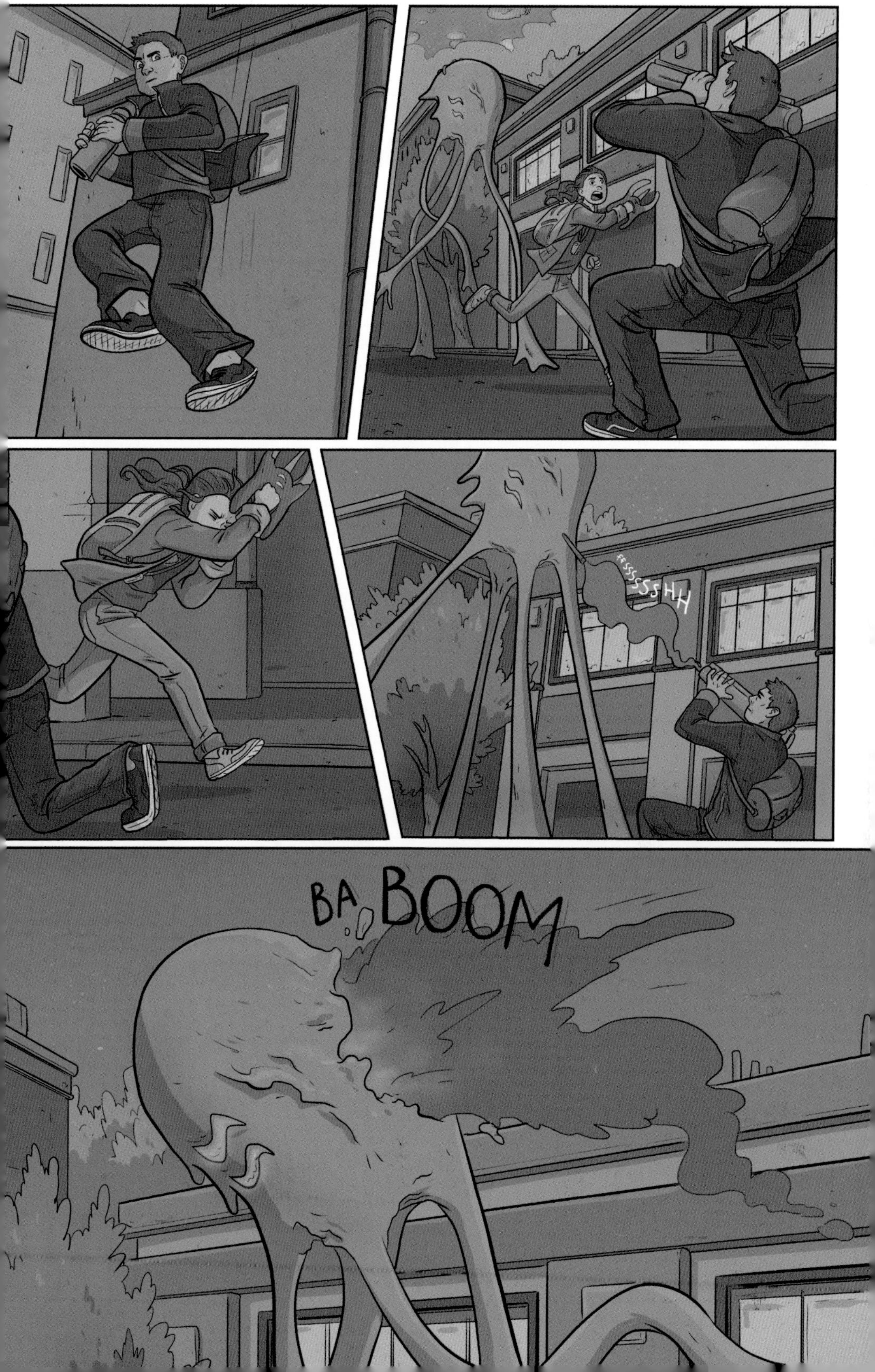
FRSSSSSSHH
BA-BOOM

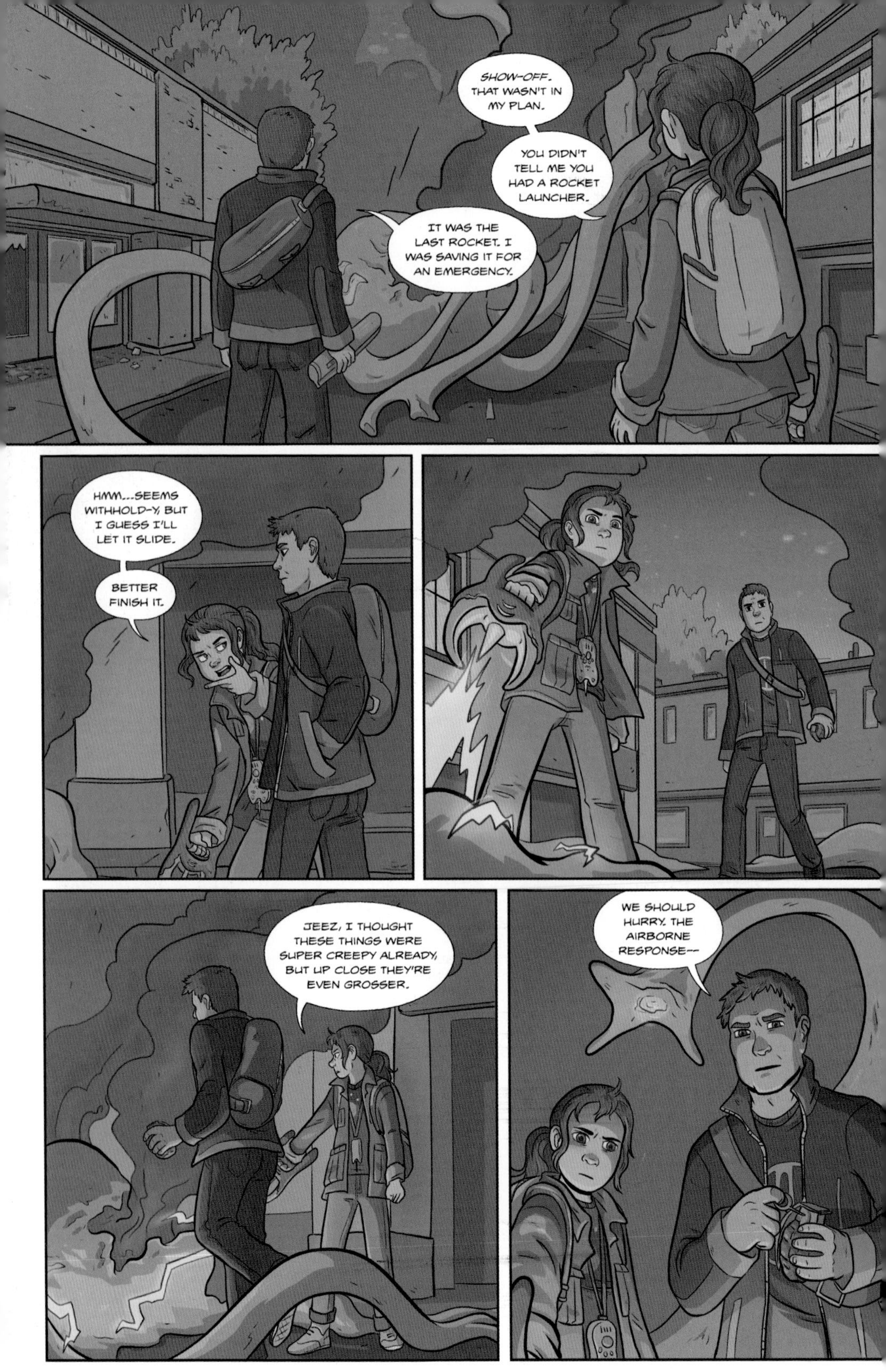
SHOW-OFF. THAT WASN'T IN MY PLAN.
YOU DIDN'T TELL ME YOU HAD A ROCKET LAUNCHER.
IT WAS THE LAST ROCKET. I WAS SAVING IT FOR AN EMERGENCY.
HMM...SEEMS WITHHOLD-Y, BUT I GUESS I'LL LET IT SLIDE.
BETTER FINISH IT.
JEEZ, I THOUGHT THESE THINGS WERE SUPER CREEPY ALREADY, BUT UP CLOSE THEY'RE EVEN GROSSER.
WE SHOULD HURRY. THE AIRBORNE RESPONSE--

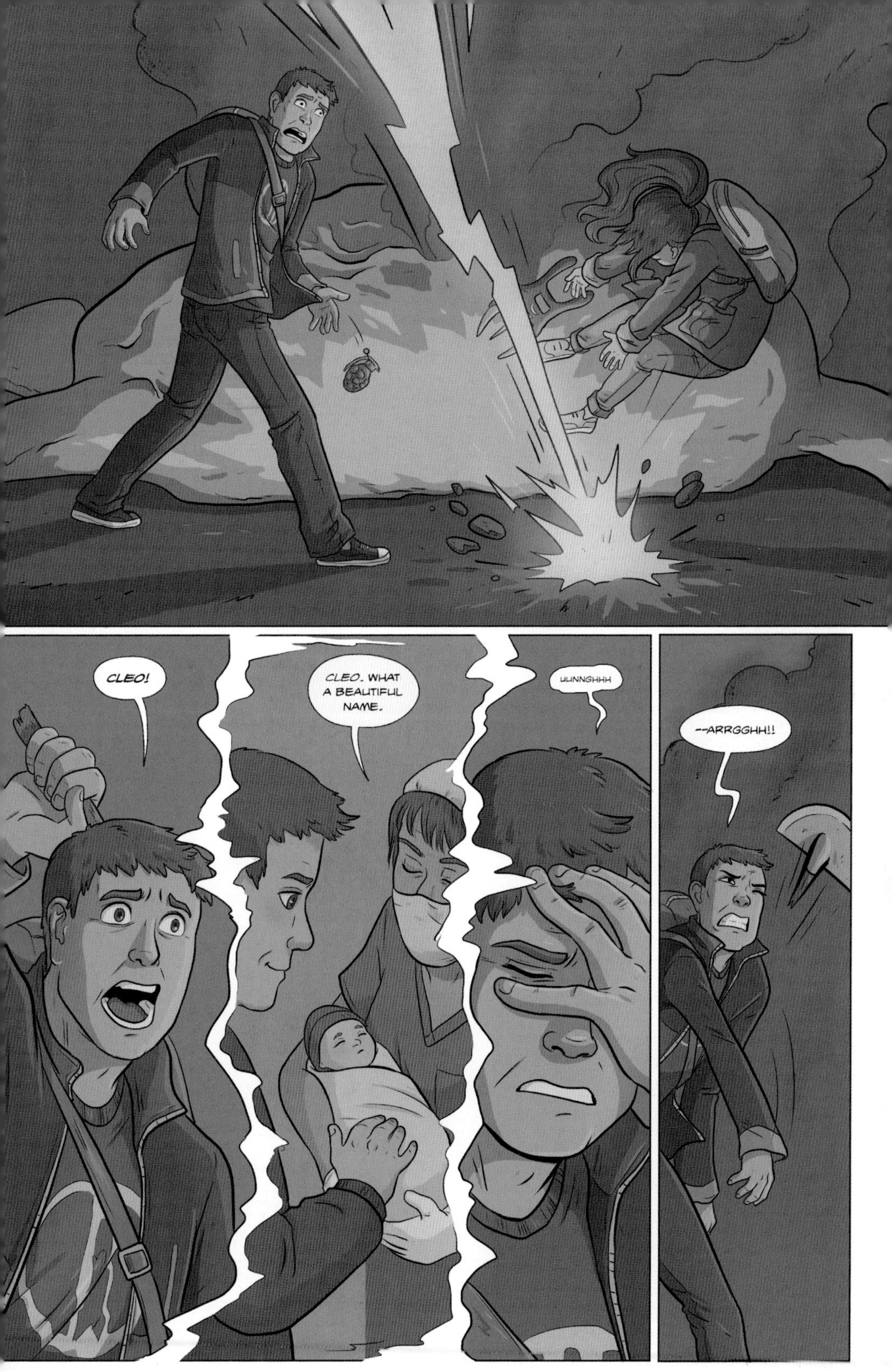
CLEO!
CLEO. WHAT A BEAUTIFUL NAME.
UUNNGHHH
--ARRGGHH!!

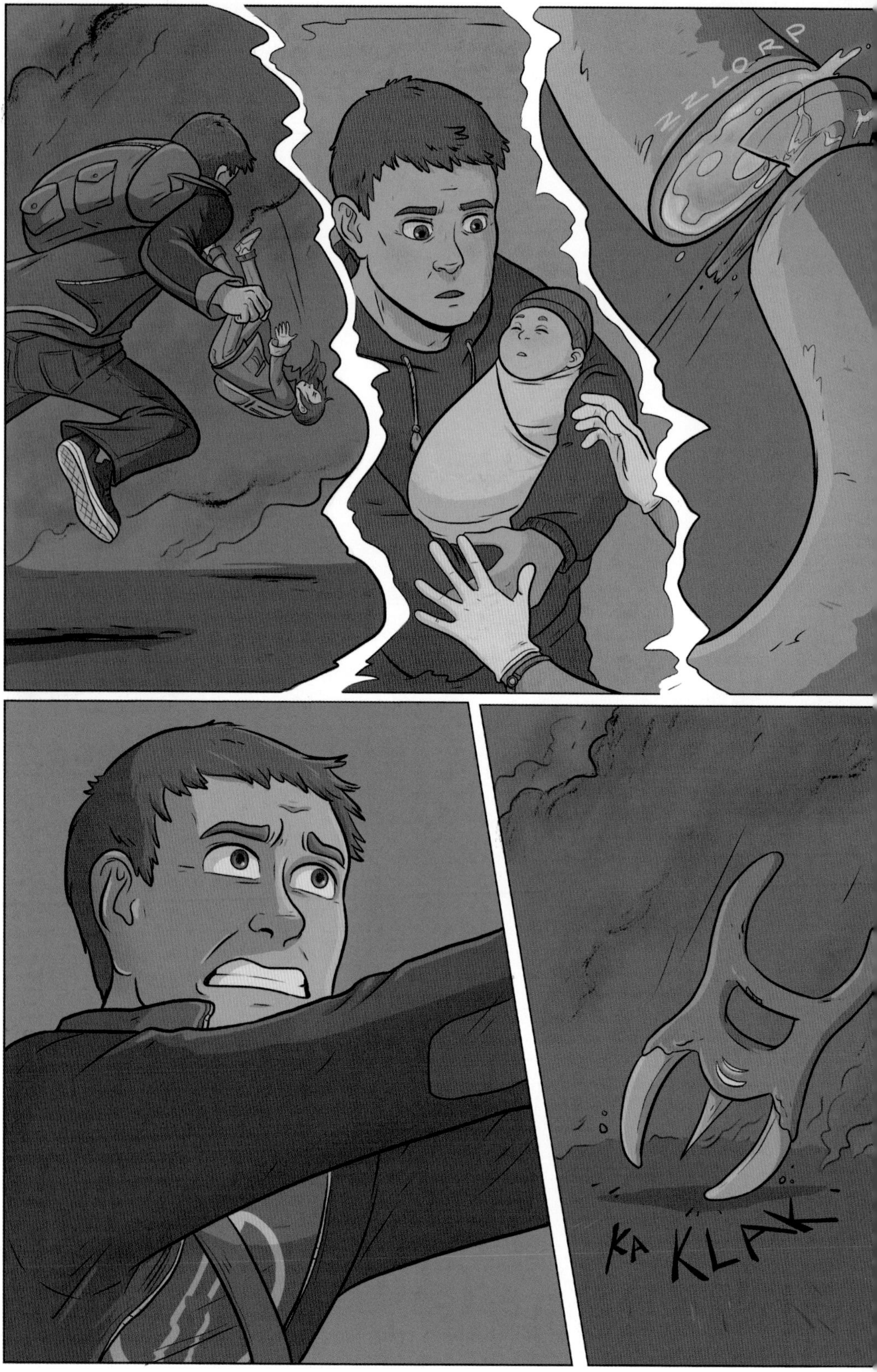
ZZLORP
KA KLAK

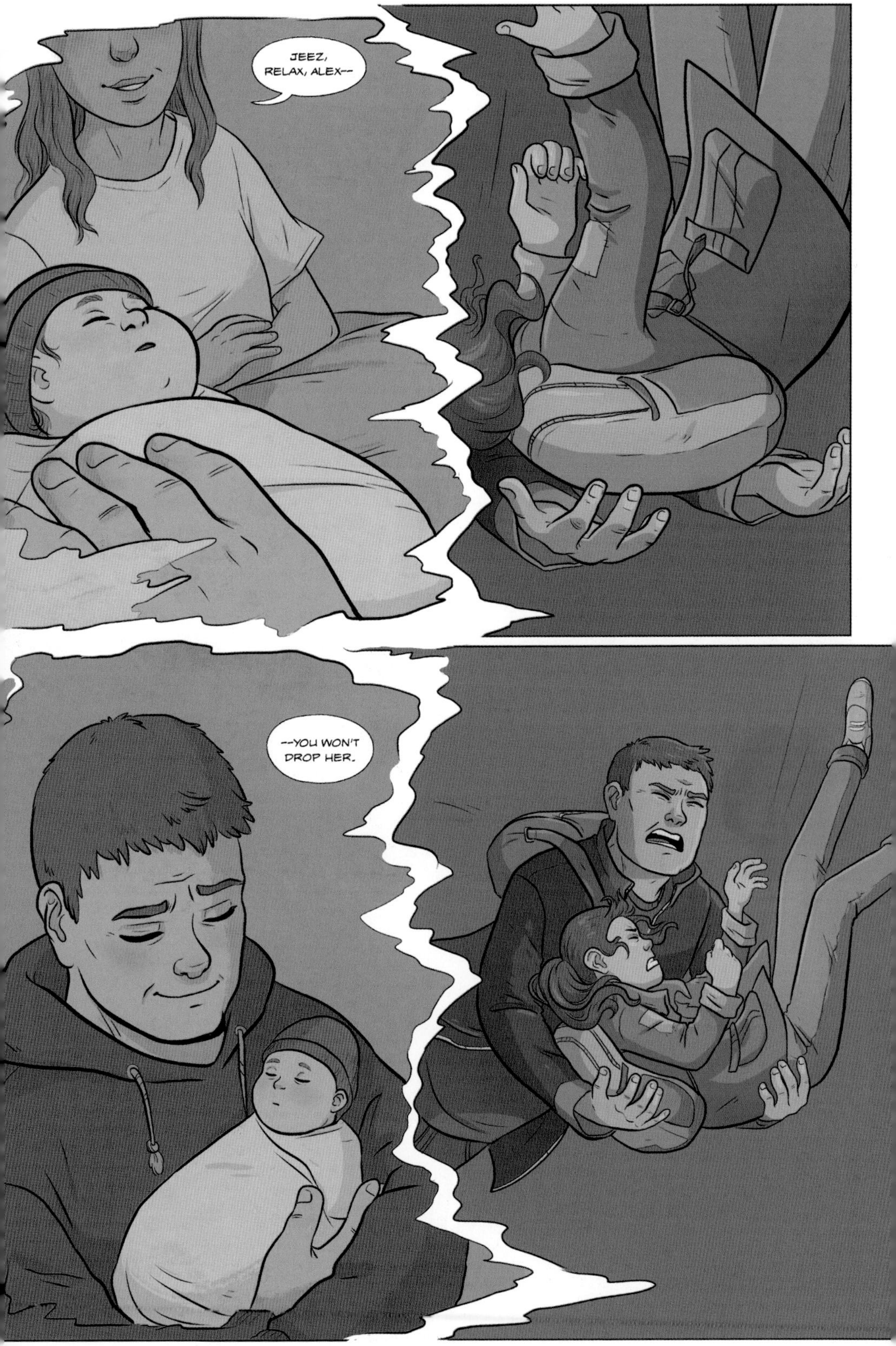
JEEZ, RELAX, ALEX--
--YOU WON'T DROP HER.

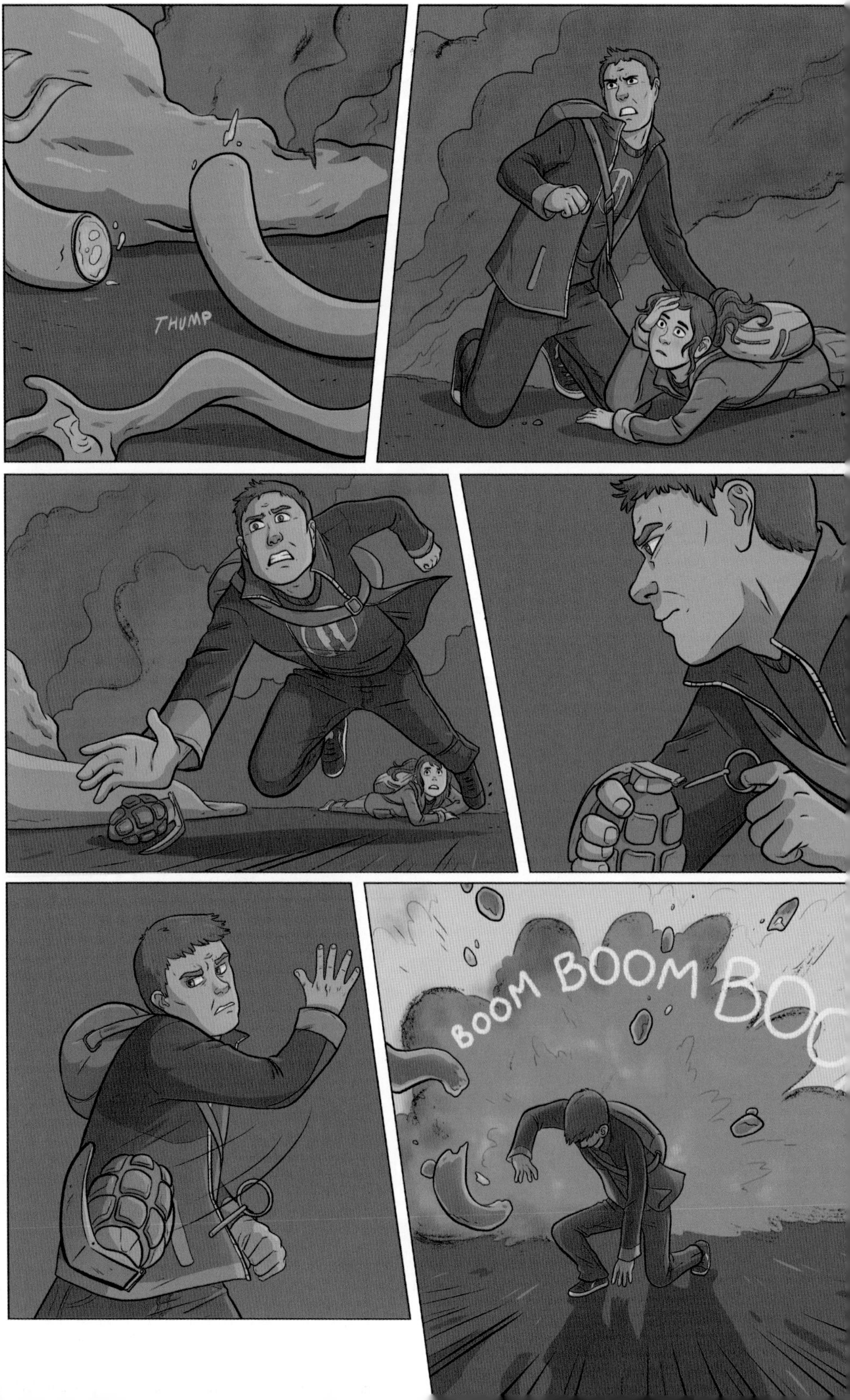
THUMP
BOOM BOOM

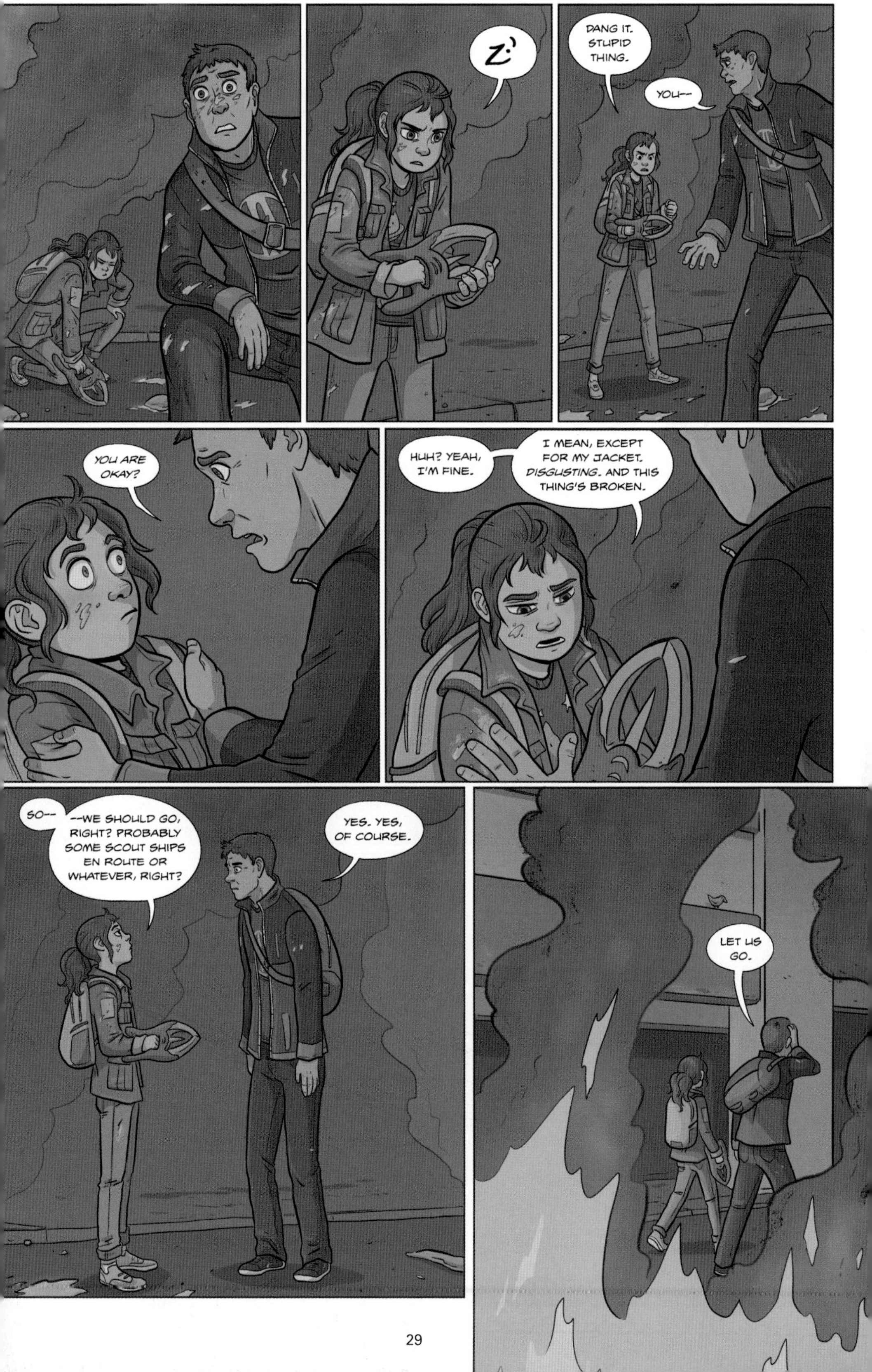
Z:
DANG IT. STUPID THING.
YOU--
YOU ARE OKAY?
HUH? YEAH, I'M FINE.
I MEAN, EXCEPT FOR MY JACKET. *DISGUSTING*. AND THIS THING'S BROKEN.
SO--
--WE SHOULD GO, RIGHT? PROBABLY SOME SCOUT SHIPS EN ROUTE OR WHATEVER, RIGHT?
YES. YES, OF COURSE.
LET US GO.

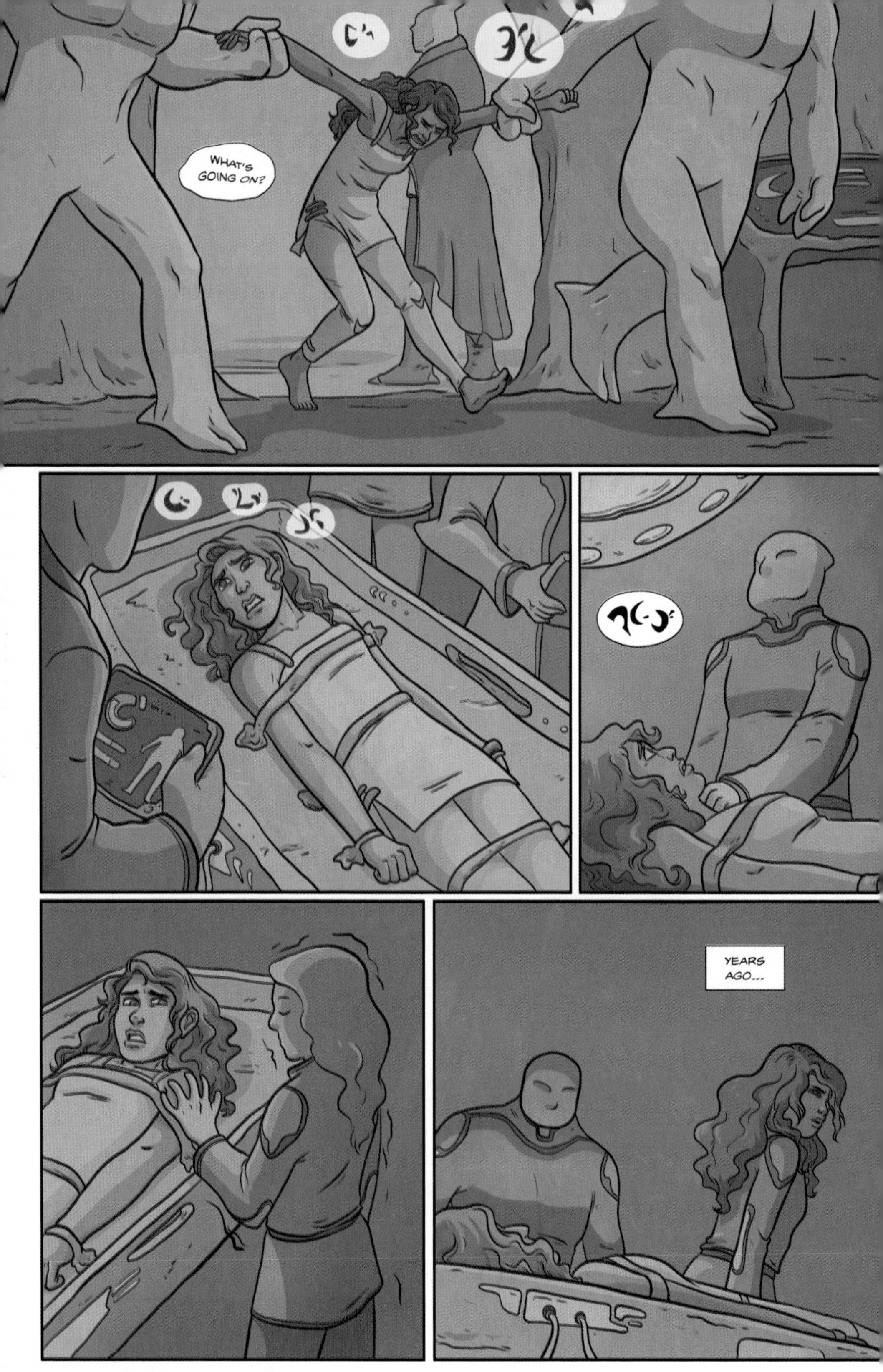

WHAT'S GOING ON?
YEARS AGO...

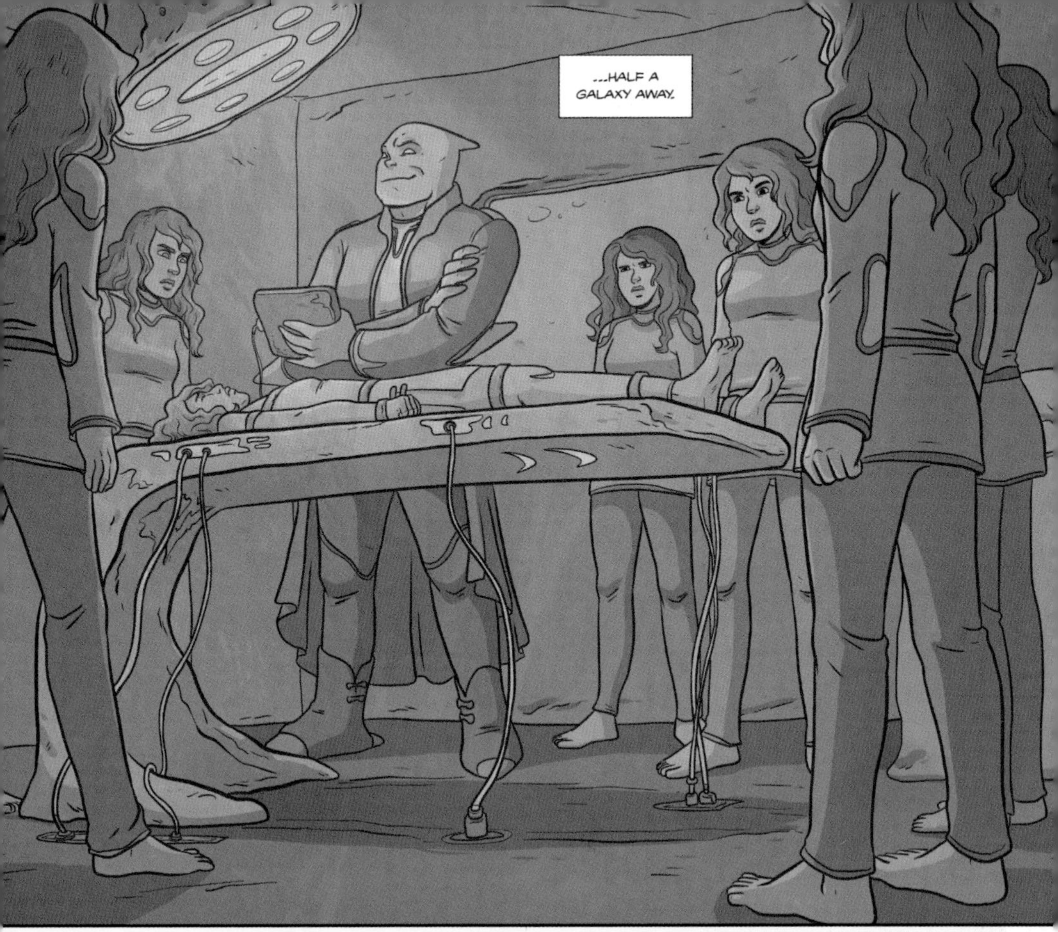
...HALF A
GALAXY AWAY.

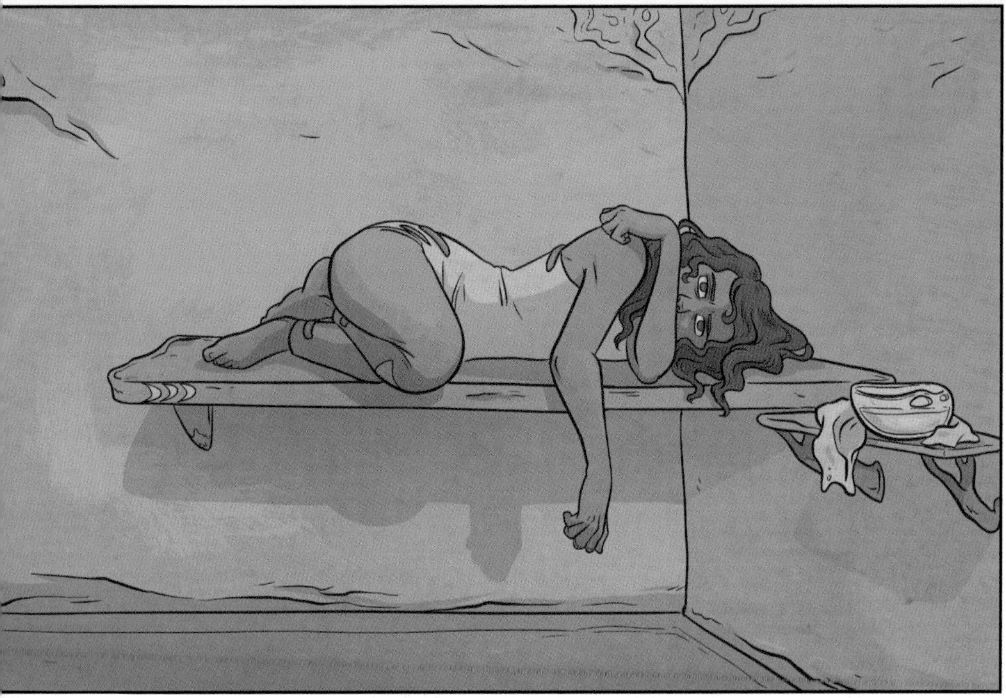

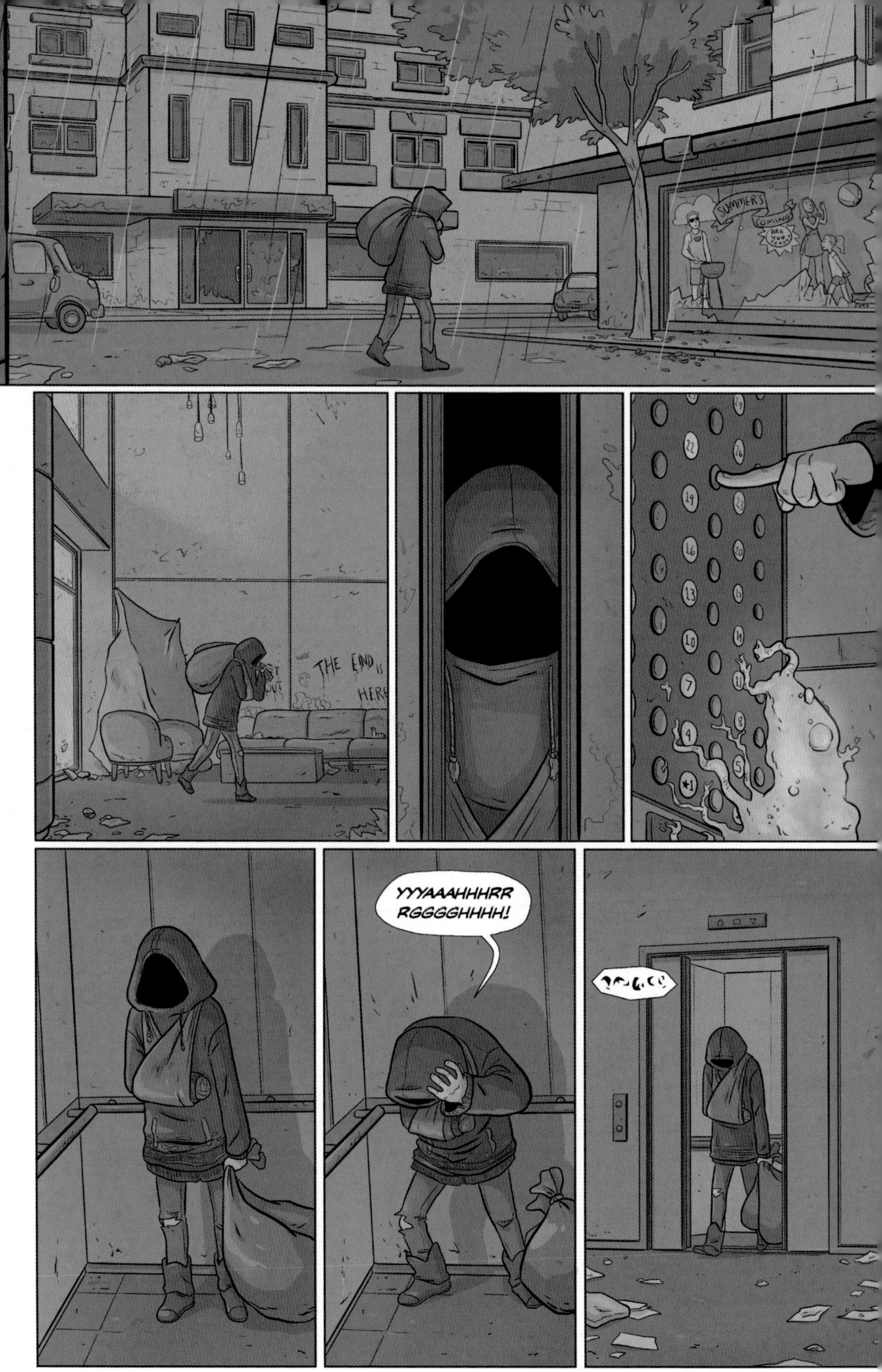
SUMMER'S COMING! ARE YOU READY?
THE END IS HERE
YYYAAAHHHRR RGGGGHHHH!

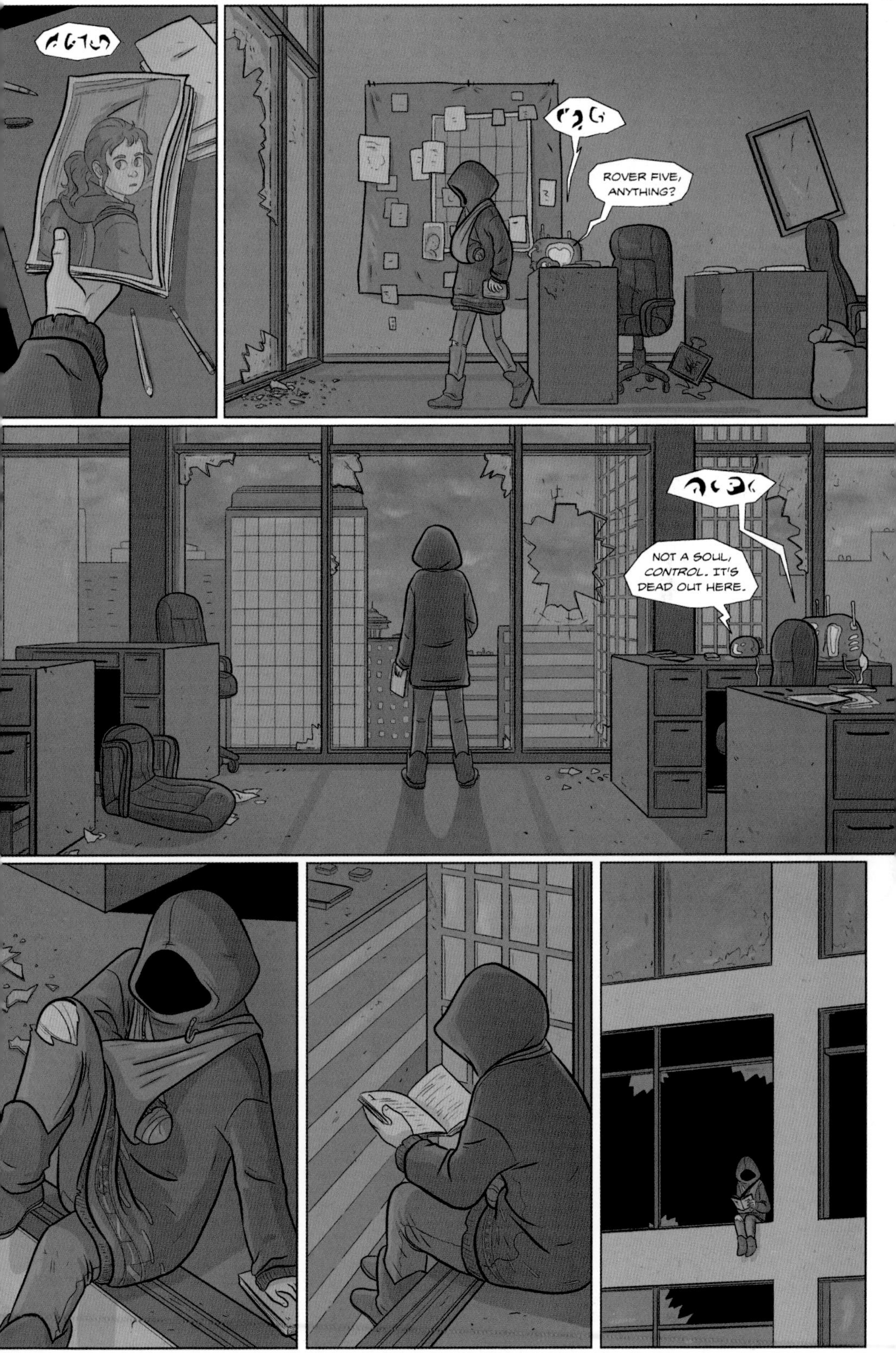
ROVER FIVE, ANYTHING?
NOT A SOUL, CONTROL. IT'S DEAD OUT HERE.

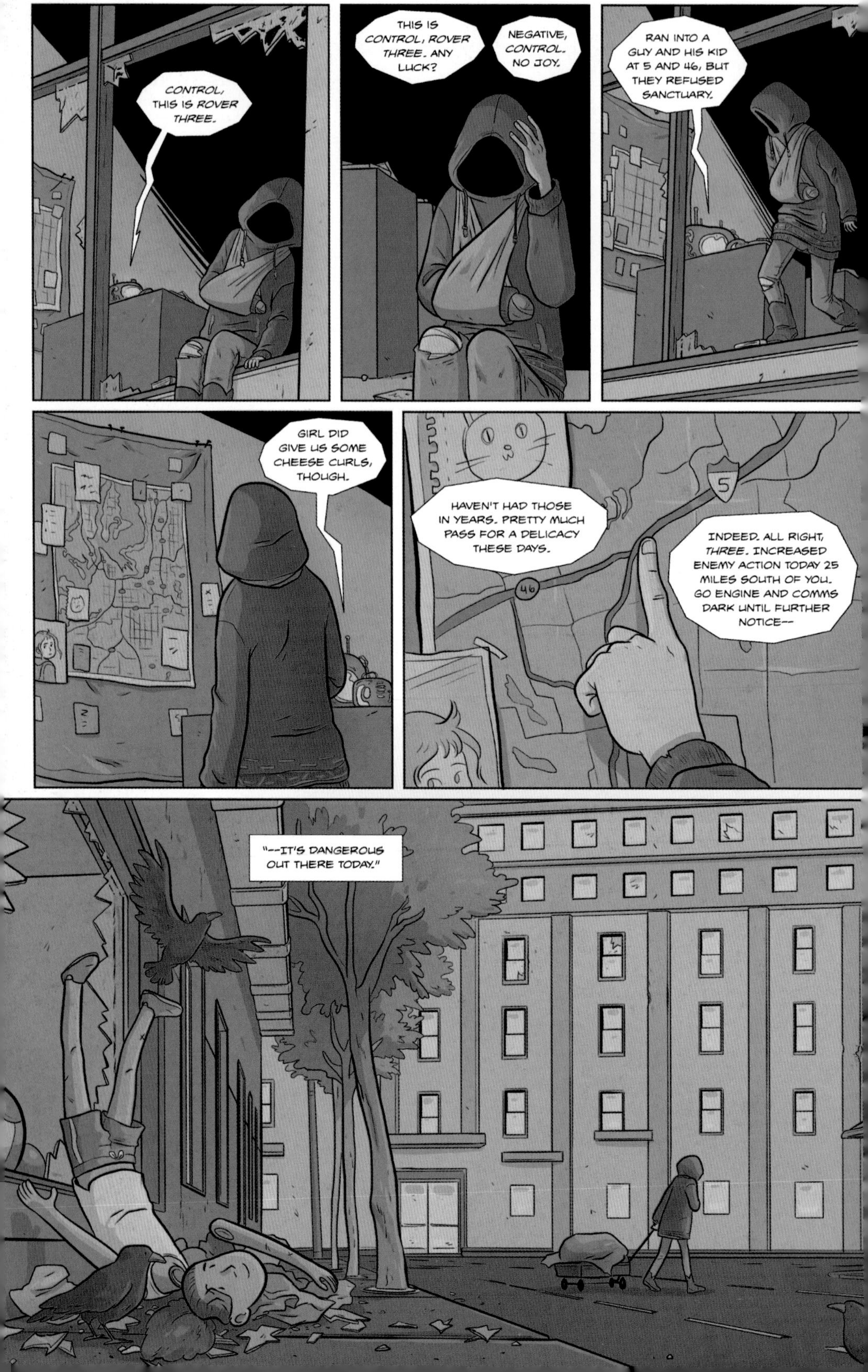
CONTROL, THIS IS ROVER THREE.
THIS IS CONTROL, ROVER THREE. ANY LUCK?
NEGATIVE, CONTROL. NO JOY.
RAN INTO A GUY AND HIS KID AT 5 AND 46, BUT THEY REFUSED SANCTUARY.
GIRL DID GIVE US SOME CHEESE CURLS, THOUGH.
HAVEN'T HAD THOSE IN YEARS. PRETTY MUCH PASS FOR A DELICACY THESE DAYS.
5
46
INDEED. ALL RIGHT, THREE. INCREASED ENEMY ACTION TODAY 25 MILES SOUTH OF YOU. GO ENGINE AND COMMS DARK UNTIL FURTHER NOTICE--
"--IT'S DANGEROUS OUT THERE TODAY."

TWO

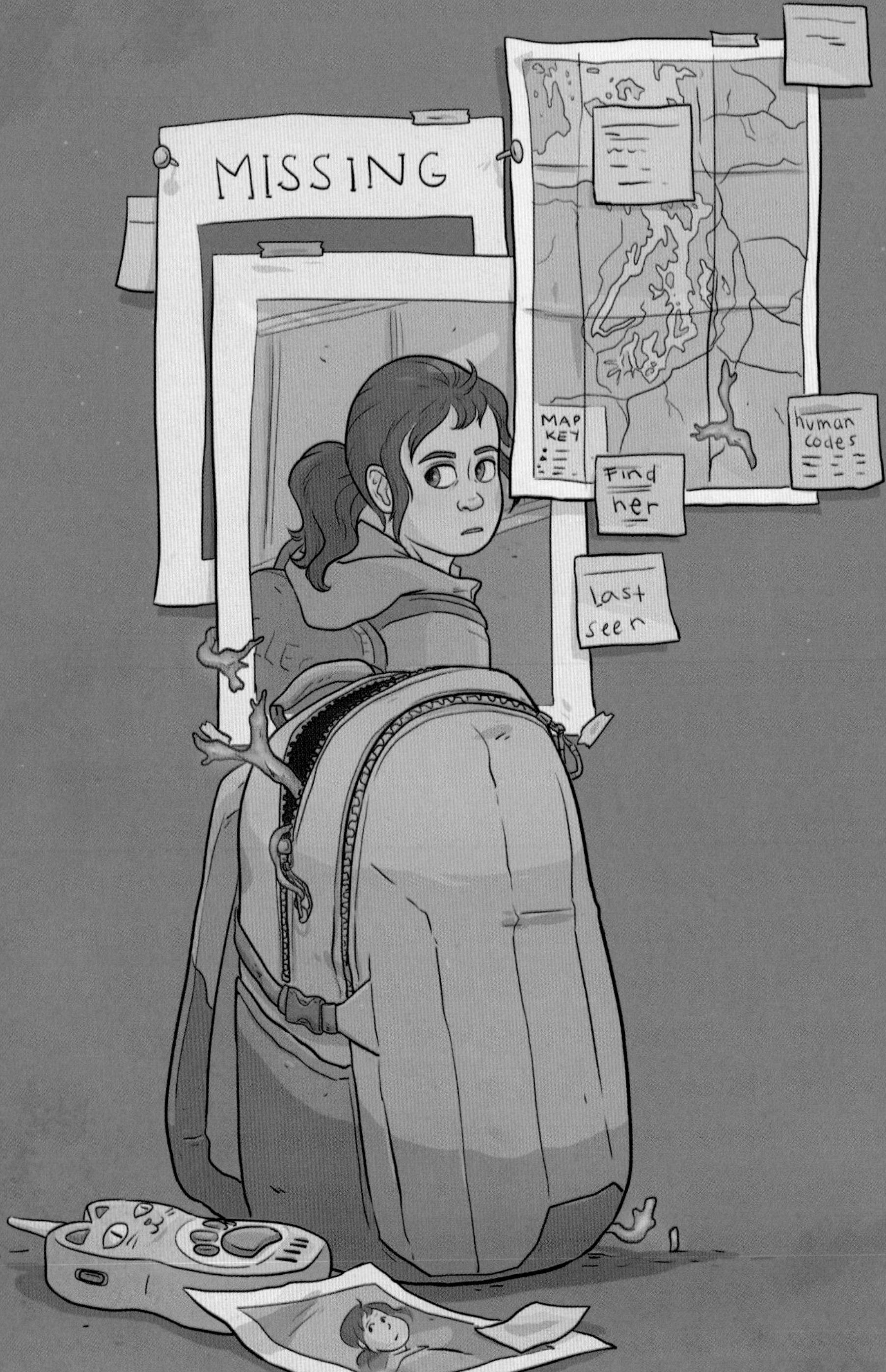
MISSING
MAP KEY
Find her
human codes
last seen

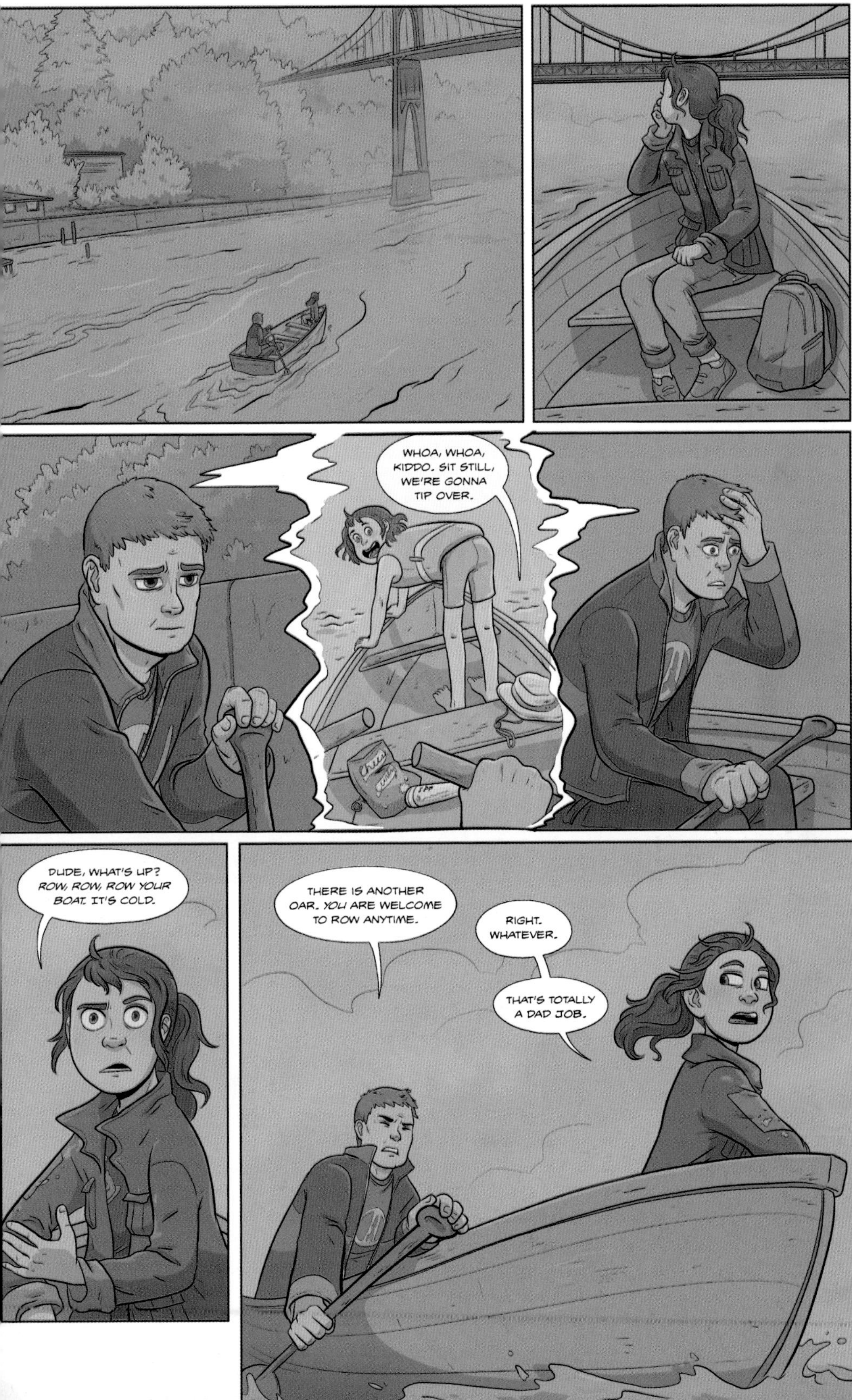
WHOA, WHOA, KIDDO. SIT STILL, WE'RE GONNA TIP OVER.
DUDE, WHAT'S UP? ROW, ROW, ROW YOUR BOAT. IT'S COLD.
THERE IS ANOTHER OAR. YOU ARE WELCOME TO ROW ANYTIME.
RIGHT. WHATEVER.
THAT'S TOTALLY A DAD JOB.

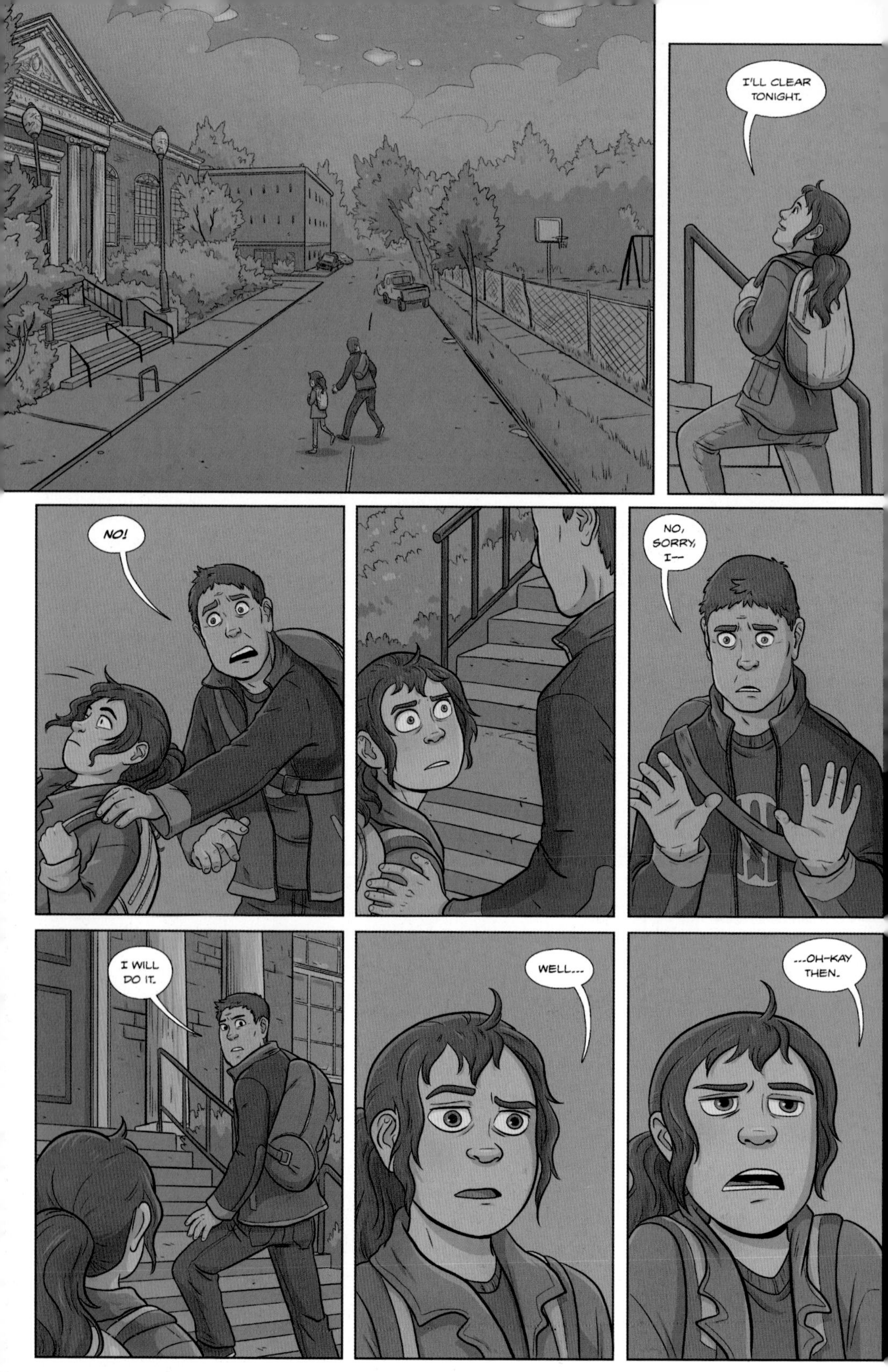
I'LL CLEAR TONIGHT.
NO!
NO, SORRY, I--
I WILL DO IT.
WELL...
...OH-KAY THEN.

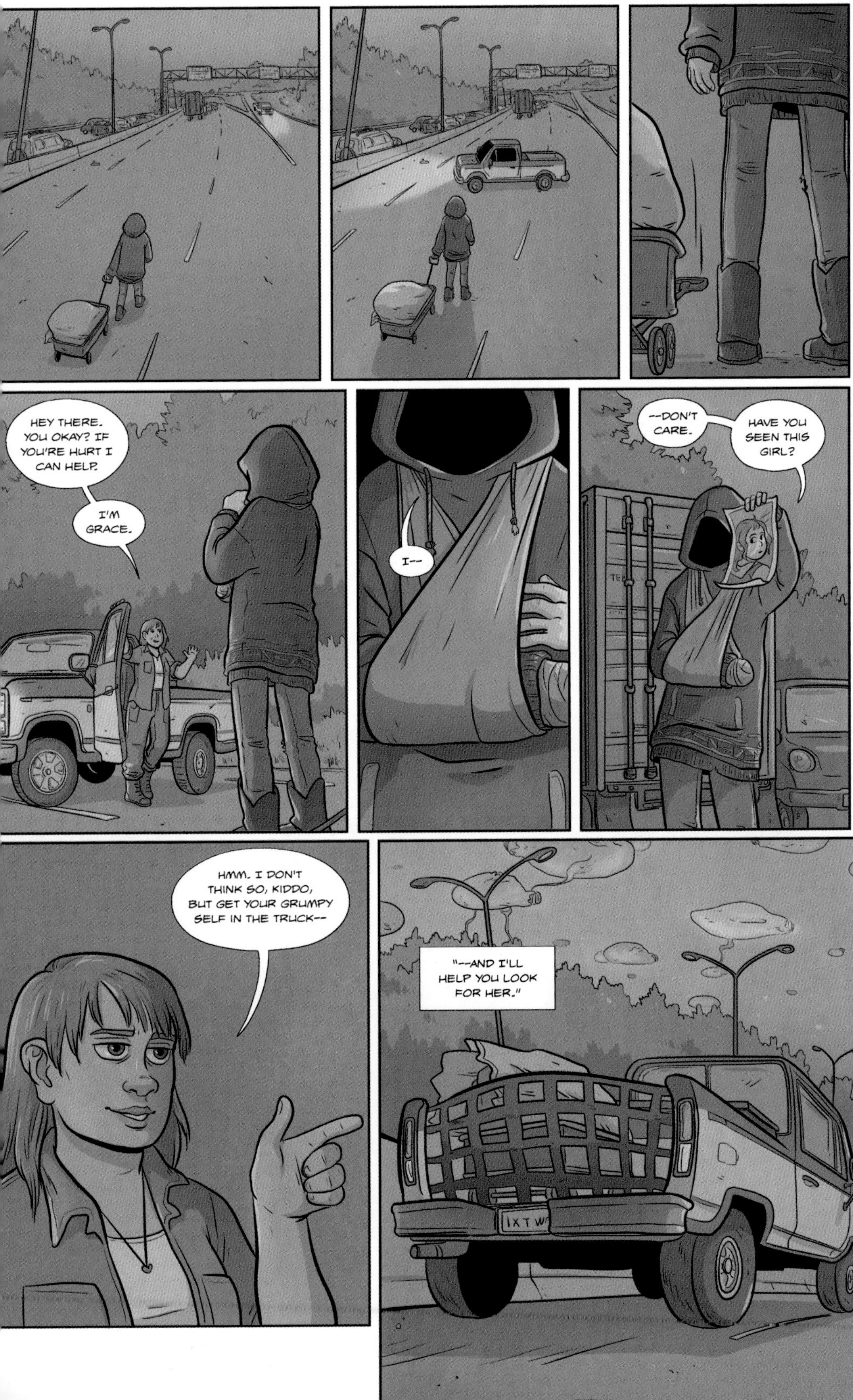

HEY THERE. YOU OKAY? IF YOU'RE HURT I CAN HELP.
I'M GRACE.
I--
--DON'T CARE.
HAVE YOU SEEN THIS GIRL?
HMM. I DON'T THINK SO, KIDDO, BUT GET YOUR GRUMPY SELF IN THE TRUCK--
"--AND I'LL HELP YOU LOOK FOR HER."

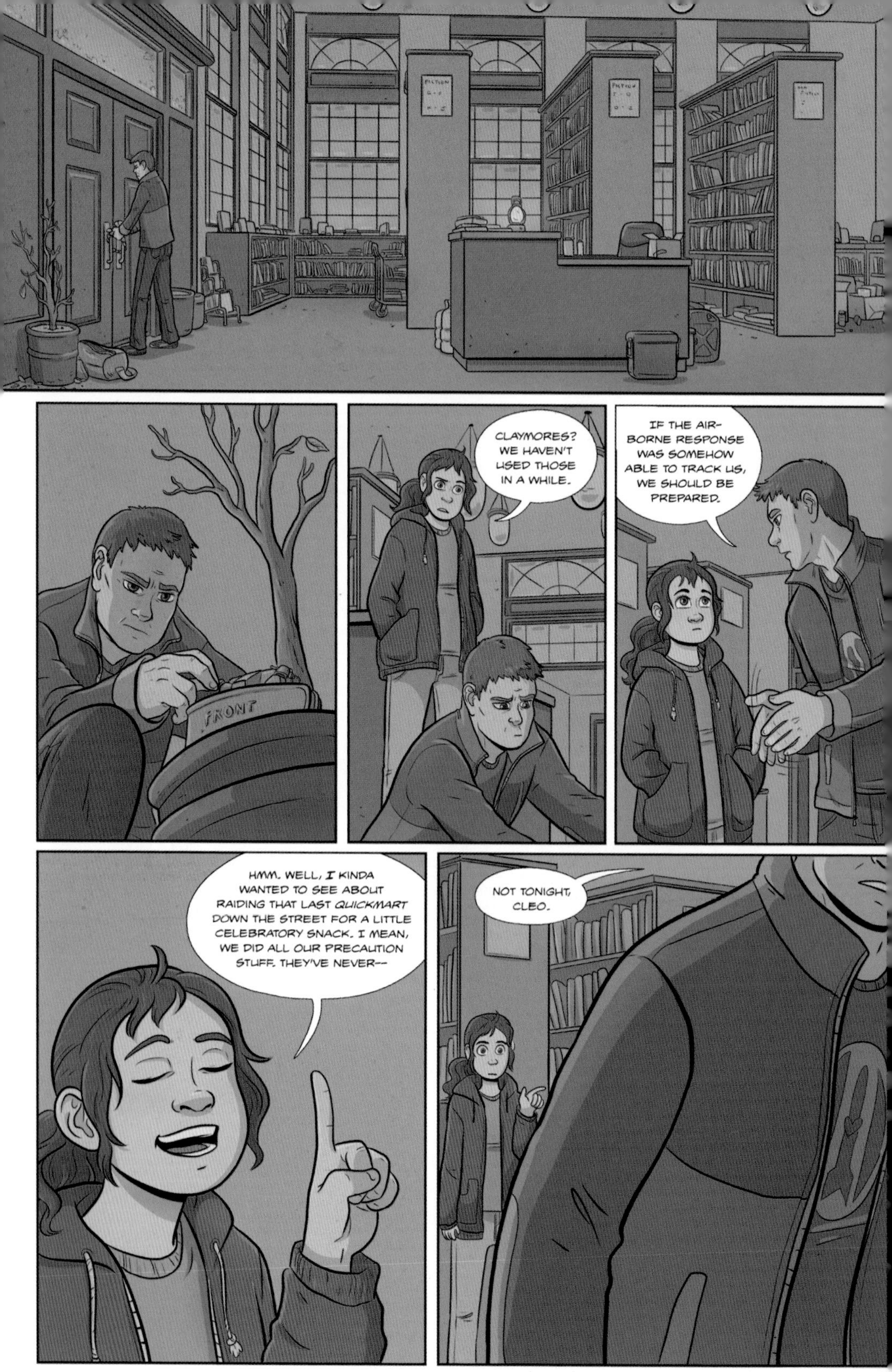
FRONT
CLAYMORES? WE HAVEN'T USED THOSE IN A WHILE.
IF THE AIR-BORNE RESPONSE WAS SOMEHOW ABLE TO TRACK US, WE SHOULD BE PREPARED.
HMM. WELL, *I* KINDA WANTED TO SEE ABOUT RAIDING THAT LAST *QUICKMART* DOWN THE STREET FOR A LITTLE CELEBRATORY SNACK. I MEAN, WE DID ALL OUR PRECAUTION STUFF. THEY'VE NEVER--
NOT TONIGHT, CLEO.

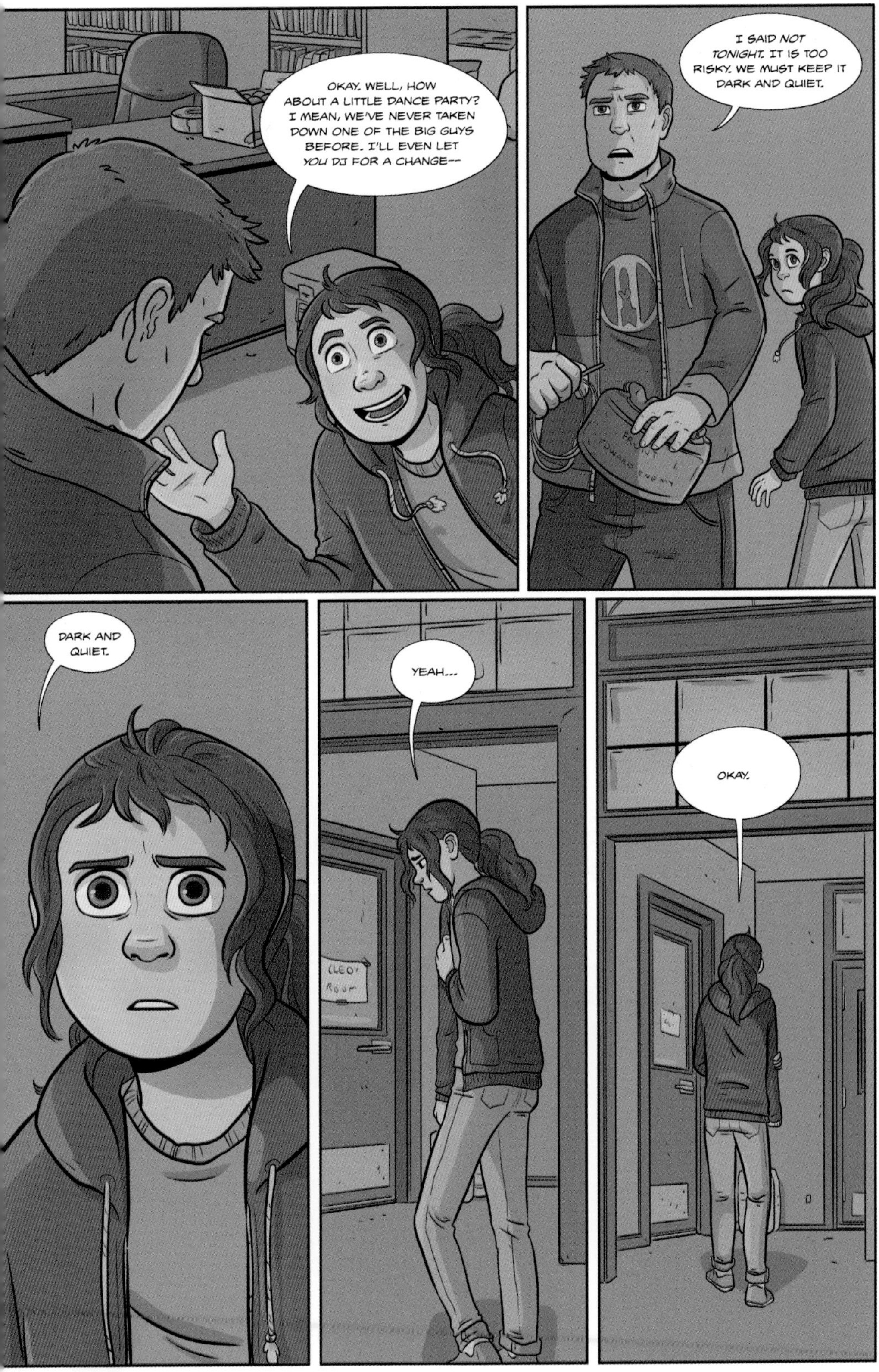
OKAY. WELL, HOW ABOUT A LITTLE DANCE PARTY? I MEAN, WE'VE NEVER TAKEN DOWN ONE OF THE BIG GUYS BEFORE. I'LL EVEN LET YOU DJ FOR A CHANGE--
I SAID NOT TONIGHT. IT IS TOO RISKY. WE MUST KEEP IT DARK AND QUIET.
FRONT TOWARD ENEMY
DARK AND QUIET.
YEAH...
CLEO'S ROOM
OKAY.

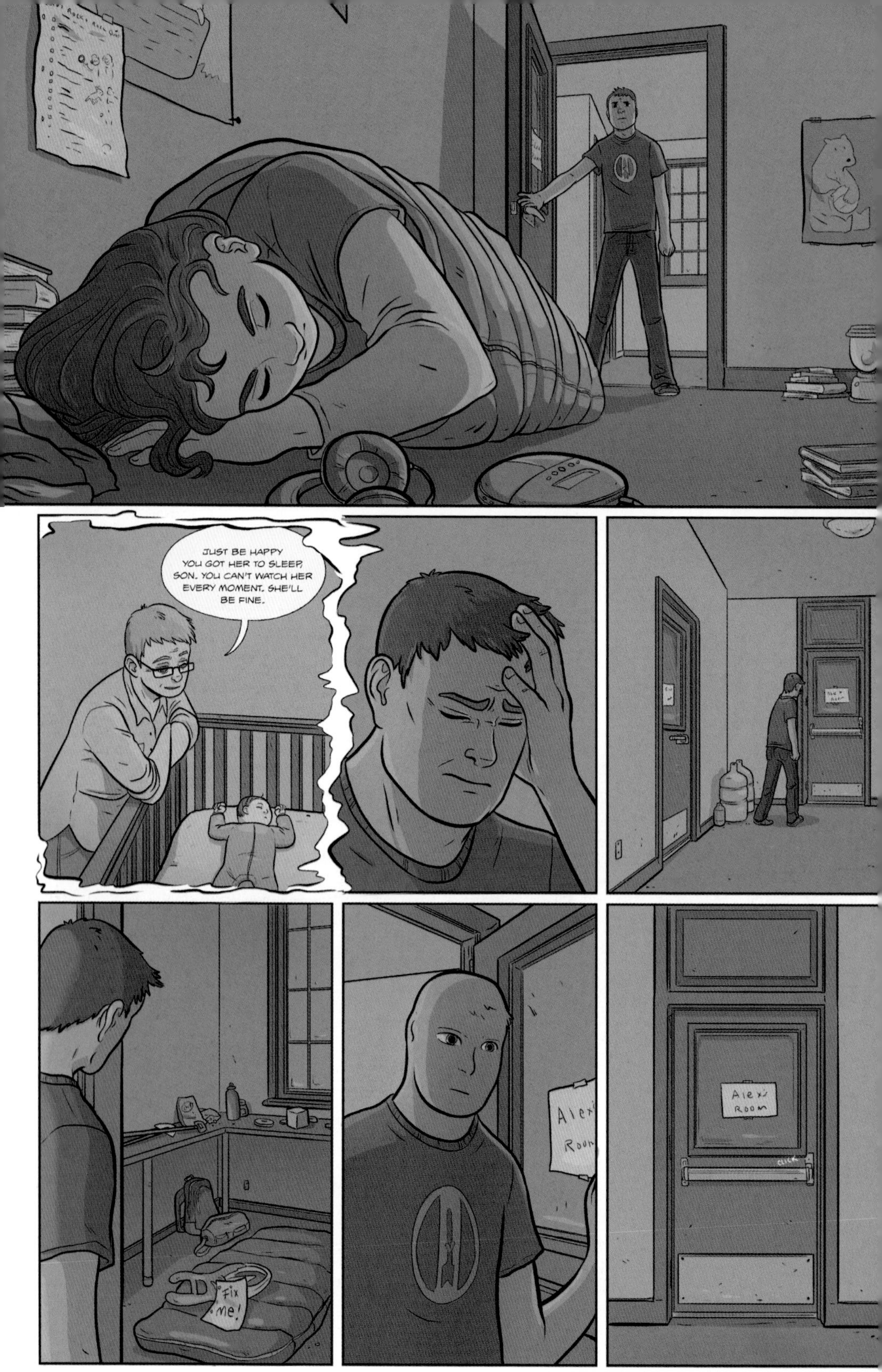
JUST BE HAPPY YOU GOT HER TO SLEEP, SON. YOU CAN'T WATCH HER EVERY MOMENT. SHE'LL BE FINE.
Fix me!
Alex's ROOM
CLICK

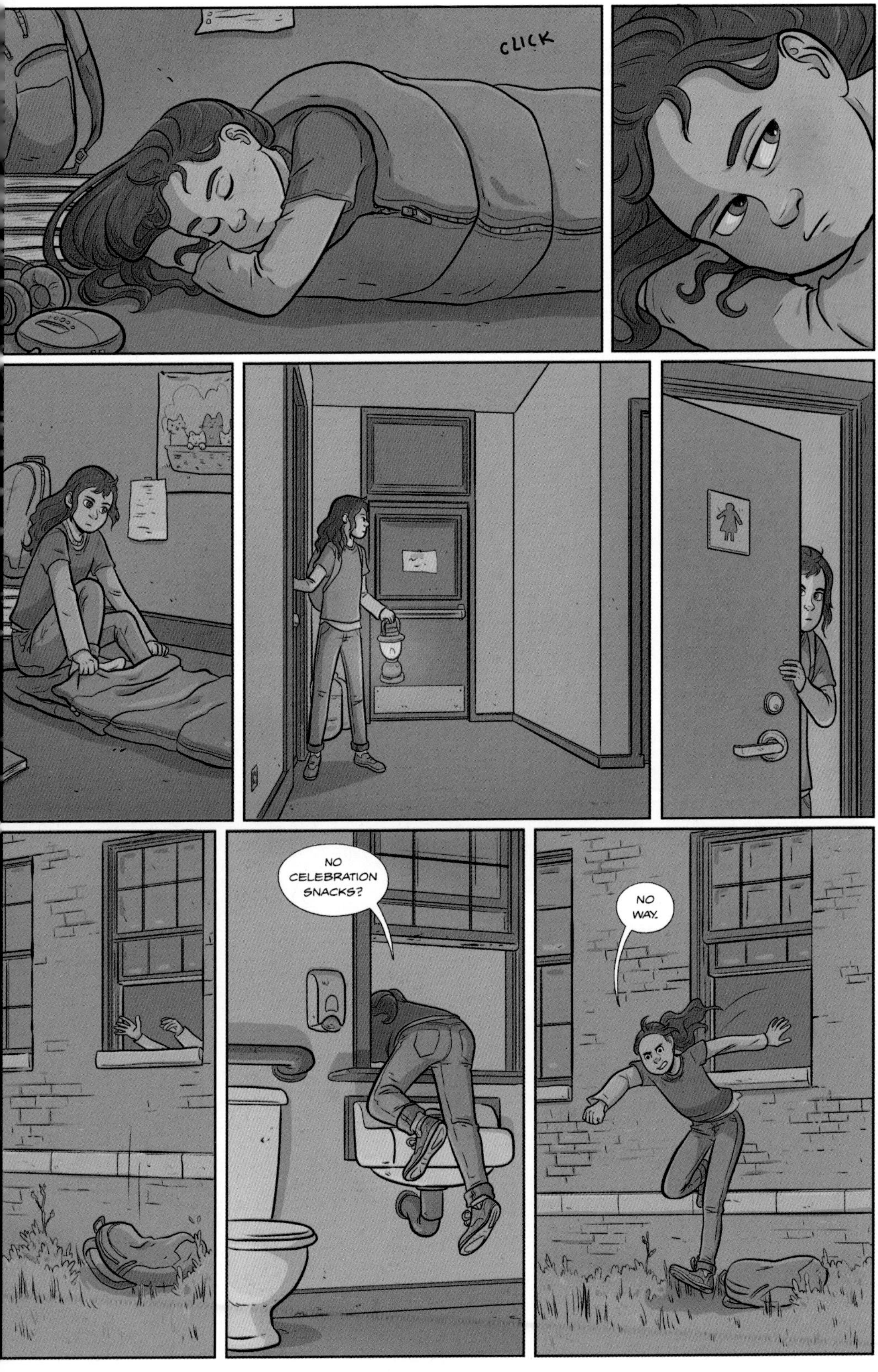
CLICK
NO CELEBRATION SNACKS?
NO WAY.

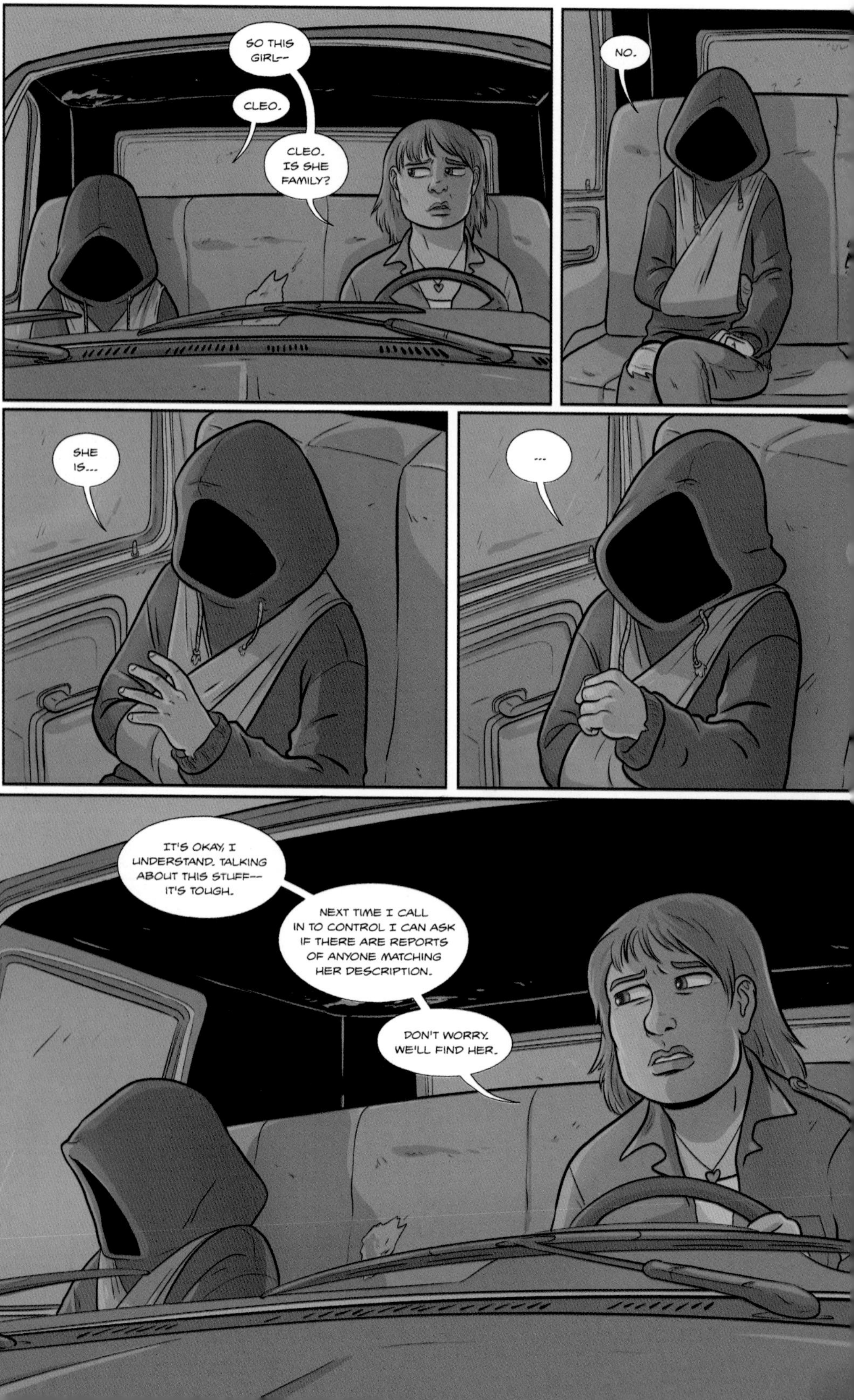
SO THIS GIRL--
CLEO.
CLEO. IS SHE FAMILY?
NO.
SHE IS...
...
IT'S OKAY, I UNDERSTAND. TALKING ABOUT THIS STUFF-- IT'S TOUGH.
NEXT TIME I CALL IN TO CONTROL I CAN ASK IF THERE ARE REPORTS OF ANYONE MATCHING HER DESCRIPTION.
DON'T WORRY. WE'LL FIND HER.

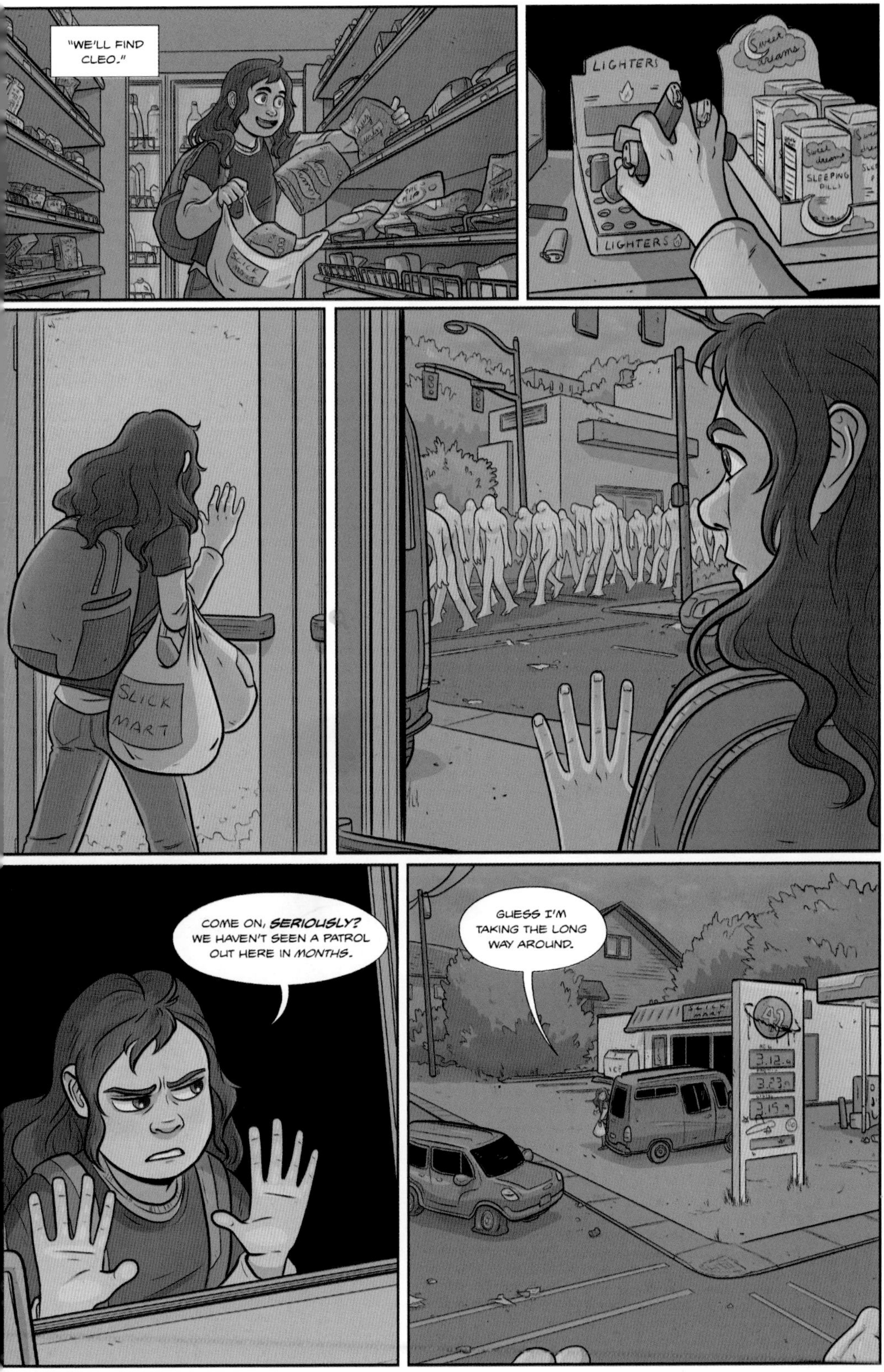
"WE'LL FIND CLEO."
LIGHTERS
LIGHTERS
SLEEPING PILLS
SLICK MART
SLICK MART
COME ON, **SERIOUSLY?** WE HAVEN'T SEEN A PATROL OUT HERE IN *MONTHS*.
GUESS I'M TAKING THE LONG WAY AROUND.

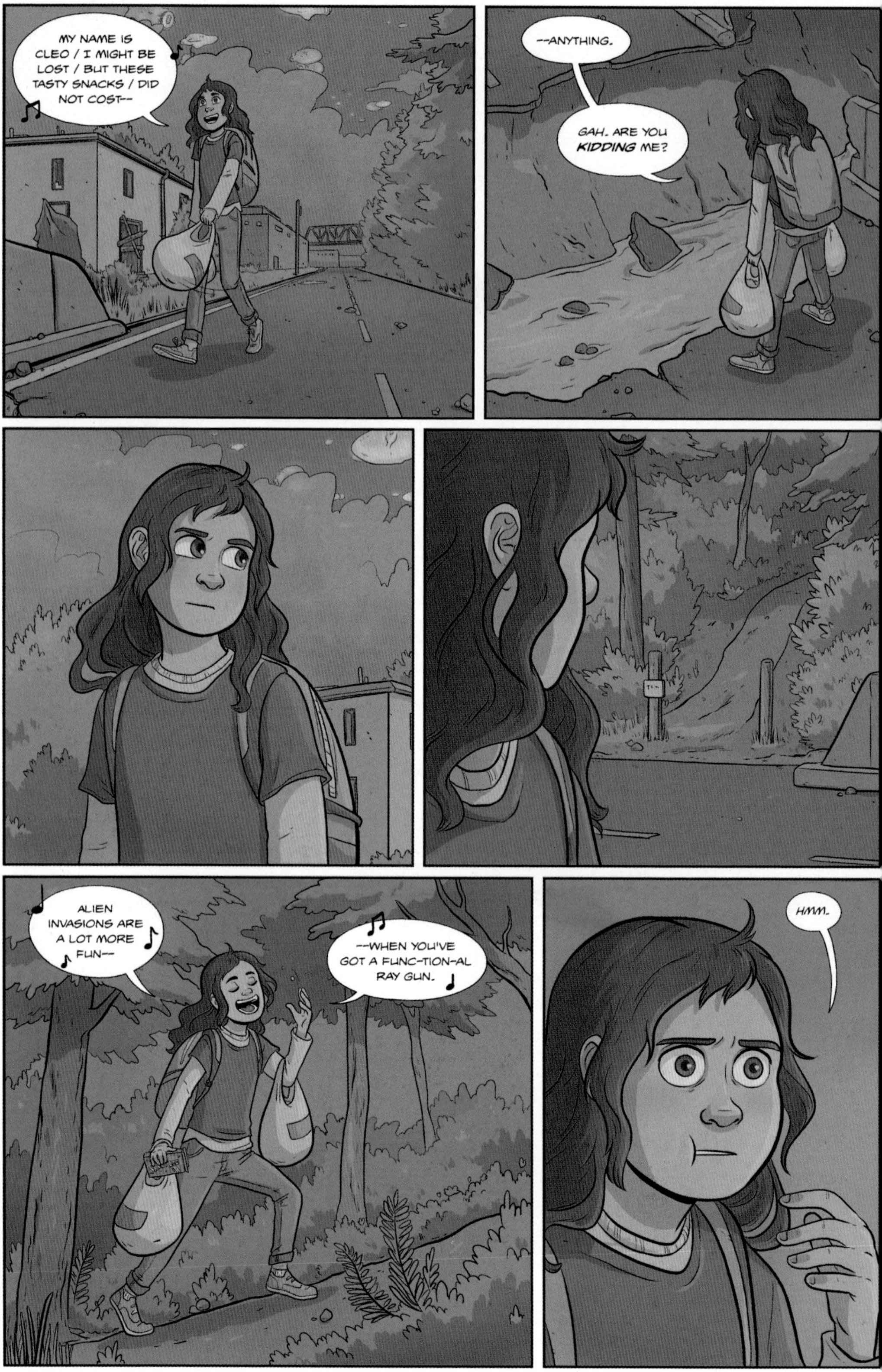
MY NAME IS CLEO / I MIGHT BE LOST / BUT THESE TASTY SNACKS / DID NOT COST--
--ANYTHING.
GAH. ARE YOU KIDDING ME?
ALIEN INVASIONS ARE A LOT MORE FUN--
--WHEN YOU'VE GOT A FUNC-TION-AL RAY GUN.
HMM.

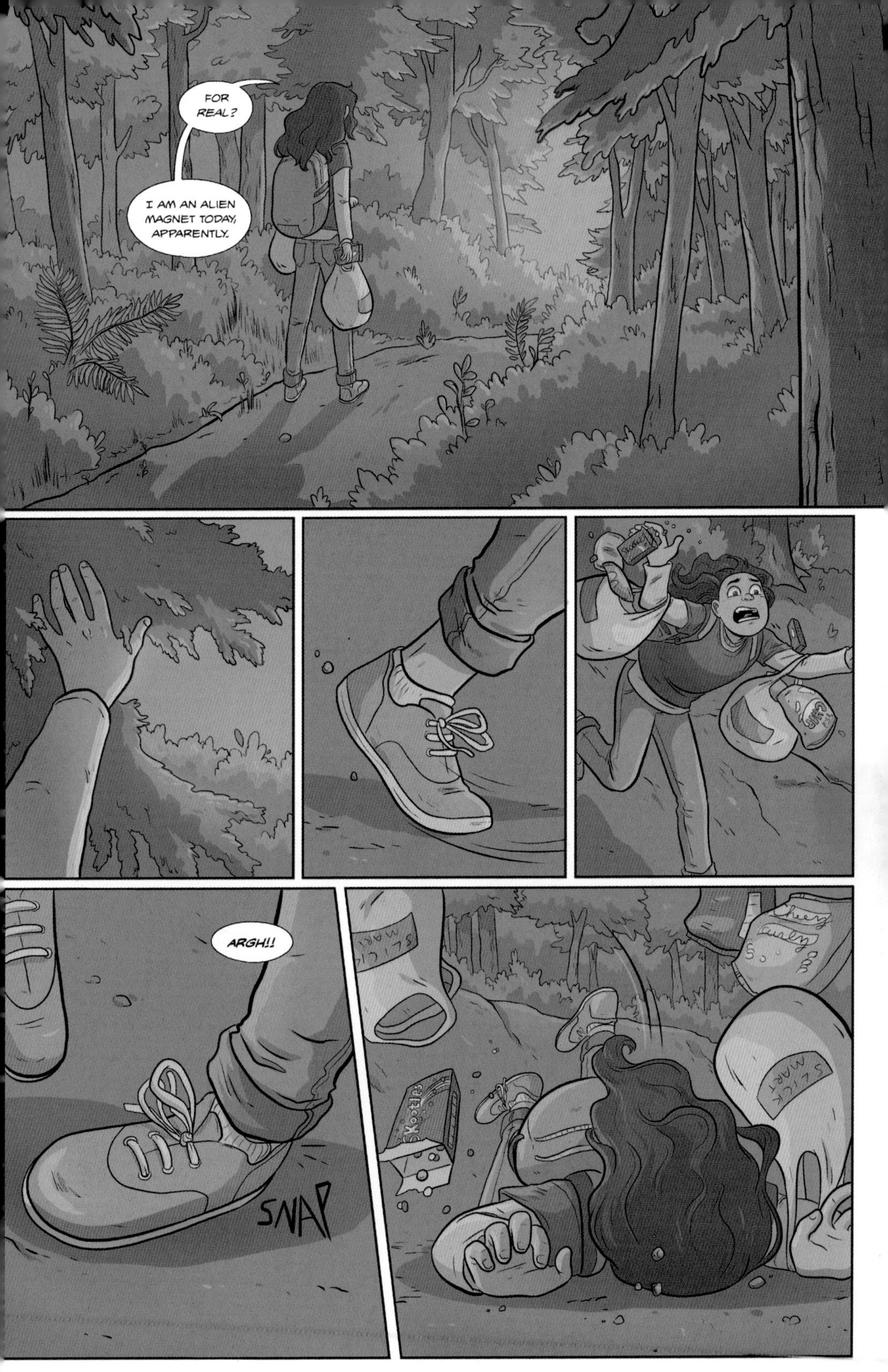
FOR REAL?
I AM AN ALIEN MAGNET TODAY, APPARENTLY.
ARGH!!
SNAP

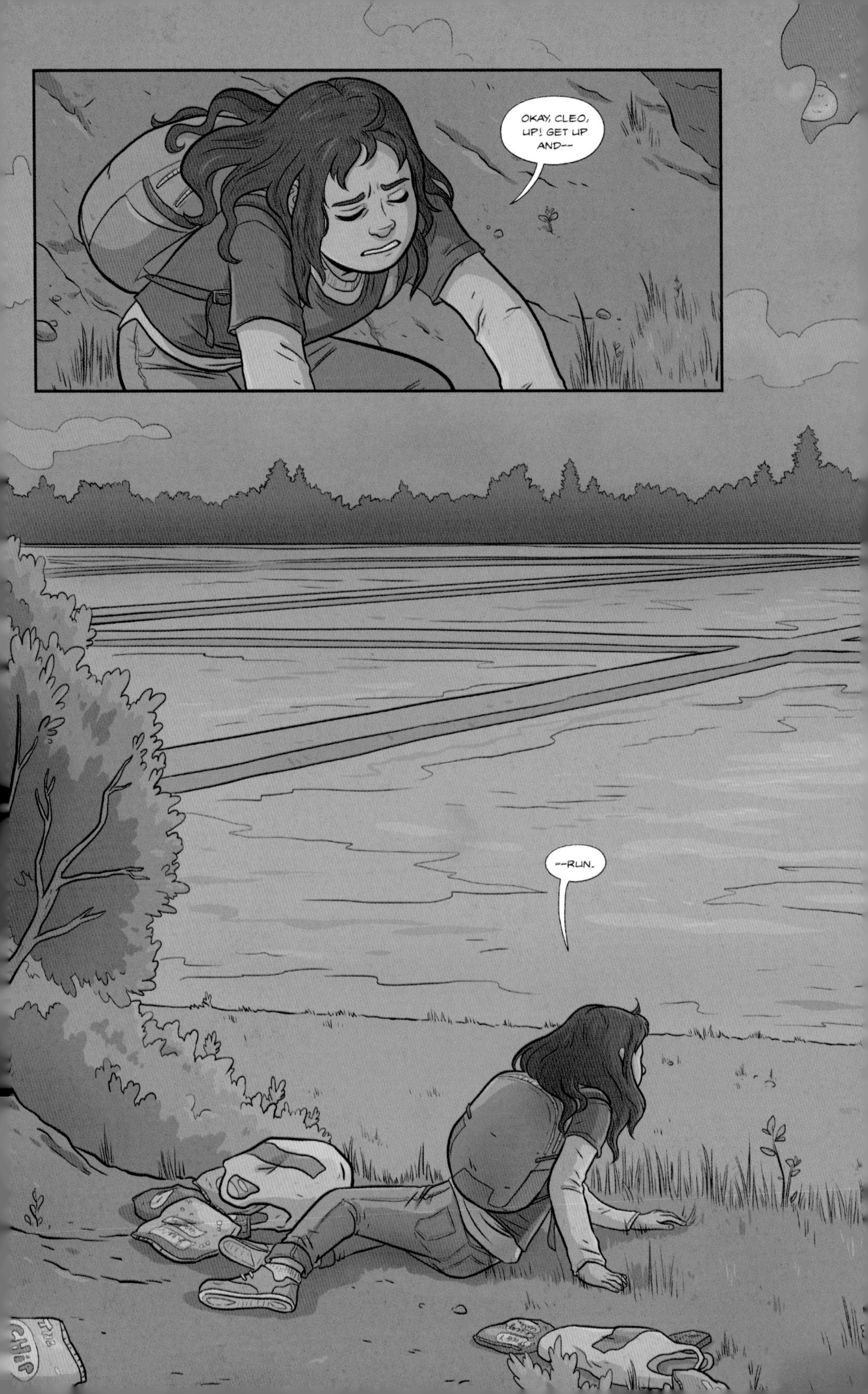
OKAY, CLEO, UP! GET UP AND--
--RUN.

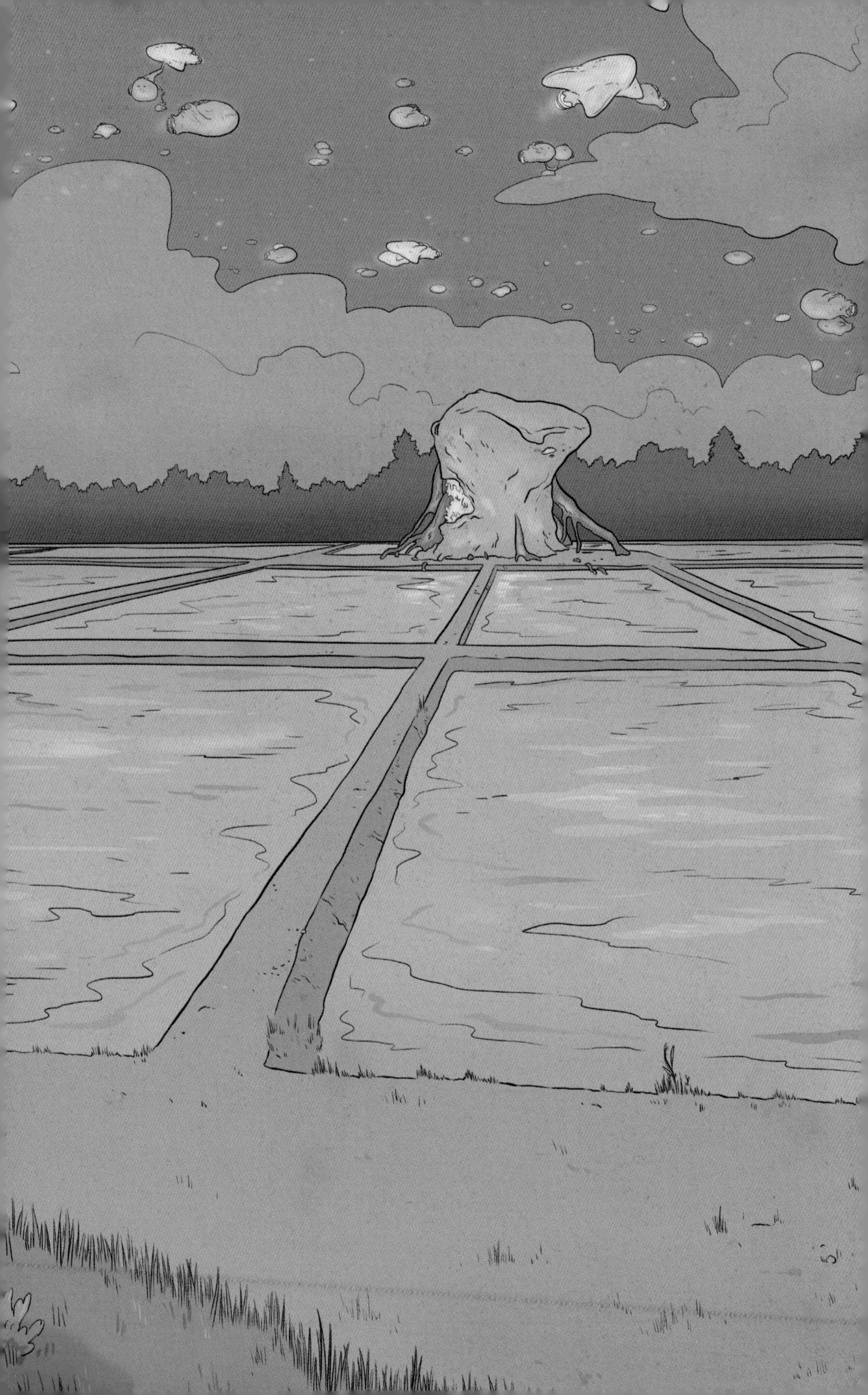

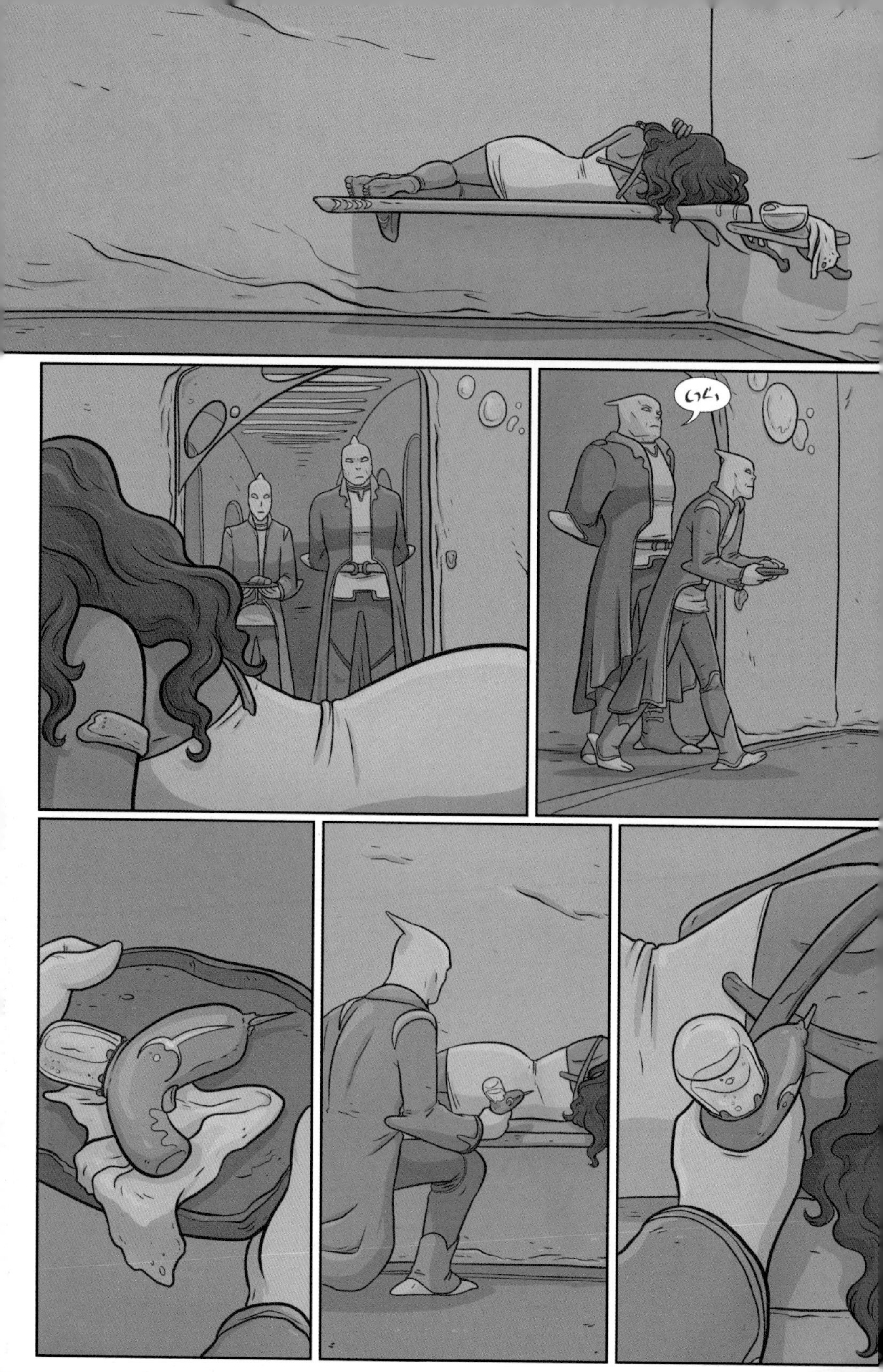

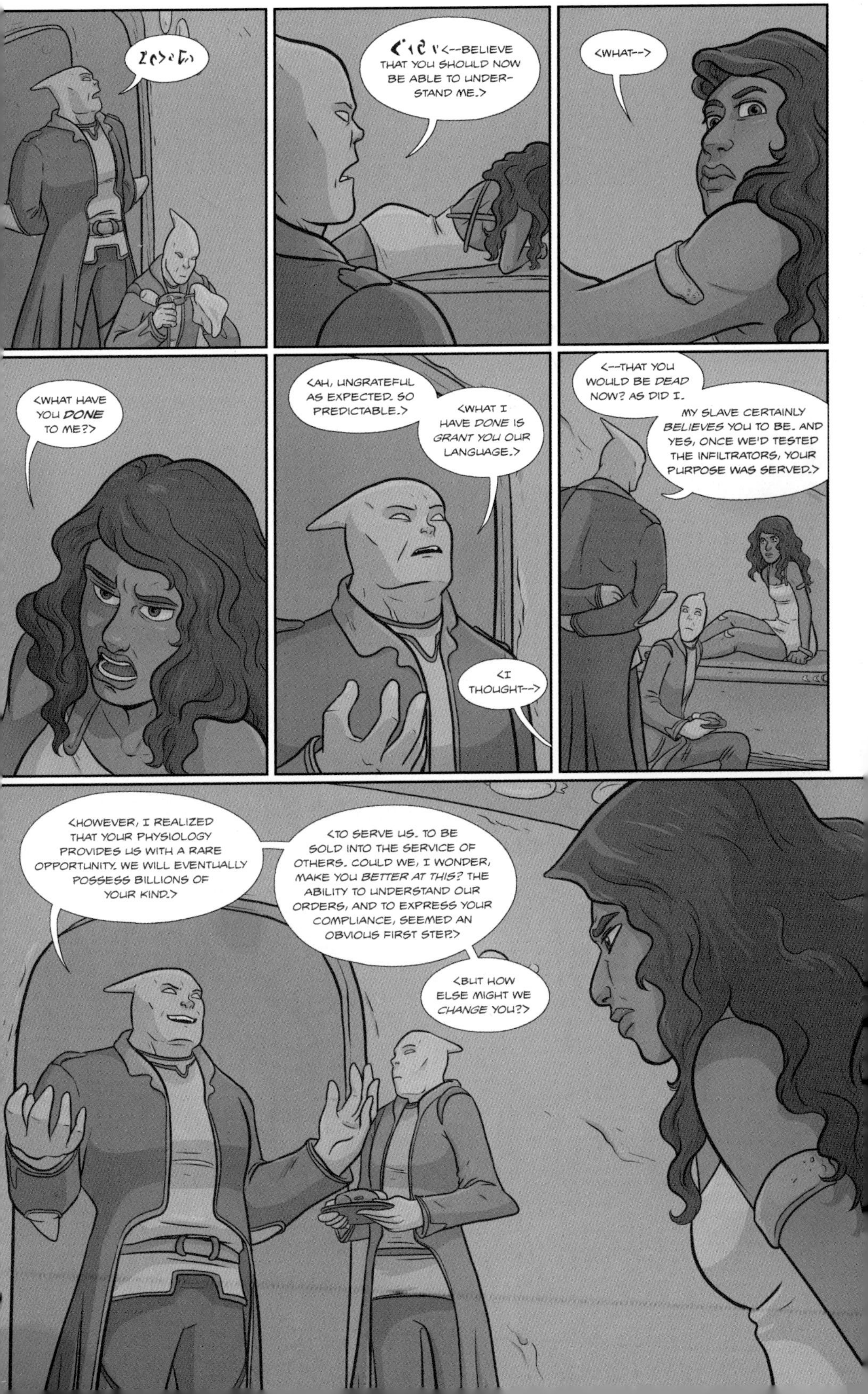

<--BELIEVE THAT YOU SHOULD NOW BE ABLE TO UNDER-STAND ME.>
<WHAT-->
<WHAT HAVE YOU *DONE* TO ME?>
<AH, UNGRATEFUL AS EXPECTED. SO PREDICTABLE.>
<WHAT I HAVE *DONE* IS *GRANT YOU OUR* LANGUAGE.>
<I THOUGHT-->
<--THAT YOU WOULD BE *DEAD* NOW? AS DID I.
MY SLAVE CERTAINLY *BELIEVES* YOU TO BE. AND YES, ONCE WE'D TESTED THE INFILTRATORS, YOUR PURPOSE WAS SERVED.>
<HOWEVER, I REALIZED THAT YOUR PHYSIOLOGY PROVIDES US WITH A RARE OPPORTUNITY. WE WILL EVENTUALLY POSSESS BILLIONS OF YOUR KIND.>
<TO SERVE US. TO BE SOLD INTO THE SERVICE OF OTHERS. COULD WE, I WONDER, MAKE YOU *BETTER AT THIS?* THE ABILITY TO UNDERSTAND OUR ORDERS, AND TO EXPRESS YOUR COMPLIANCE, SEEMED AN OBVIOUS FIRST STEP.>
<BUT HOW ELSE MIGHT WE *CHANGE* YOU?>

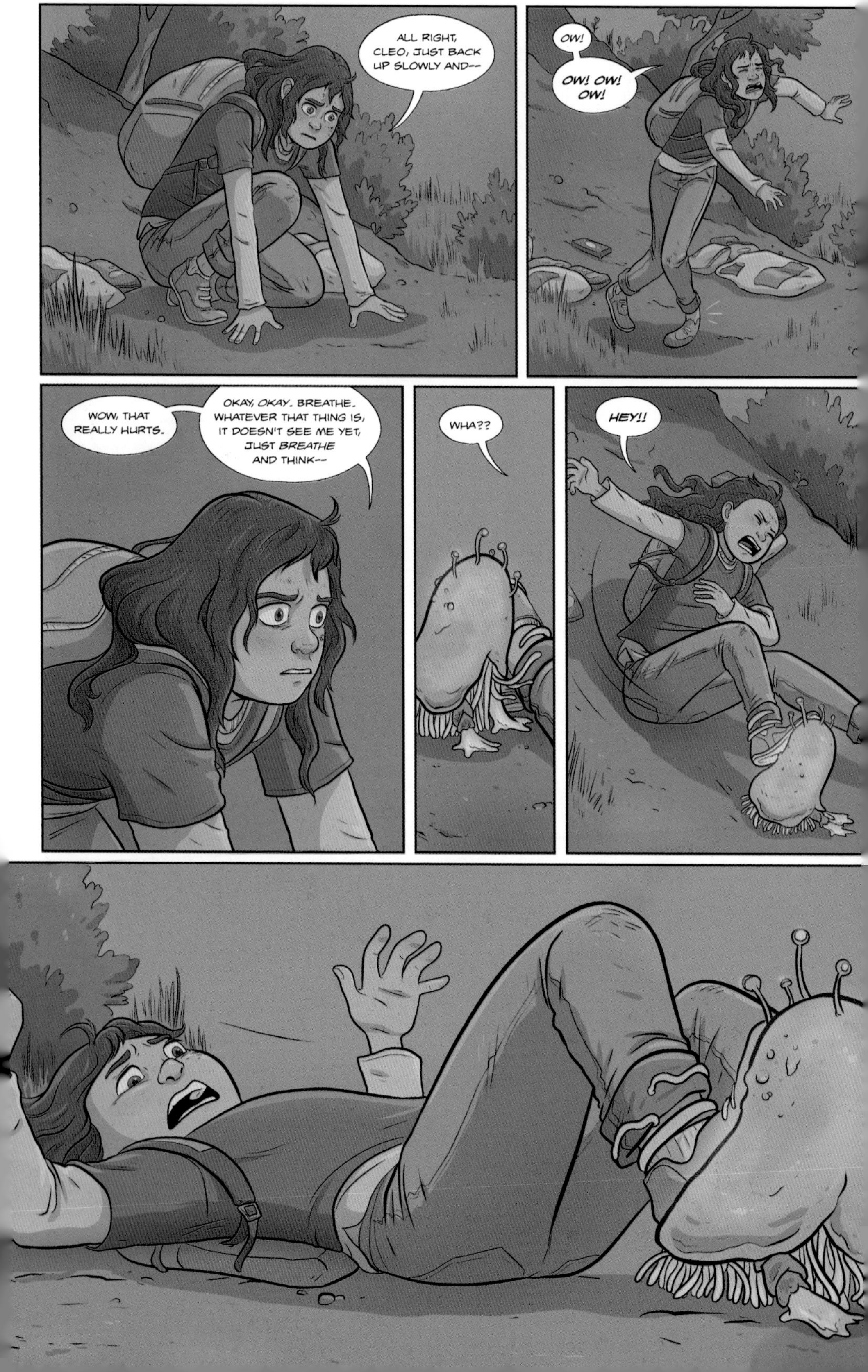
ALL RIGHT, CLEO, JUST BACK UP SLOWLY AND--
OW!
OW! OW! OW!
WOW, THAT REALLY HURTS.
OKAY, *OKAY*. BREATHE. WHATEVER THAT THING IS, IT DOESN'T SEE ME YET, JUST *BREATHE* AND THINK--
WHA??
HEY!!

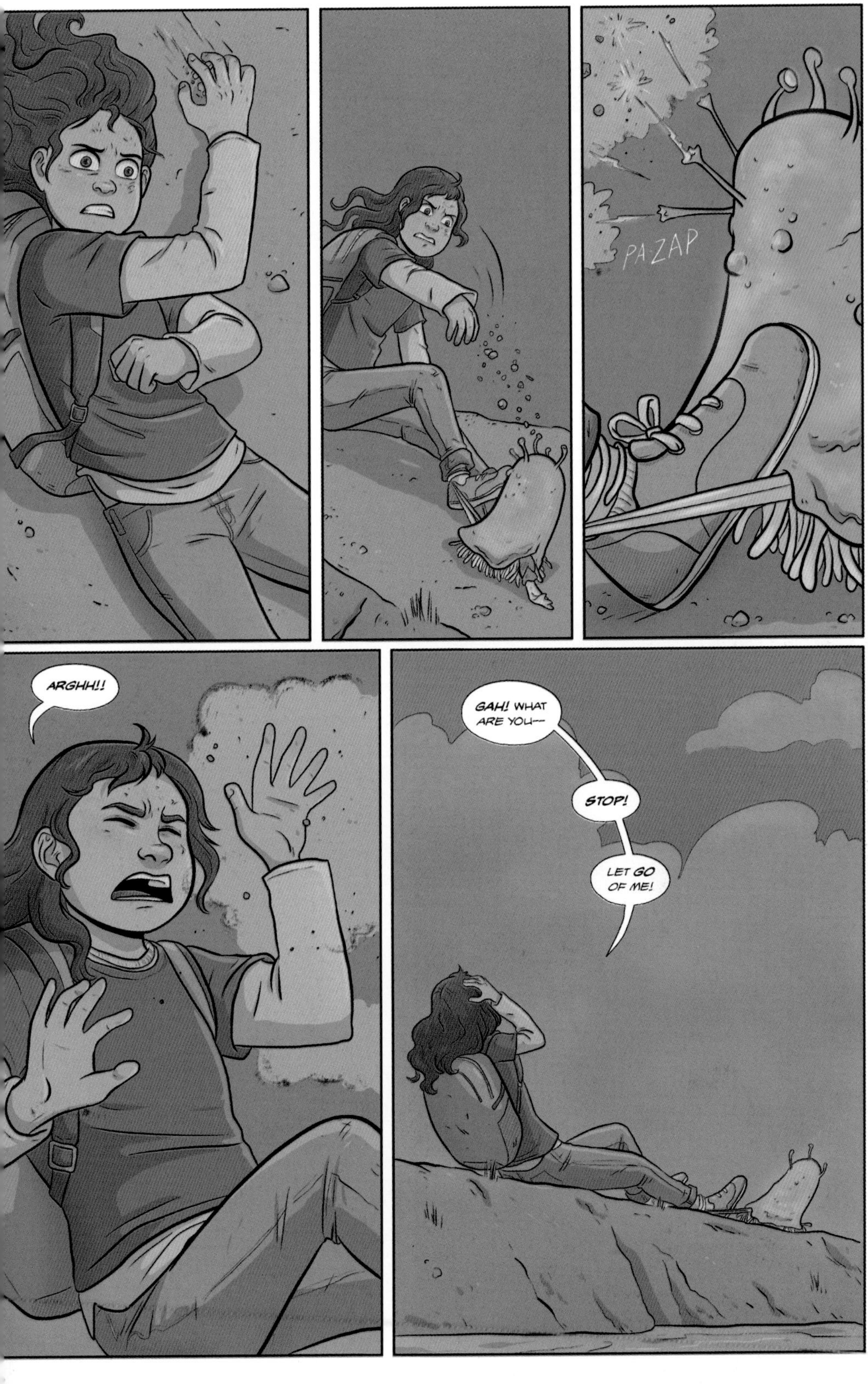
PA·ZAP
ARGHH!!
GAH! WHAT ARE YOU--
STOP!
LET GO OF ME!

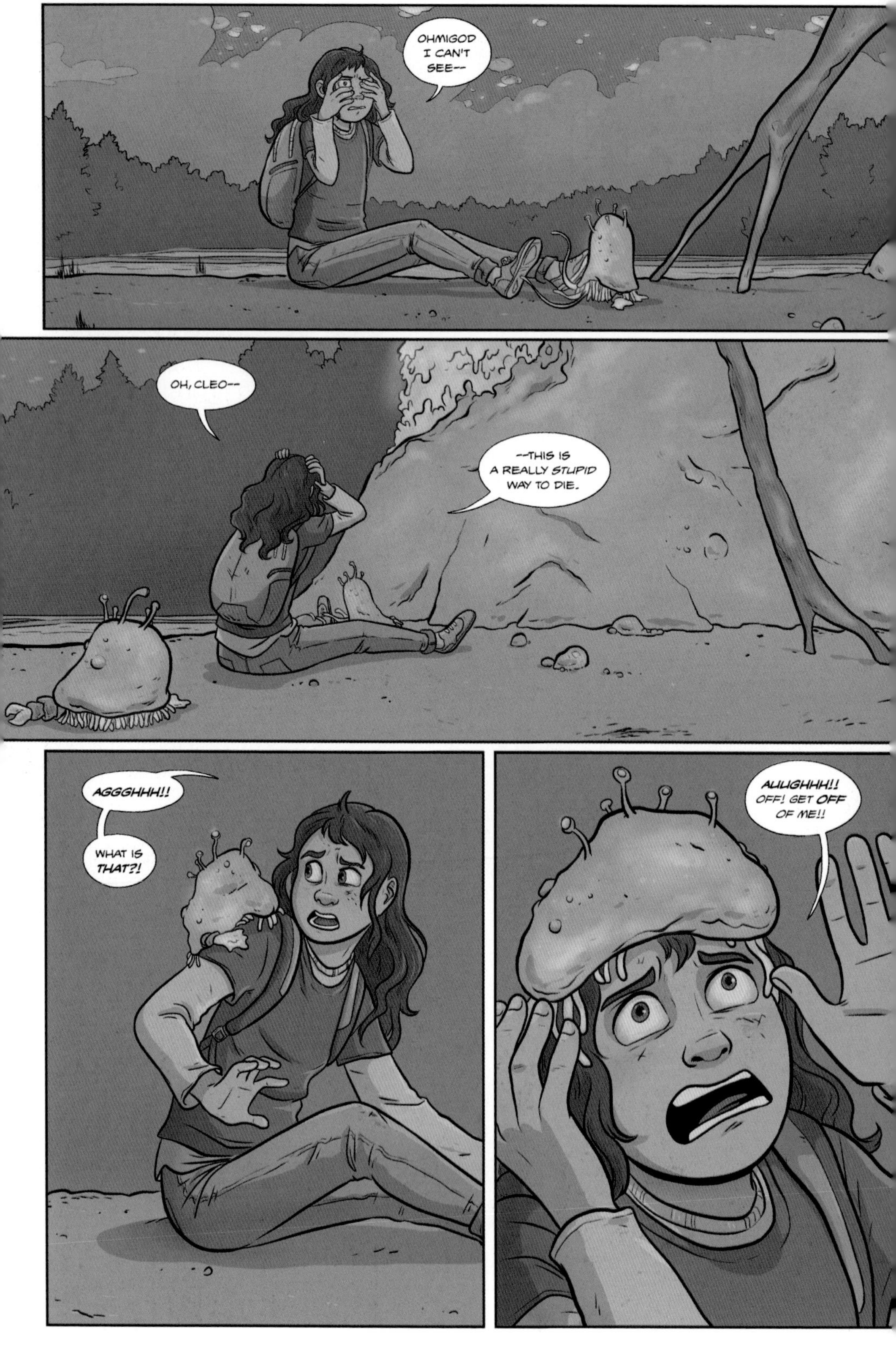
OHMIGOD I CAN'T SEE--
OH, CLEO--
--THIS IS A REALLY *STUPID* WAY TO DIE.
AGGGHHH!!
WHAT IS *THAT?!*
AUUGHHH!! OFF! GET *OFF* OF ME!!

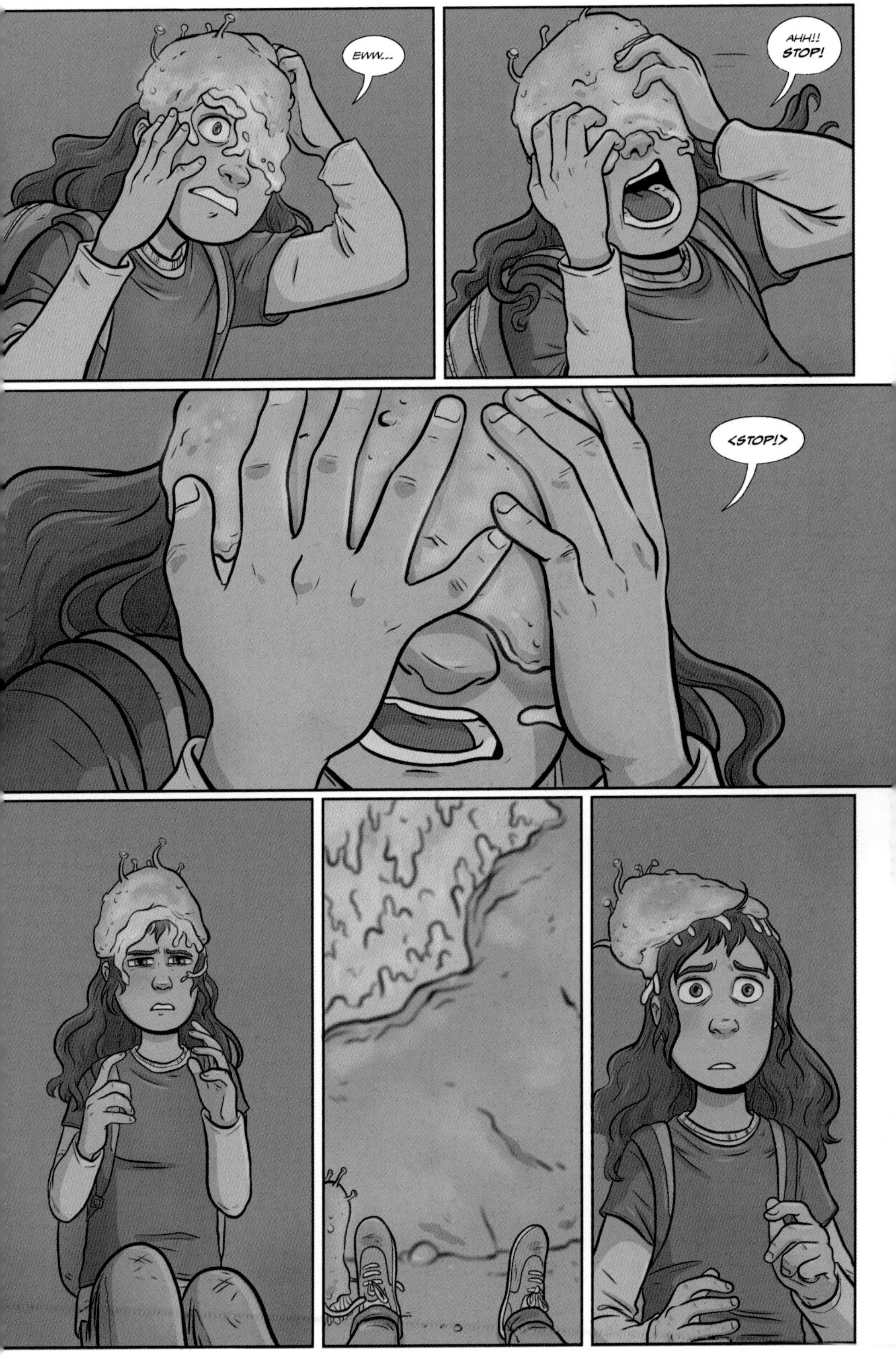
EWW...
AHH!!
STOP!
<STOP!>

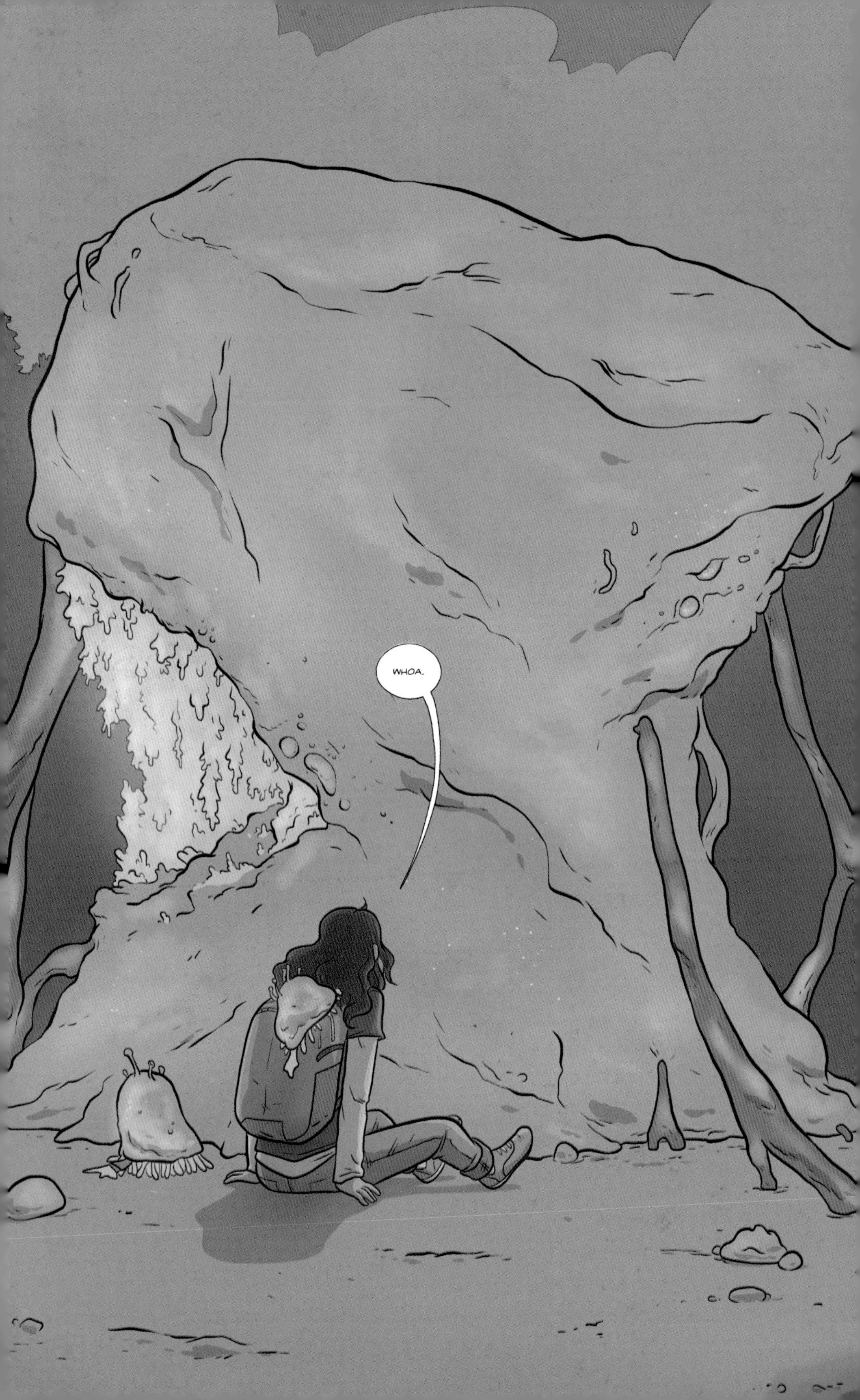
WHOA.

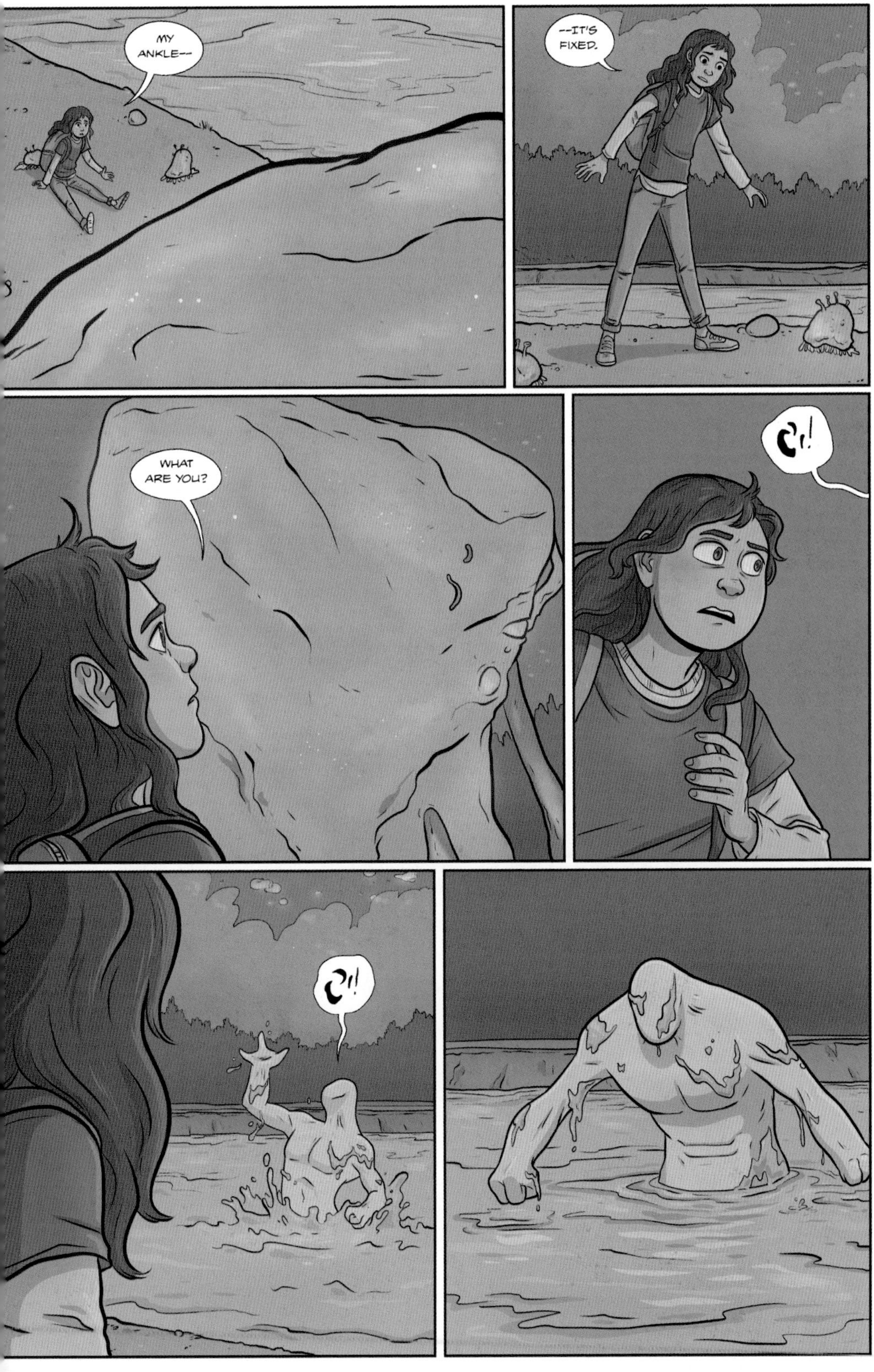
MY ANKLE--
--IT'S FIXED.
WHAT ARE YOU?

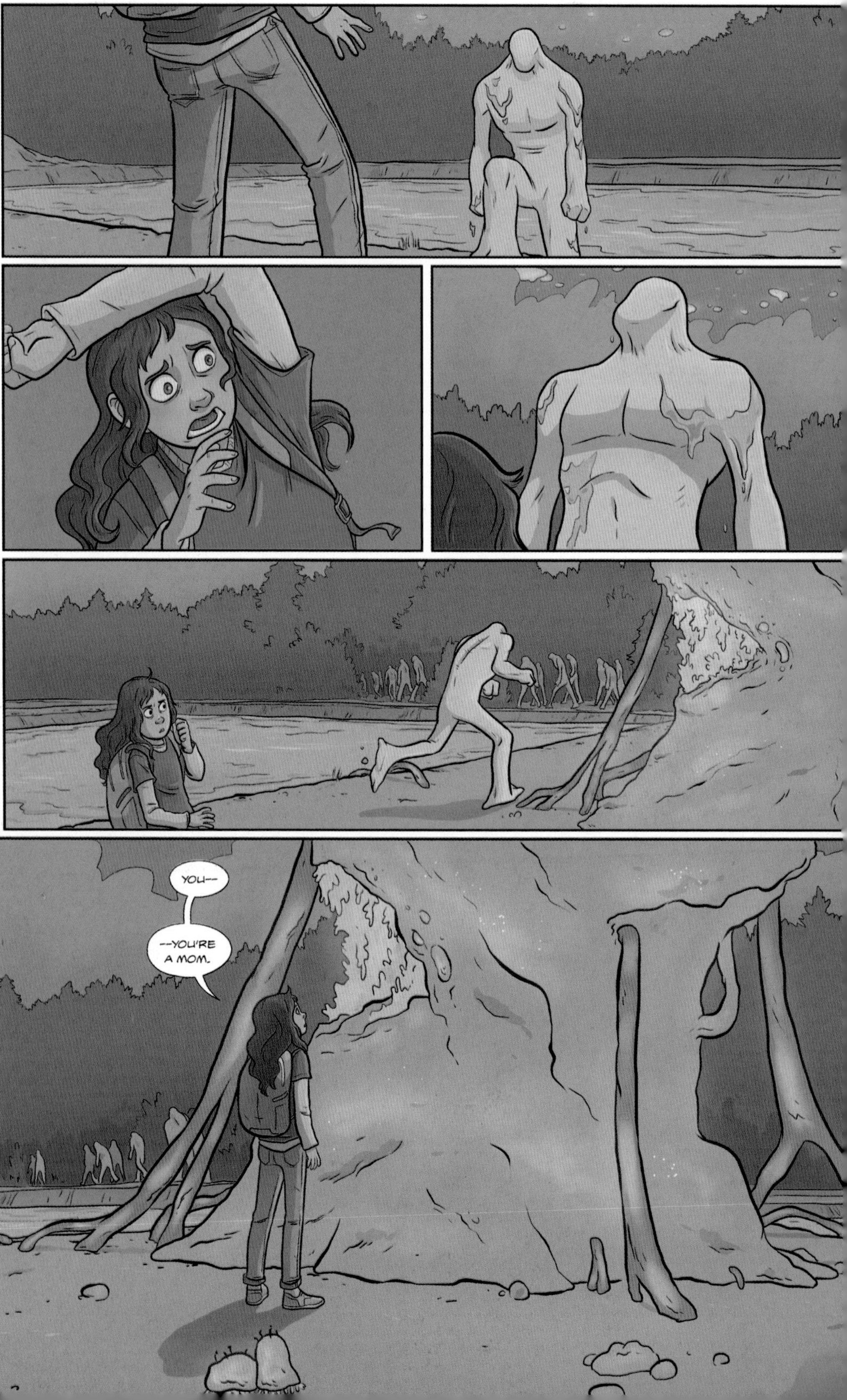
YOU--
--YOU'RE A MOM.

THREE

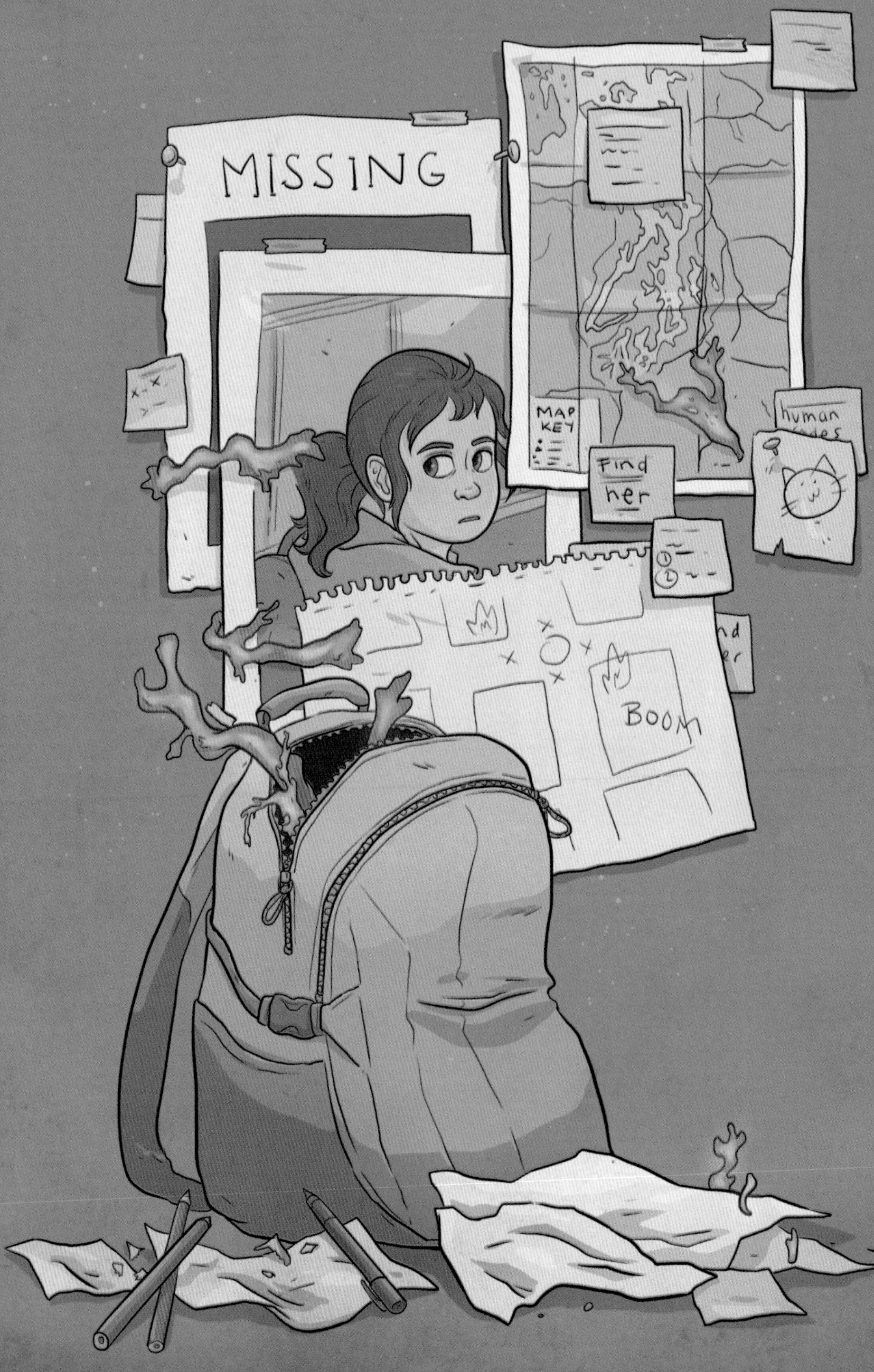
MISSING
MAP KEY
Find her
human
BOOM

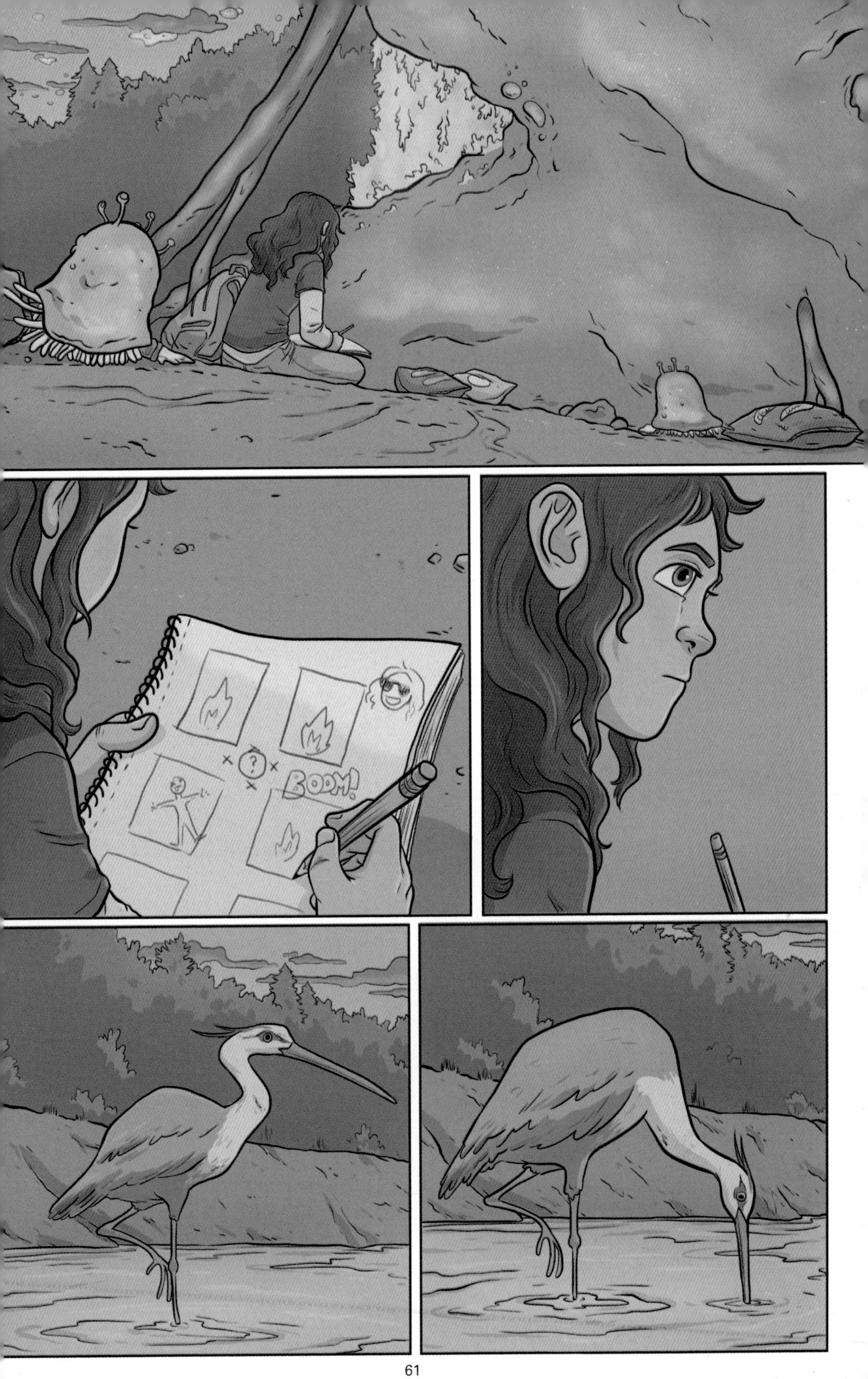
BOOM!

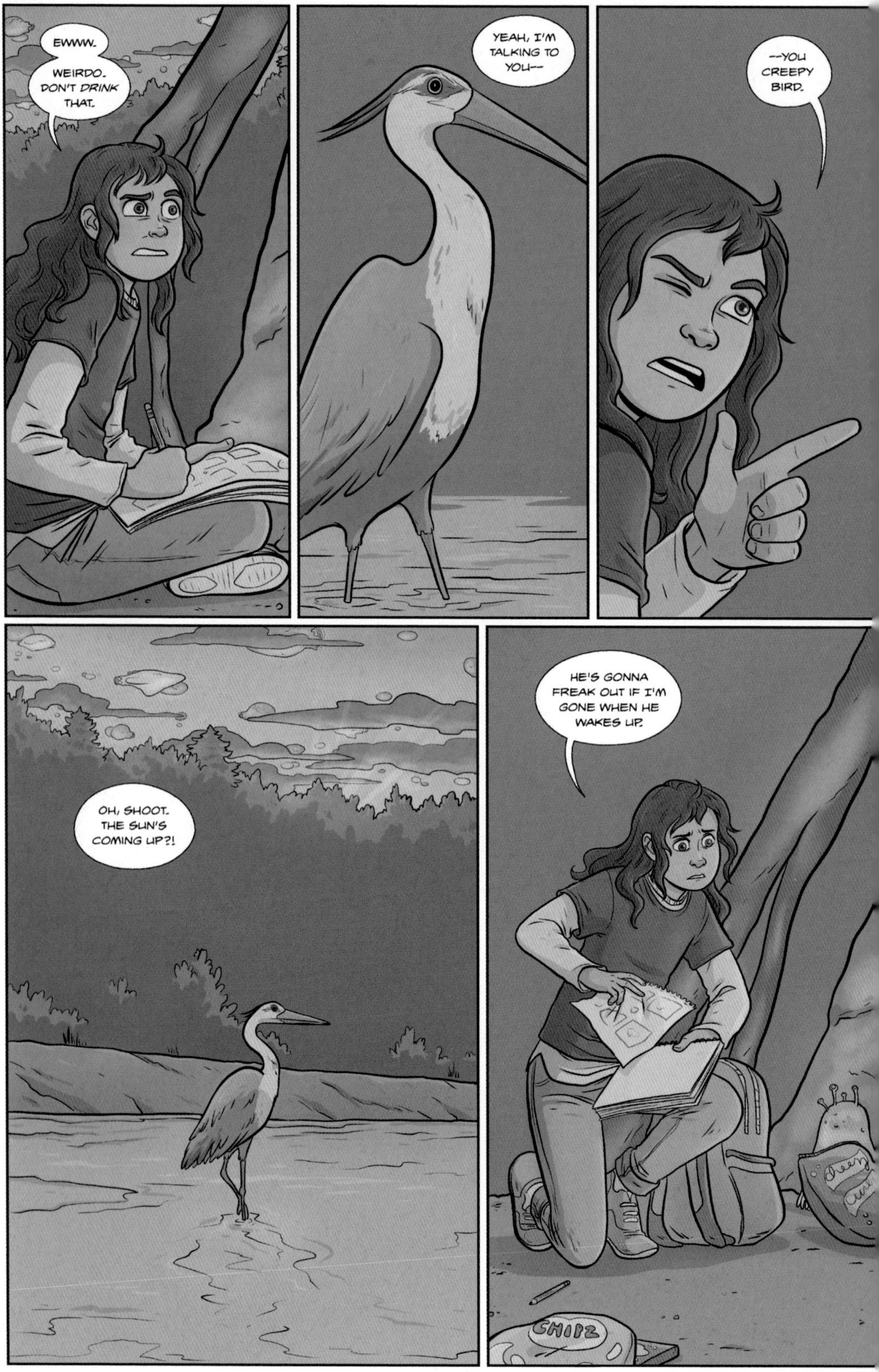
EWWW.
WEIRDO. DON'T *DRINK* THAT.
YEAH, I'M TALKING TO YOU--
--YOU CREEPY BIRD.
OH, SHOOT. THE SUN'S COMING UP?!
HE'S GONNA FREAK OUT IF I'M GONE WHEN HE WAKES UP.
CHIPZ

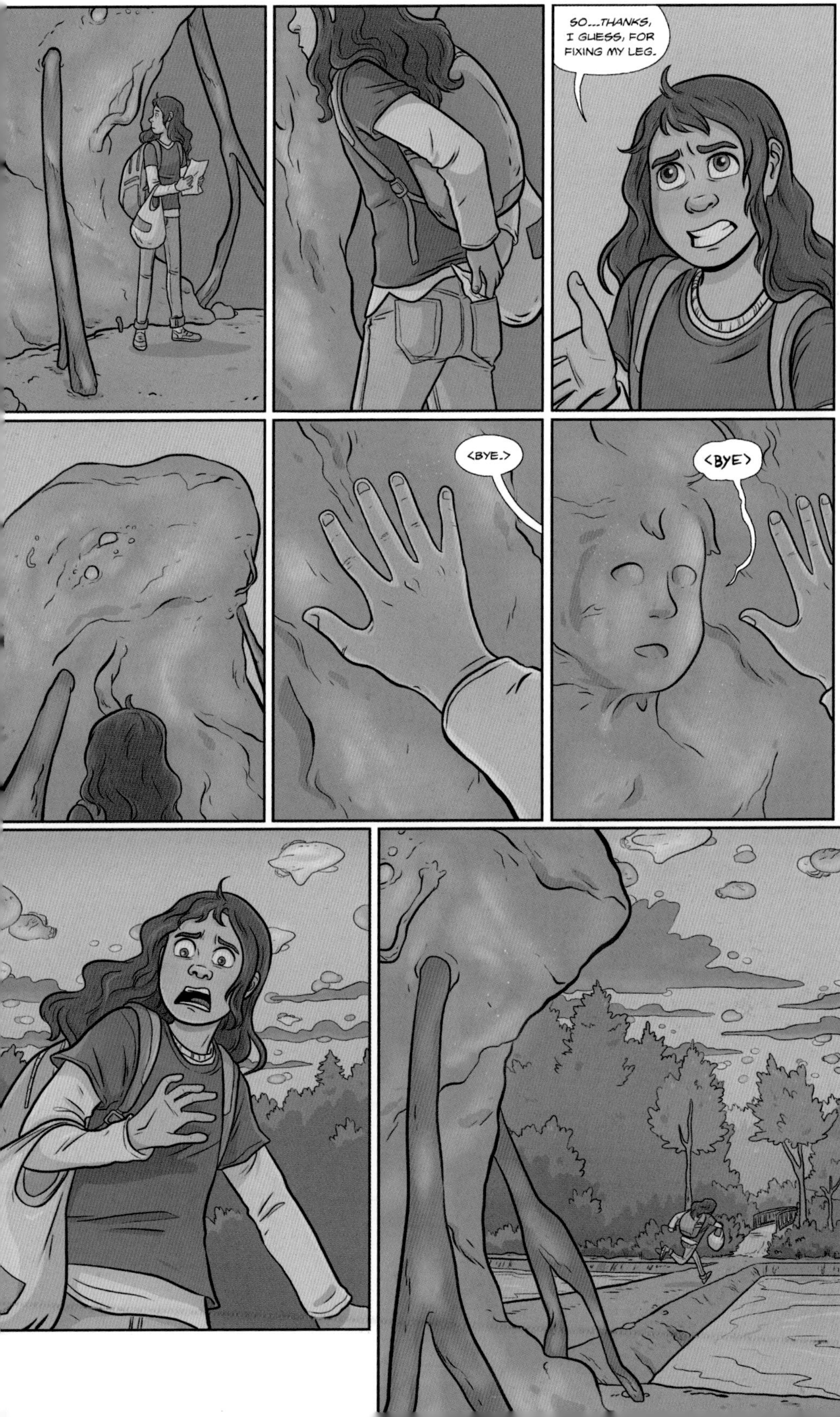
SO...THANKS, I GUESS, FOR FIXING MY LEG.
<BYE.>
<BYE>

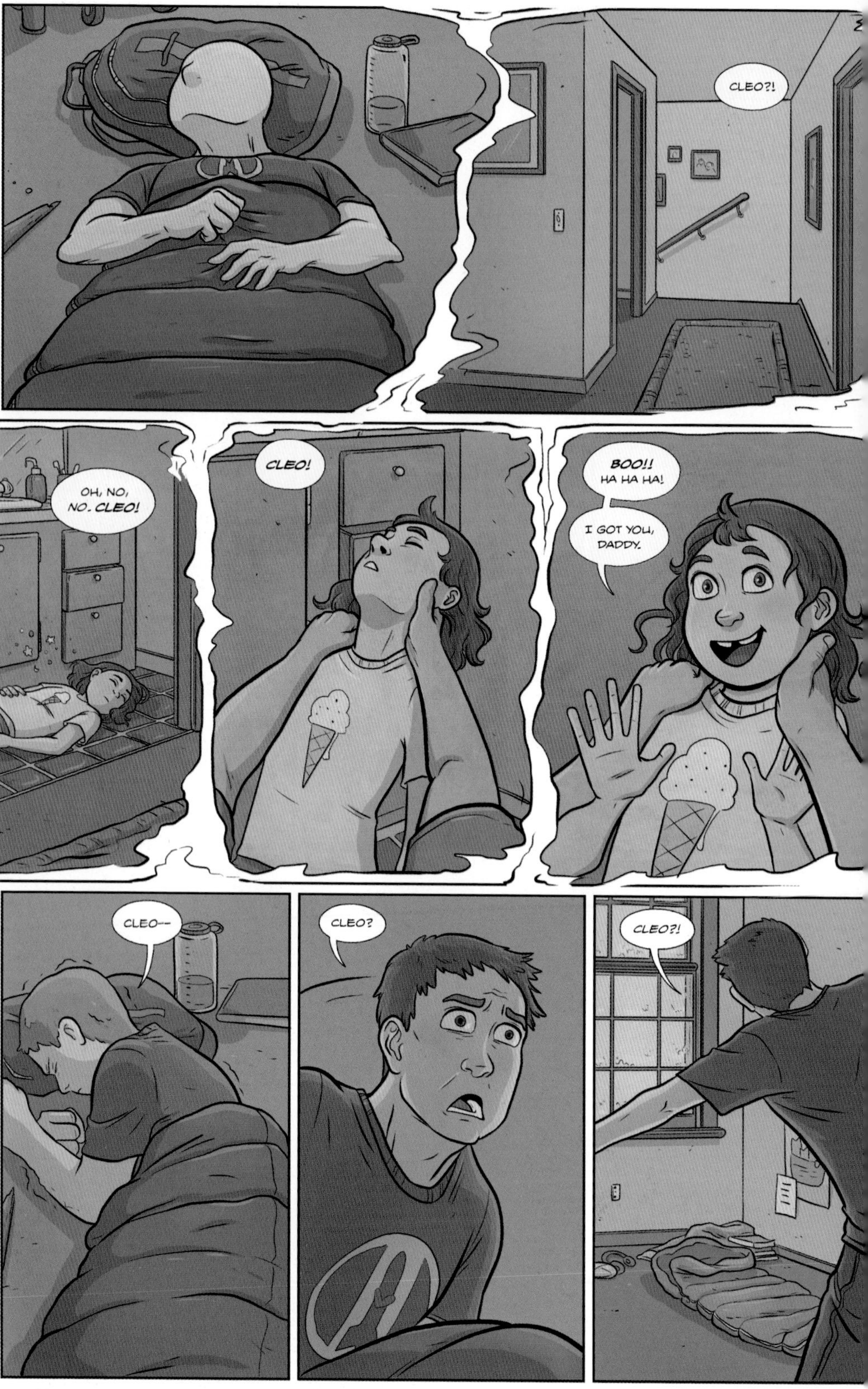
CLEO?!
OH, NO, NO. CLEO!
CLEO!
BOO!! HA HA HA!
I GOT YOU, DADDY.
CLEO--
CLEO?
CLEO?!

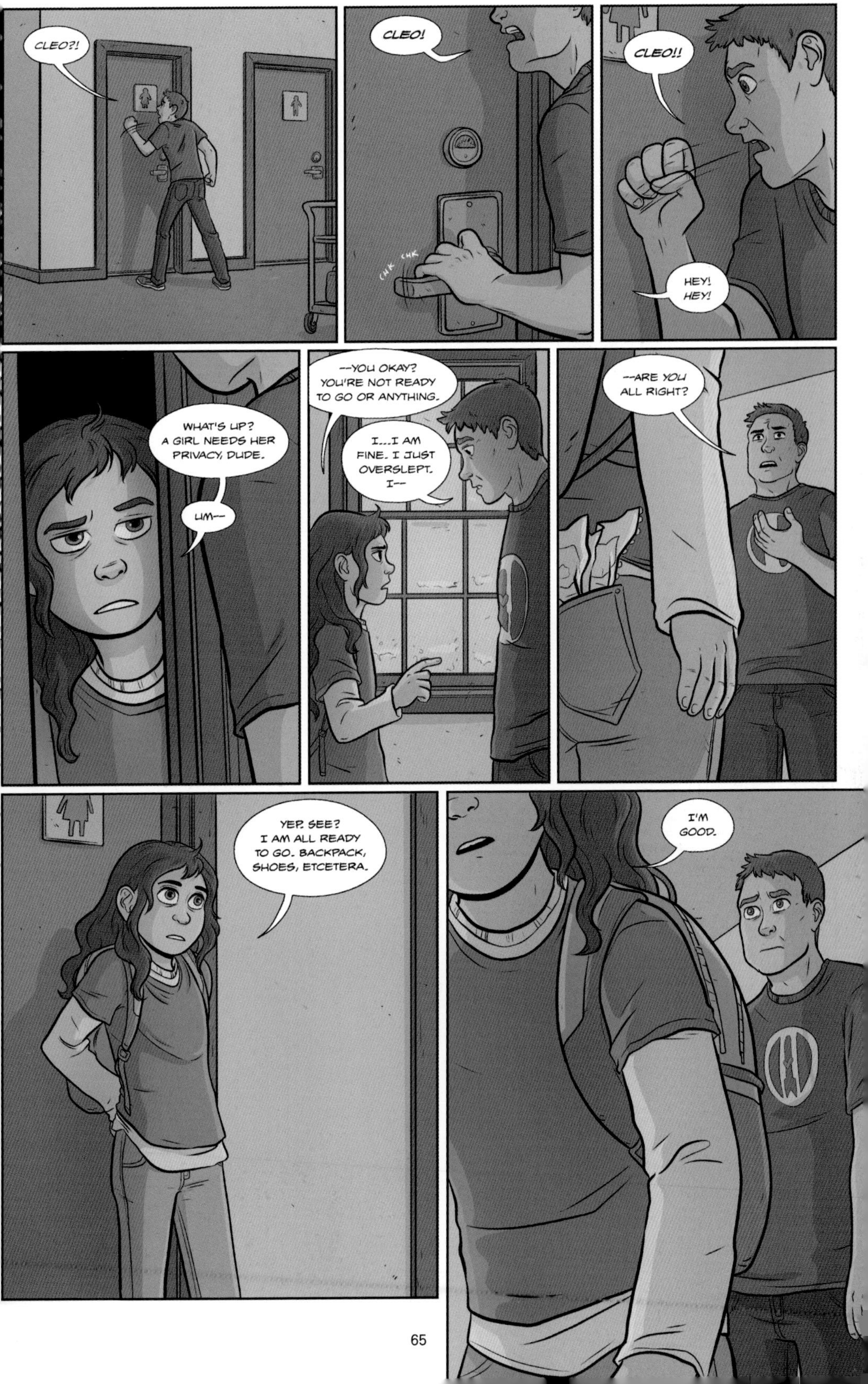
CLEO?!
CLEO!
CHK CHK
CLEO!!
HEY! HEY!
WHAT'S UP? A GIRL NEEDS HER PRIVACY, DUDE.
UM--
--YOU OKAY? YOU'RE NOT READY TO GO OR ANYTHING.
I...I AM FINE. I JUST OVERSLEPT. I--
--ARE YOU ALL RIGHT?
YEP. SEE? I AM ALL READY TO GO. BACKPACK, SHOES, ETCETERA.
I'M GOOD.

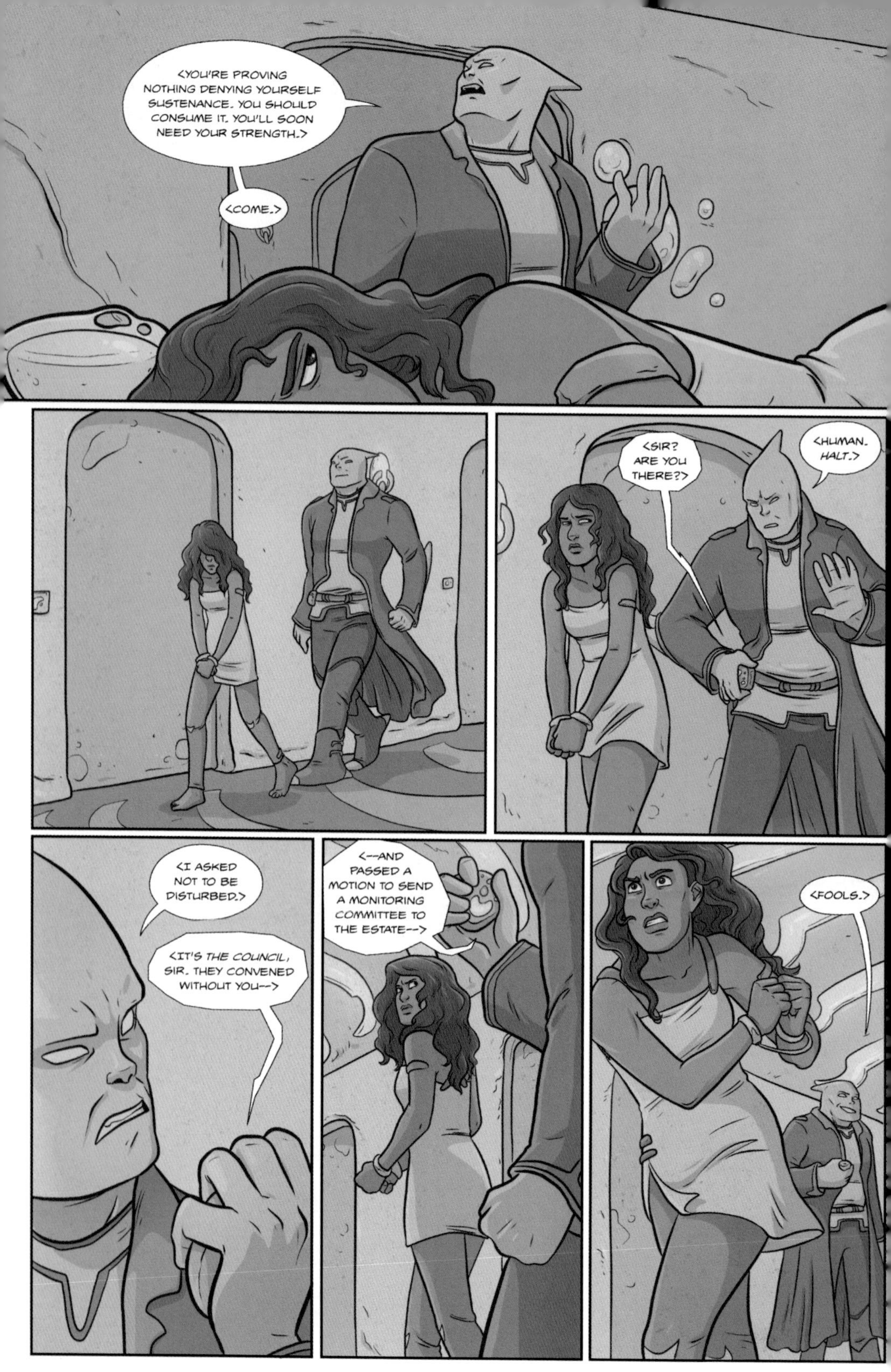
<YOU'RE PROVING NOTHING DENYING YOURSELF SUSTENANCE. YOU SHOULD CONSUME IT. YOU'LL SOON NEED YOUR STRENGTH.>
<COME.>
<SIR? ARE YOU THERE?>
<HUMAN. HALT.>
<I ASKED NOT TO BE DISTURBED.>
<IT'S *THE COUNCIL*, SIR. THEY CONVENED WITHOUT YOU-->
<--AND PASSED A MOTION TO SEND A MONITORING COMMITTEE TO THE ESTATE-->
<FOOLS.>

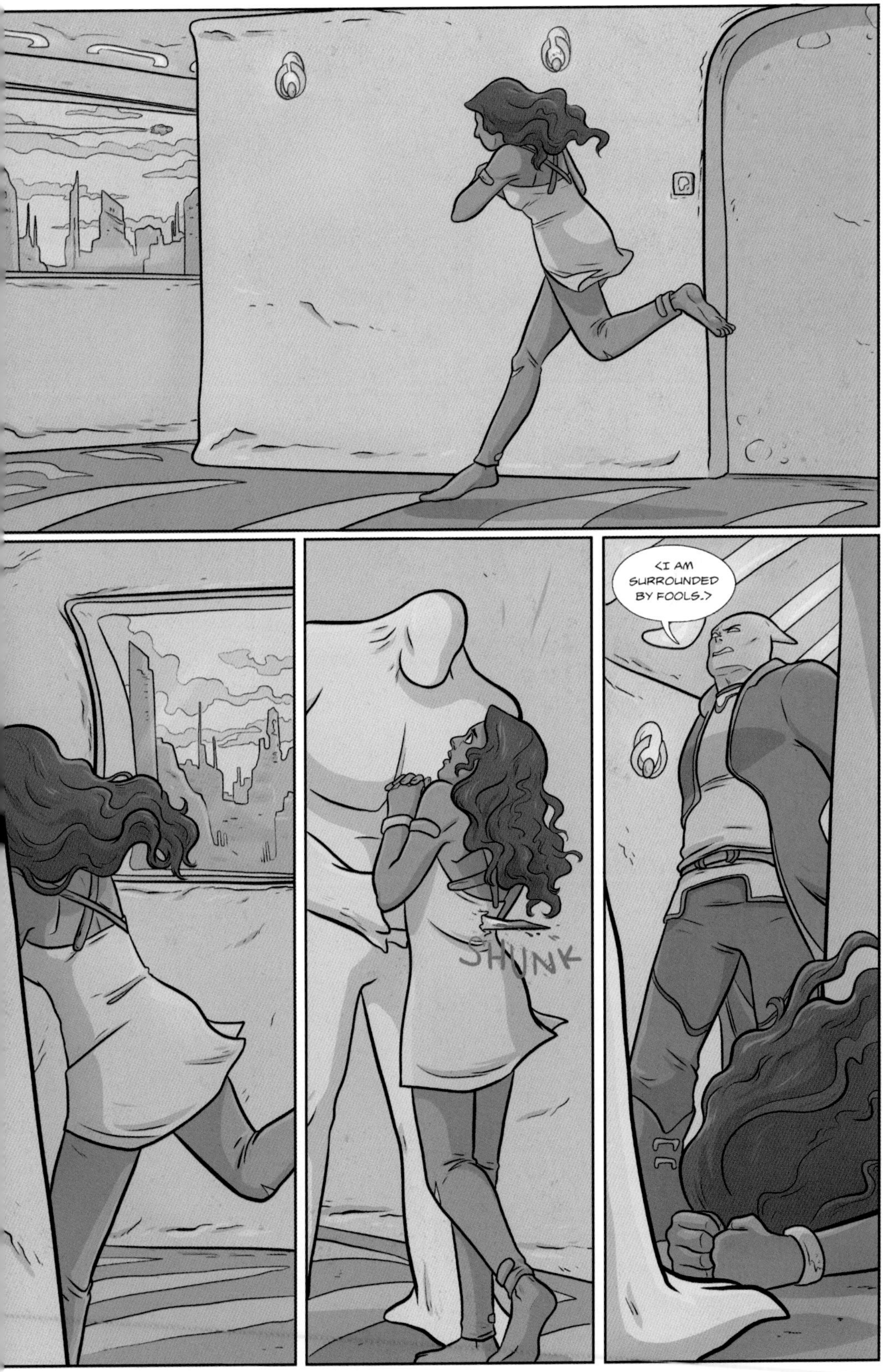
SHUNK
<I AM SURROUNDED BY FOOLS.>

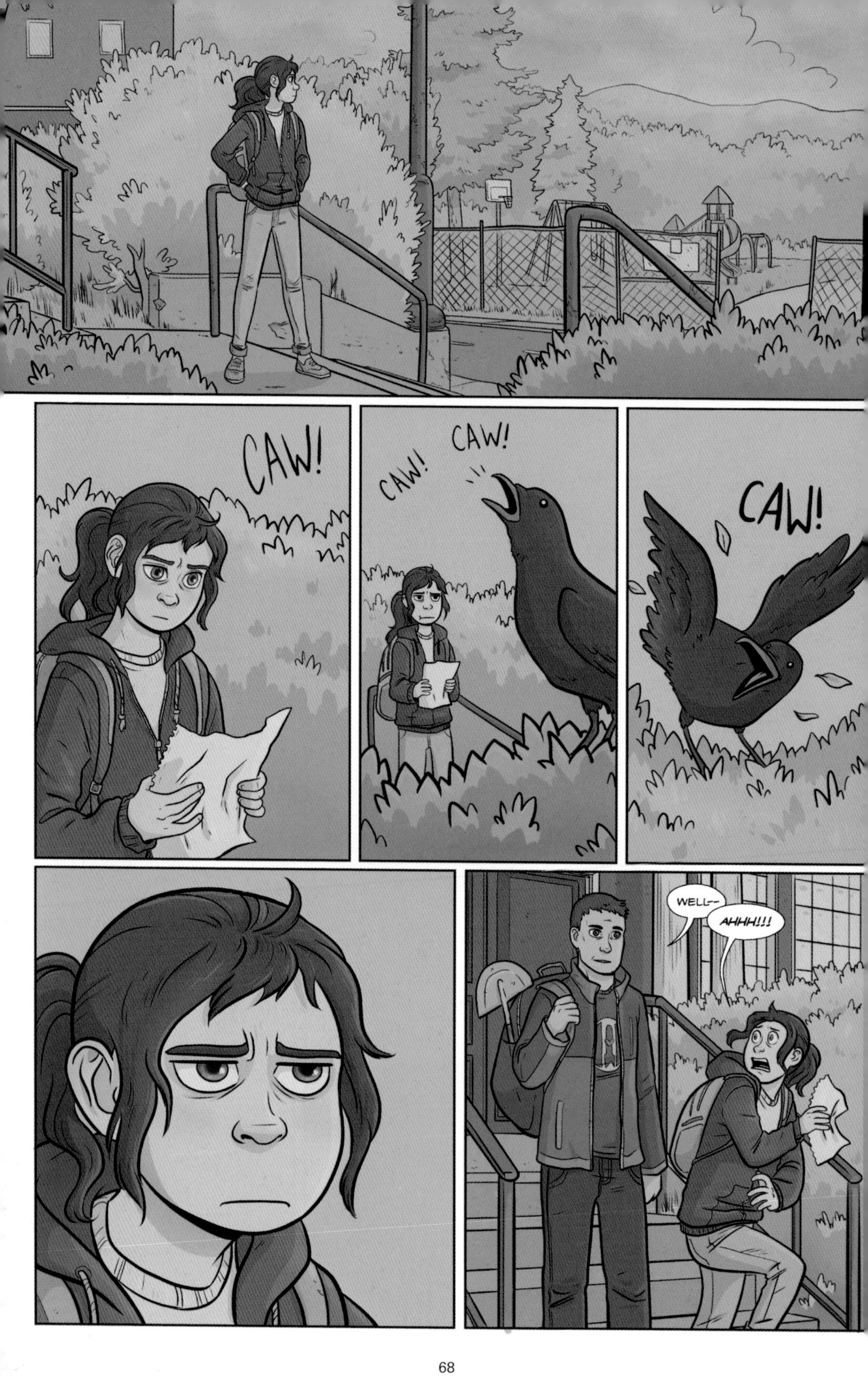
CAW!
CAW!
CAW!
CAW!
WELL--
AHHH!!!

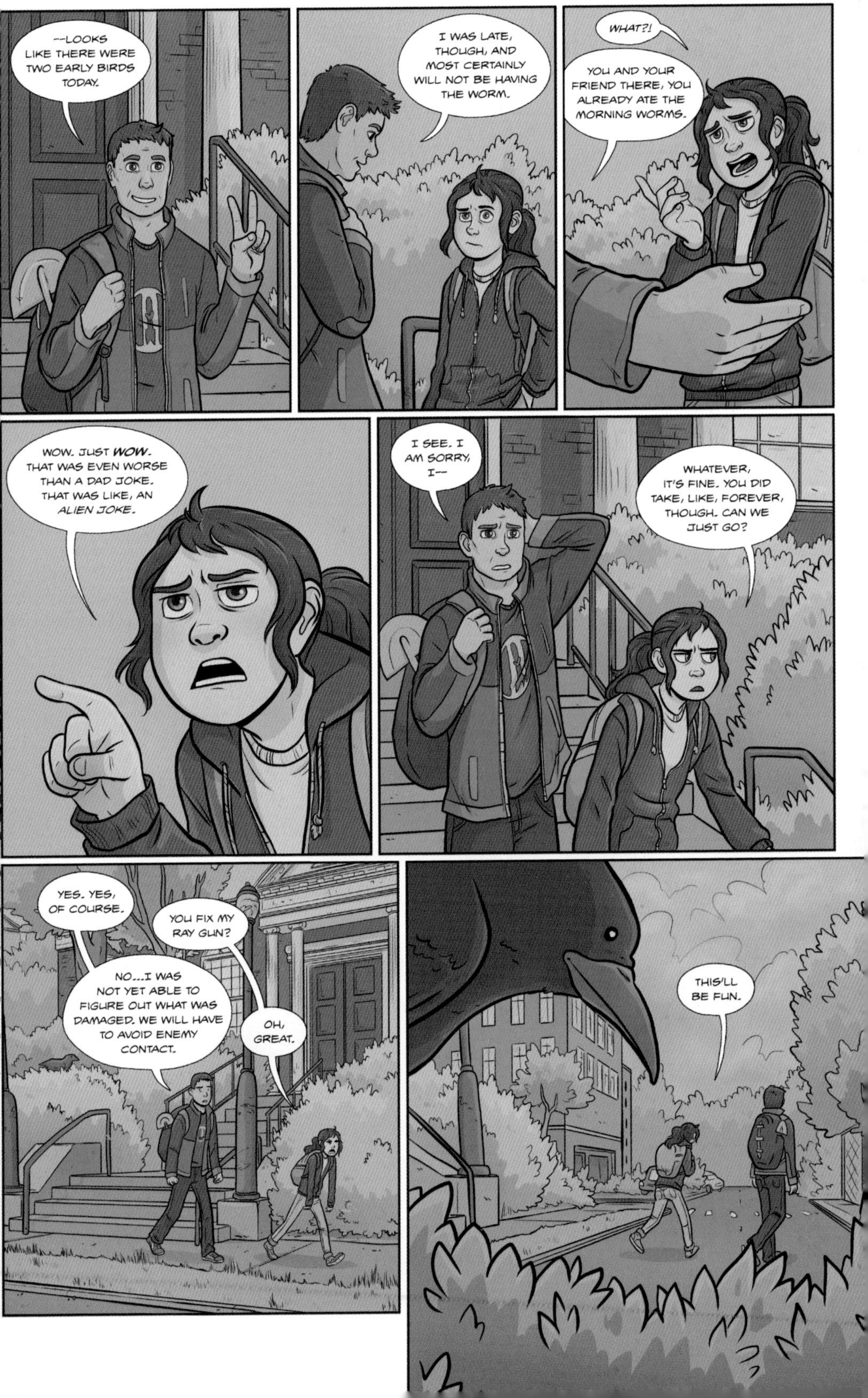
--LOOKS LIKE THERE WERE TWO EARLY BIRDS TODAY.
I WAS LATE, THOUGH, AND MOST CERTAINLY WILL NOT BE HAVING THE WORM.
WHAT?!
YOU AND YOUR FRIEND THERE, YOU ALREADY ATE THE MORNING WORMS.
WOW. JUST WOW. THAT WAS EVEN WORSE THAN A DAD JOKE. THAT WAS LIKE, AN ALIEN JOKE.
I SEE. I AM SORRY, I--
WHATEVER, IT'S FINE. YOU DID TAKE, LIKE, FOREVER, THOUGH. CAN WE JUST GO?
YES. YES, OF COURSE.
YOU FIX MY RAY GUN?
NO...I WAS NOT YET ABLE TO FIGURE OUT WHAT WAS DAMAGED. WE WILL HAVE TO AVOID ENEMY CONTACT.
OH, GREAT.
THIS'LL BE FUN.

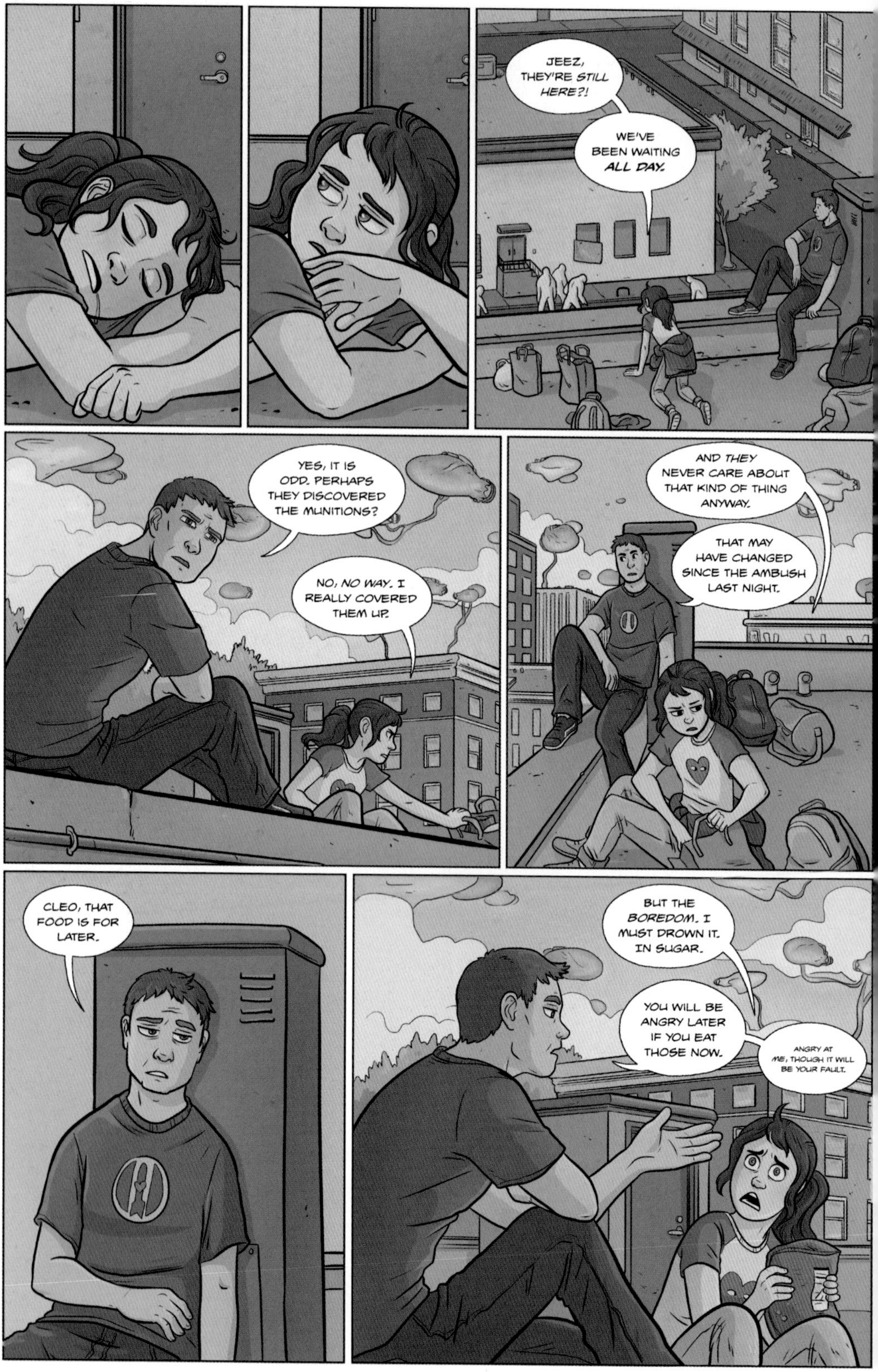
JEEZ, THEY'RE STILL HERE?!
WE'VE BEEN WAITING ALL DAY.
YES, IT IS ODD. PERHAPS THEY DISCOVERED THE MUNITIONS?
NO, NO WAY. I REALLY COVERED THEM UP.
AND THEY NEVER CARE ABOUT THAT KIND OF THING ANYWAY.
THAT MAY HAVE CHANGED SINCE THE AMBUSH LAST NIGHT.
CLEO, THAT FOOD IS FOR LATER.
BUT THE BOREDOM. I MUST DROWN IT IN SUGAR.
YOU WILL BE ANGRY LATER IF YOU EAT THOSE NOW.
ANGRY AT ME, THOUGH IT WILL BE YOUR FAULT.

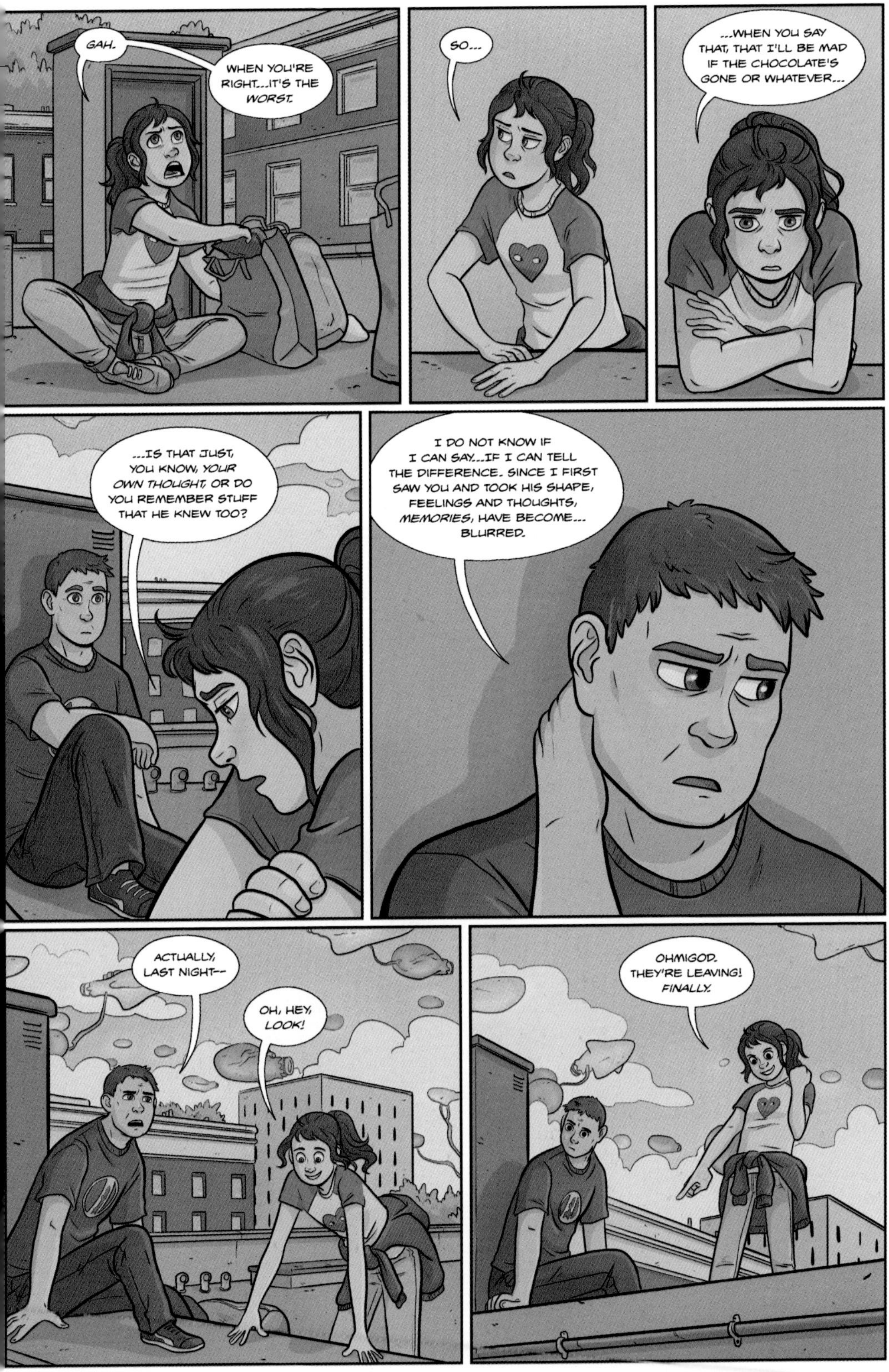
GAH.
WHEN YOU'RE RIGHT...IT'S THE *WORST.*
SO...
...WHEN YOU SAY THAT, THAT I'LL BE MAD IF THE CHOCOLATE'S GONE OR WHATEVER...
...IS THAT JUST, YOU KNOW, *YOUR OWN THOUGHT,* OR DO YOU REMEMBER STUFF THAT HE KNEW TOO?
I DO NOT KNOW IF I CAN SAY...IF I CAN TELL THE DIFFERENCE. SINCE I FIRST SAW YOU AND TOOK HIS SHAPE, FEELINGS AND THOUGHTS, *MEMORIES,* HAVE BECOME... BLURRED.
ACTUALLY, LAST NIGHT--
OH, HEY, *LOOK!*
OHMIGOD. THEY'RE LEAVING! *FINALLY.*

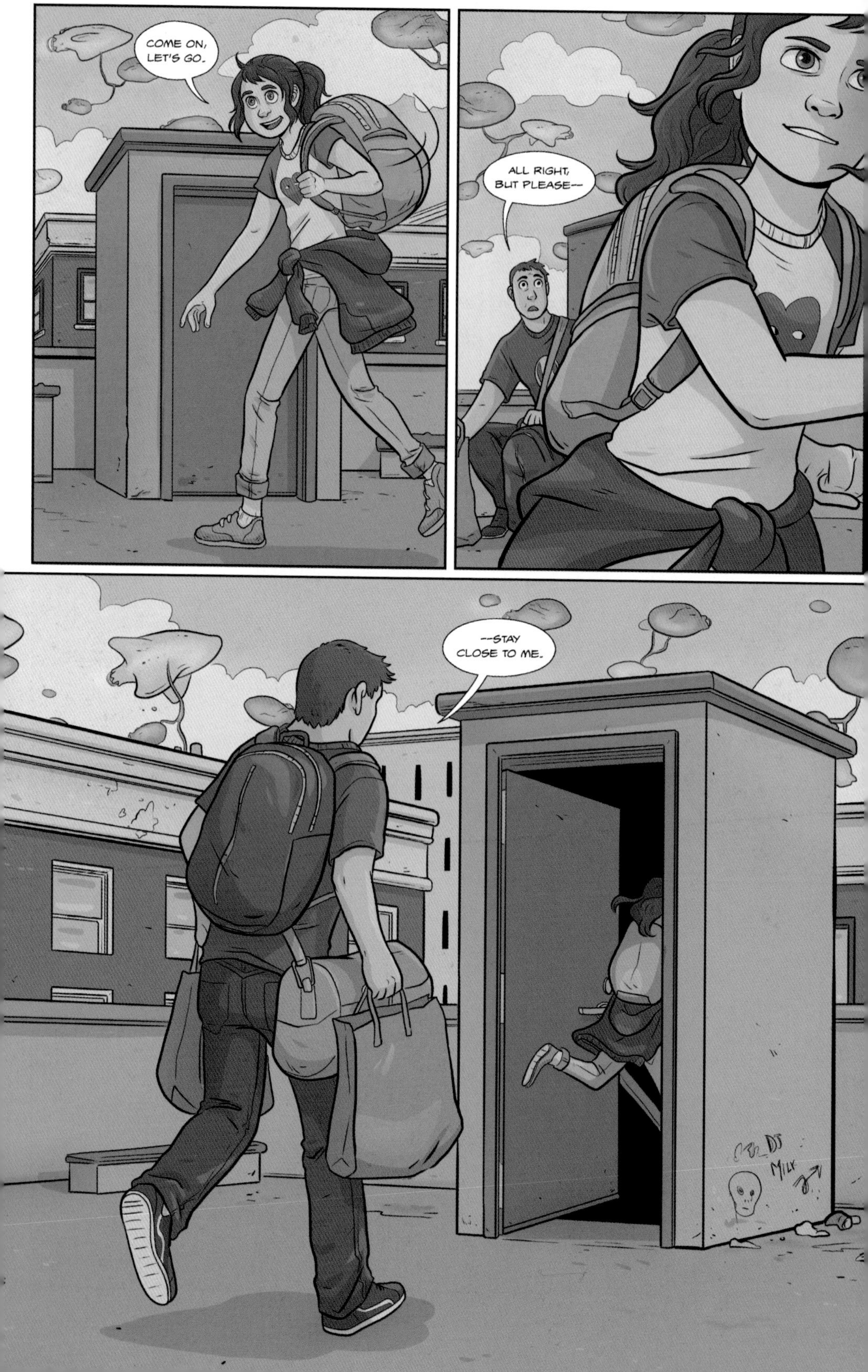
COME ON, LET'S GO.
ALL RIGHT, BUT PLEASE--
--STAY CLOSE TO ME.
DJ MILK

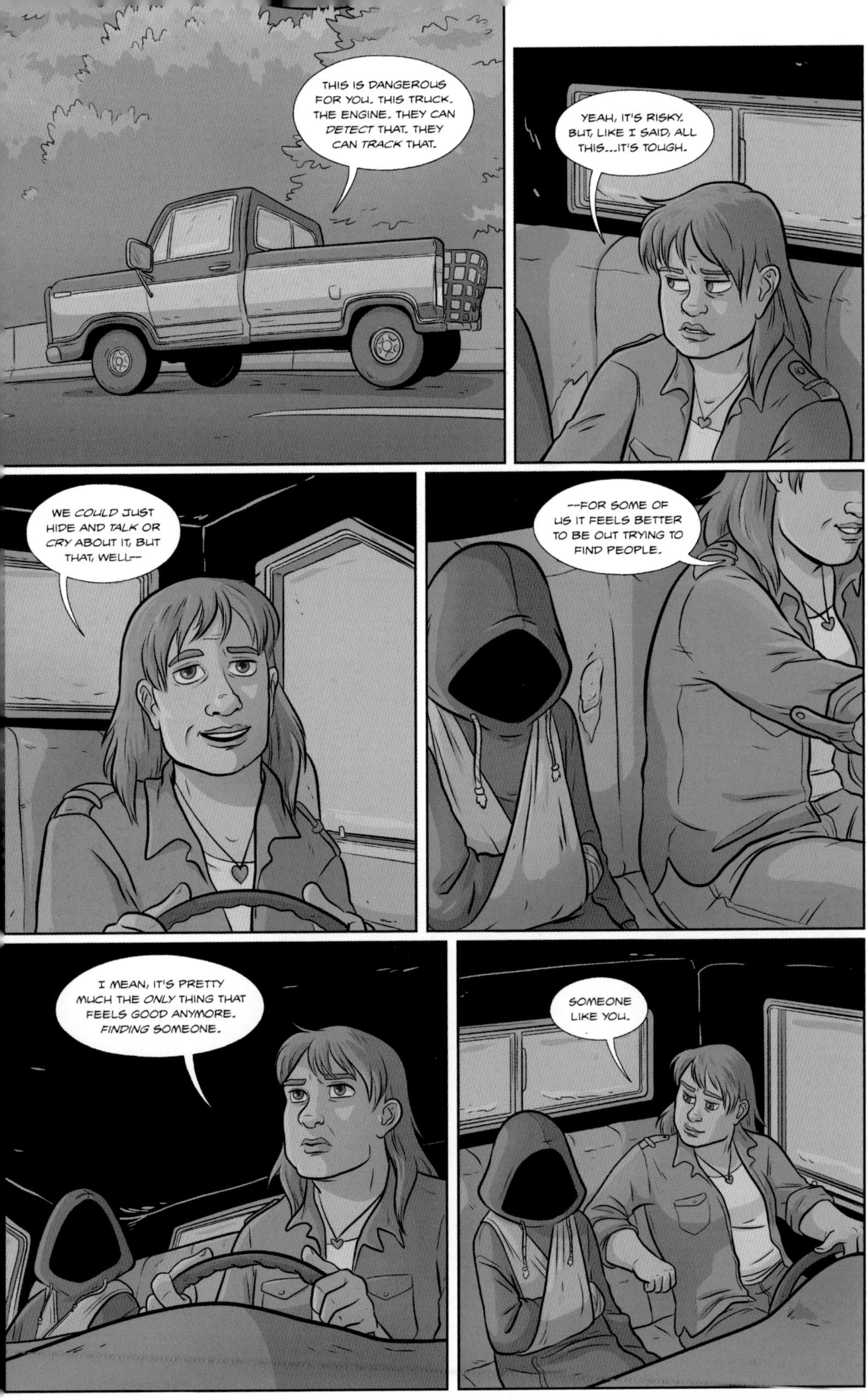
THIS IS DANGEROUS FOR YOU. THIS TRUCK. THE ENGINE. THEY CAN *DETECT* THAT. THEY CAN *TRACK* THAT.
YEAH, IT'S RISKY. BUT, LIKE I SAID, ALL THIS...IT'S TOUGH.
WE *COULD* JUST HIDE AND *TALK* OR *CRY* ABOUT IT, BUT THAT, WELL--
--FOR SOME OF US IT FEELS BETTER TO BE OUT TRYING TO FIND PEOPLE.
I MEAN, IT'S PRETTY MUCH THE *ONLY* THING THAT FEELS GOOD ANYMORE. *FINDING* SOMEONE.
SOMEONE LIKE YOU.

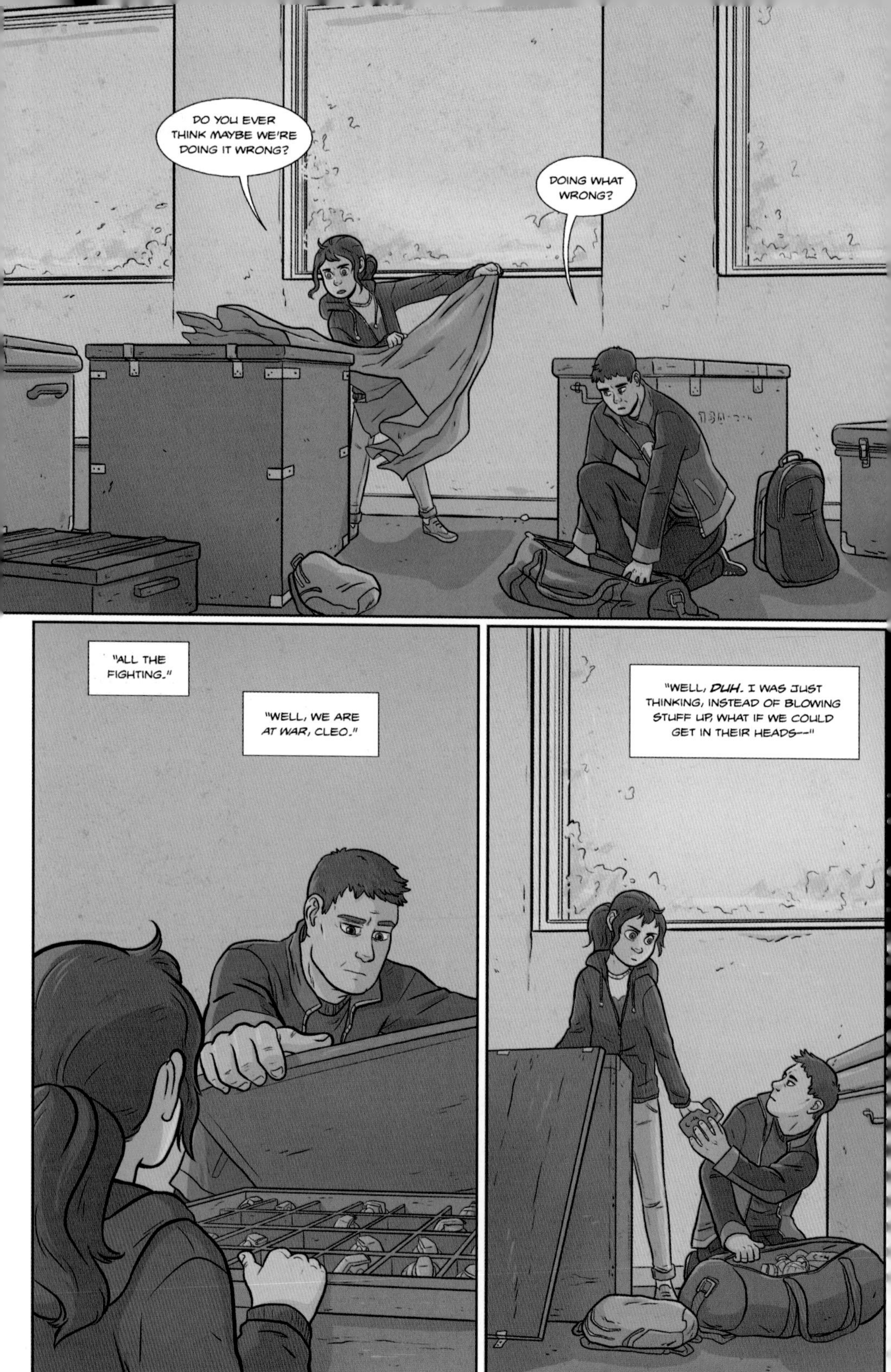
DO YOU EVER THINK MAYBE WE'RE DOING IT WRONG?
DOING WHAT WRONG?
"ALL THE FIGHTING."
"WELL, WE ARE *AT WAR*, CLEO."
"WELL, *DUH*. I WAS JUST THINKING, INSTEAD OF BLOWING STUFF UP, WHAT IF WE COULD GET IN THEIR HEADS--"

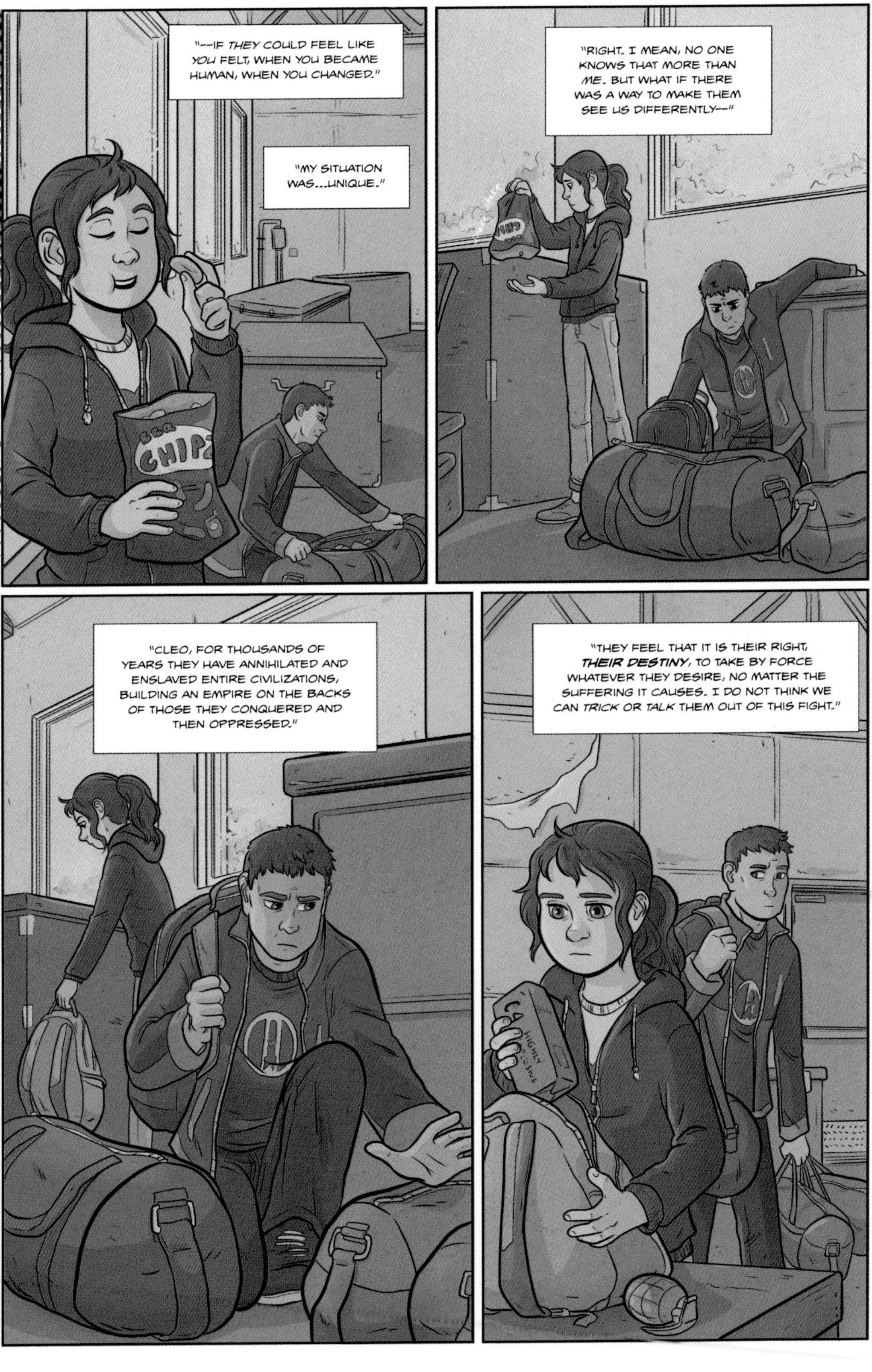
"--IF *THEY* COULD FEEL LIKE *YOU* FELT, WHEN YOU BECAME HUMAN, WHEN YOU CHANGED."
"MY SITUATION WAS...UNIQUE."
"RIGHT. I MEAN, NO ONE KNOWS THAT MORE THAN *ME*. BUT WHAT IF THERE WAS A WAY TO MAKE THEM SEE US DIFFERENTLY--"
"CLEO, FOR THOUSANDS OF YEARS THEY HAVE ANNIHILATED AND ENSLAVED ENTIRE CIVILIZATIONS, BUILDING AN EMPIRE ON THE BACKS OF THOSE THEY CONQUERED AND THEN OPPRESSED."
"THEY FEEL THAT IT IS THEIR RIGHT, ***THEIR DESTINY***, TO TAKE BY FORCE WHATEVER THEY DESIRE, NO MATTER THE SUFFERING IT CAUSES. I DO NOT THINK WE CAN *TRICK* OR *TALK* THEM OUT OF THIS FIGHT."

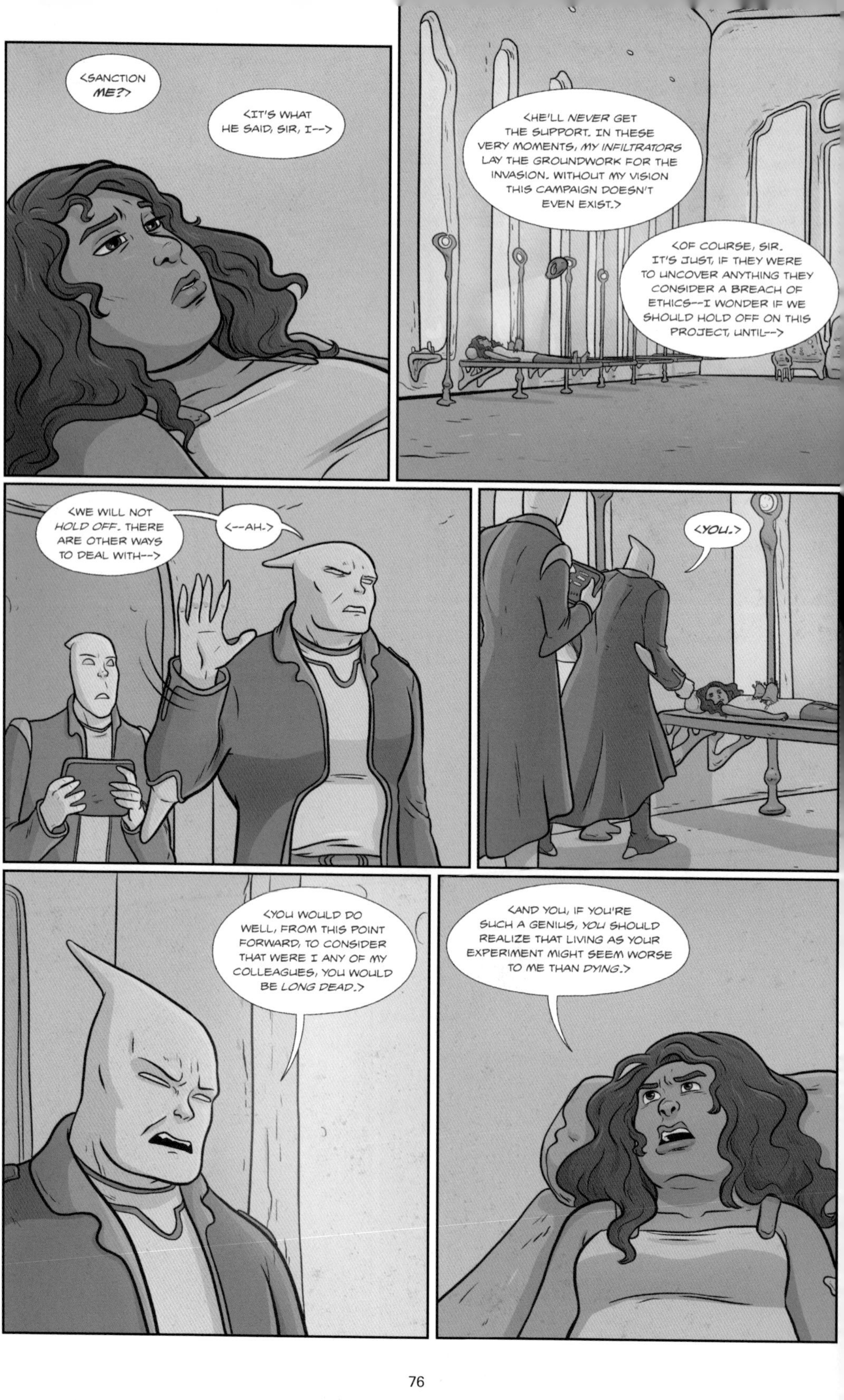
<SANCTION ME?>
<IT'S WHAT HE SAID, SIR, I-->
<HE'LL NEVER GET THE SUPPORT. IN THESE VERY MOMENTS, MY INFILTRATORS LAY THE GROUNDWORK FOR THE INVASION. WITHOUT MY VISION THIS CAMPAIGN DOESN'T EVEN EXIST.>
<OF COURSE, SIR. IT'S JUST, IF THEY WERE TO UNCOVER ANYTHING THEY CONSIDER A BREACH OF ETHICS--I WONDER IF WE SHOULD HOLD OFF ON THIS PROJECT, UNTIL-->
<WE WILL NOT HOLD OFF. THERE ARE OTHER WAYS TO DEAL WITH-->
<--AH.>
<YOU.>
<YOU WOULD DO WELL, FROM THIS POINT FORWARD, TO CONSIDER THAT WERE I ANY OF MY COLLEAGUES, YOU WOULD BE LONG DEAD.>
<AND YOU, IF YOU'RE SUCH A GENIUS, YOU SHOULD REALIZE THAT LIVING AS YOUR EXPERIMENT MIGHT SEEM WORSE TO ME THAN DYING.>

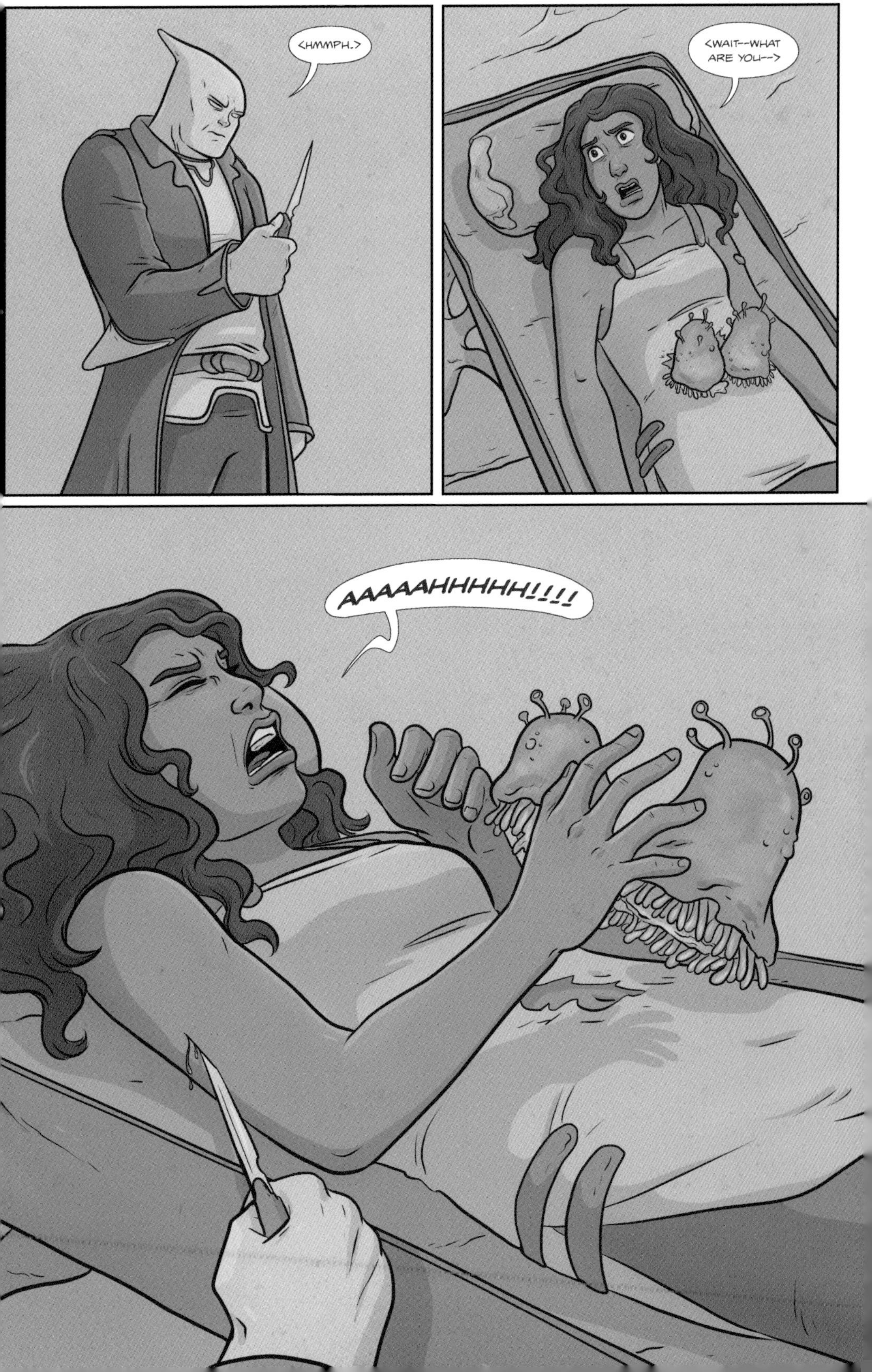
<HMMPH.>
<WAIT--WHAT ARE YOU-->
AAAAAHHHHH!!!!

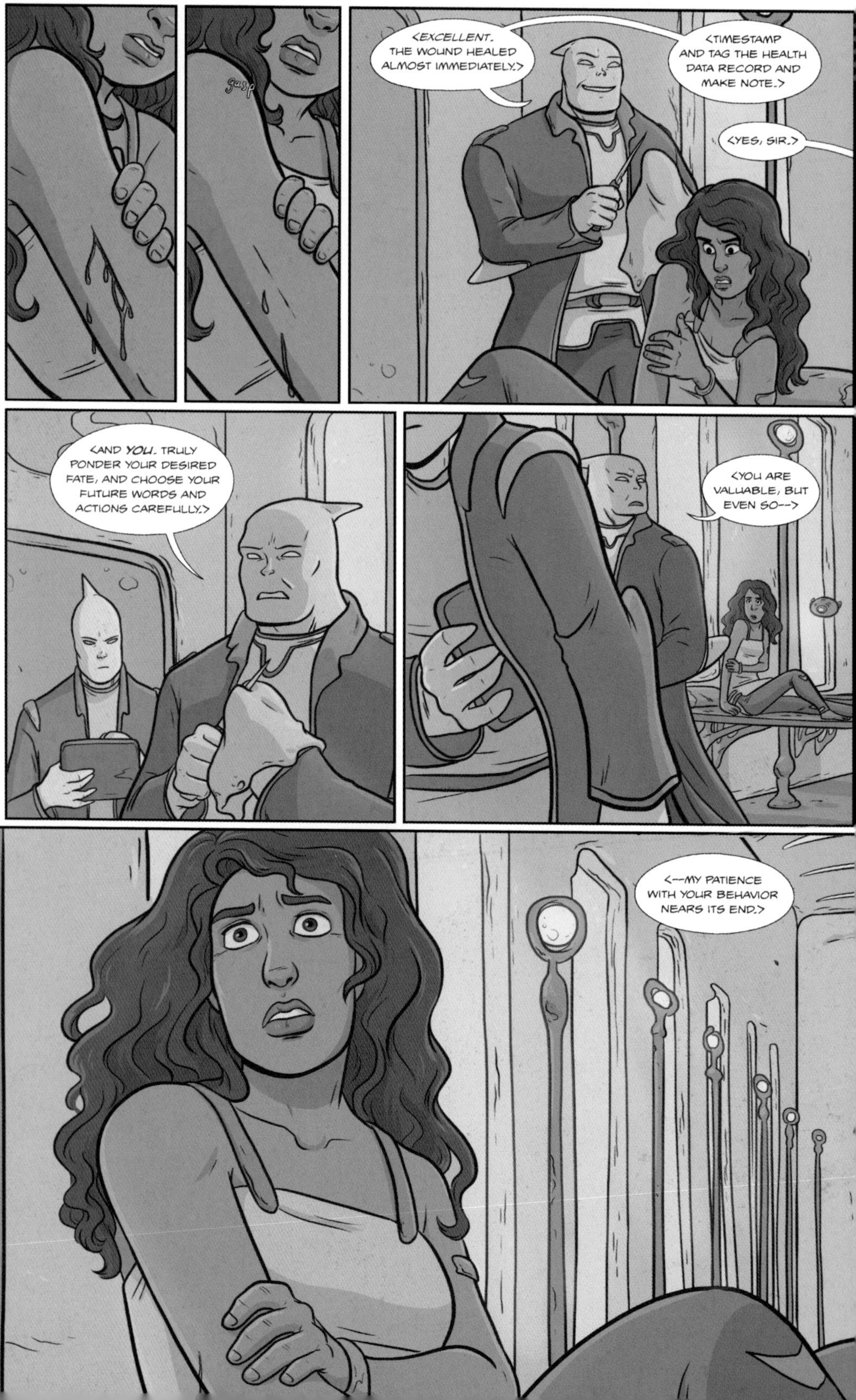
gasp
<EXCELLENT. THE WOUND HEALED ALMOST IMMEDIATELY.>
<TIMESTAMP AND TAG THE HEALTH DATA RECORD AND MAKE NOTE.>
<YES, SIR.>
<AND *YOU*. TRULY PONDER YOUR DESIRED FATE, AND CHOOSE YOUR FUTURE WORDS AND ACTIONS CAREFULLY.>
<YOU ARE VALUABLE, BUT EVEN SO-->
<--MY PATIENCE WITH YOUR BEHAVIOR NEARS ITS END.>

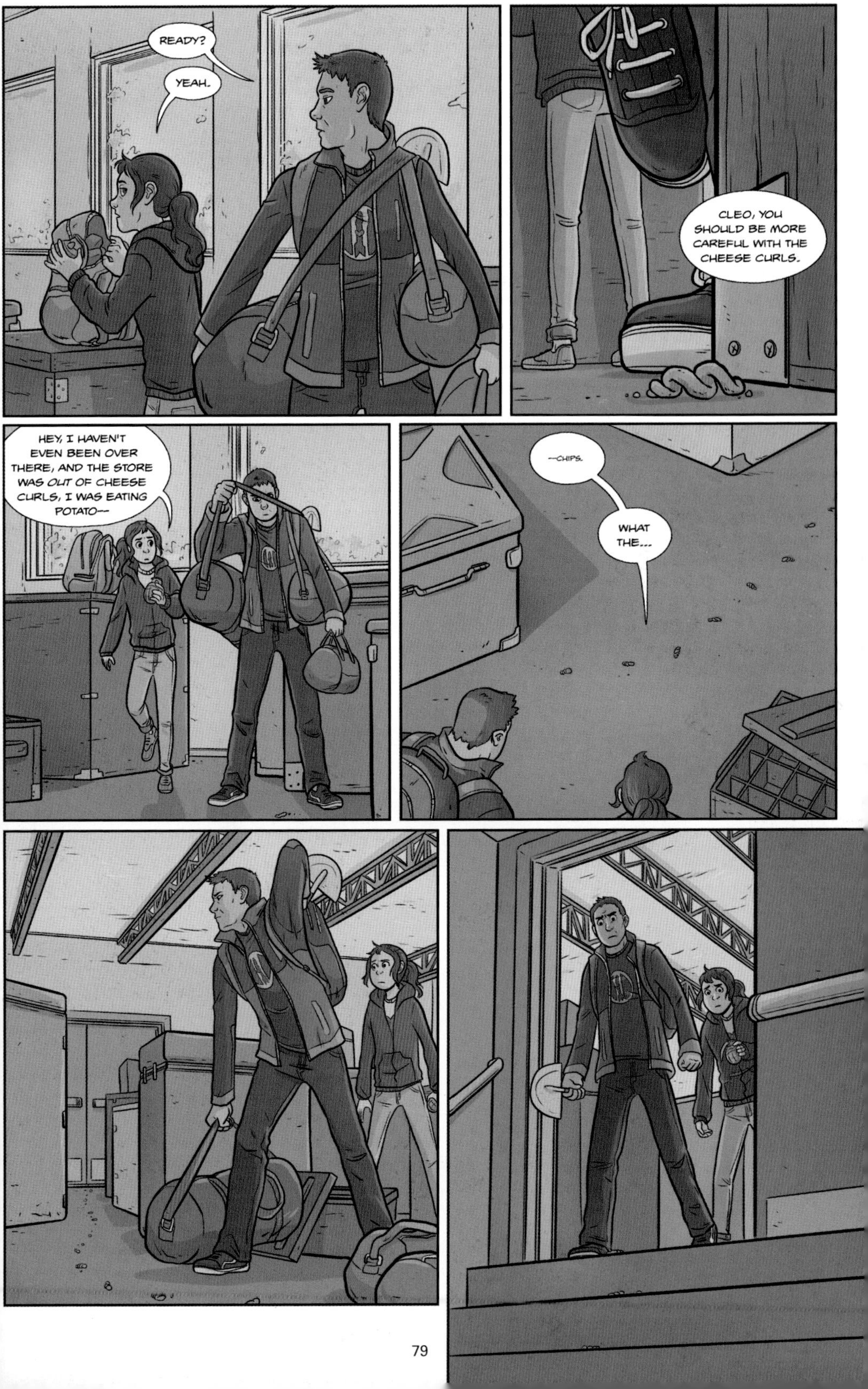
READY?
YEAH.
CLEO, YOU SHOULD BE MORE CAREFUL WITH THE CHEESE CURLS.
HEY, I HAVEN'T EVEN BEEN OVER THERE, AND THE STORE WAS *OUT* OF CHEESE CURLS, I WAS EATING POTATO--
--CHIPS.
WHAT THE...

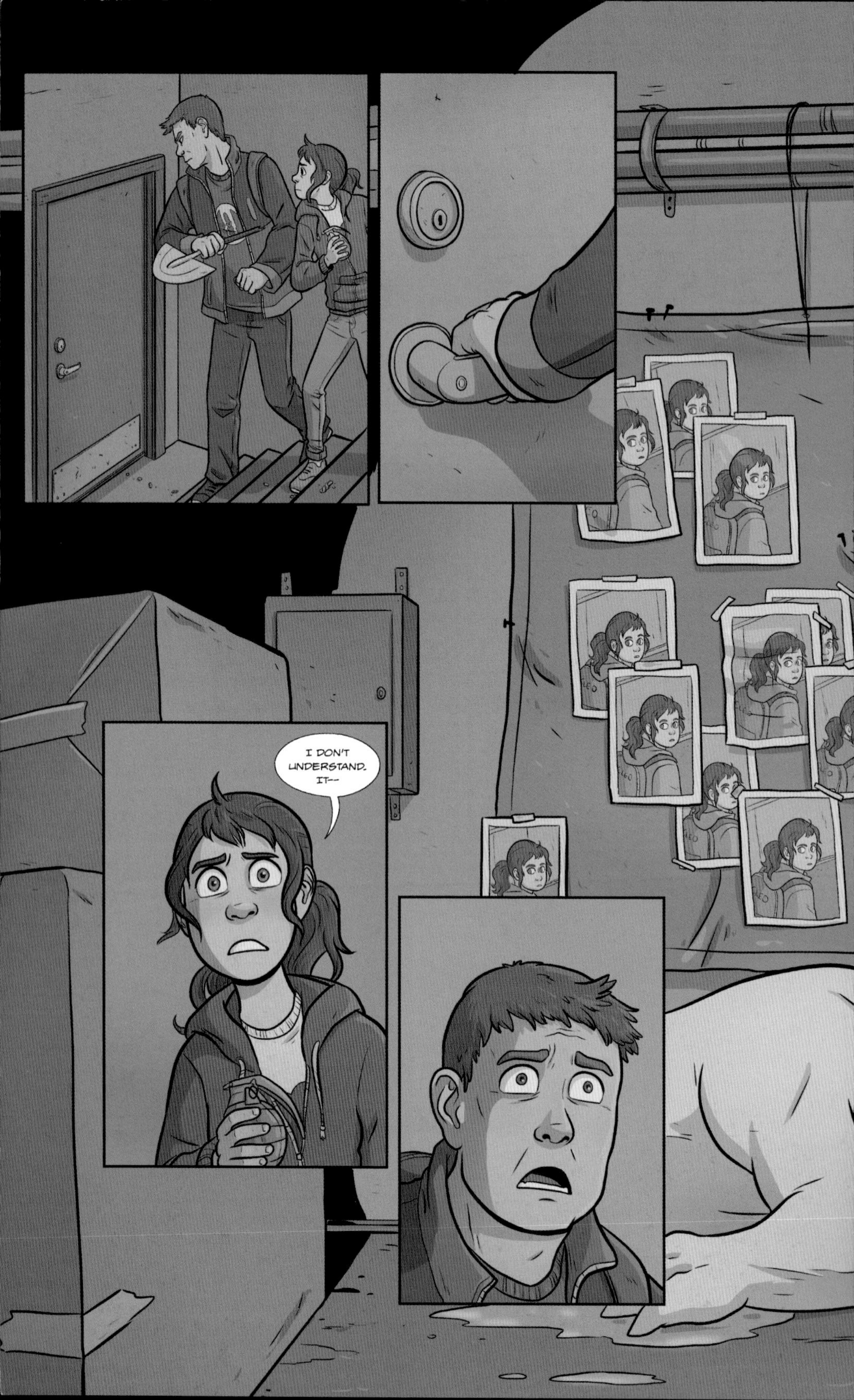
I DON'T UNDERSTAND. IT--

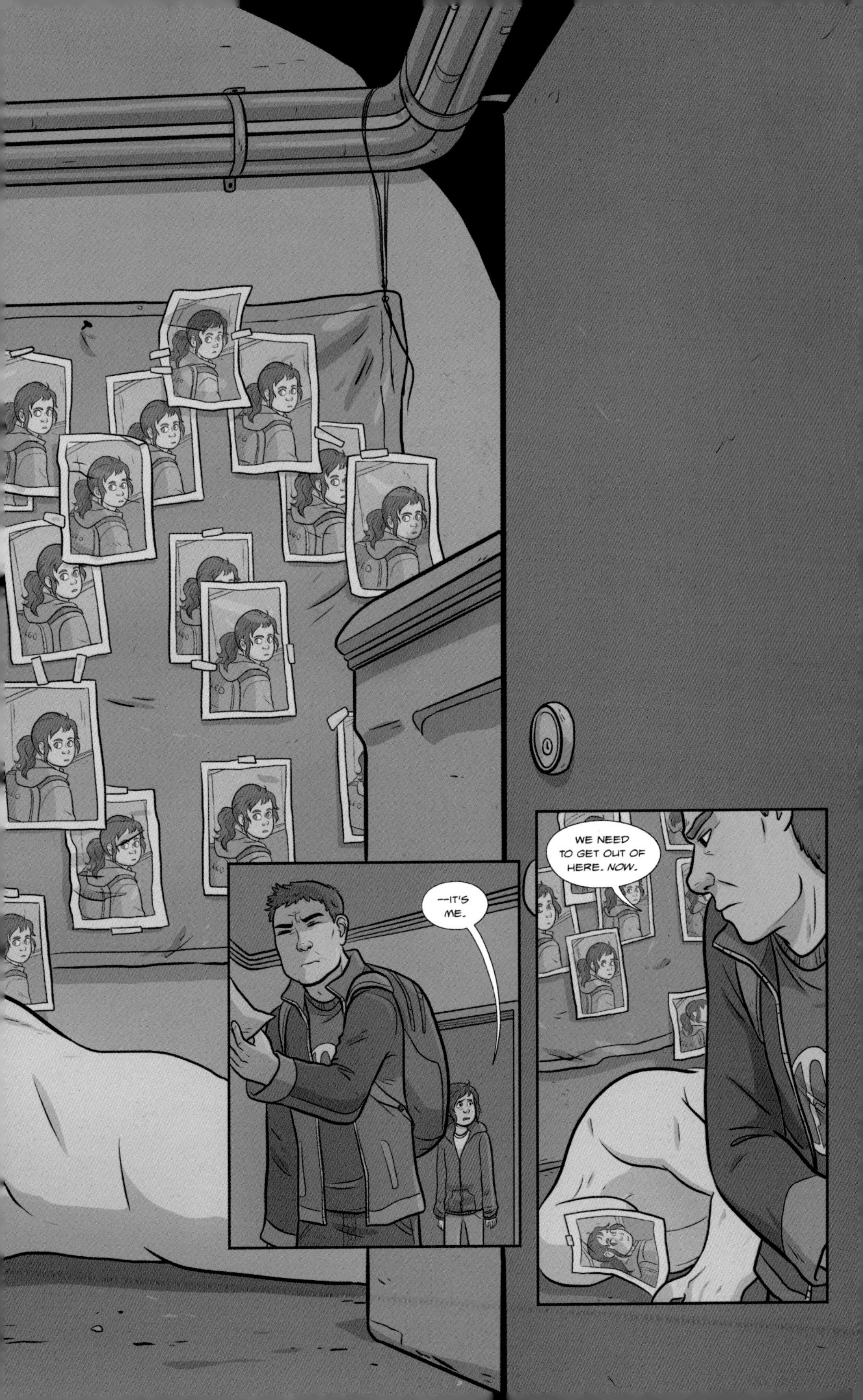
--IT'S
ME.
WE NEED
TO GET OUT OF
HERE. NOW.

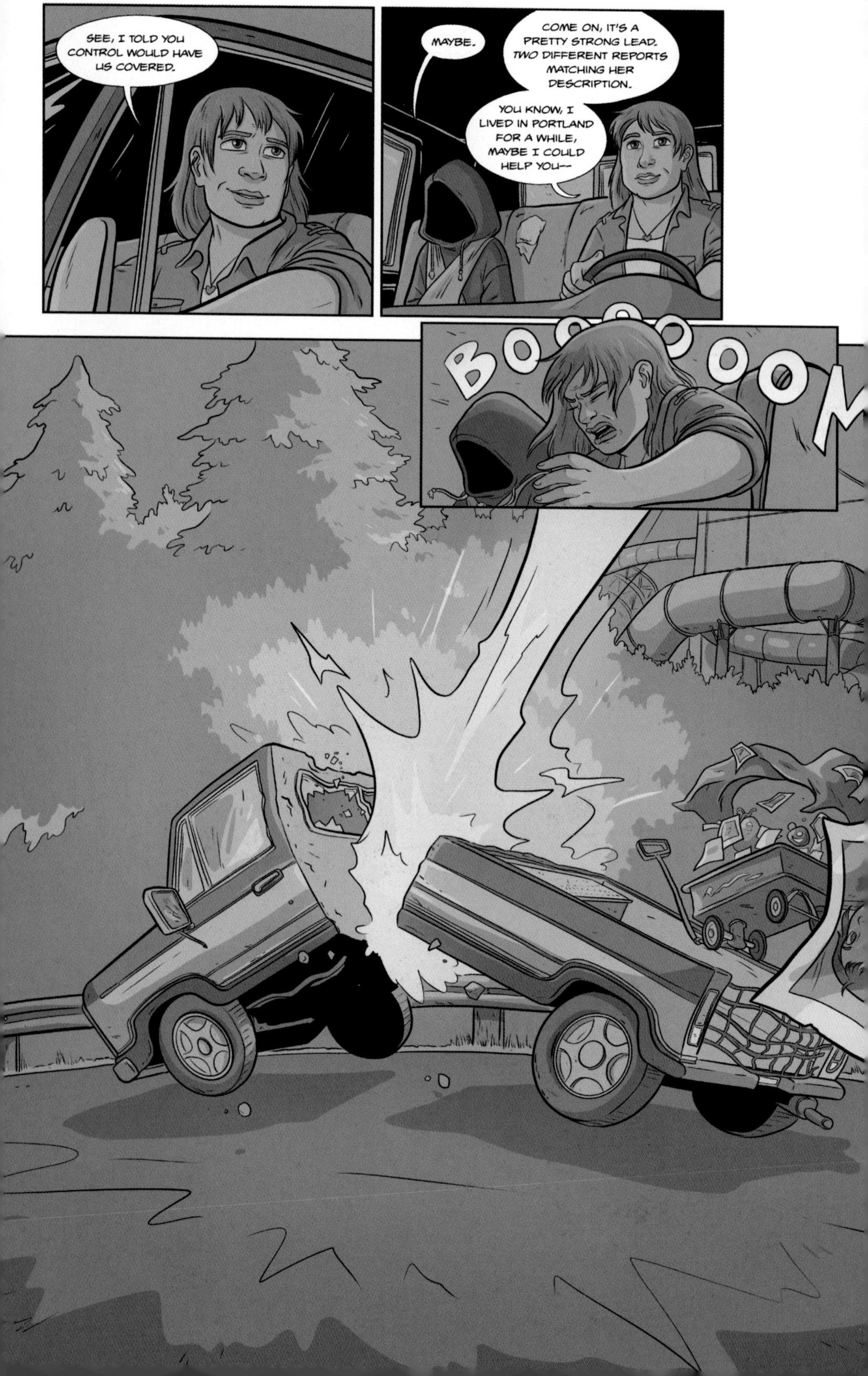
SEE, I TOLD YOU CONTROL WOULD HAVE US COVERED.
MAYBE.
COME ON, IT'S A PRETTY STRONG LEAD. *TWO* DIFFERENT REPORTS MATCHING HER DESCRIPTION.
YOU KNOW, I LIVED IN PORTLAND FOR A WHILE, MAYBE I COULD HELP YOU--
BOOOOOOM

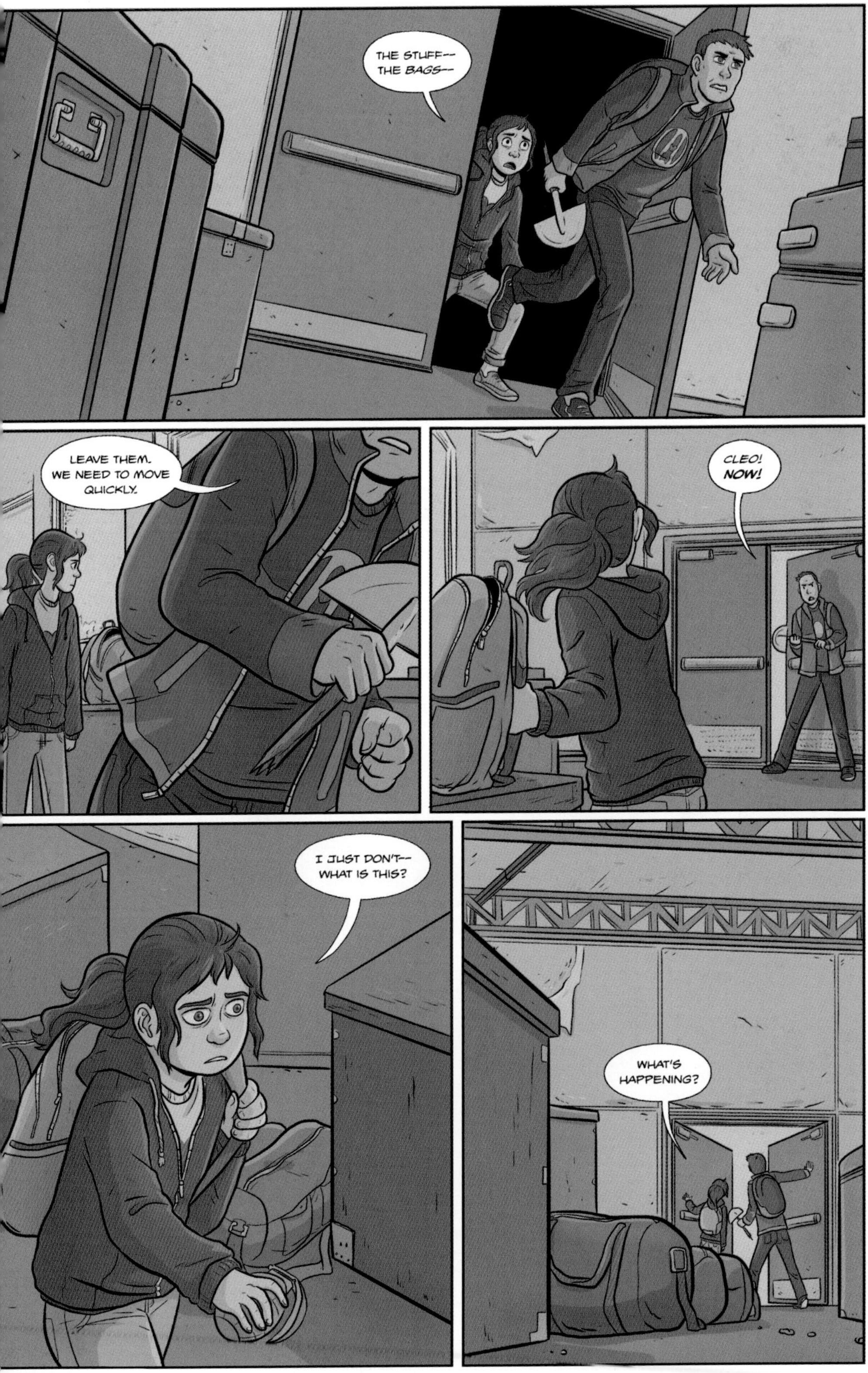
THE STUFF--
THE BAGS--
LEAVE THEM. WE NEED TO MOVE QUICKLY.
CLEO! NOW!
I JUST DON'T-- WHAT IS THIS?
WHAT'S HAPPENING?

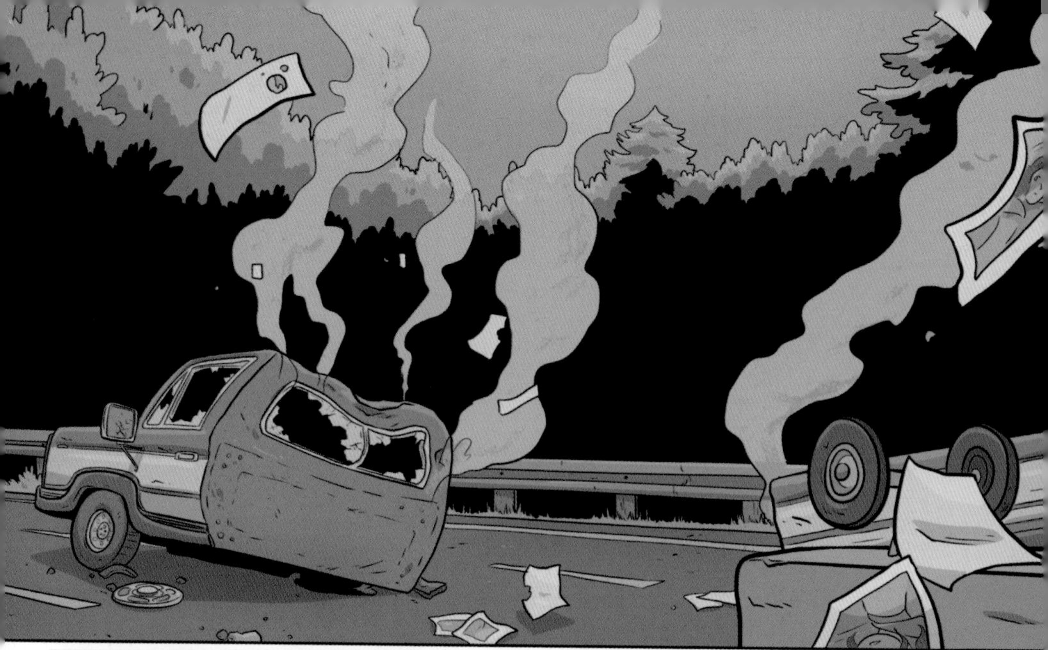

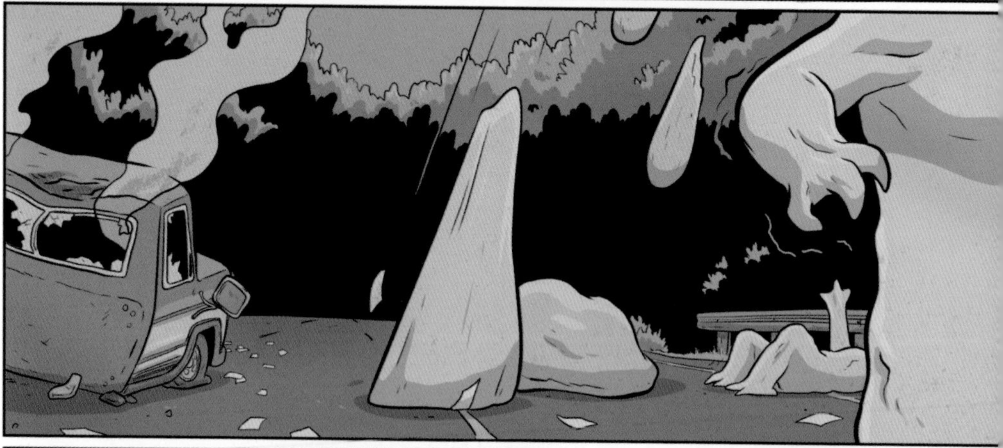

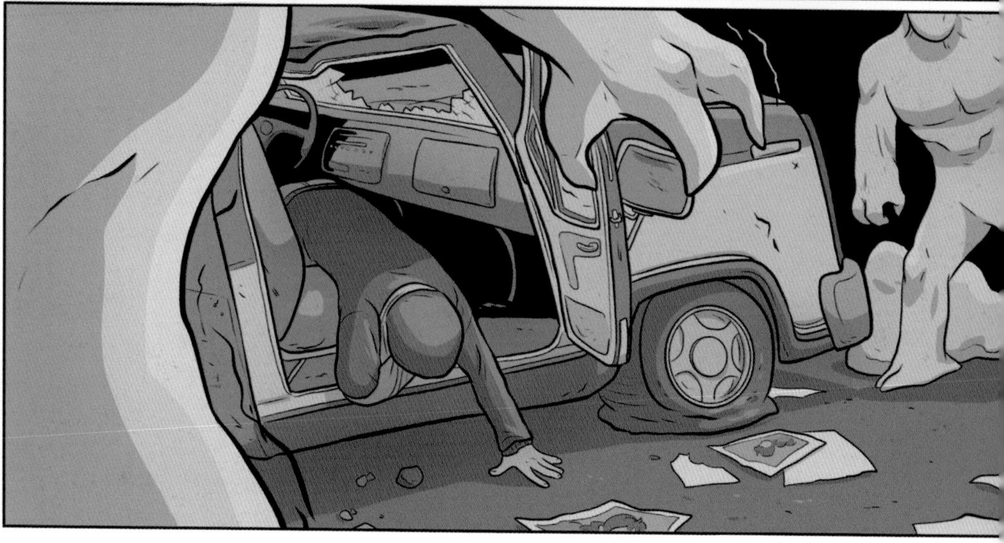

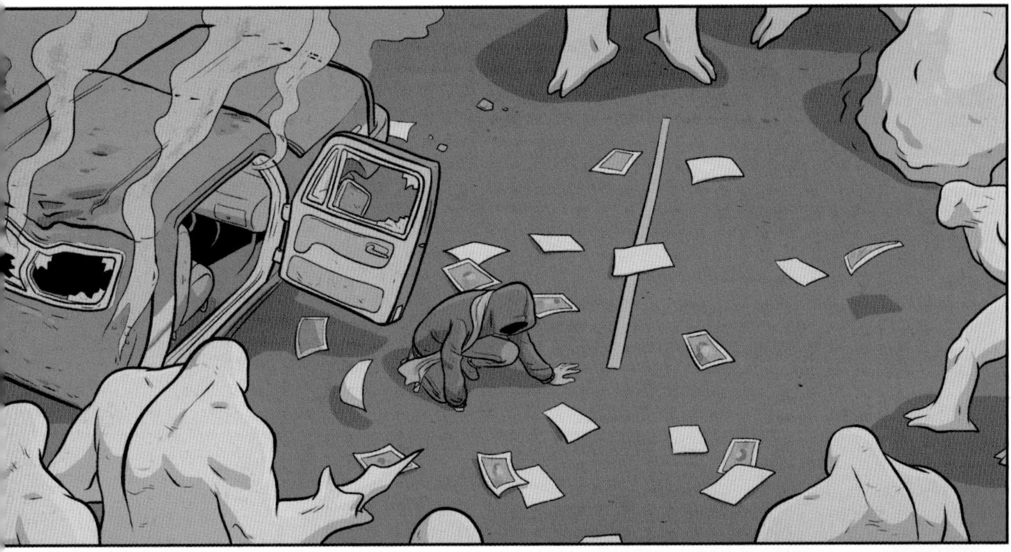

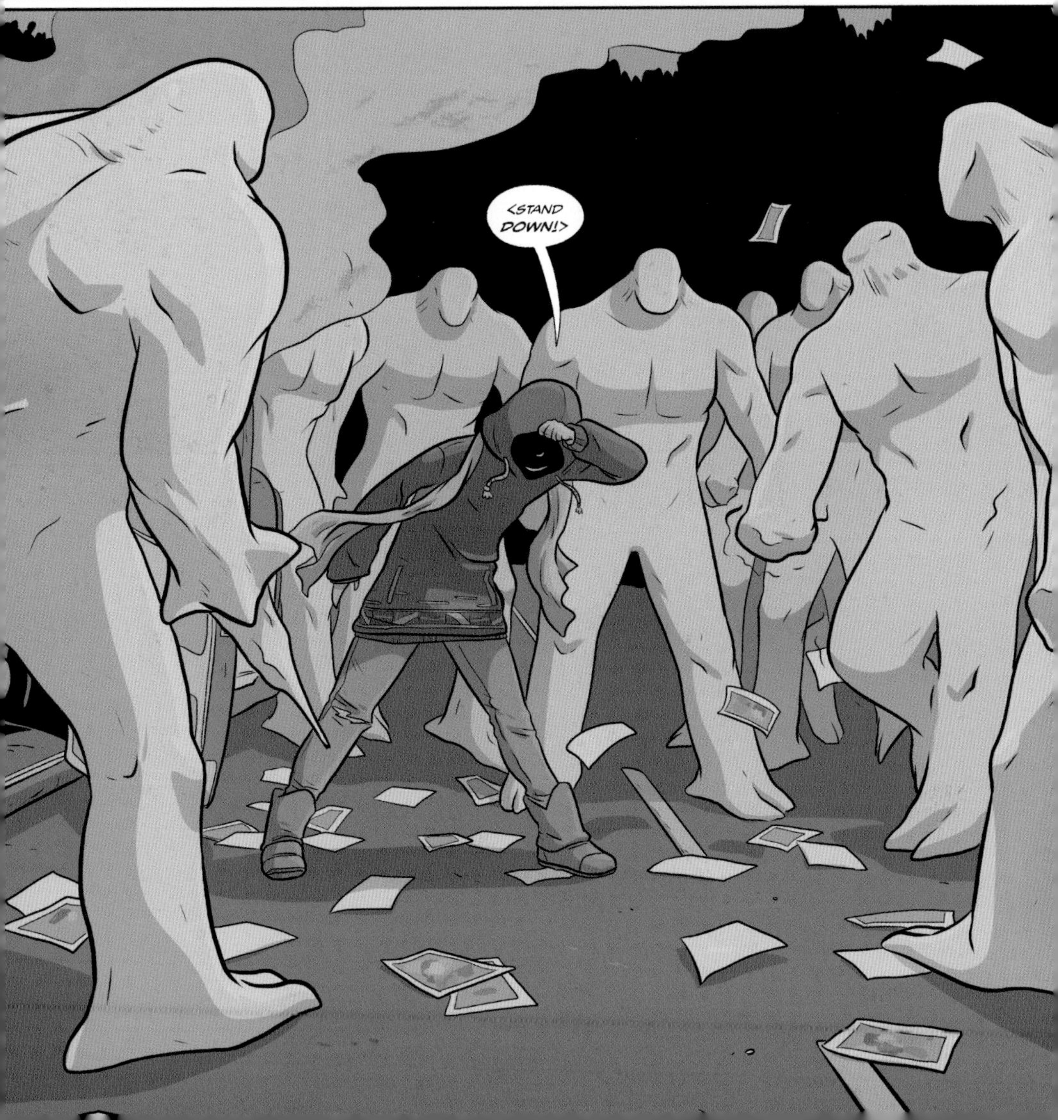
<STAND DOWN!>

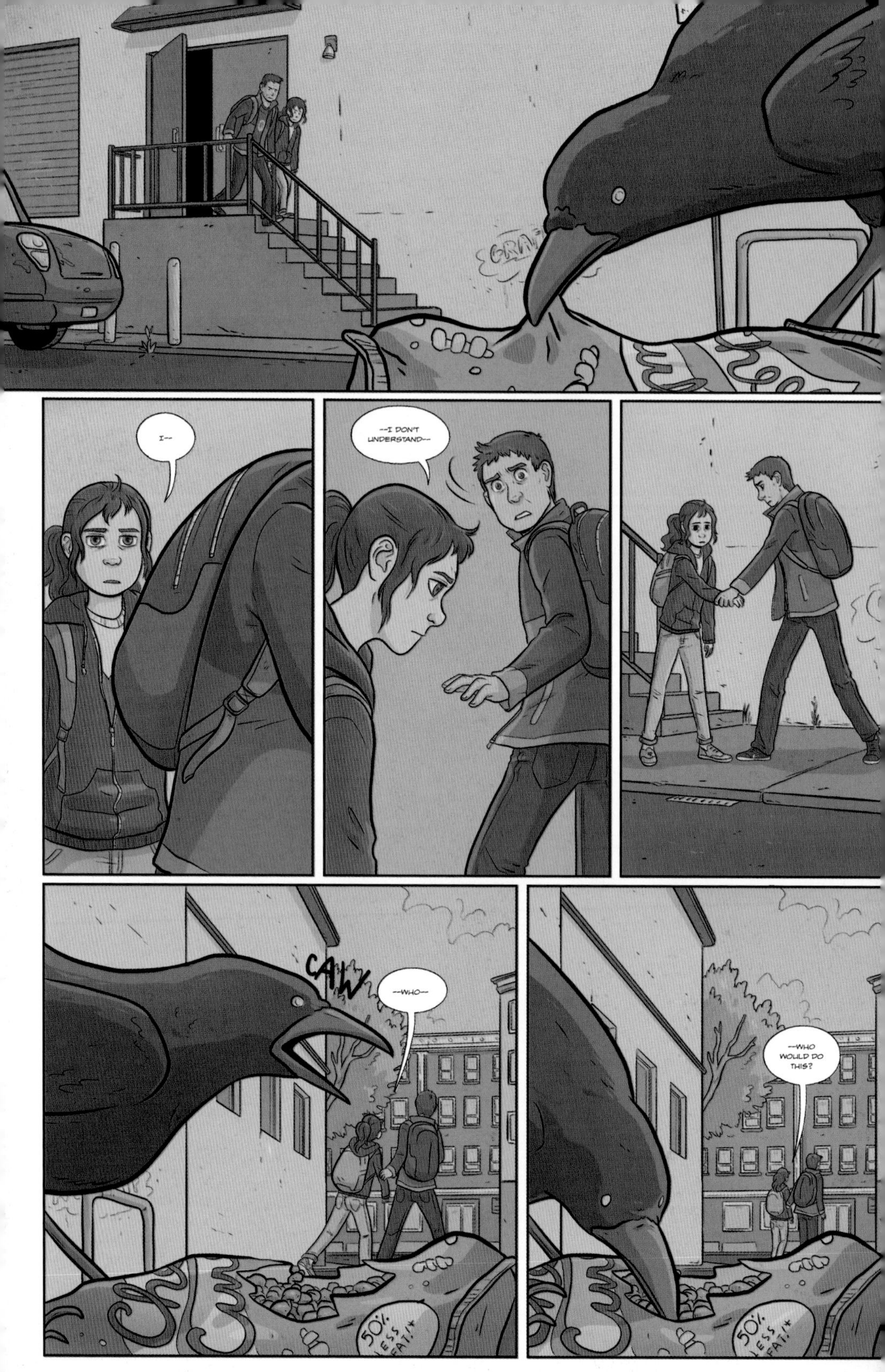
I--
--I DON'T UNDERSTAND--
CAW
--WHO--
50% LESS FAT!*
--WHO WOULD DO THIS?
50% LESS FAT!*

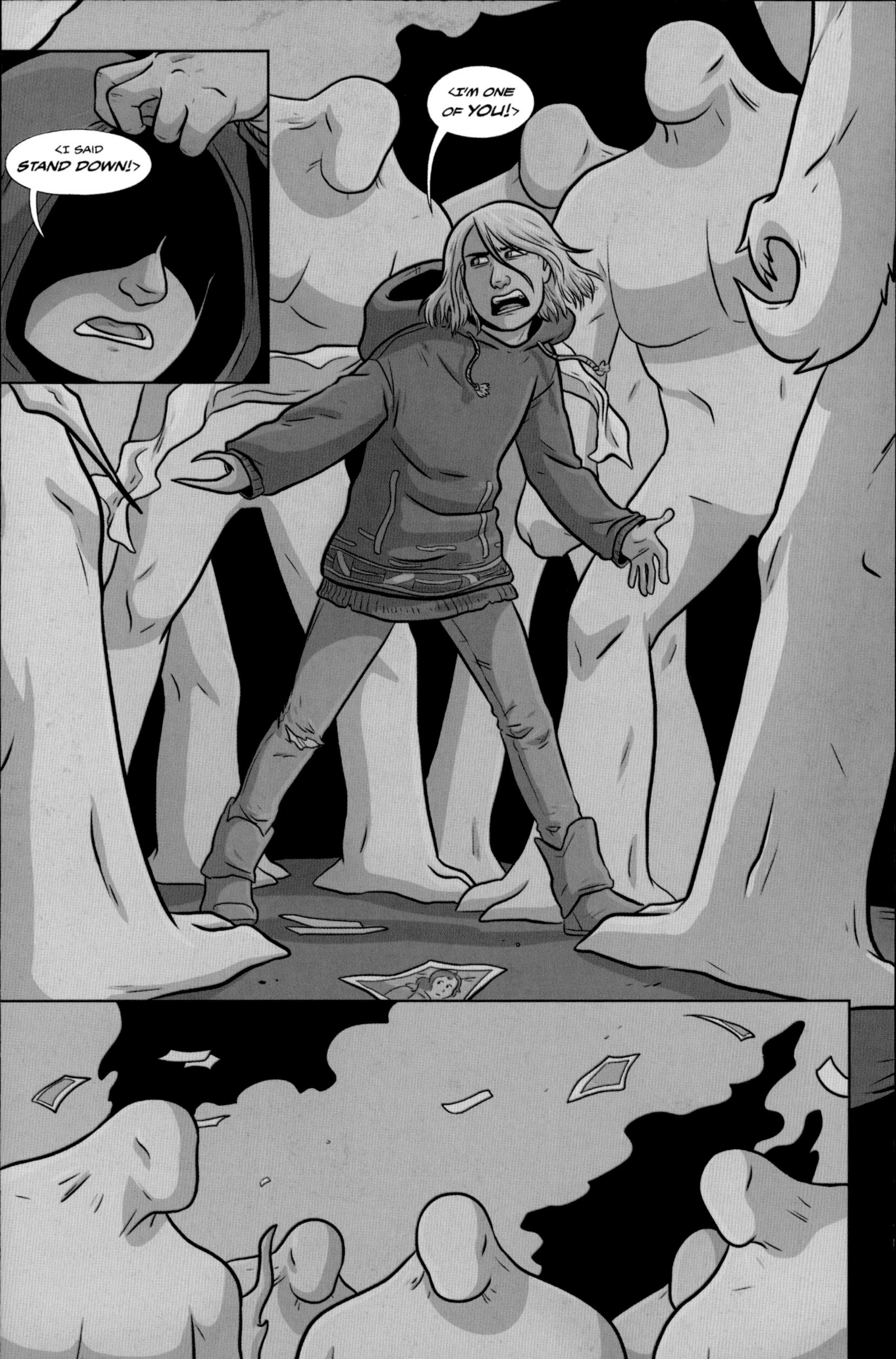
<I SAID STAND DOWN!>
<I'M ONE OF YOU!>

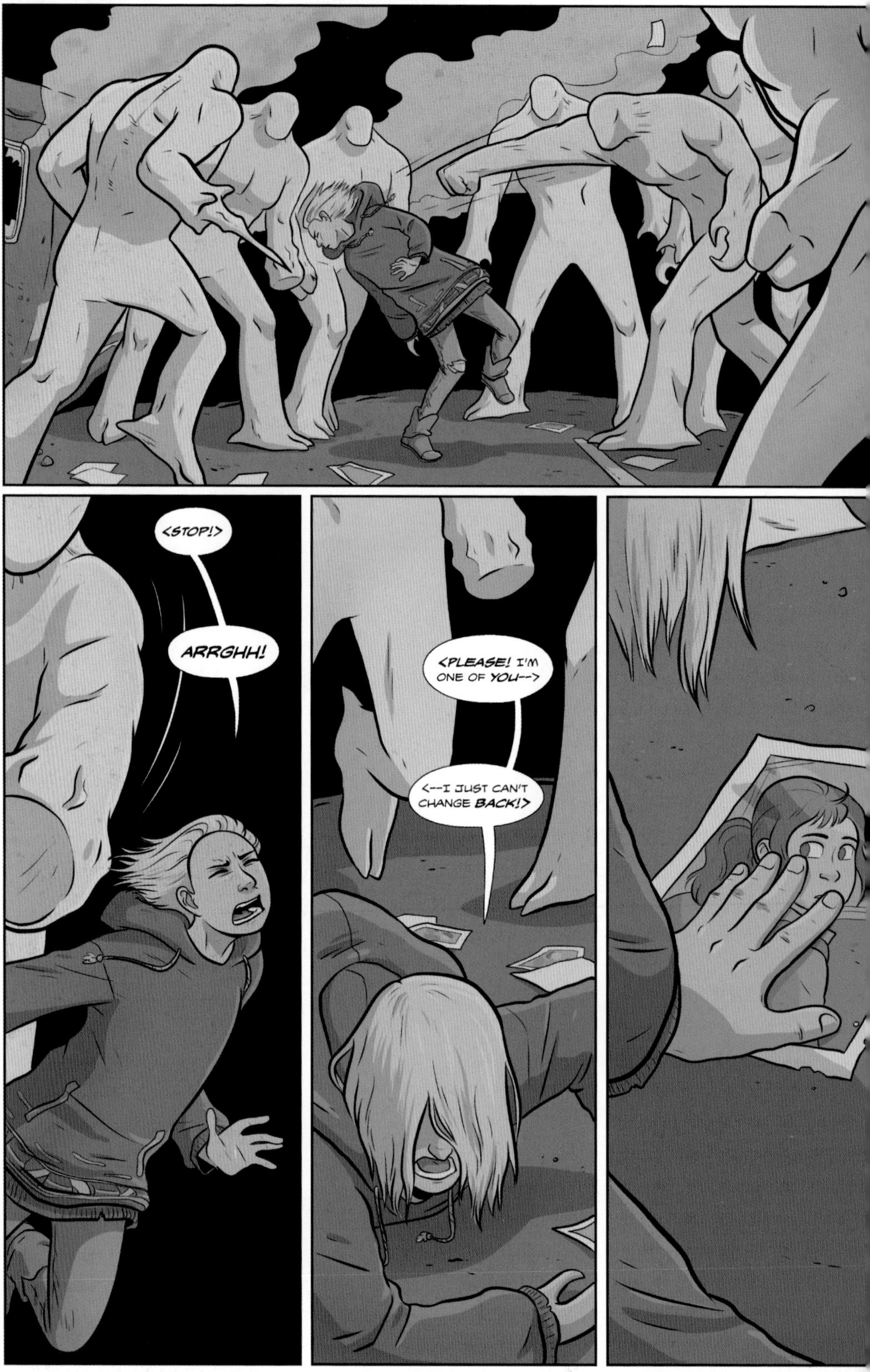
<STOP!>
ARRGHH!
<PLEASE! I'M ONE OF YOU-->
<--I JUST CAN'T CHANGE BACK!>

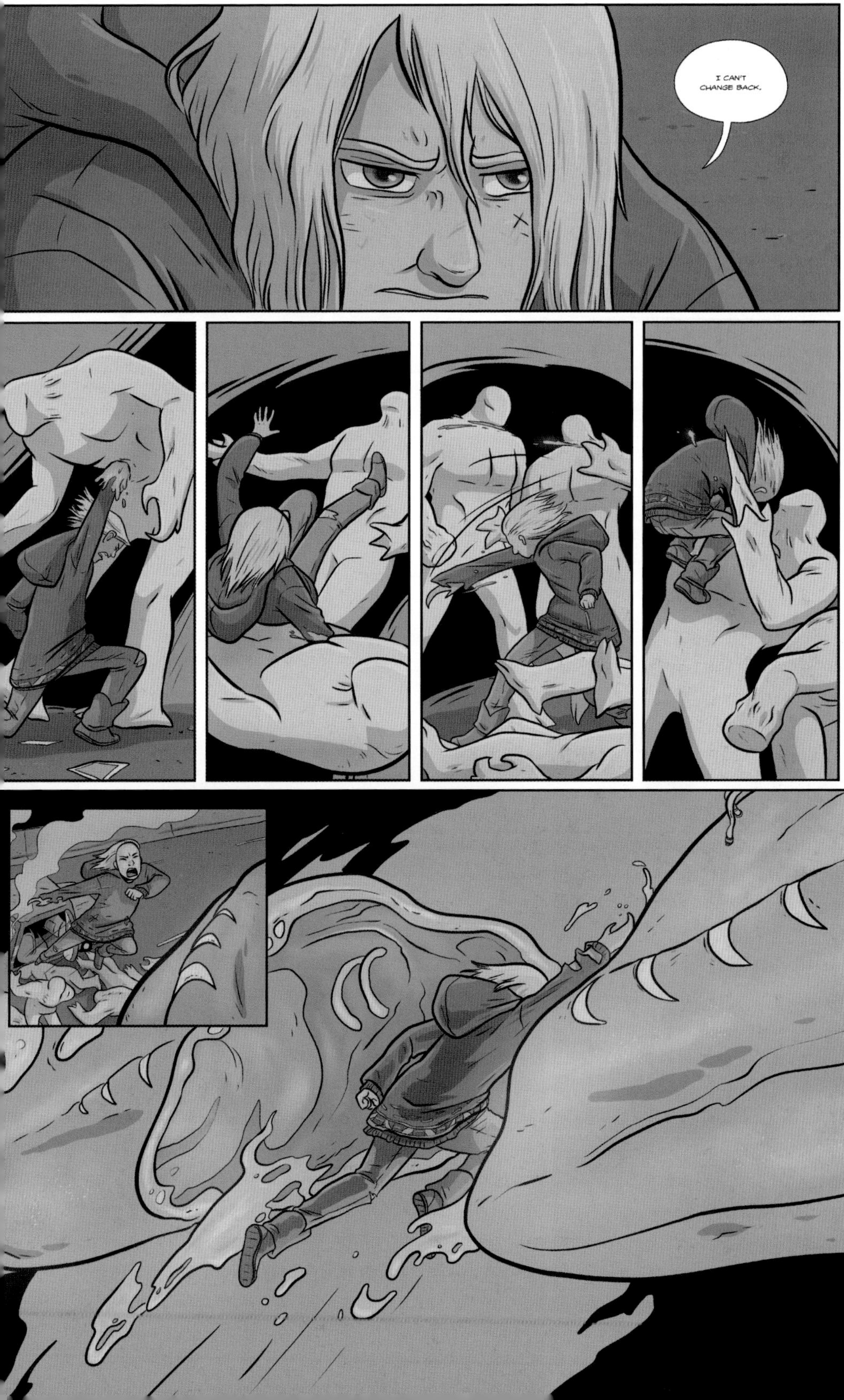
I CAN'T CHANGE BACK.

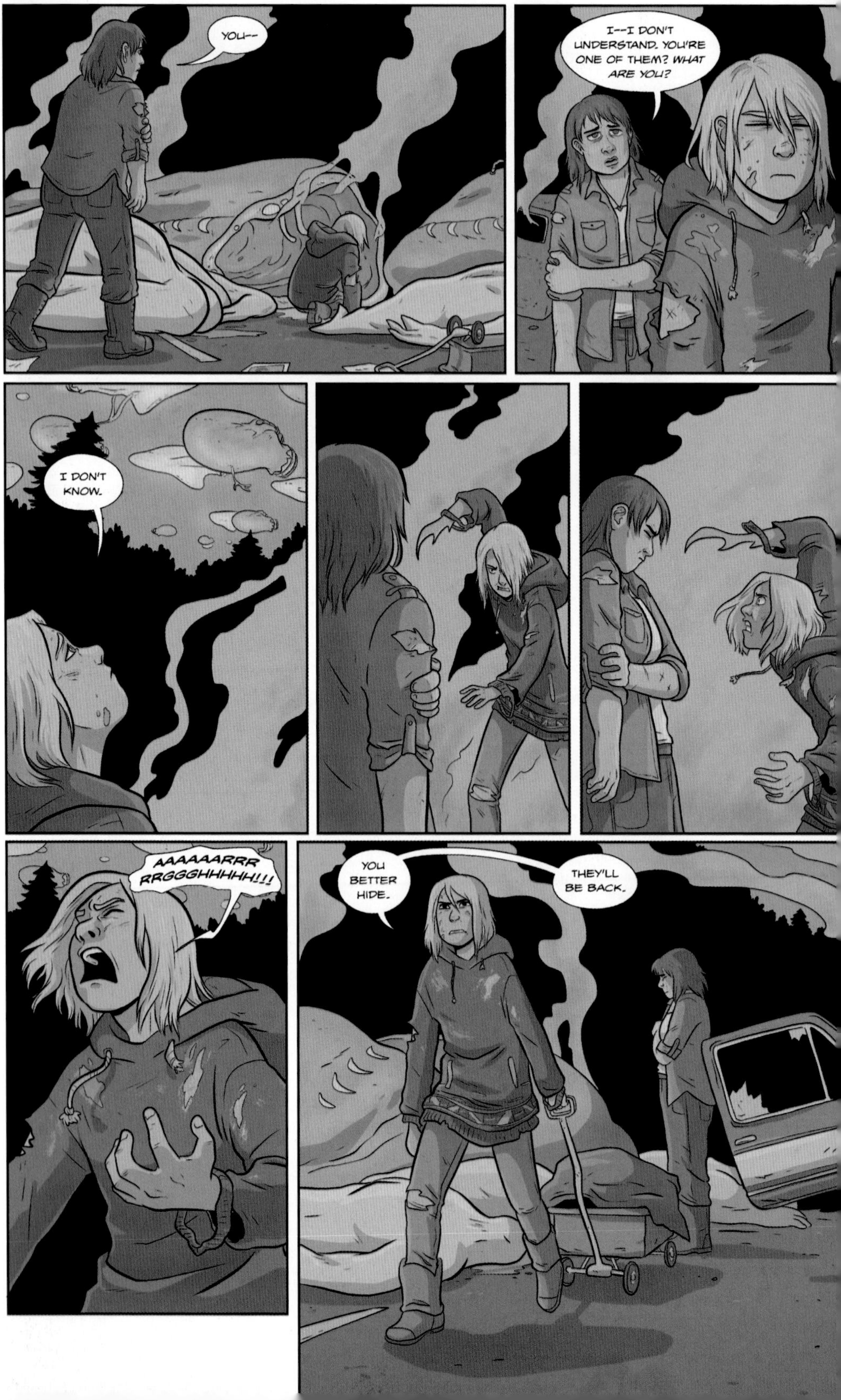
YOU--
I--I DON'T UNDERSTAND. YOU'RE ONE OF THEM? WHAT ARE YOU?
I DON'T KNOW.
AAAAAARRR RRGGGHHHHH!!!
YOU BETTER HIDE.
THEY'LL BE BACK.

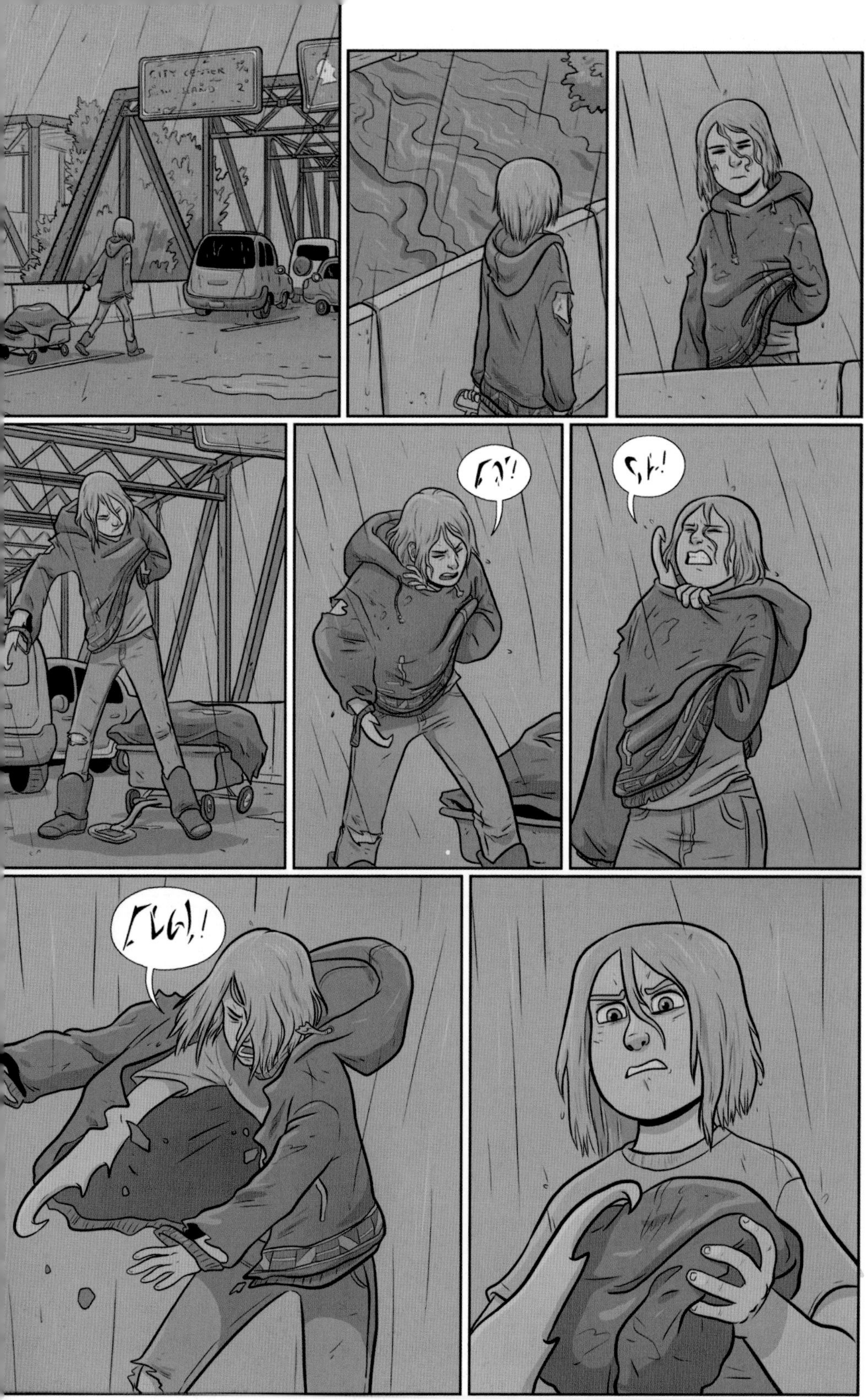

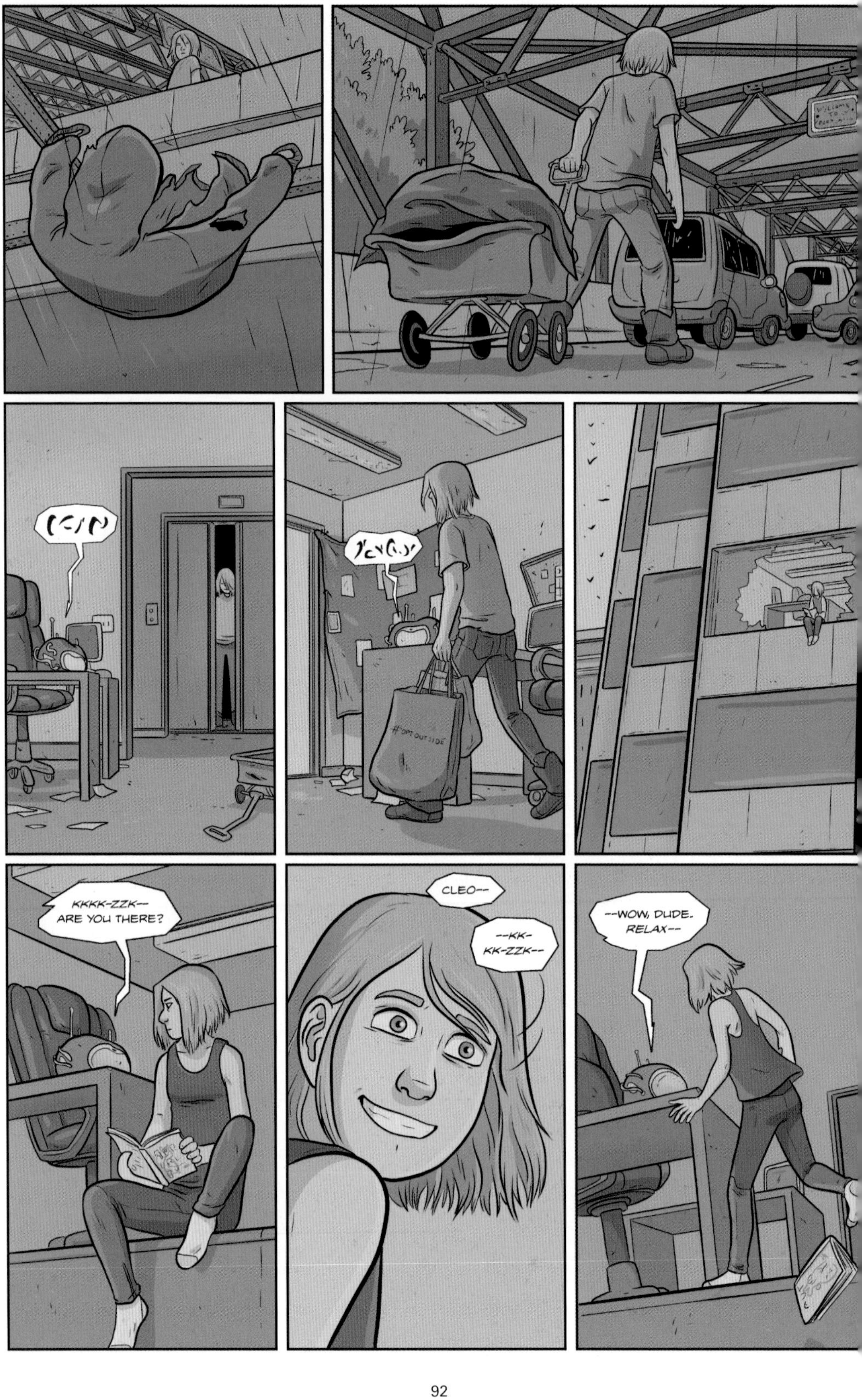
KKKK-ZZK--
ARE YOU THERE?
CLEO--
--KK-
KK-ZZK--
--WOW, DUDE.
RELAX--

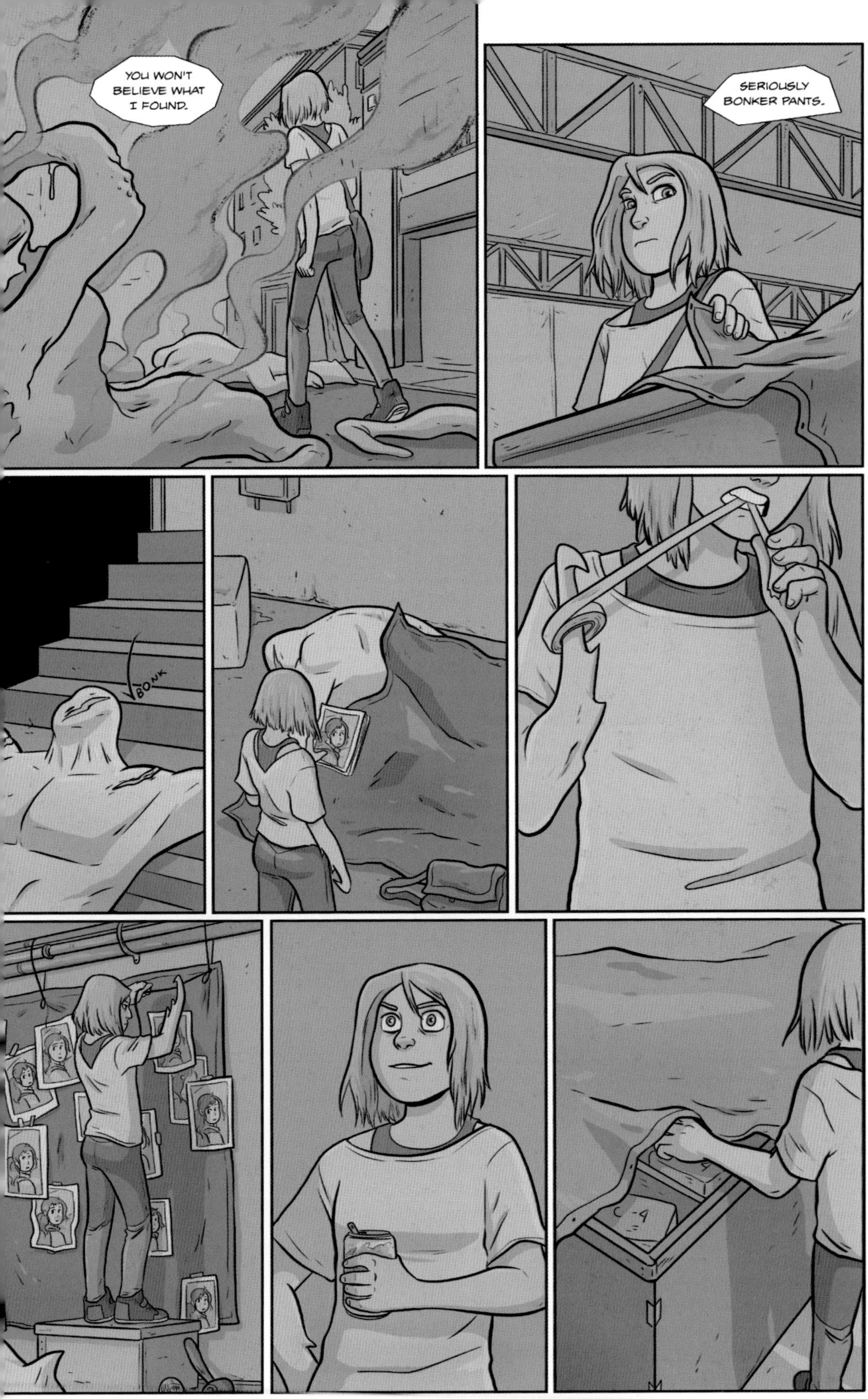
YOU WON'T BELIEVE WHAT I FOUND.
SERIOUSLY BONKER PANTS.
BONK
C-4

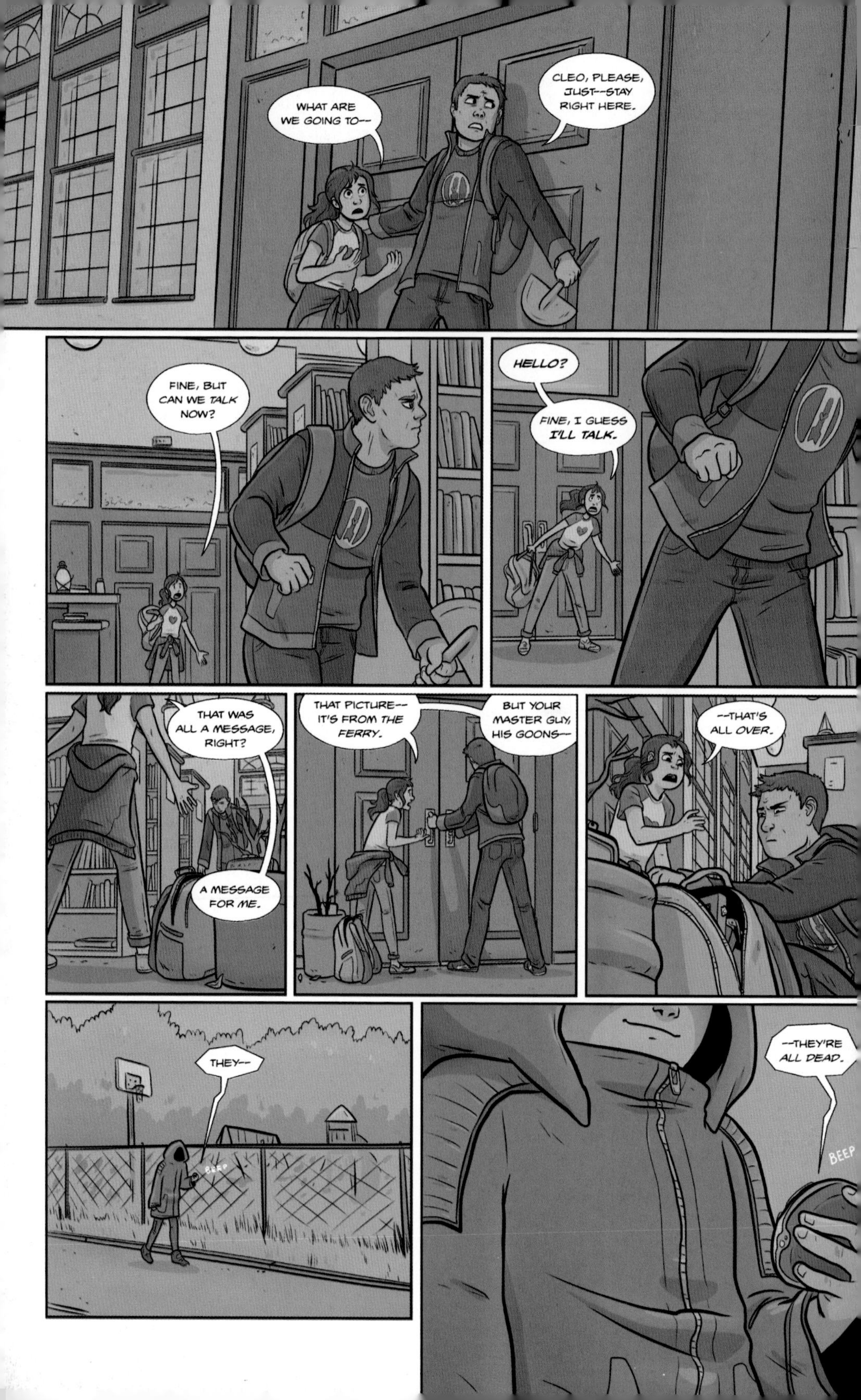
WHAT ARE WE GOING TO--
CLEO, PLEASE, JUST--STAY RIGHT HERE.
FINE, BUT CAN WE *TALK* NOW?
HELLO?
FINE, I GUESS ***I'LL TALK.***
THAT WAS ALL A MESSAGE, RIGHT?
A MESSAGE FOR *ME*.
THAT PICTURE-- IT'S FROM *THE FERRY*.
BUT YOUR MASTER GUY, HIS GOONS--
--THAT'S ALL *OVER*.
THEY--
BEEP
--THEY'RE *ALL DEAD*.
BEEP

FOUR

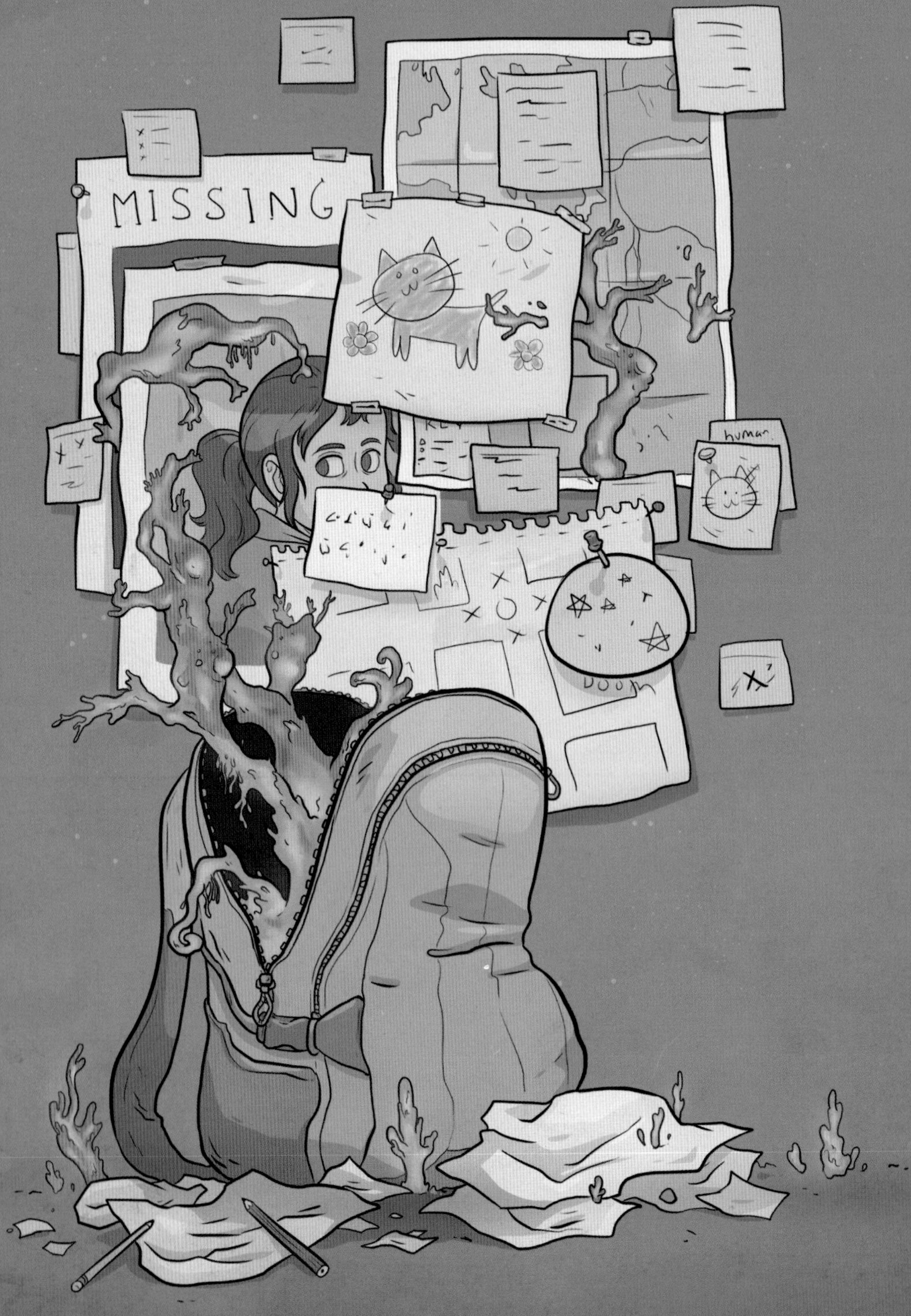
MISSING
human

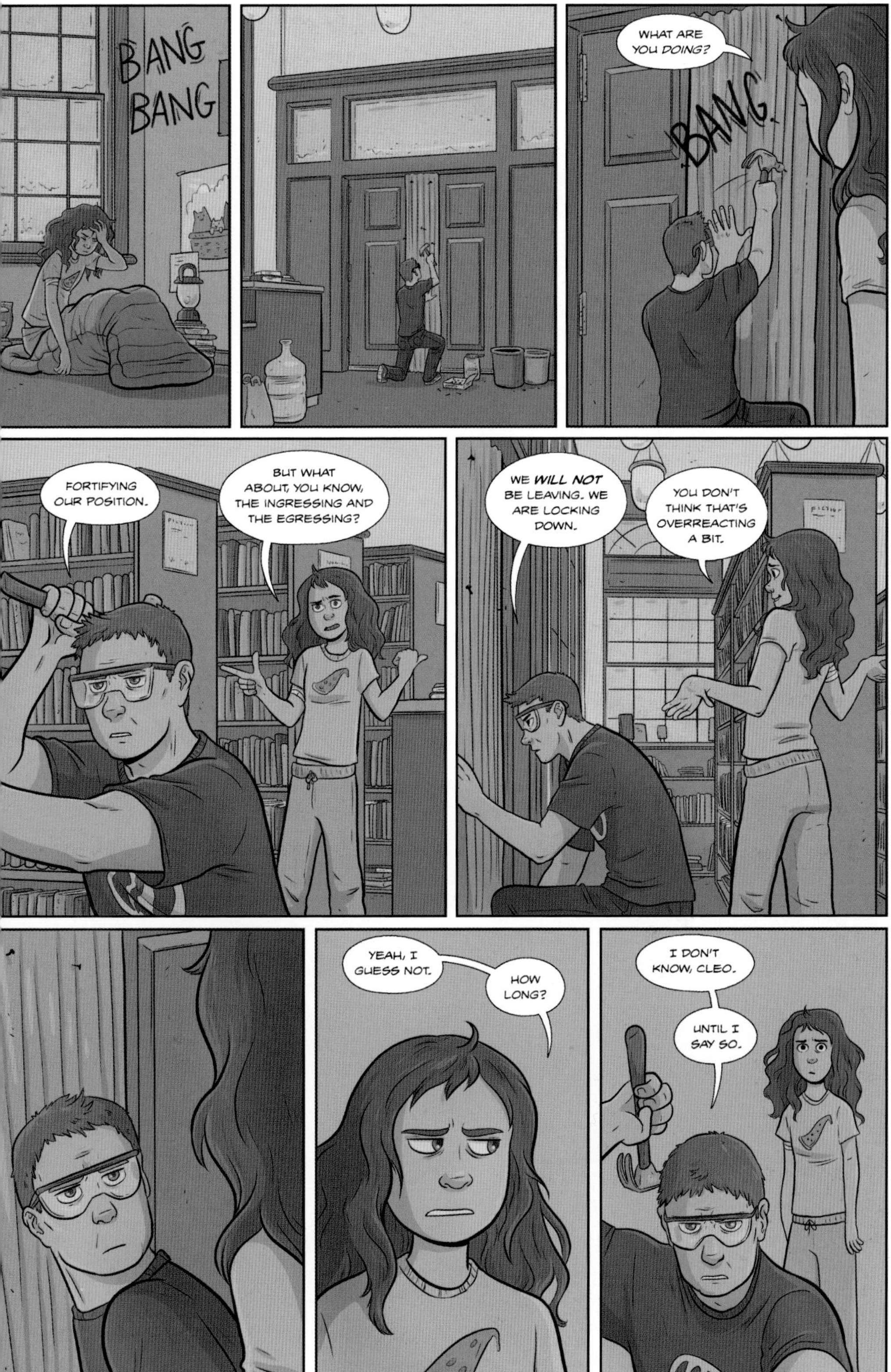
BANG
BANG
WHAT ARE YOU DOING?
BANG.
FORTIFYING OUR POSITION.
BUT WHAT ABOUT, YOU KNOW, THE INGRESSING AND THE EGRESSING?
WE **WILL NOT** BE LEAVING. WE ARE LOCKING DOWN.
YOU DON'T THINK THAT'S OVERREACTING A BIT.
YEAH, I GUESS NOT.
HOW LONG?
I DON'T KNOW, CLEO.
UNTIL I SAY SO.

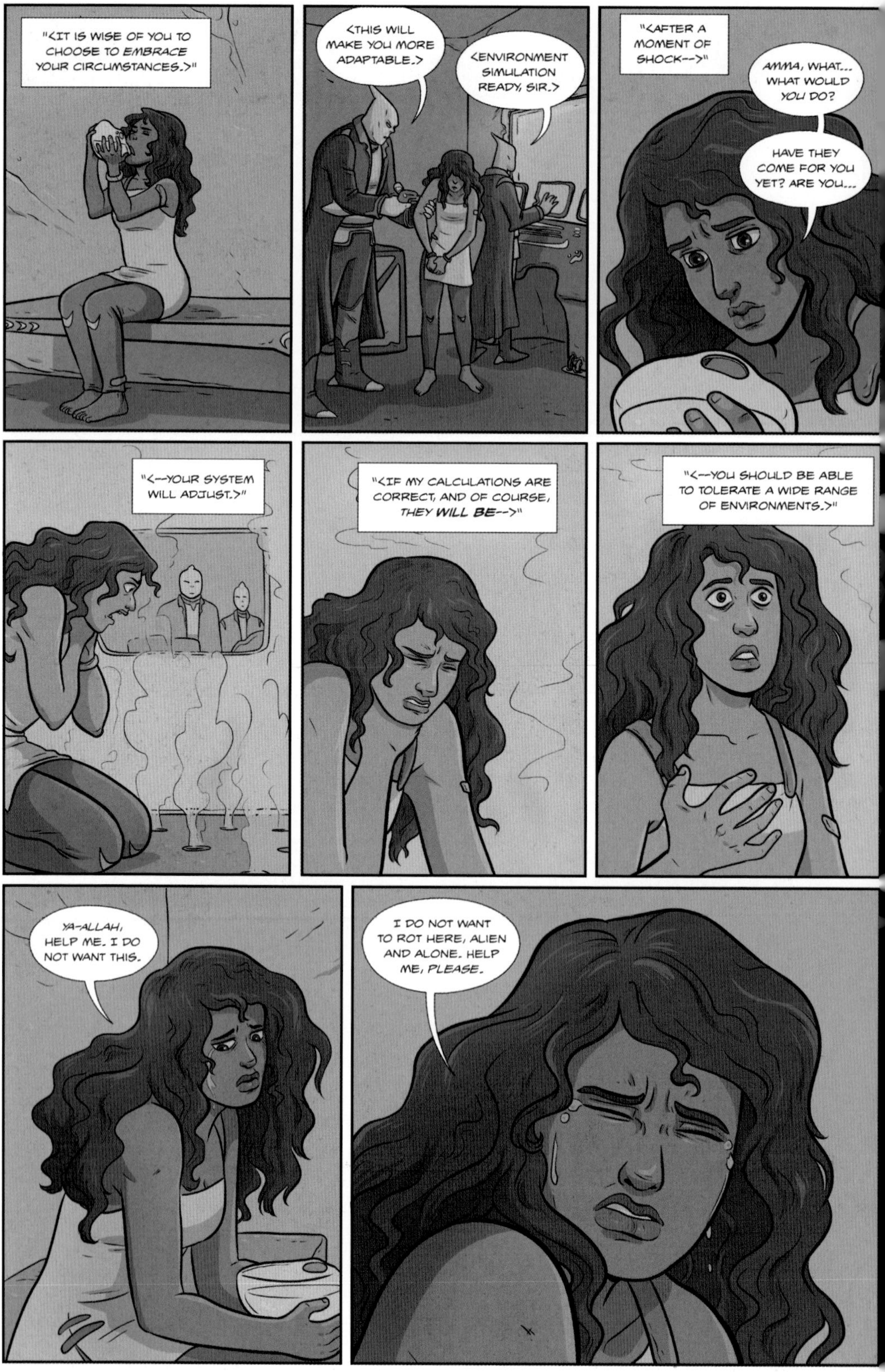
"<IT IS WISE OF YOU TO CHOOSE TO *EMBRACE* YOUR CIRCUMSTANCES.>"
<THIS WILL MAKE YOU MORE ADAPTABLE.>
<ENVIRONMENT SIMULATION READY, SIR.>
"<AFTER A MOMENT OF SHOCK-->"
AMMA, WHAT... WHAT WOULD YOU DO?
HAVE THEY COME FOR YOU YET? ARE YOU...
"<--YOUR SYSTEM WILL ADJUST.>"
"<IF MY CALCULATIONS ARE CORRECT, AND OF COURSE, *THEY **WILL** BE*-->"
"<--YOU SHOULD BE ABLE TO TOLERATE A WIDE RANGE OF ENVIRONMENTS.>"
YA-ALLAH, HELP ME. I DO NOT WANT THIS.
I DO NOT WANT TO ROT HERE, ALIEN AND ALONE. HELP ME, *PLEASE*.

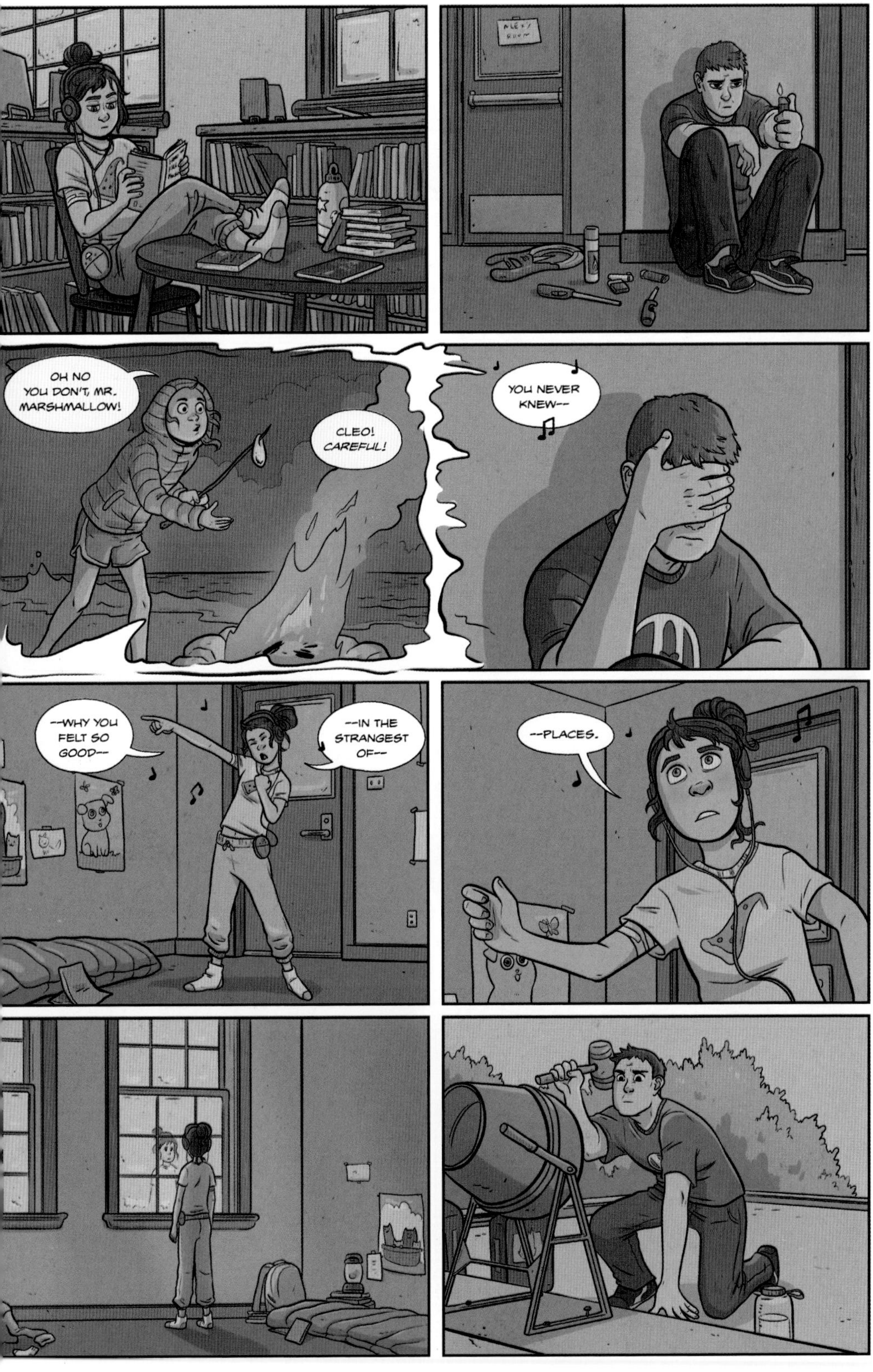
OH NO YOU DON'T, MR. MARSHMALLOW!
CLEO! CAREFUL!
YOU NEVER KNEW--
--WHY YOU FELT SO GOOD--
--IN THE STRANGEST OF--
--PLACES.

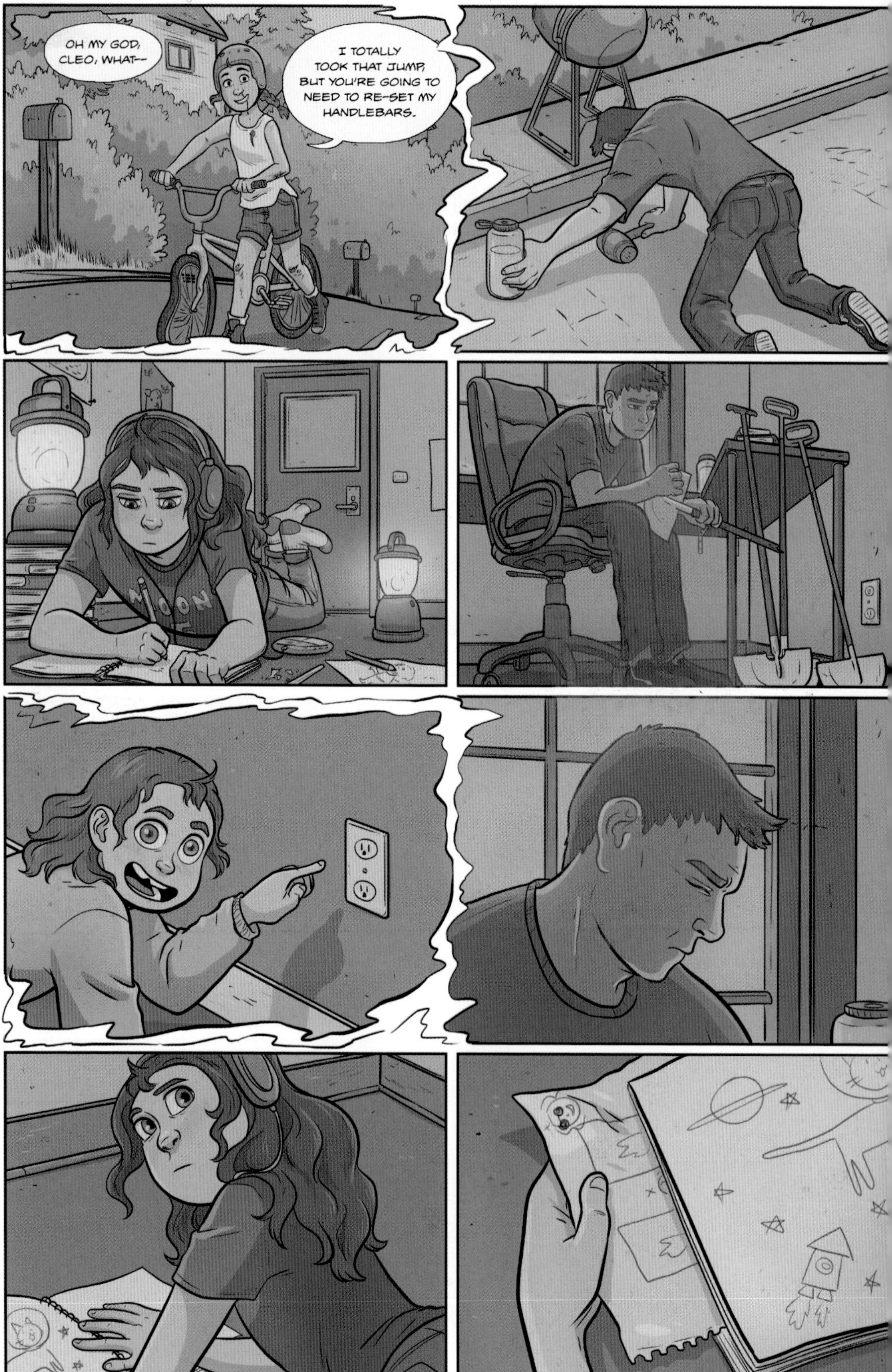
OH MY GOD, CLEO, WHAT--
I TOTALLY TOOK THAT JUMP, BUT YOU'RE GOING TO NEED TO RE-SET MY HANDLEBARS.

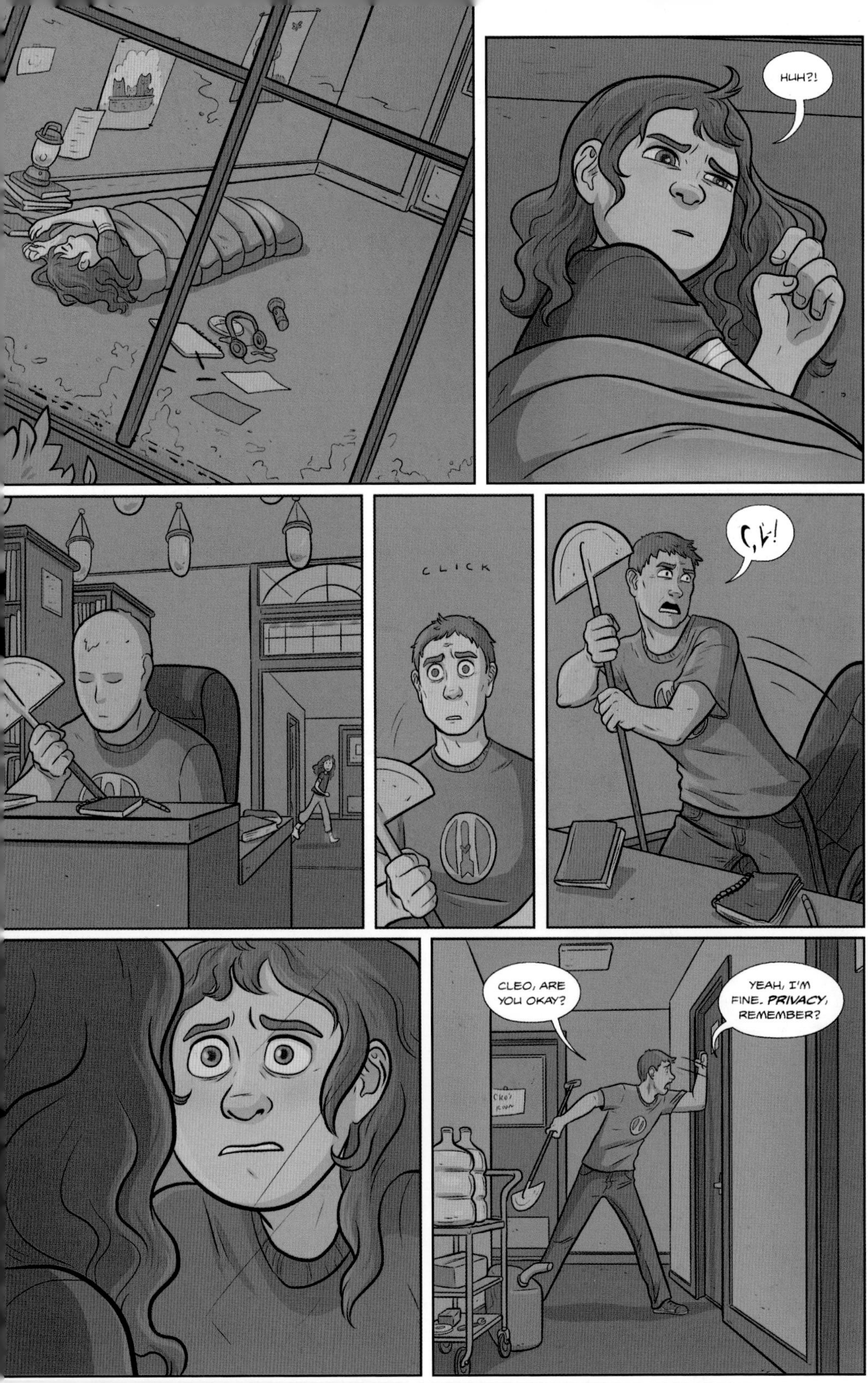
HUH?!
CLICK
CLEO, ARE YOU OKAY?
YEAH, I'M FINE. **PRIVACY**, REMEMBER?

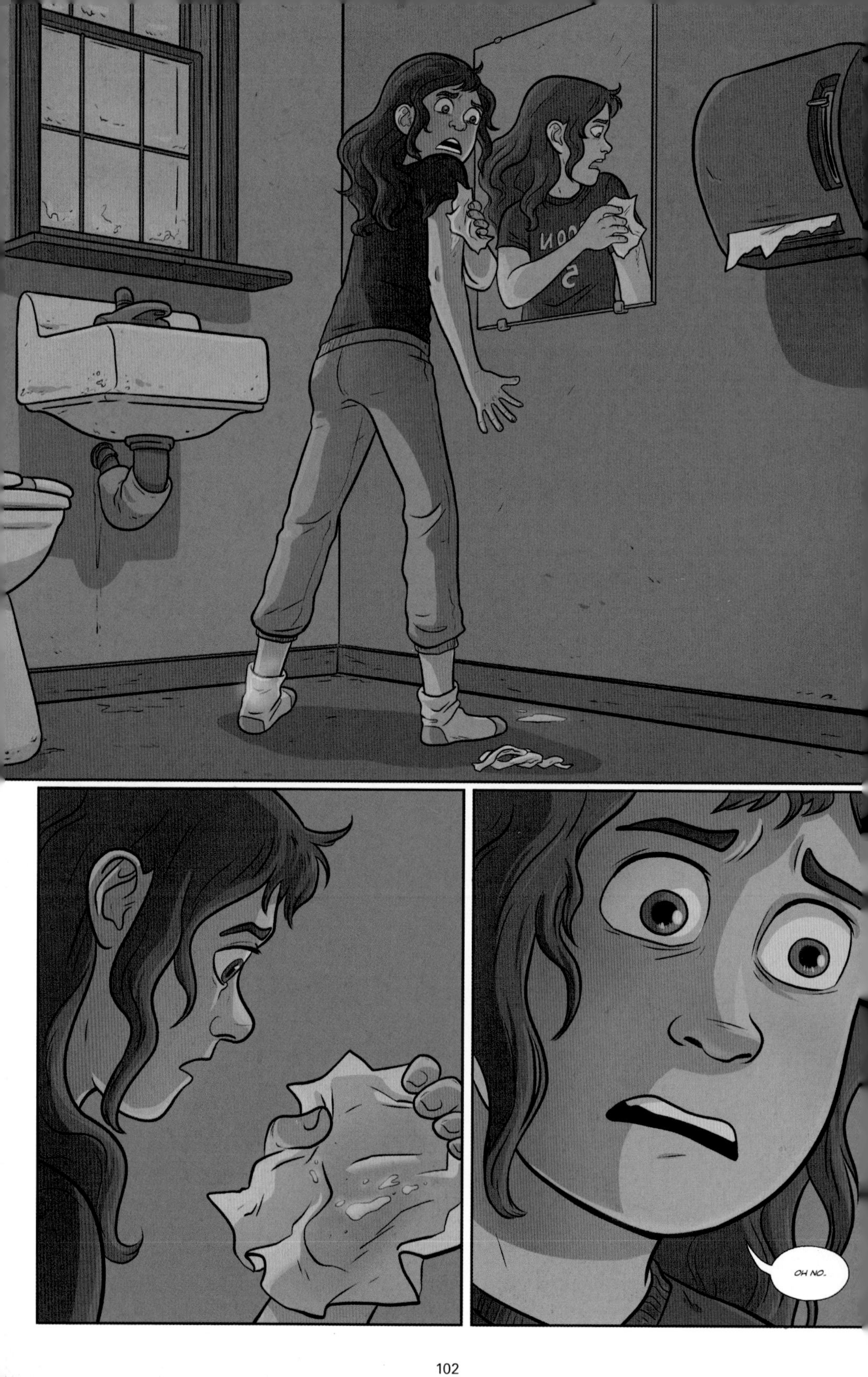
OH NO.

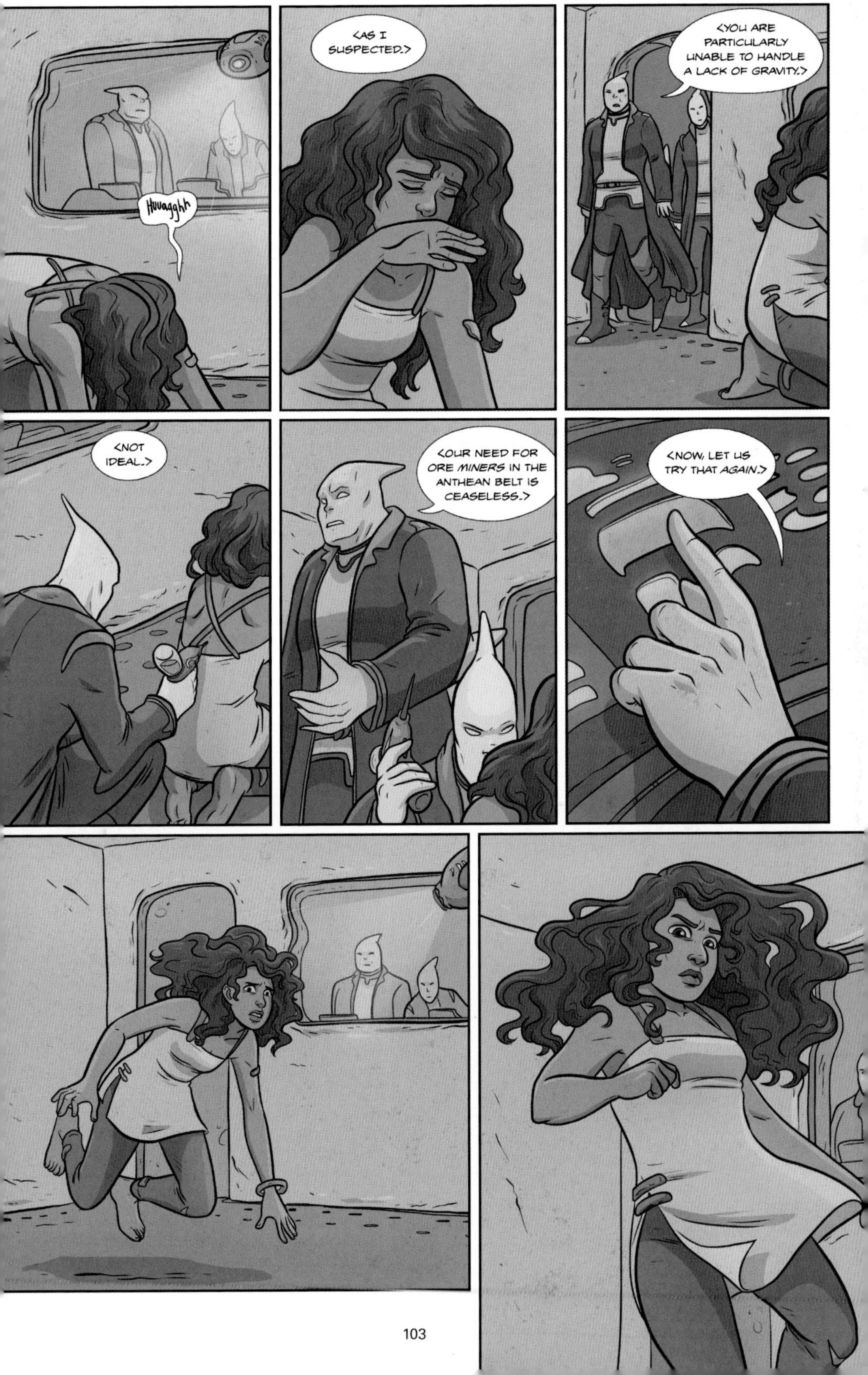
Huuagghh
<AS I SUSPECTED.>
<YOU ARE PARTICULARLY UNABLE TO HANDLE A LACK OF GRAVITY.>
<NOT IDEAL.>
<OUR NEED FOR ORE *MINERS* IN THE ANTHEAN BELT IS CEASELESS.>
<NOW, LET US TRY THAT *AGAIN*.>

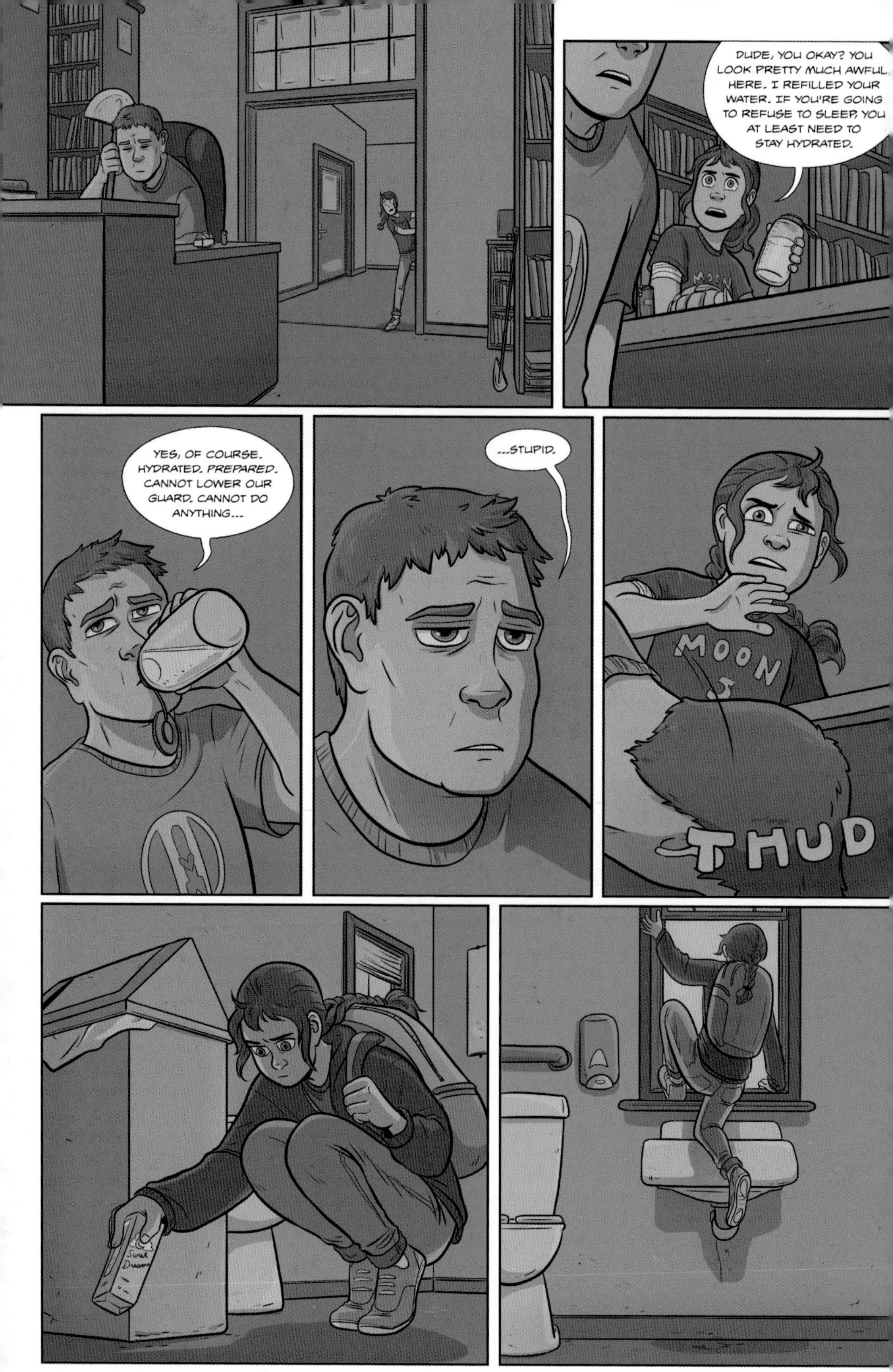
DUDE, YOU OKAY? YOU LOOK PRETTY MUCH AWFUL HERE. I REFILLED YOUR WATER. IF YOU'RE GOING TO REFUSE TO SLEEP, YOU AT LEAST NEED TO STAY HYDRATED.
YES, OF COURSE. HYDRATED. PREPARED. CANNOT LOWER OUR GUARD. CANNOT DO ANYTHING...
...STUPID.
MOON
THUD

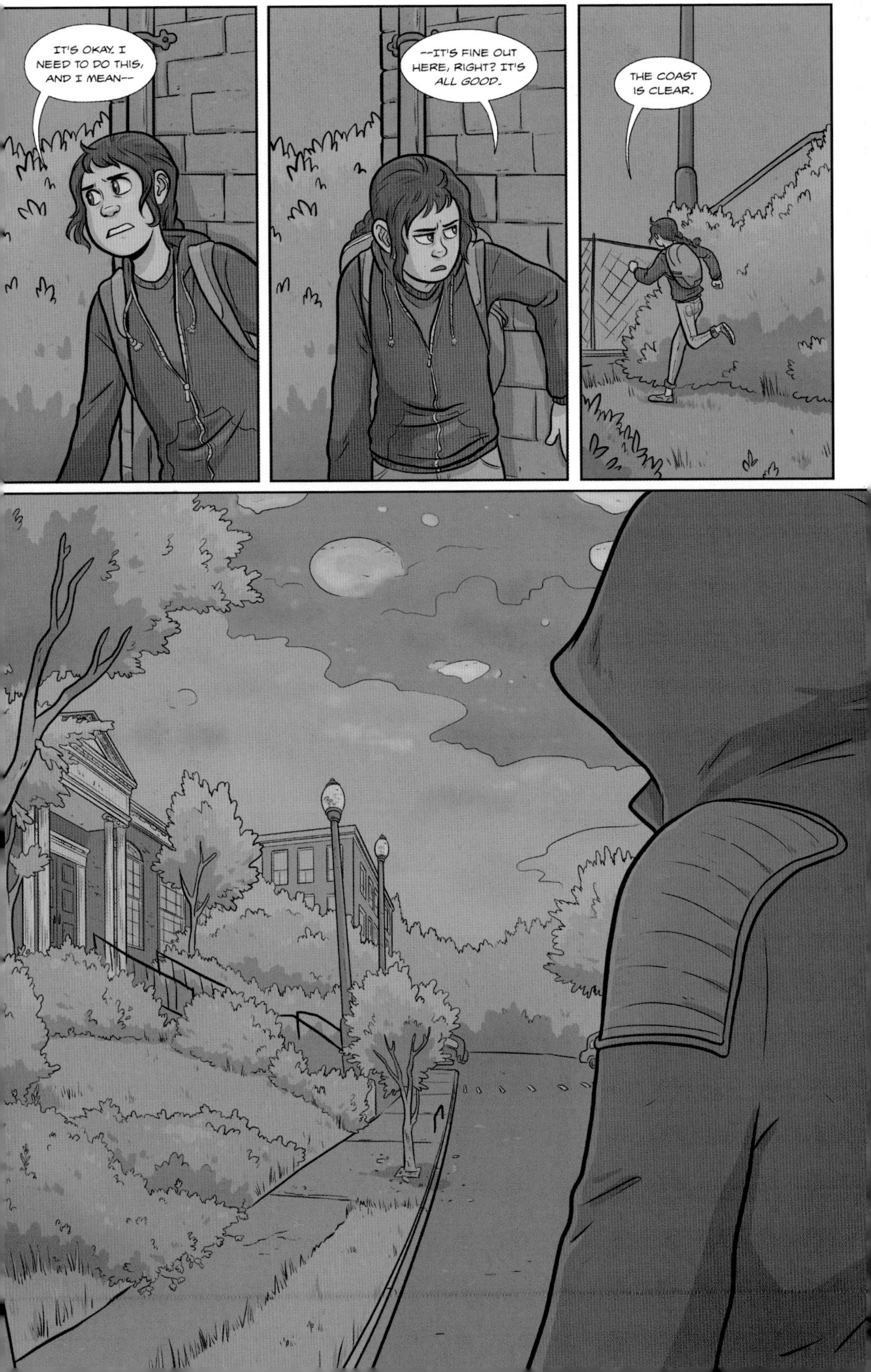
IT'S OKAY. I NEED TO DO THIS, AND I MEAN--
--IT'S FINE OUT HERE, RIGHT? IT'S ALL GOOD.
THE COAST IS CLEAR.

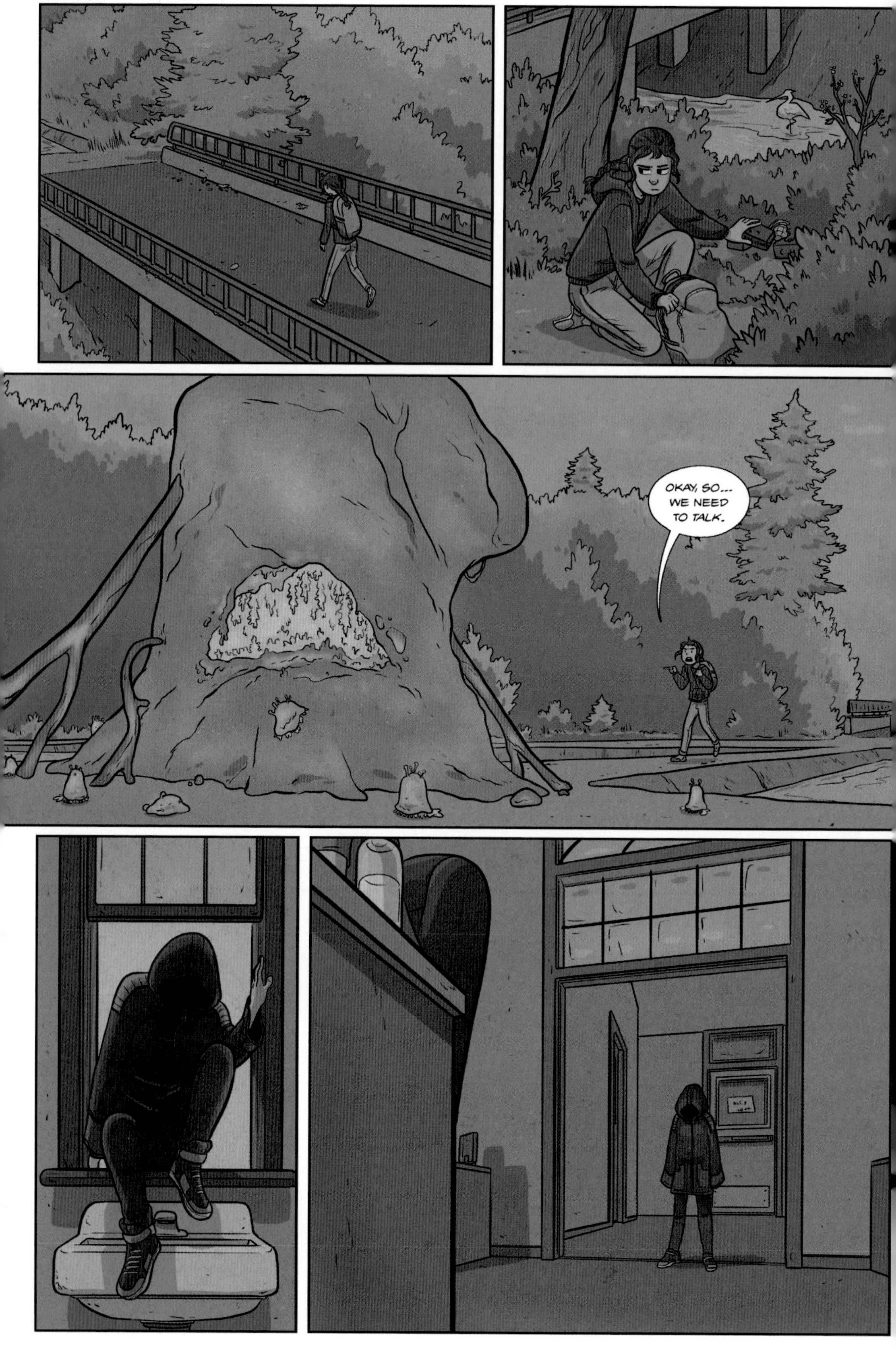
OKAY, SO...
WE NEED
TO TALK.

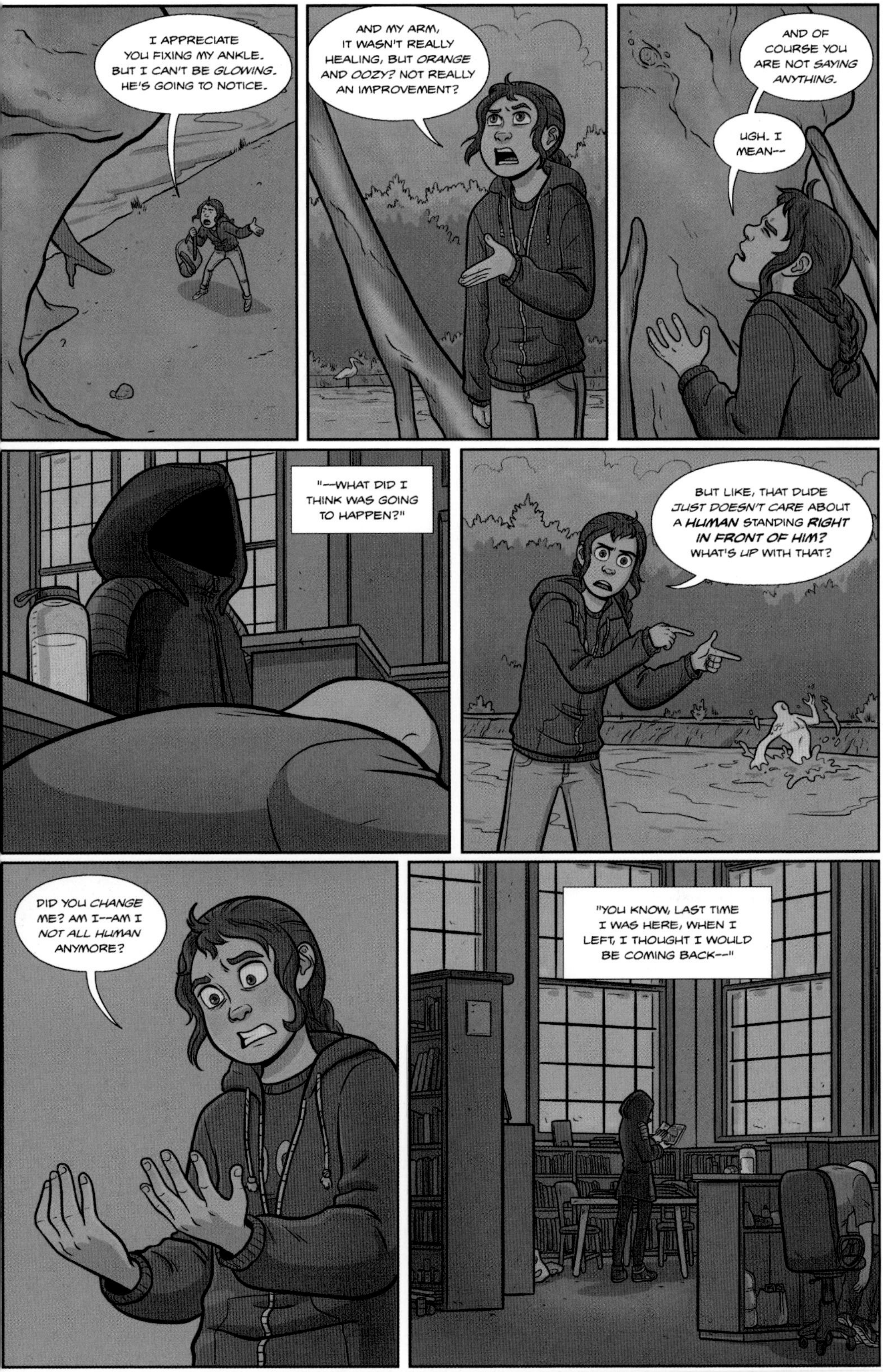
I APPRECIATE YOU FIXING MY ANKLE. BUT I CAN'T BE *GLOWING.* HE'S GOING TO NOTICE.
AND MY ARM, IT WASN'T REALLY HEALING, BUT *ORANGE* AND *OOZY?* NOT REALLY AN IMPROVEMENT?
AND OF COURSE YOU ARE NOT *SAYING* ANYTHING.
UGH. I MEAN--
"--WHAT DID I THINK WAS GOING TO HAPPEN?"
BUT LIKE, THAT DUDE *JUST DOESN'T CARE* ABOUT A **HUMAN** STANDING ***RIGHT IN FRONT OF HIM?*** WHAT'S *UP* WITH THAT?
DID YOU *CHANGE* ME? AM I--AM I *NOT ALL HUMAN* ANYMORE?
"YOU KNOW, LAST TIME I WAS HERE, WHEN I LEFT, I THOUGHT I WOULD BE COMING BACK--"

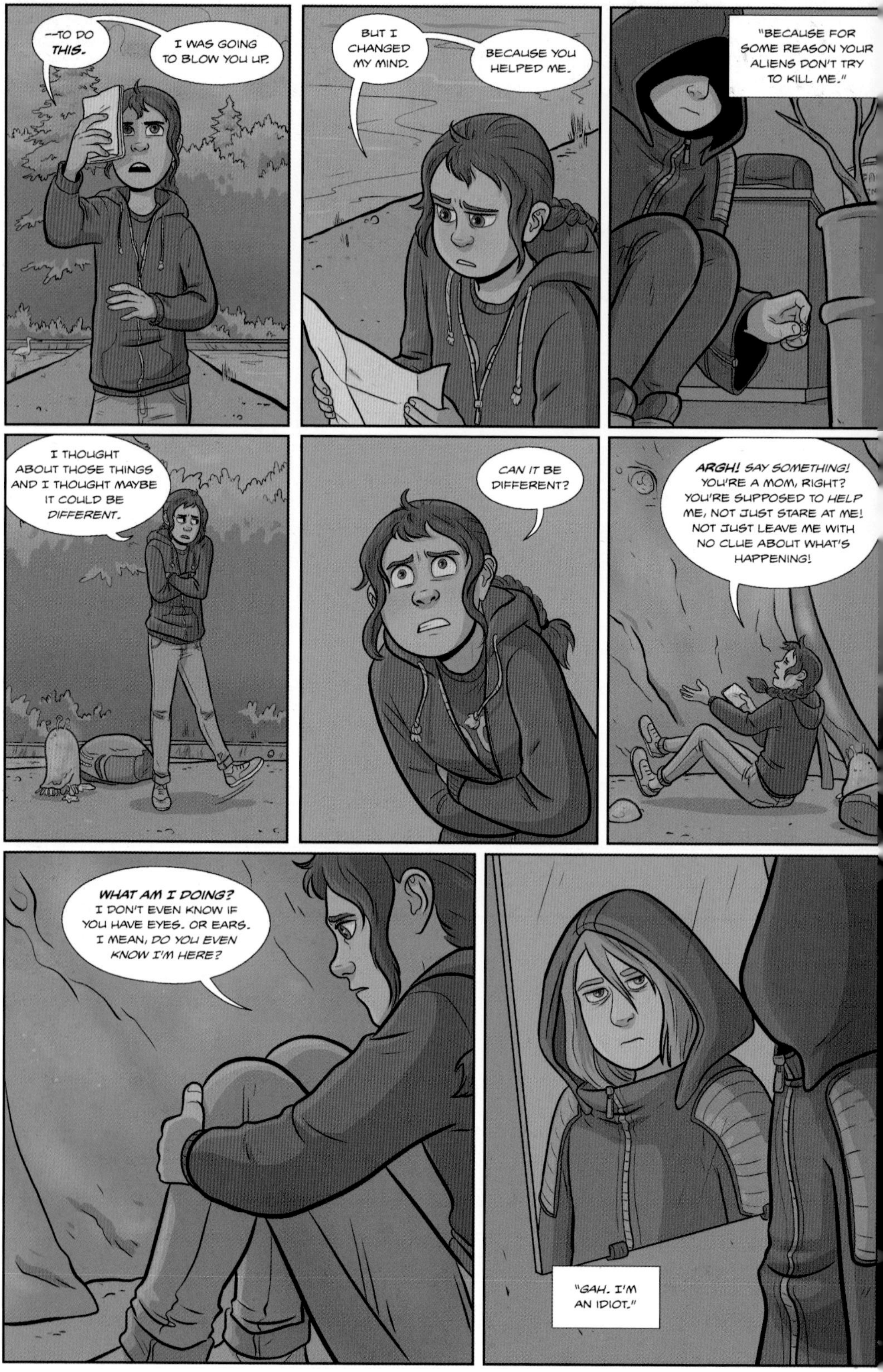
--TO DO THIS.
I WAS GOING TO BLOW YOU UP.
BUT I CHANGED MY MIND.
BECAUSE YOU HELPED ME.
"BECAUSE FOR SOME REASON YOUR ALIENS DON'T TRY TO KILL ME."
I THOUGHT ABOUT THOSE THINGS AND I THOUGHT MAYBE IT COULD BE DIFFERENT.
CAN IT BE DIFFERENT?
ARGH! SAY SOMETHING! YOU'RE A MOM, RIGHT? YOU'RE SUPPOSED TO HELP ME, NOT JUST STARE AT ME! NOT JUST LEAVE ME WITH NO CLUE ABOUT WHAT'S HAPPENING!
WHAT AM I DOING? I DON'T EVEN KNOW IF YOU HAVE EYES. OR EARS. I MEAN, DO YOU EVEN KNOW I'M HERE?
"GAH. I'M AN IDIOT."

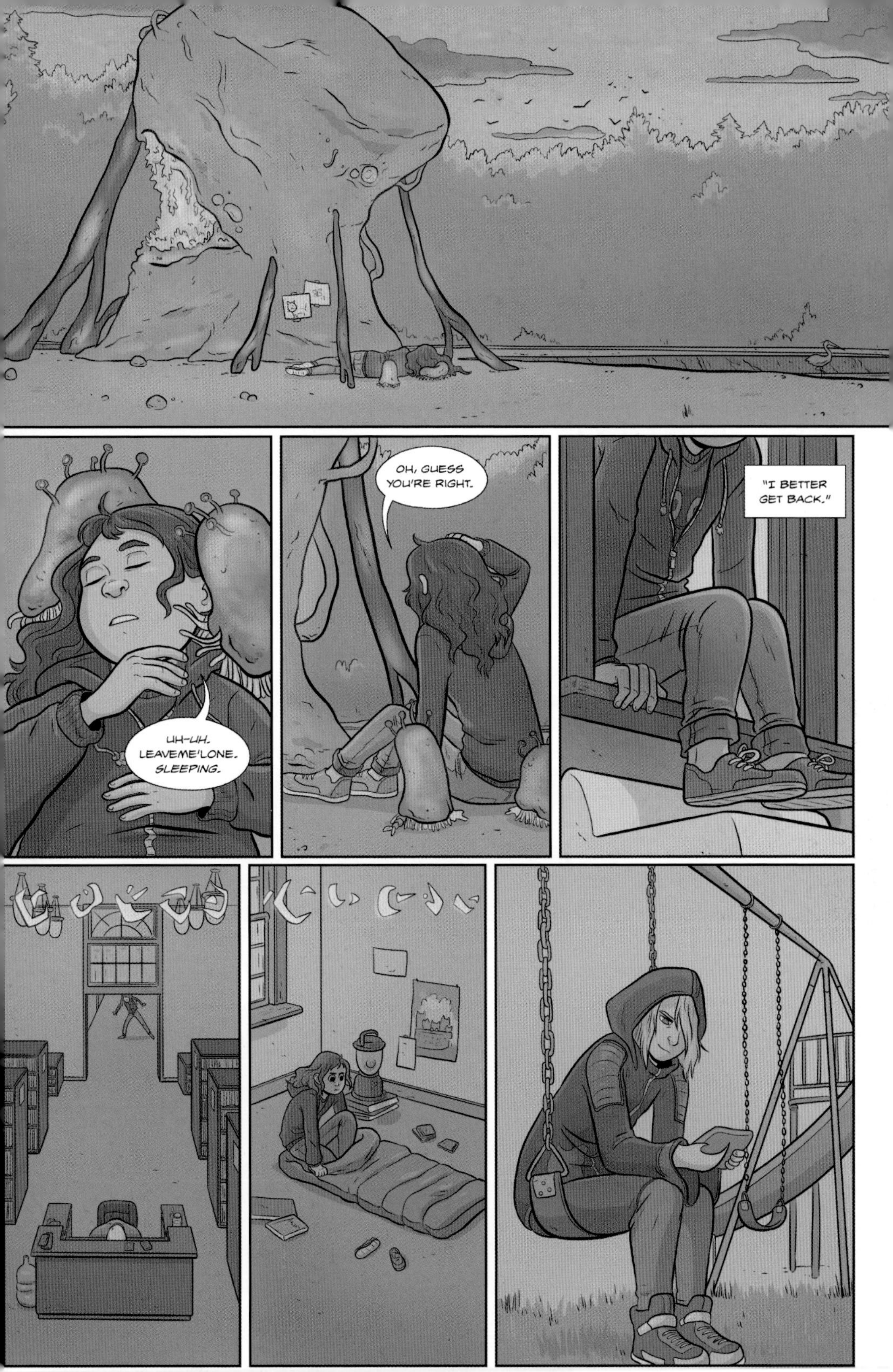
UH-UH.
LEAVEME'LONE.
SLEEPING.
OH, GUESS YOU'RE RIGHT.
"I BETTER GET BACK."

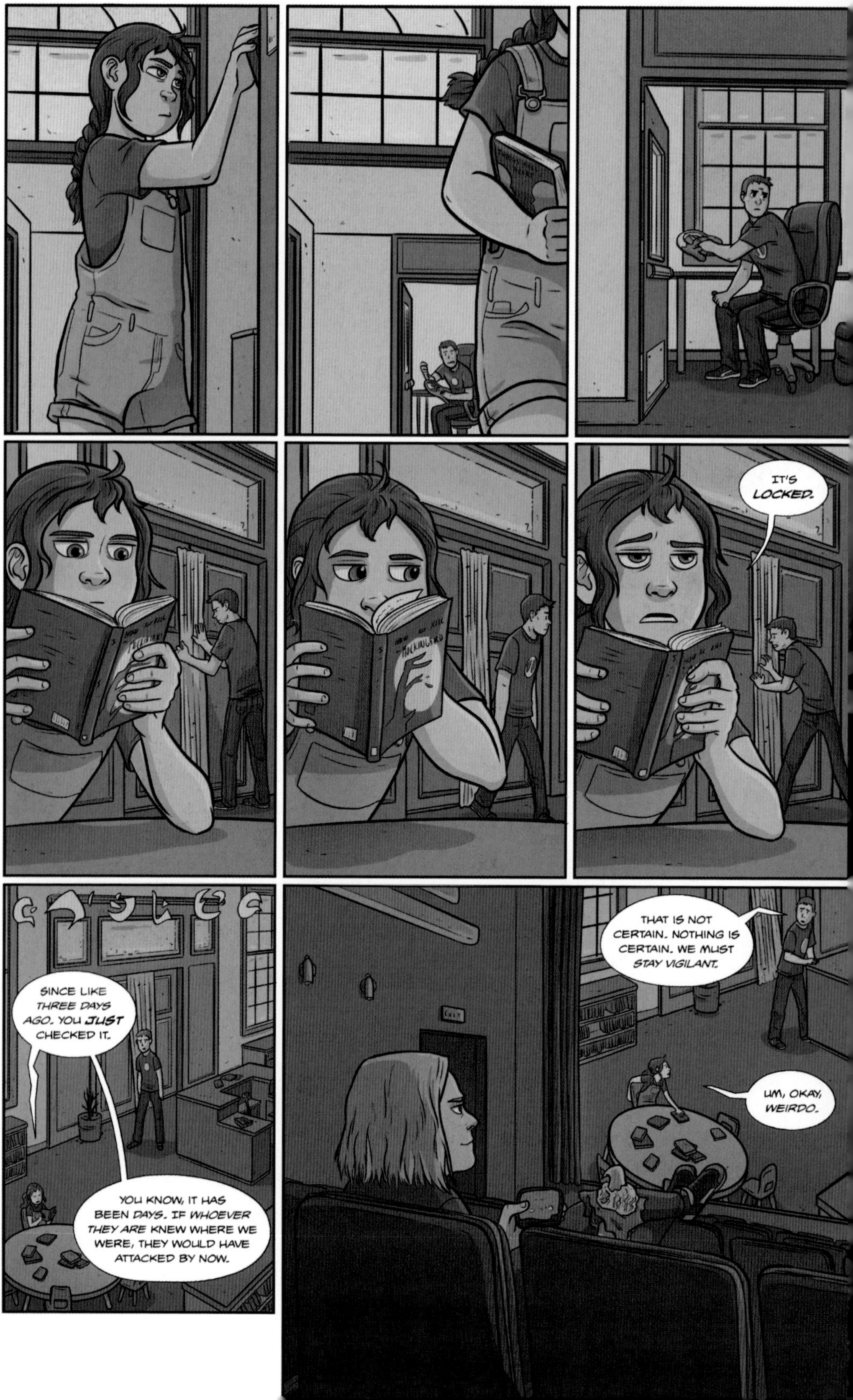
IT'S
LOCKED.
SINCE LIKE *THREE DAYS* AGO. YOU ***JUST*** CHECKED IT.
YOU KNOW, IT HAS BEEN *DAYS*. IF *WHOEVER THEY ARE* KNEW WHERE WE WERE, THEY WOULD HAVE ATTACKED BY NOW.
THAT IS NOT CERTAIN. NOTHING IS CERTAIN. WE MUST *STAY VIGILANT.*
UM, OKAY, *WEIRDO.*

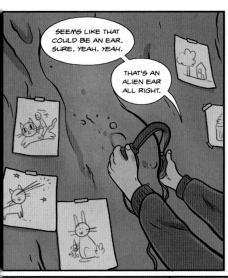

SEEMS LIKE THAT COULD BE AN EAR. SURE. YEAH. YEAH.

THAT'S AN ALIEN EAR ALL RIGHT.

"SO, WHAT DO YOU THINK?"

OH, *THIS!* THIS, RIGHT HERE!

"THIS IS MY FAVORITE PART."

HEY, I'VE BEEN WONDERING—

"—DO YOU NOTICE WHEN THEY LEAVE?"

EXTRA ORDIN
CHAPTER 3

DO YOU FEEL IT?

DOES IT MAKE YOU SAD?

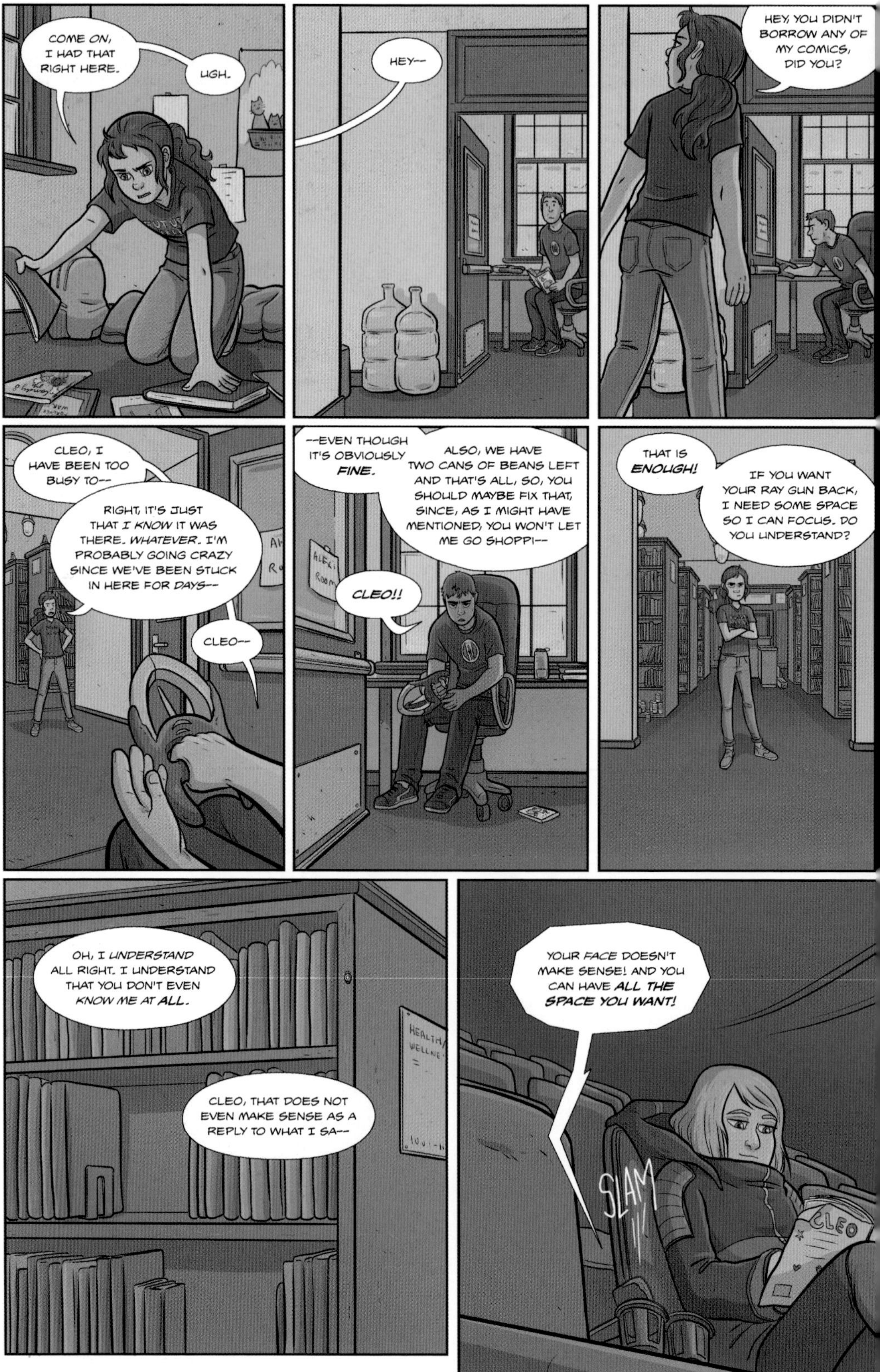
COME ON, I HAD THAT RIGHT HERE.
UGH.
HEY--
HEY, YOU DIDN'T BORROW ANY OF MY COMICS, DID YOU?
CLEO, I HAVE BEEN TOO BUSY TO--
RIGHT, IT'S JUST THAT I KNOW IT WAS THERE. WHATEVER. I'M PROBABLY GOING CRAZY SINCE WE'VE BEEN STUCK IN HERE FOR DAYS--
CLEO--
--EVEN THOUGH IT'S OBVIOUSLY FINE.
ALSO, WE HAVE TWO CANS OF BEANS LEFT AND THAT'S ALL, SO, YOU SHOULD MAYBE FIX THAT, SINCE, AS I MIGHT HAVE MENTIONED, YOU WON'T LET ME GO SHOPPI--
CLEO!!
THAT IS ENOUGH!
IF YOU WANT YOUR RAY GUN BACK, I NEED SOME SPACE SO I CAN FOCUS. DO YOU UNDERSTAND?
OH, I UNDERSTAND ALL RIGHT. I UNDERSTAND THAT YOU DON'T EVEN KNOW ME AT ALL.
CLEO, THAT DOES NOT EVEN MAKE SENSE AS A REPLY TO WHAT I SA--
YOUR FACE DOESN'T MAKE SENSE! AND YOU CAN HAVE ALL THE SPACE YOU WANT!
SLAM
CLEO

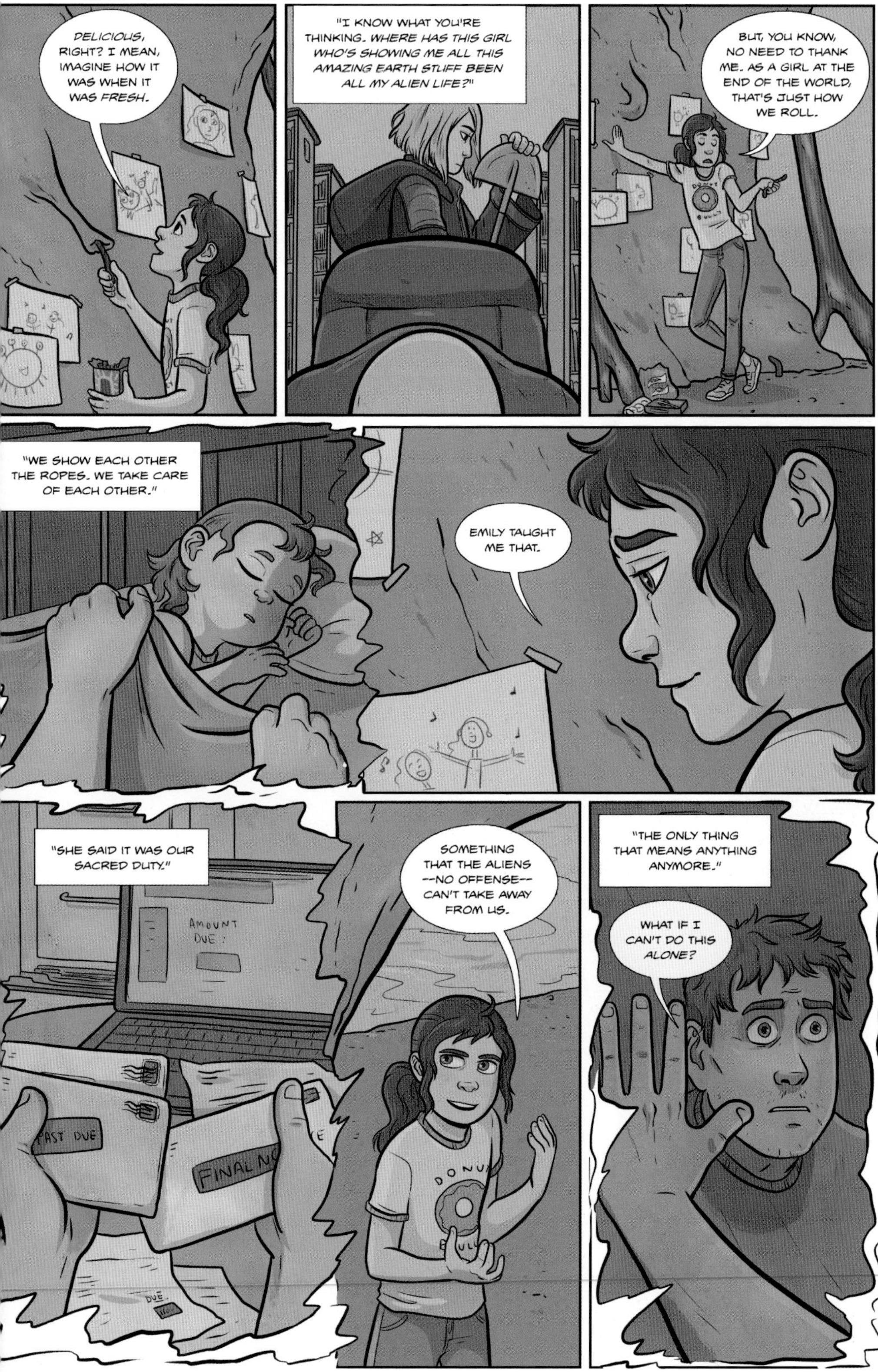
DELICIOUS, RIGHT? I MEAN, IMAGINE HOW IT WAS WHEN IT WAS FRESH.
"I KNOW WHAT YOU'RE THINKING. WHERE HAS THIS GIRL WHO'S SHOWING ME ALL THIS AMAZING EARTH STUFF BEEN ALL MY ALIEN LIFE?"
BUT, YOU KNOW, NO NEED TO THANK ME. AS A GIRL AT THE END OF THE WORLD, THAT'S JUST HOW WE ROLL.
"WE SHOW EACH OTHER THE ROPES. WE TAKE CARE OF EACH OTHER."
EMILY TAUGHT ME THAT.
"SHE SAID IT WAS OUR SACRED DUTY."
AMOUNT DUE:
PAST DUE
SOMETHING THAT THE ALIENS --NO OFFENSE-- CAN'T TAKE AWAY FROM US.
"THE ONLY THING THAT MEANS ANYTHING ANYMORE."
WHAT IF I CAN'T DO THIS ALONE?

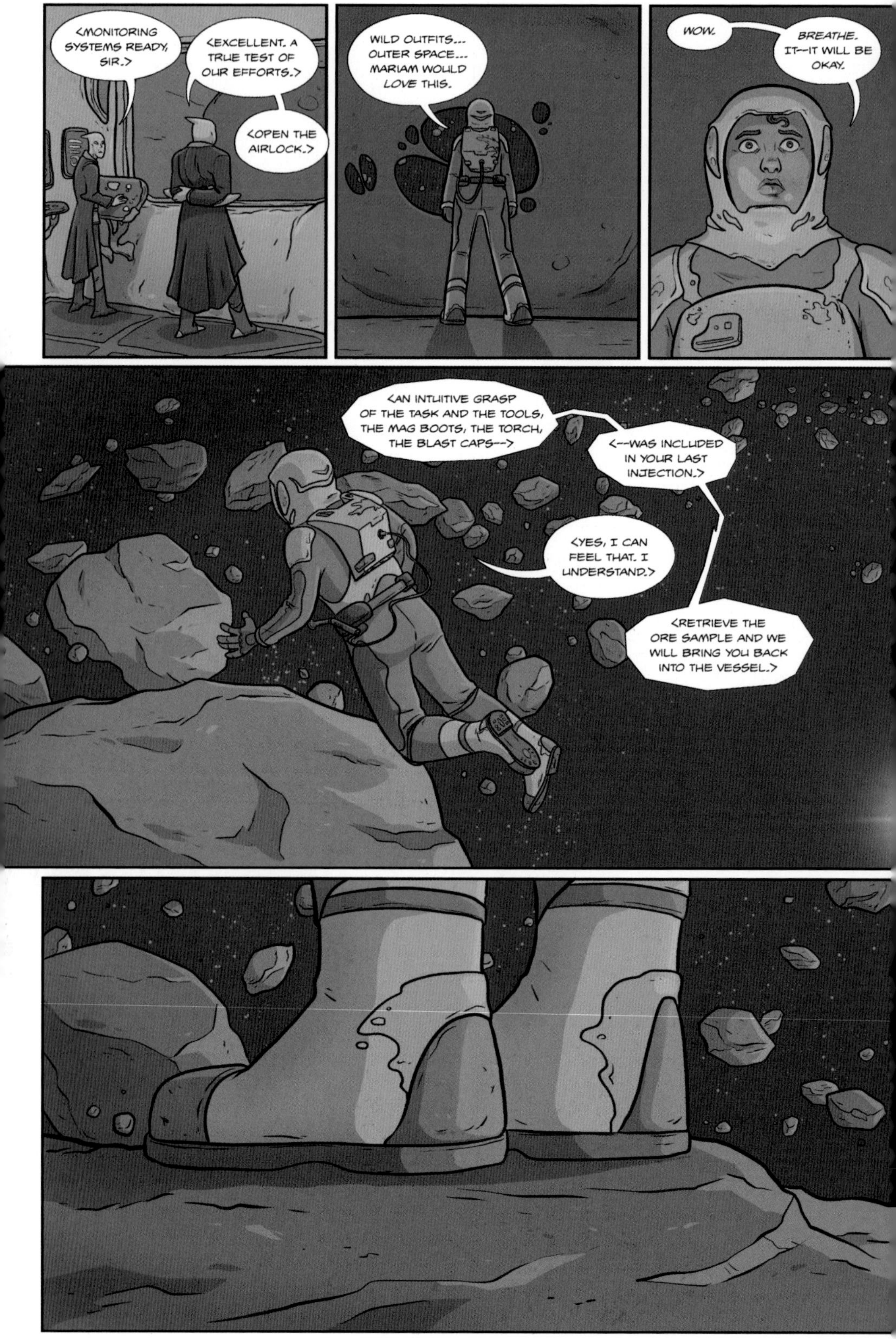
<MONITORING SYSTEMS READY, SIR.>
<EXCELLENT. A TRUE TEST OF OUR EFFORTS.>
<OPEN THE AIRLOCK.>
WILD OUTFITS... OUTER SPACE... MARIAM WOULD LOVE THIS.
WOW.
BREATHE. IT--IT WILL BE OKAY.
<AN INTUITIVE GRASP OF THE TASK AND THE TOOLS, THE MAG BOOTS, THE TORCH, THE BLAST CAPS-->
<--WAS INCLUDED IN YOUR LAST INJECTION.>
<YES, I CAN FEEL THAT. I UNDERSTAND.>
<RETRIEVE THE ORE SAMPLE AND WE WILL BRING YOU BACK INTO THE VESSEL.>

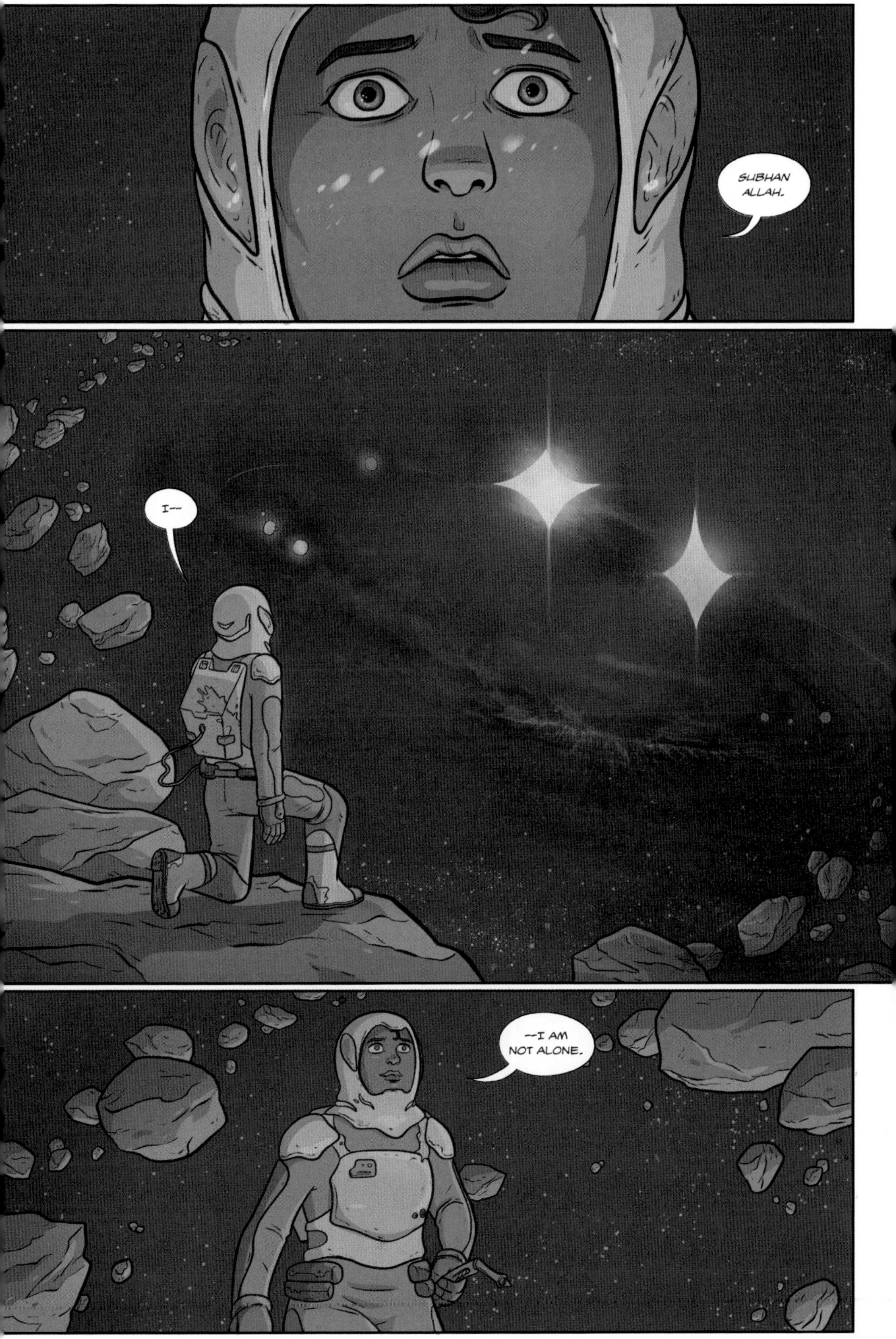
SUBHAN ALLAH.
I--
--I AM NOT ALONE.

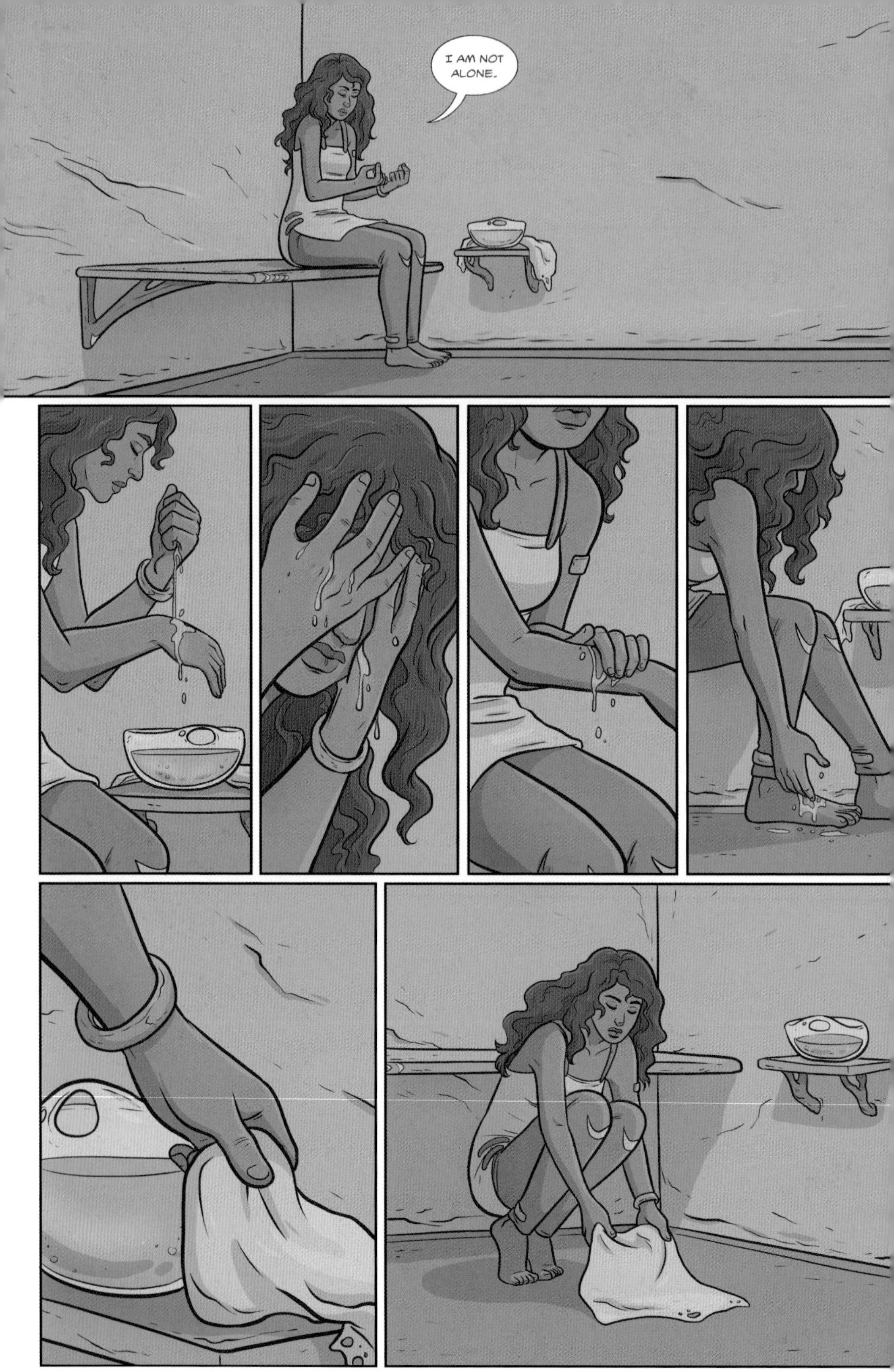
I AM NOT ALONE.

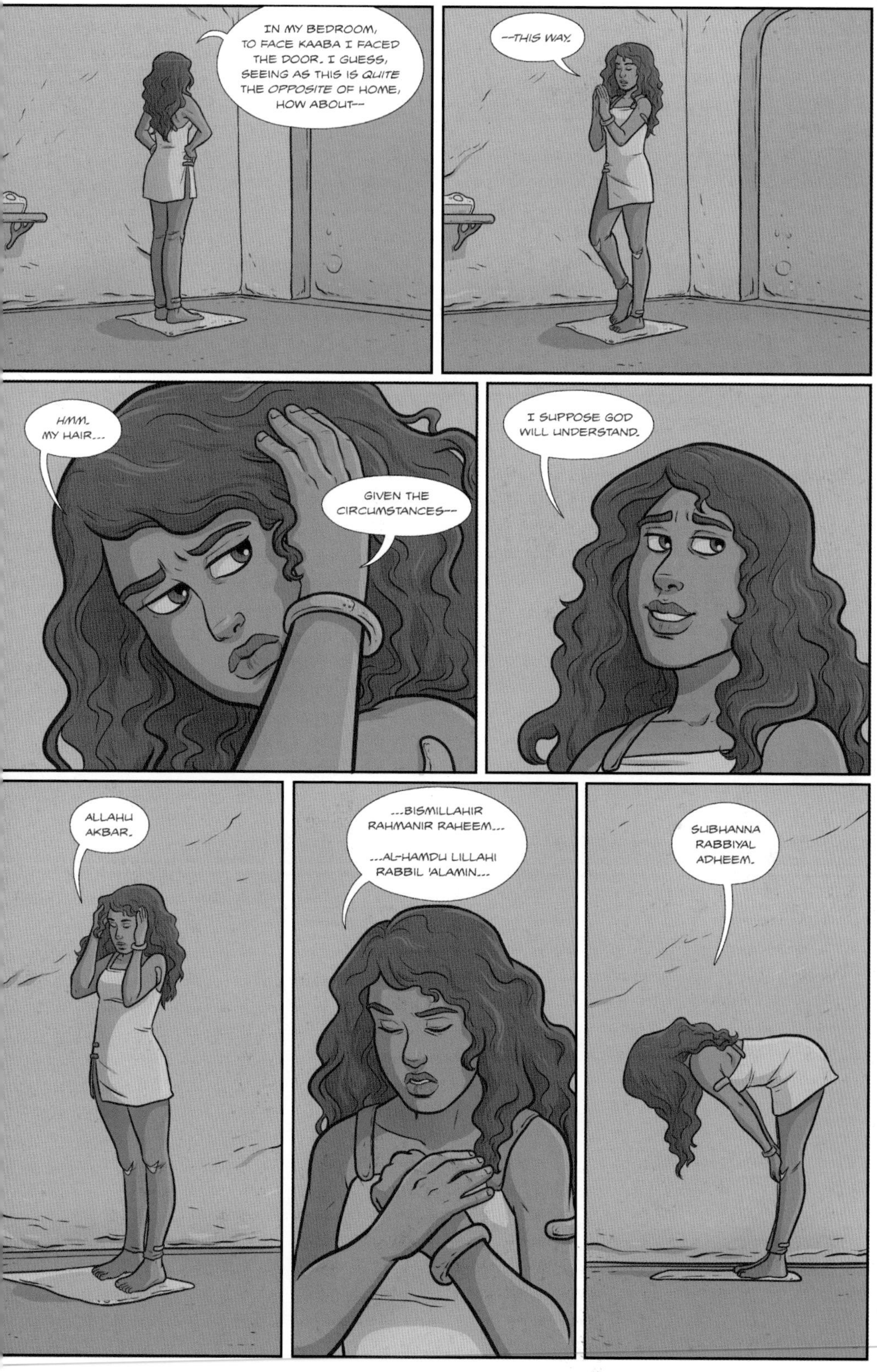
IN MY BEDROOM, TO FACE KAABA I FACED THE DOOR. I GUESS, SEEING AS THIS IS *QUITE* THE *OPPOSITE* OF HOME, HOW ABOUT--
--THIS WAY.
HMM. MY HAIR...
GIVEN THE CIRCUMSTANCES--
I SUPPOSE GOD WILL UNDERSTAND.
ALLAHU AKBAR.
...BISMILLAHIR RAHMANIR RAHEEM...
...AL-HAMDU LILLAHI RABBIL 'ALAMIN...
SUBHANNA RABBIYAL ADHEEM.

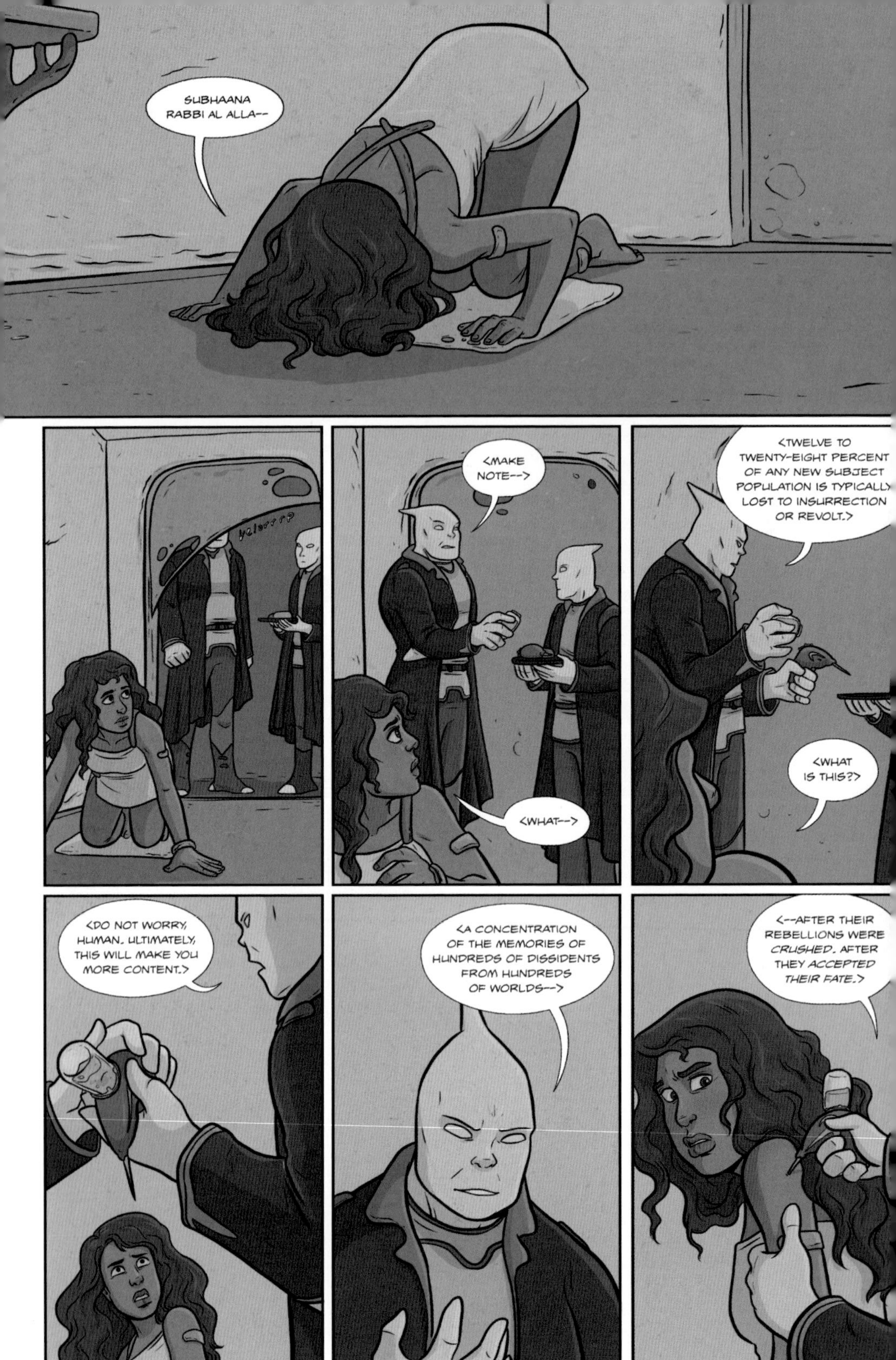
SUBHAANA RABBI AL ALLA--
<MAKE NOTE-->
<WHAT-->
<TWELVE TO TWENTY-EIGHT PERCENT OF ANY NEW SUBJECT POPULATION IS TYPICALLY LOST TO INSURRECTION OR REVOLT.>
<WHAT IS THIS?>
<DO NOT WORRY, HUMAN. ULTIMATELY, THIS WILL MAKE YOU MORE CONTENT.>
<A CONCENTRATION OF THE MEMORIES OF HUNDREDS OF DISSIDENTS FROM HUNDREDS OF WORLDS-->
<--AFTER THEIR REBELLIONS WERE *CRUSHED*. AFTER THEY *ACCEPTED THEIR FATE*.>

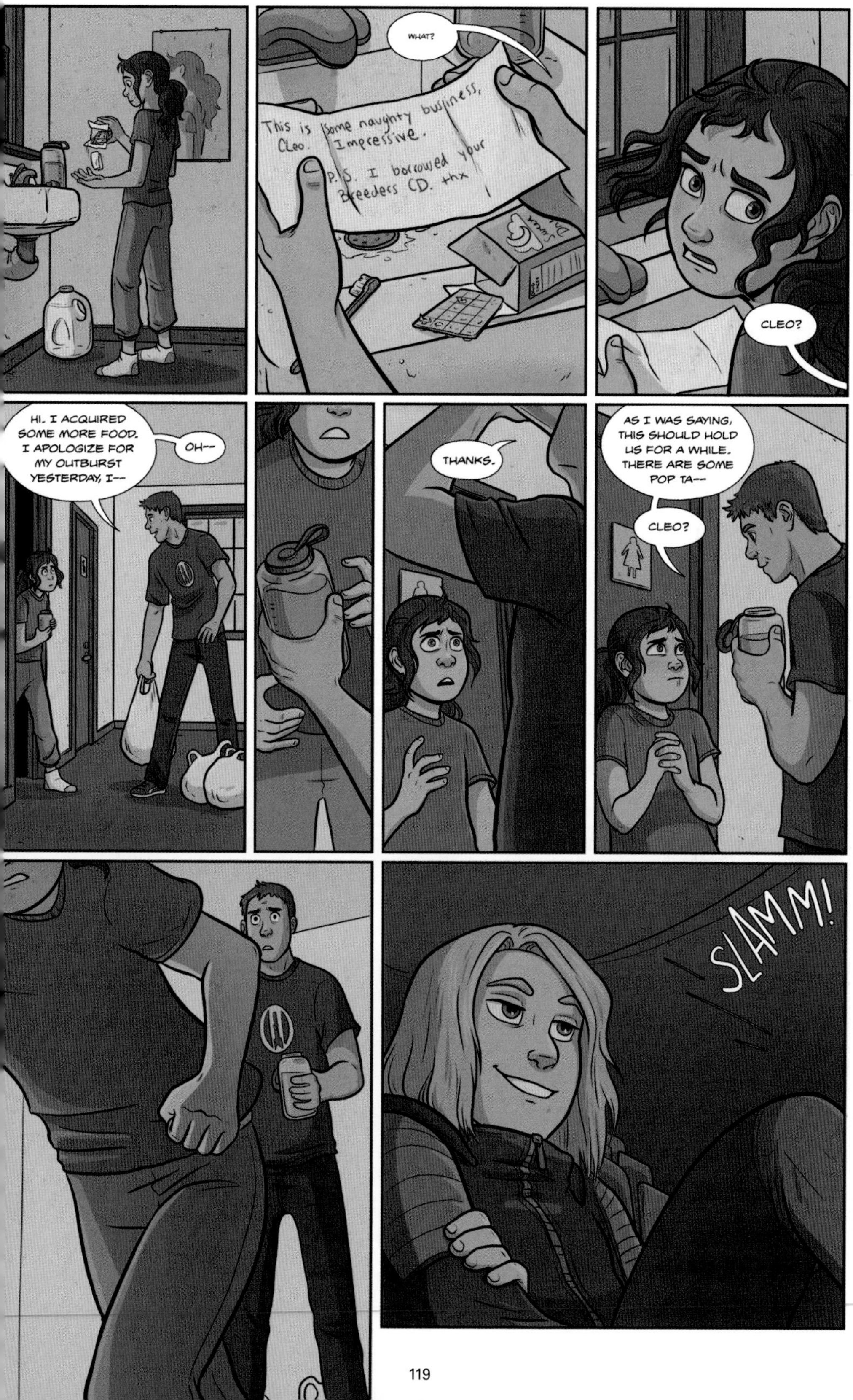
WHAT?
This is some naughty business, Cleo. Impressive.
P.S. I borrowed your Breeders CD. thx
CLEO?
HI. I ACQUIRED SOME MORE FOOD. I APOLOGIZE FOR MY OUTBURST YESTERDAY, I--
OH--
THANKS.
AS I WAS SAYING, THIS SHOULD HOLD US FOR A WHILE. THERE ARE SOME POP TA--
CLEO?
SLAMM!

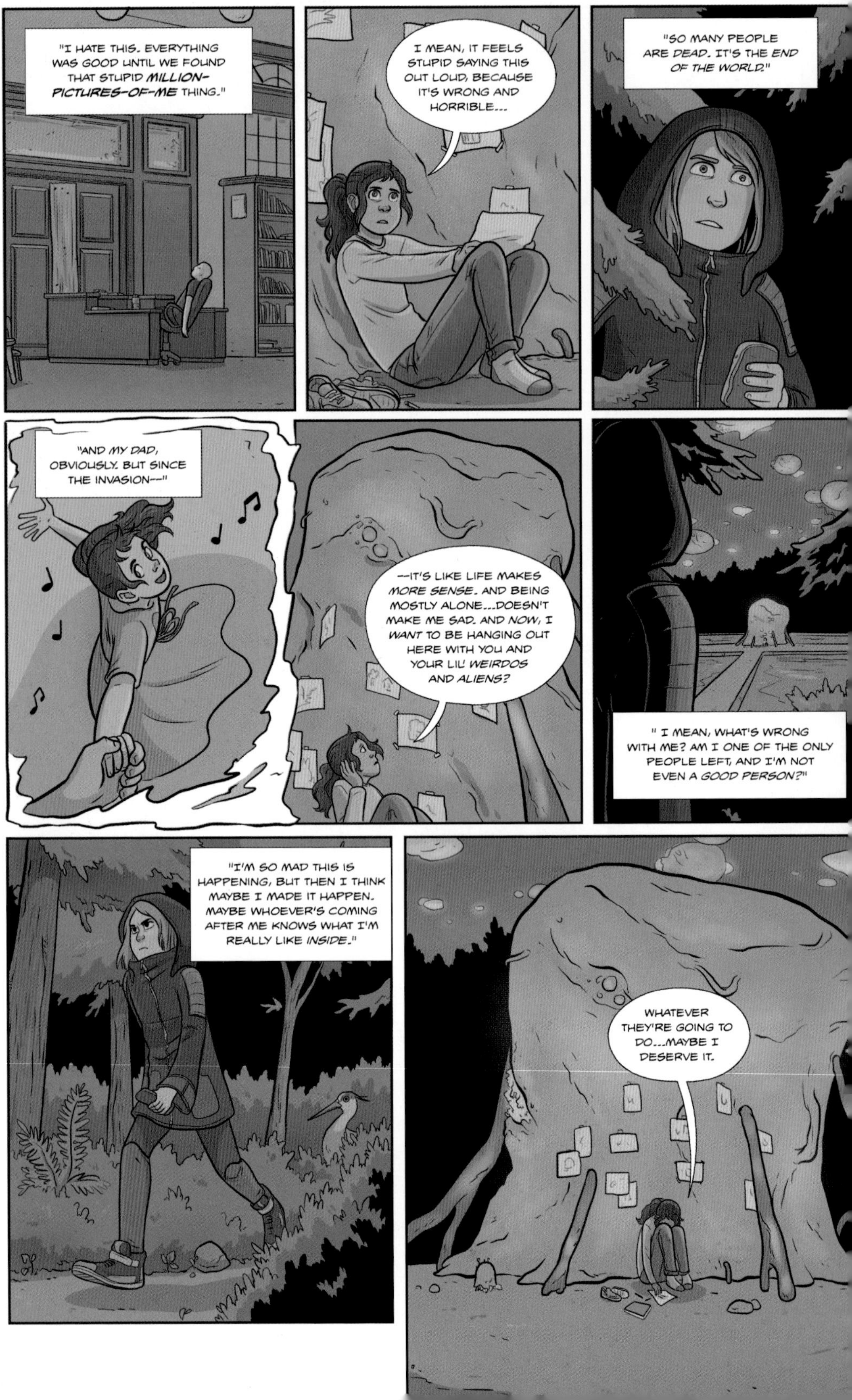
"I HATE THIS. EVERYTHING WAS GOOD UNTIL WE FOUND THAT STUPID MILLION-PICTURES-OF-ME THING."
I MEAN, IT FEELS STUPID SAYING THIS OUT LOUD, BECAUSE IT'S WRONG AND HORRIBLE...
"SO MANY PEOPLE ARE DEAD. IT'S THE END OF THE WORLD."
"AND MY DAD, OBVIOUSLY. BUT SINCE THE INVASION--"
--IT'S LIKE LIFE MAKES MORE SENSE. AND BEING MOSTLY ALONE...DOESN'T MAKE ME SAD. AND NOW, I WANT TO BE HANGING OUT HERE WITH YOU AND YOUR LIL' WEIRDOS AND ALIENS?
" I MEAN, WHAT'S WRONG WITH ME? AM I ONE OF THE ONLY PEOPLE LEFT, AND I'M NOT EVEN A GOOD PERSON?"
"I'M SO MAD THIS IS HAPPENING, BUT THEN I THINK MAYBE I MADE IT HAPPEN. MAYBE WHOEVER'S COMING AFTER ME KNOWS WHAT I'M REALLY LIKE INSIDE."
WHATEVER THEY'RE GOING TO DO...MAYBE I DESERVE IT.

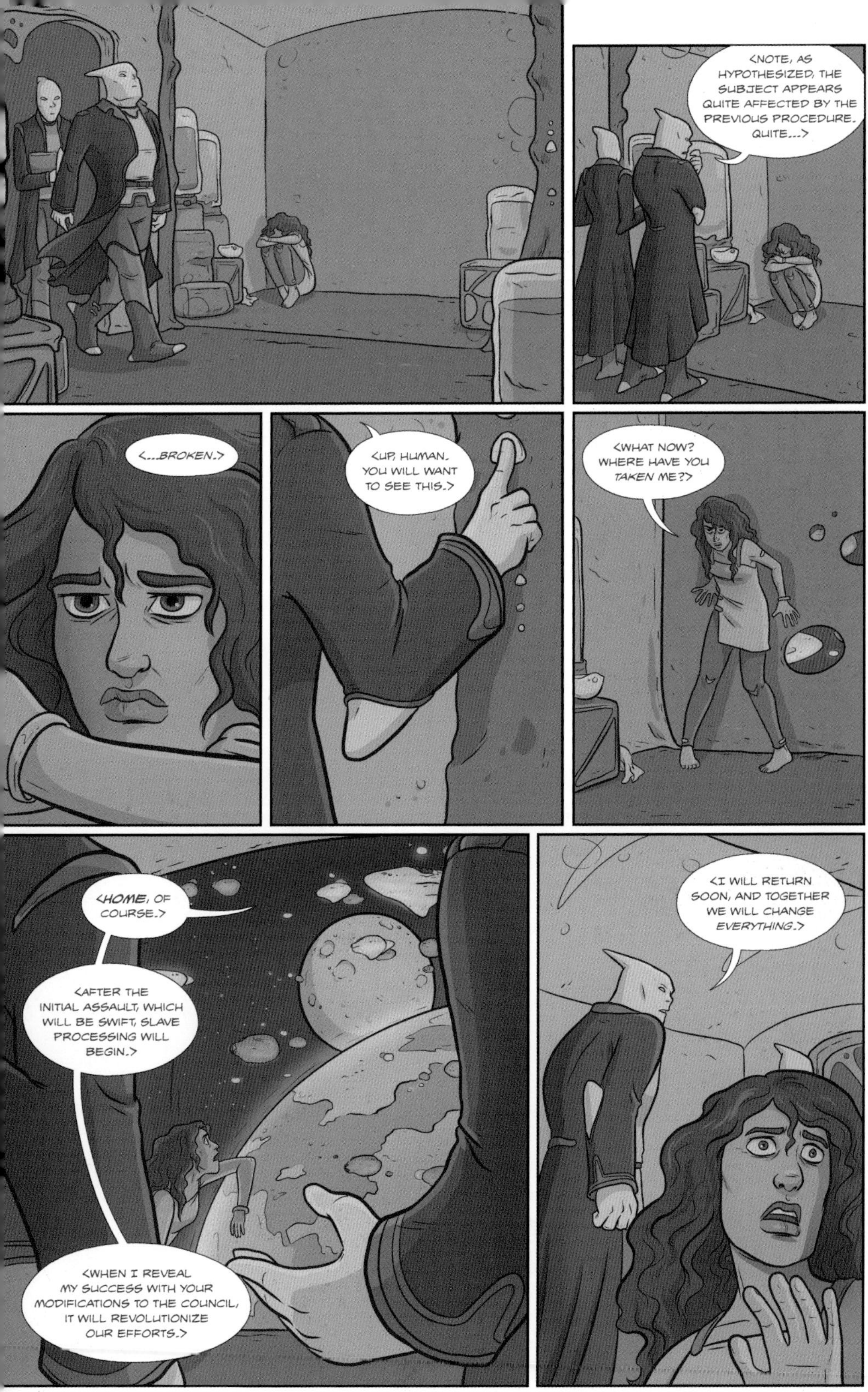
<NOTE, AS HYPOTHESIZED, THE SUBJECT APPEARS QUITE AFFECTED BY THE PREVIOUS PROCEDURE. QUITE...>
<...BROKEN.>
<UP, HUMAN. YOU WILL WANT TO SEE THIS.>
<WHAT NOW? WHERE HAVE YOU *TAKEN* ME?>
<***HOME***, OF COURSE.>
<AFTER THE INITIAL ASSAULT, WHICH WILL BE SWIFT, SLAVE PROCESSING WILL BEGIN.>
<WHEN I REVEAL MY SUCCESS WITH YOUR MODIFICATIONS TO THE COUNCIL, IT WILL REVOLUTIONIZE OUR EFFORTS.>
<I WILL RETURN SOON, AND TOGETHER WE WILL CHANGE *EVERYTHING*.>

CLEO, I HAVE BEEN THINKING.

I DO NOT THINK THAT IT WILL FEEL SAFE HERE AGAIN AND—

—WE SHOULD MOVE TO A NEW CITY.

WHAT?!

I *LIKE* IT HERE.

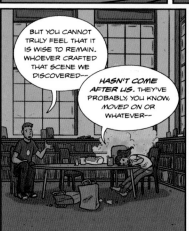

BUT YOU CANNOT TRULY FEEL THAT IT IS WISE TO REMAIN. WHOEVER CRAFTED THAT SCENE WE DISCOVERED—

HASN'T COME AFTER US. THEY'VE PROBABLY, YOU KNOW, *MOVED ON* OR WHATEVER—

IT SEEMS *UNLIKELY* THAT THEY WOULD ABANDON WHAT APPEARS TO BE AN ELABORATELY CONCEIVED PLAN.

MORE LIKELY THEY ARE WAITING FOR US TO MAKE A *MISTAKE.* TO RESUME OUR ACTIVITIES AND EXPOSE OURSELVES.

WELL, YOU KNOW WHAT? *FINE.* IF THAT'S THE CASE, *BRING IT ON.*

EXIT

AT LEAST THEN WE'D *KNOW.* AT LEAST THEN SOMETHING WOULD *MAKE SENSE.*

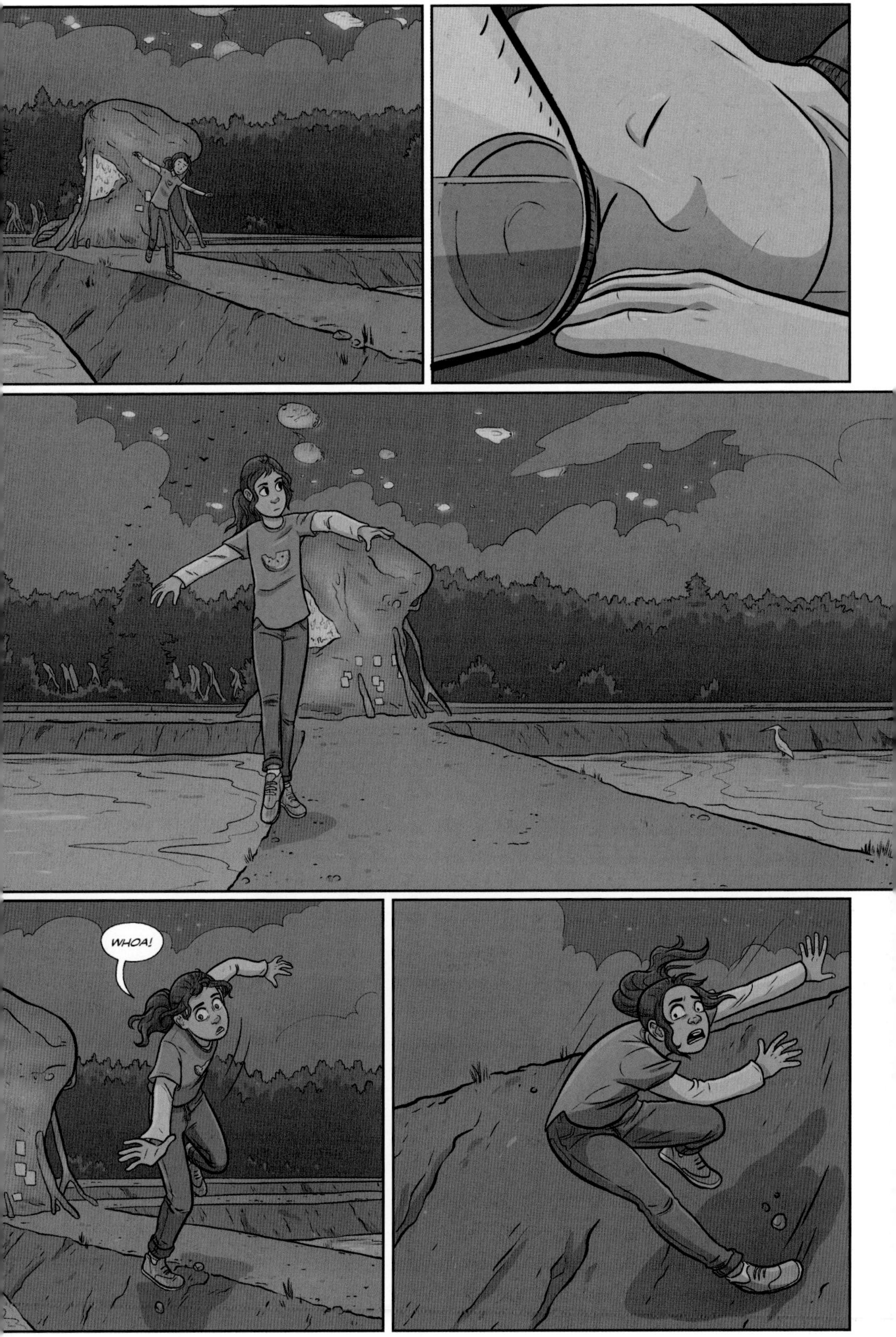
WHOA!

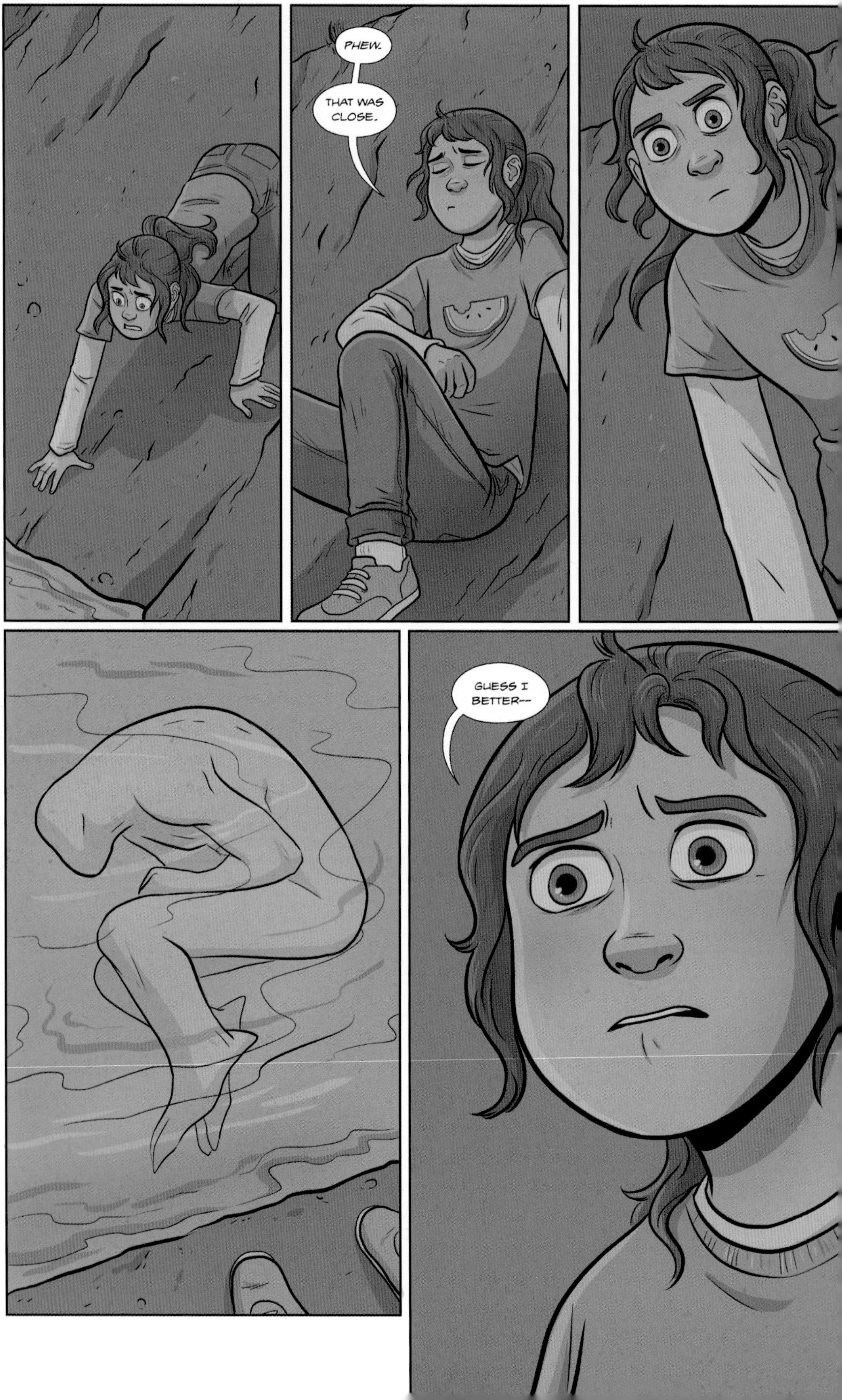
PHEW.
THAT WAS CLOSE.
GUESS I BETTER--

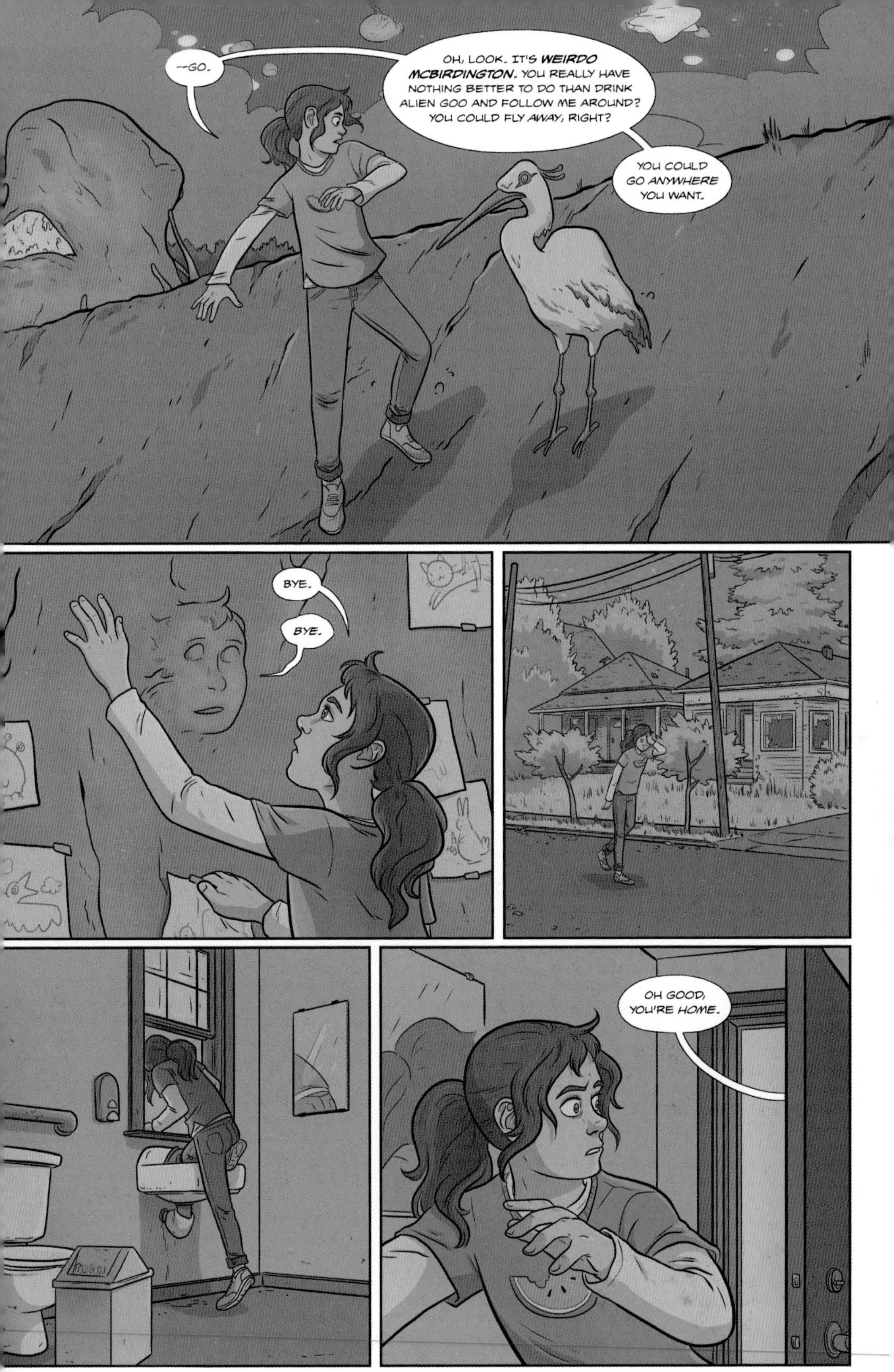
--GO.
OH, LOOK. IT'S WEIRDO MCBIRDINGTON. YOU REALLY HAVE NOTHING BETTER TO DO THAN DRINK ALIEN GOO AND FOLLOW ME AROUND? YOU COULD FLY AWAY, RIGHT?
YOU COULD GO ANYWHERE YOU WANT.
BYE.
BYE.
OH GOOD, YOU'RE HOME.

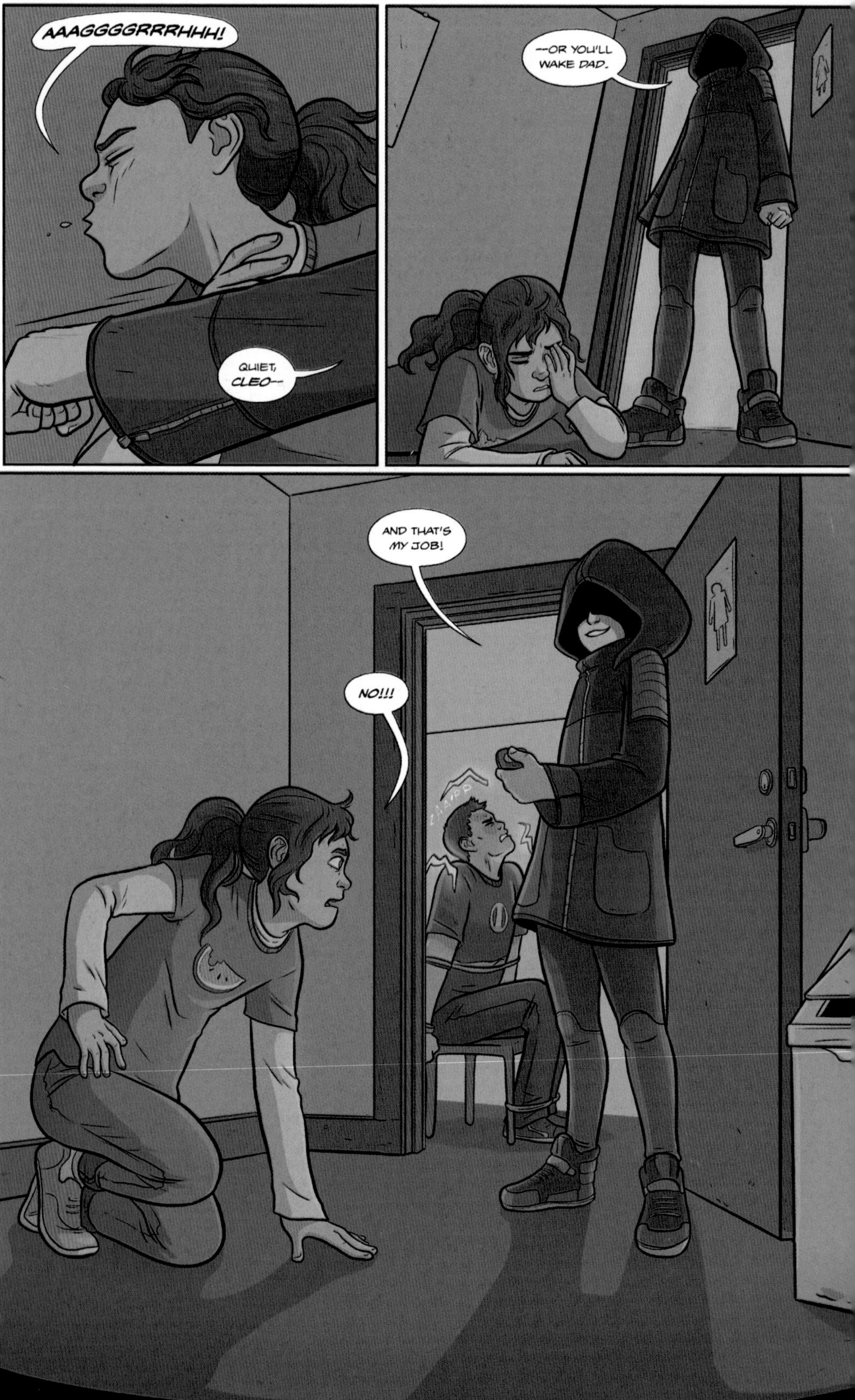
AAAGGGGRRRHHH!
QUIET, CLEO--
--OR YOU'LL WAKE DAD.
AND THAT'S MY JOB!
NO!!!

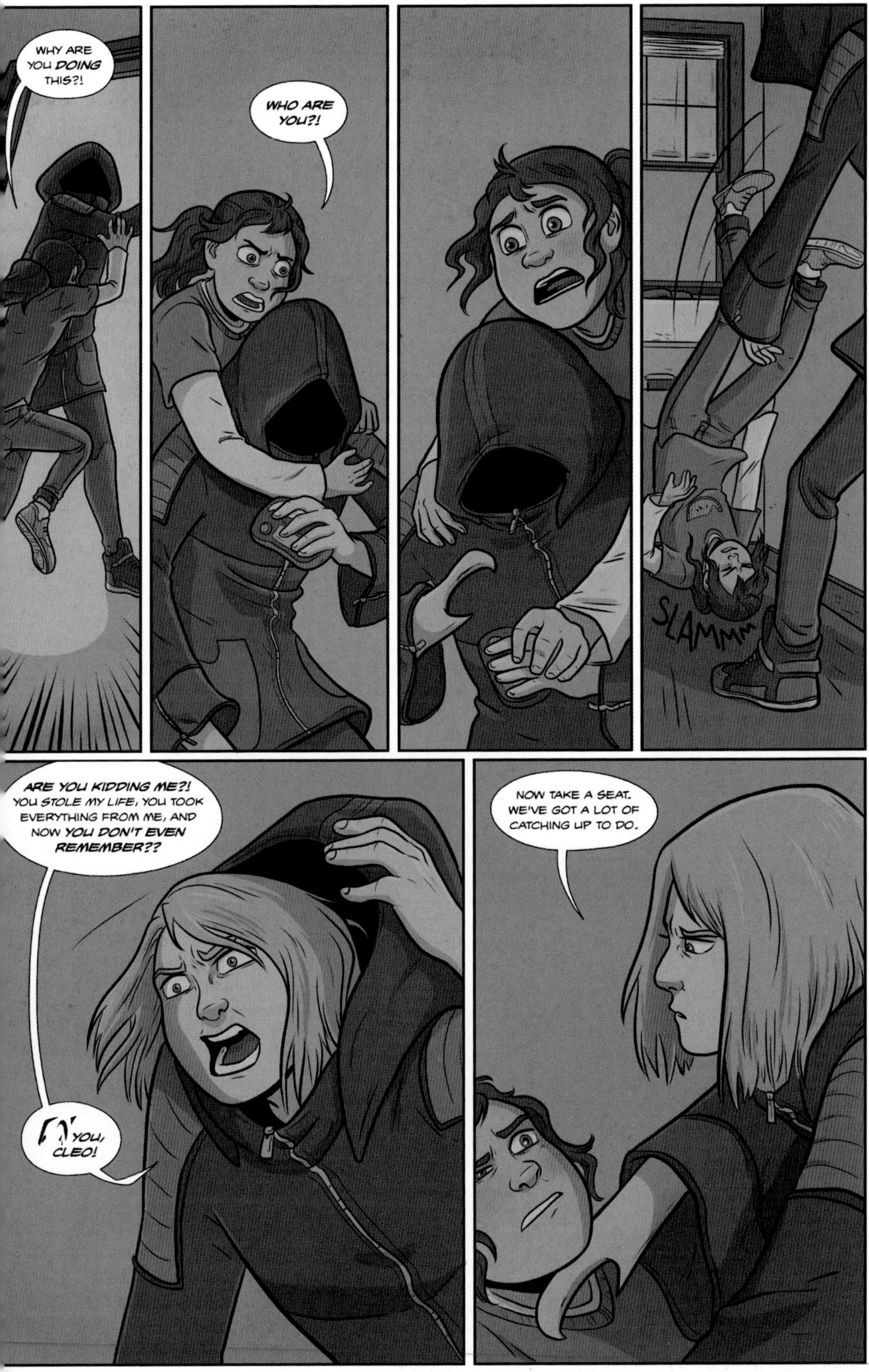
WHY ARE YOU DOING THIS?!
WHO ARE YOU?!
SLAMMM
ARE YOU KIDDING ME?! YOU STOLE MY LIFE, YOU TOOK EVERYTHING FROM ME, AND NOW YOU DON'T EVEN REMEMBER??
YOU, CLEO!
NOW TAKE A SEAT. WE'VE GOT A LOT OF CATCHING UP TO DO.

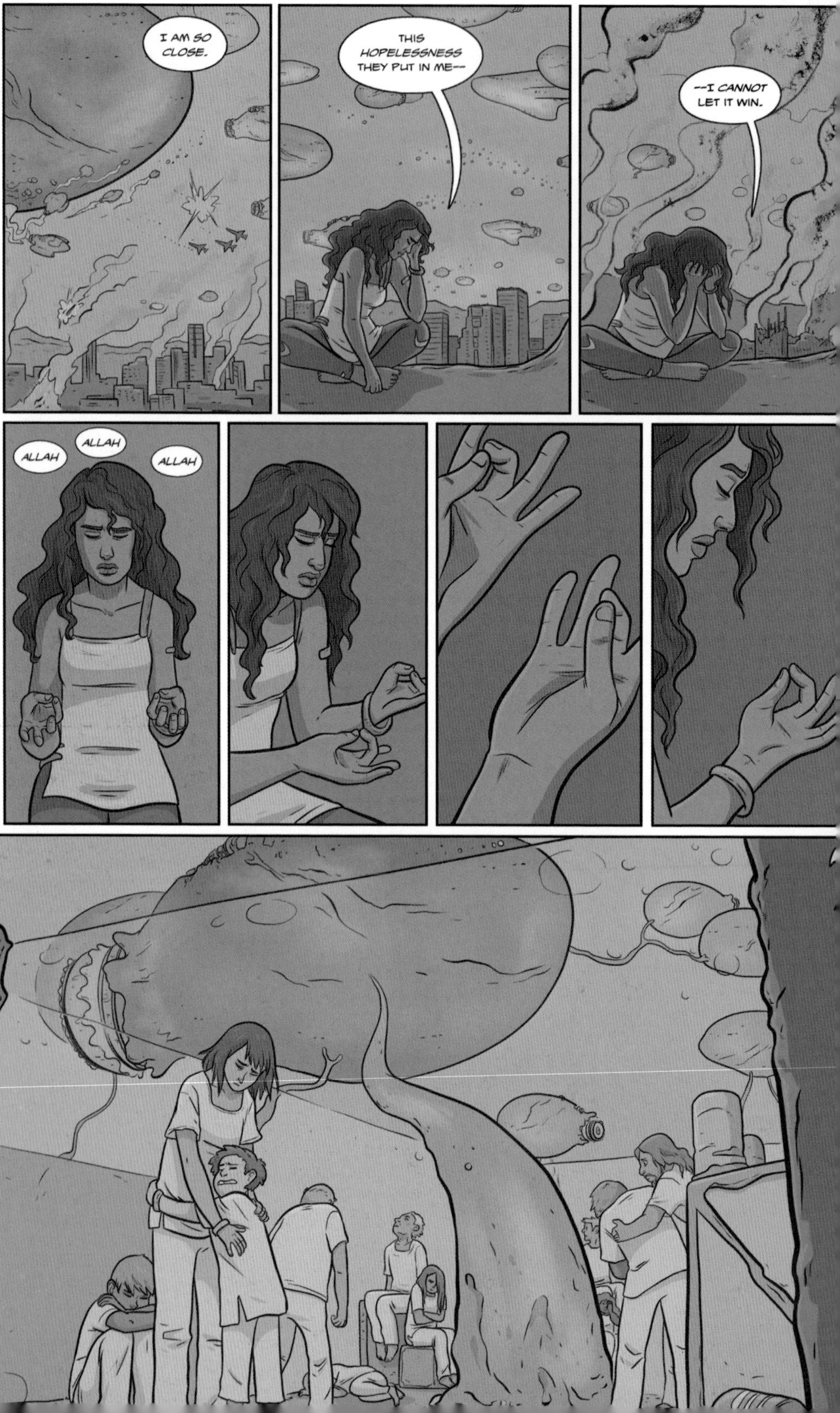
I AM SO CLOSE.
THIS HOPELESSNESS THEY PUT IN ME--
--I CANNOT LET IT WIN.
ALLAH
ALLAH
ALLAH

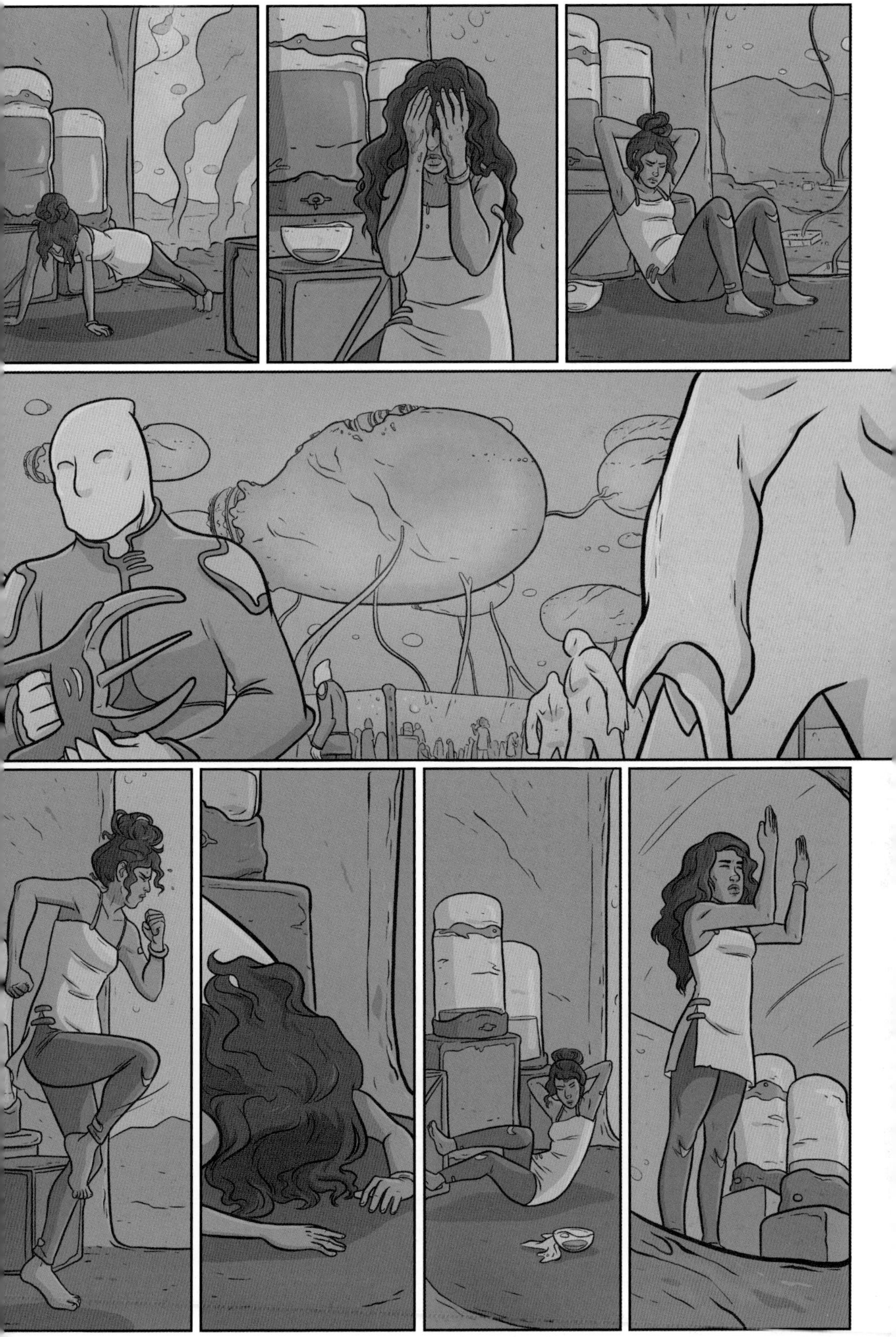

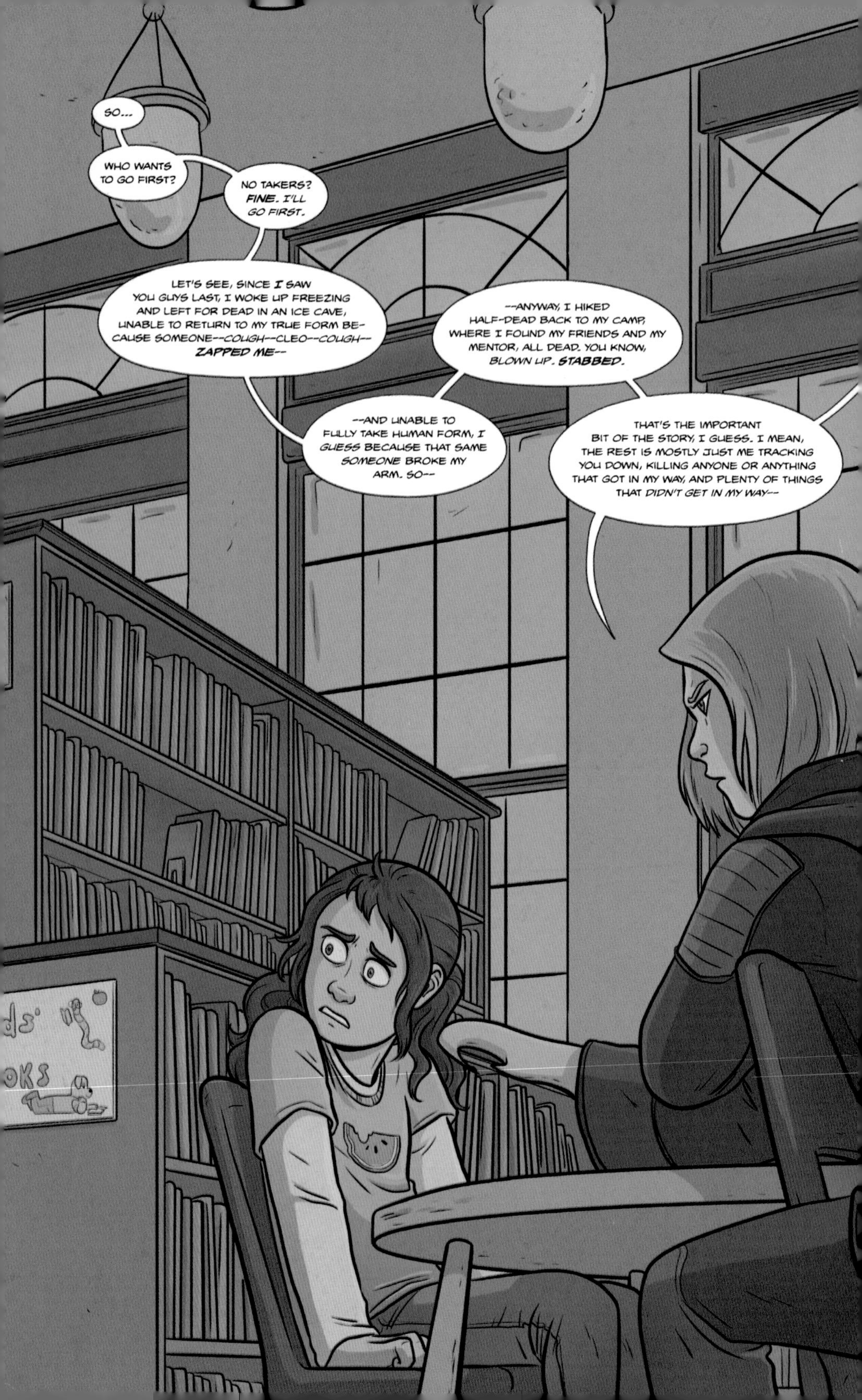
SO...
WHO WANTS TO GO FIRST?
NO TAKERS? FINE. I'LL GO FIRST.
LET'S SEE, SINCE I SAW YOU GUYS LAST, I WOKE UP FREEZING AND LEFT FOR DEAD IN AN ICE CAVE, UNABLE TO RETURN TO MY TRUE FORM BE-CAUSE SOMEONE--COUGH--CLEO--COUGH--ZAPPED ME--
--AND UNABLE TO FULLY TAKE HUMAN FORM, I GUESS BECAUSE THAT SAME SOMEONE BROKE MY ARM. SO--
--ANYWAY, I HIKED HALF-DEAD BACK TO MY CAMP, WHERE I FOUND MY FRIENDS AND MY MENTOR, ALL DEAD. YOU KNOW, BLOWN UP. STABBED.
THAT'S THE IMPORTANT BIT OF THE STORY, I GUESS. I MEAN, THE REST IS MOSTLY JUST ME TRACKING YOU DOWN, KILLING ANYONE OR ANYTHING THAT GOT IN MY WAY, AND PLENTY OF THINGS THAT DIDN'T GET IN MY WAY--

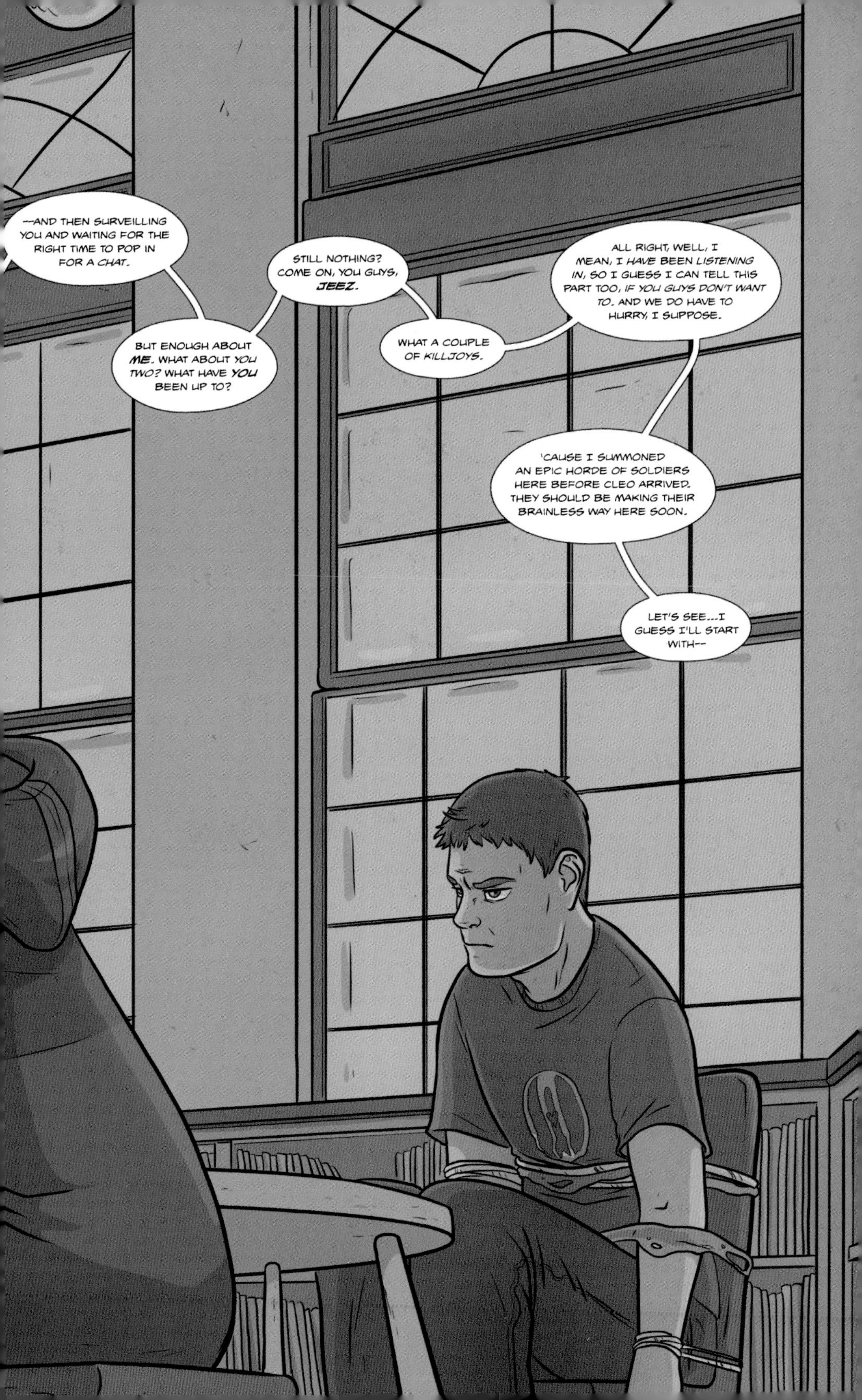
--AND THEN SURVEILLING YOU AND WAITING FOR THE RIGHT TIME TO POP IN FOR A *CHAT*.
BUT ENOUGH ABOUT ***ME***. WHAT ABOUT *YOU TWO*? WHAT HAVE ***YOU*** BEEN UP TO?
STILL NOTHING? COME ON, YOU GUYS, ***JEEZ***.
WHAT A COUPLE OF *KILLJOYS*.
ALL RIGHT, WELL, I MEAN, I *HAVE* BEEN *LISTENING IN*, SO I GUESS I CAN TELL THIS PART TOO, *IF YOU GUYS DON'T WANT TO*. AND WE DO HAVE TO HURRY, I SUPPOSE.
'CAUSE I SUMMONED AN EPIC HORDE OF SOLDIERS HERE BEFORE CLEO ARRIVED. THEY SHOULD BE MAKING THEIR BRAINLESS WAY HERE SOON.
LET'S SEE...I GUESS I'LL START WITH--

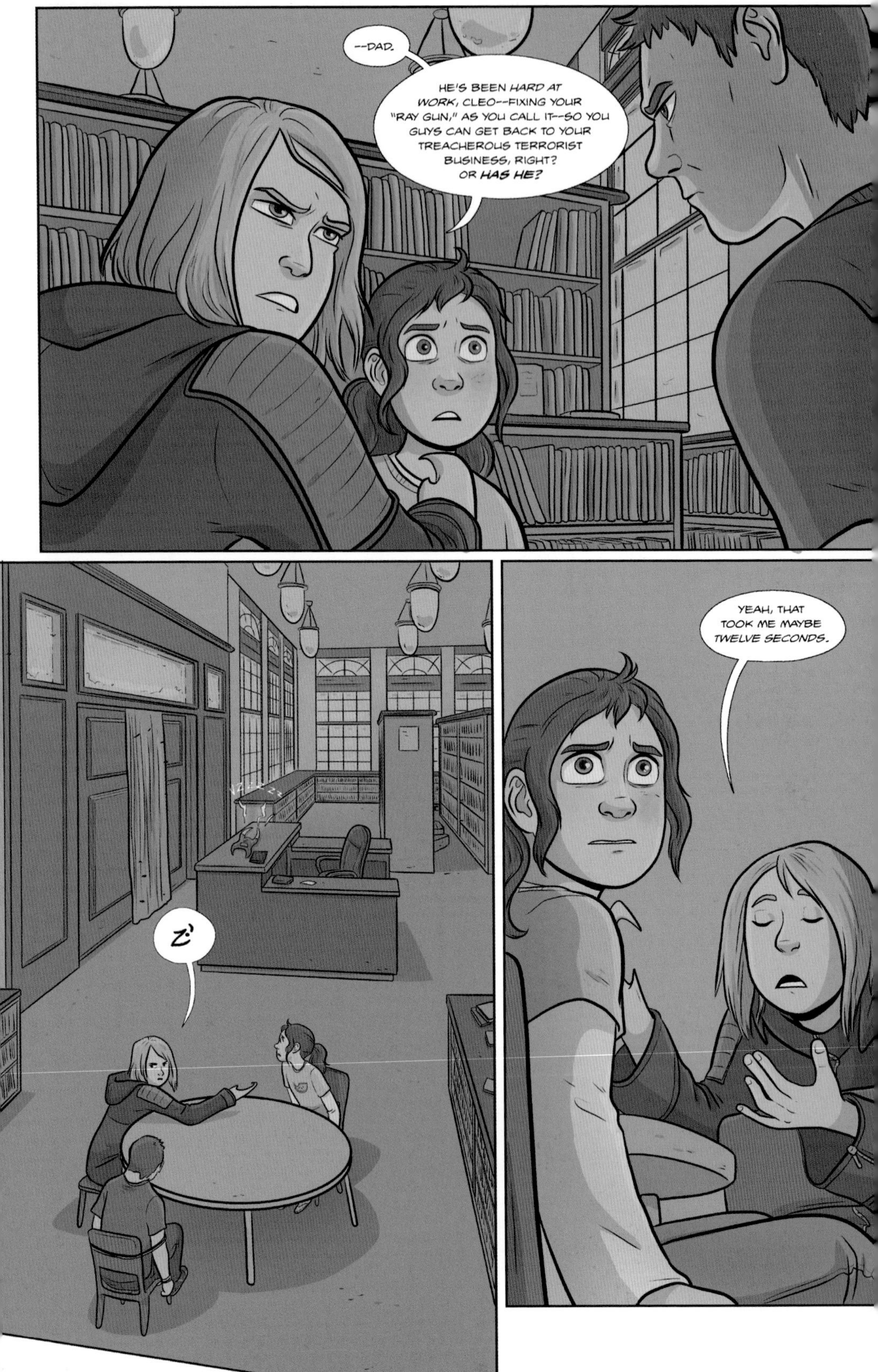
--DAD.
HE'S BEEN *HARD AT WORK*, CLEO--FIXING YOUR "RAY GUN," AS YOU CALL IT--SO YOU GUYS CAN GET BACK TO YOUR TREACHEROUS TERRORIST BUSINESS, RIGHT? OR ***HAS HE?***
YEAH, THAT TOOK ME MAYBE *TWELVE SECONDS*.

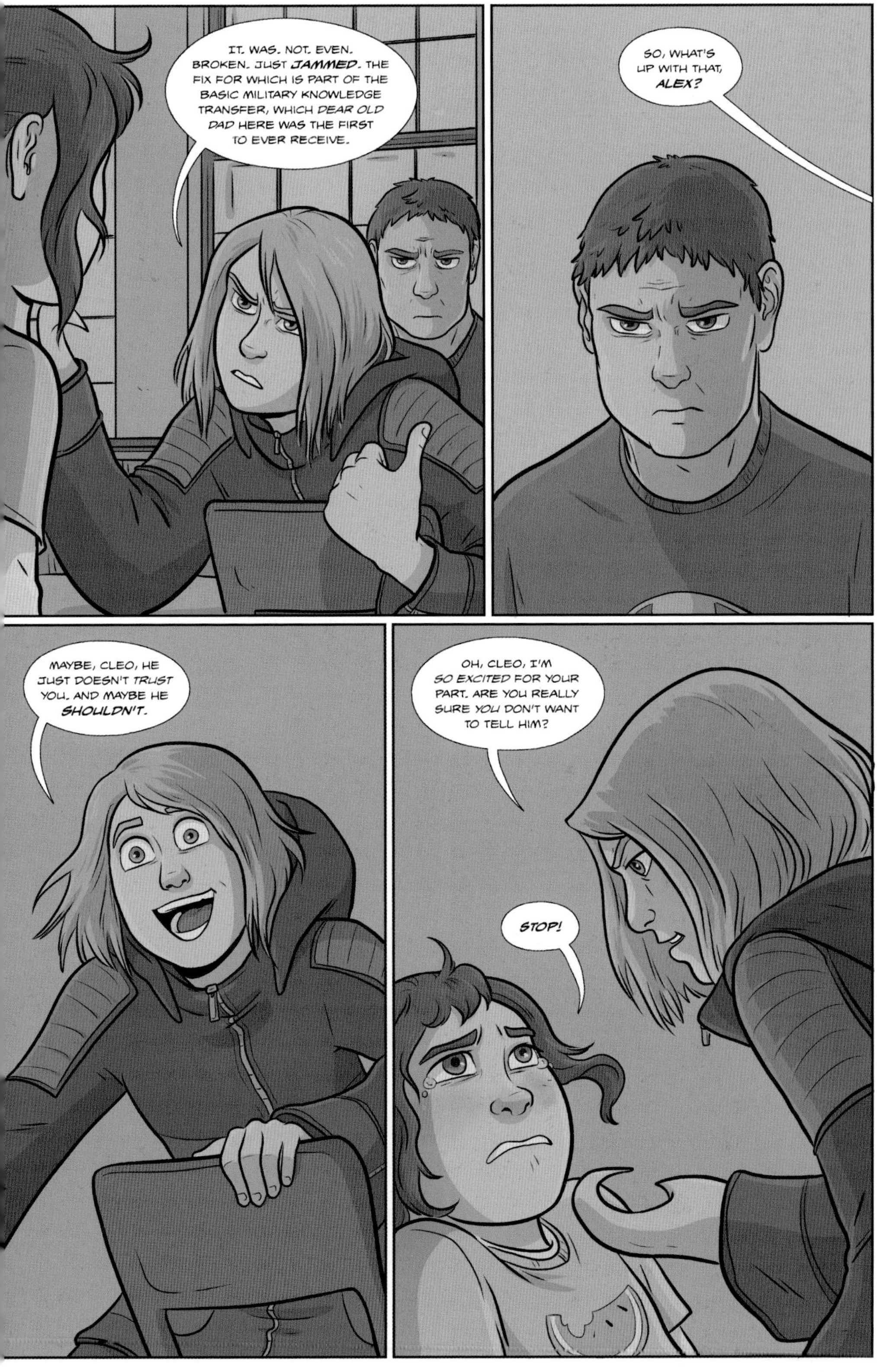
IT. WAS. NOT. EVEN. BROKEN. JUST JAMMED. THE FIX FOR WHICH IS PART OF THE BASIC MILITARY KNOWLEDGE TRANSFER, WHICH DEAR OLD DAD HERE WAS THE FIRST TO EVER RECEIVE.
SO, WHAT'S UP WITH THAT, ALEX?
MAYBE, CLEO, HE JUST DOESN'T TRUST YOU. AND MAYBE HE SHOULDN'T.
OH, CLEO, I'M SO EXCITED FOR YOUR PART. ARE YOU REALLY SURE YOU DON'T WANT TO TELL HIM?
STOP!

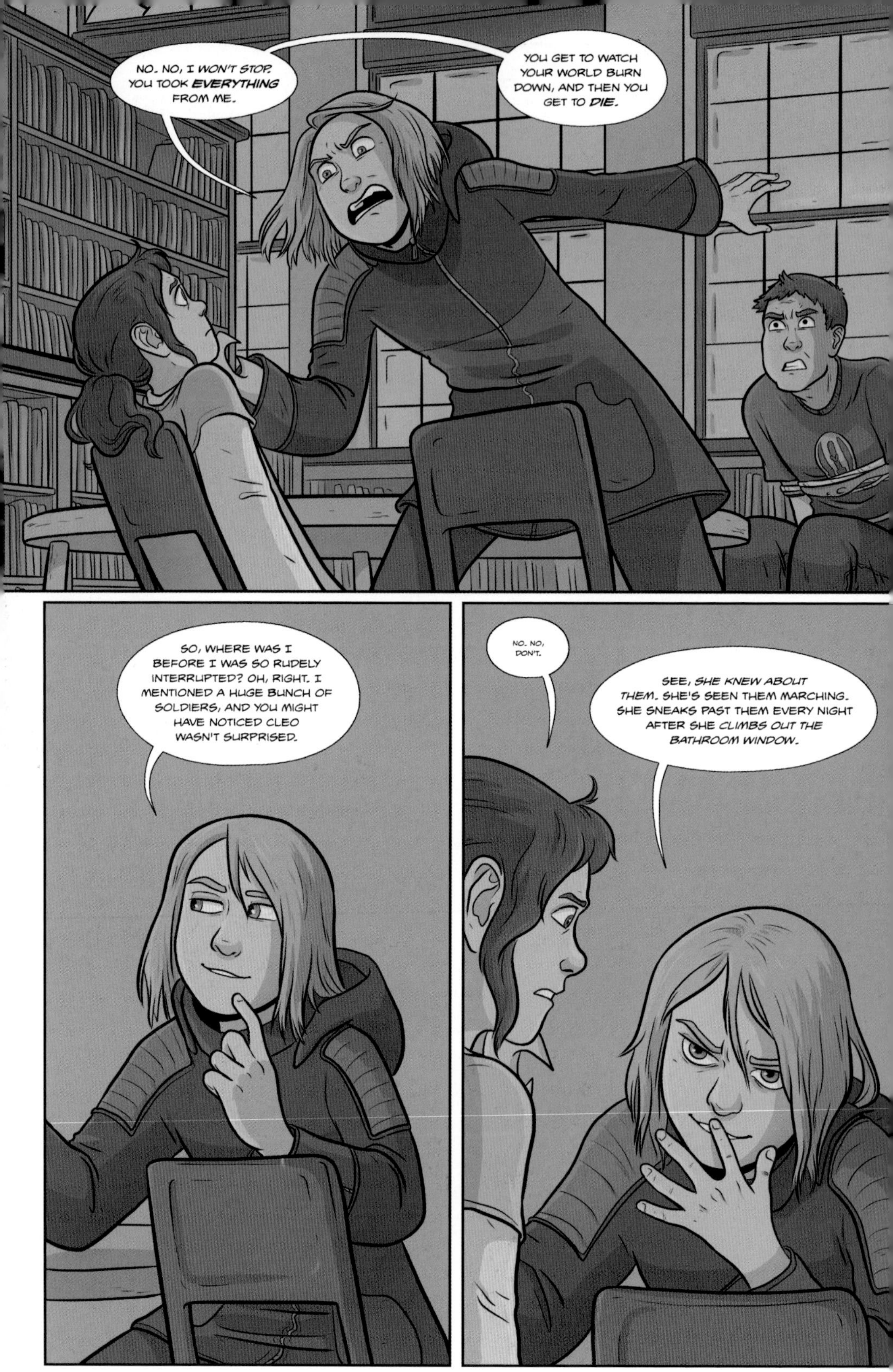
NO. NO, I *WON'T STOP.* YOU TOOK **EVERYTHING** FROM ME.
YOU GET TO WATCH YOUR WORLD BURN DOWN, AND THEN YOU GET TO ***DIE.***
SO, WHERE WAS I BEFORE I WAS SO RUDELY INTERRUPTED? OH, RIGHT. I MENTIONED A HUGE BUNCH OF SOLDIERS, AND YOU MIGHT HAVE NOTICED CLEO WASN'T SURPRISED.
NO. NO, DON'T.
SEE, *SHE KNEW ABOUT THEM.* SHE'S SEEN THEM MARCHING. SHE SNEAKS PAST THEM EVERY NIGHT AFTER SHE *CLIMBS OUT THE BATHROOM WINDOW.*

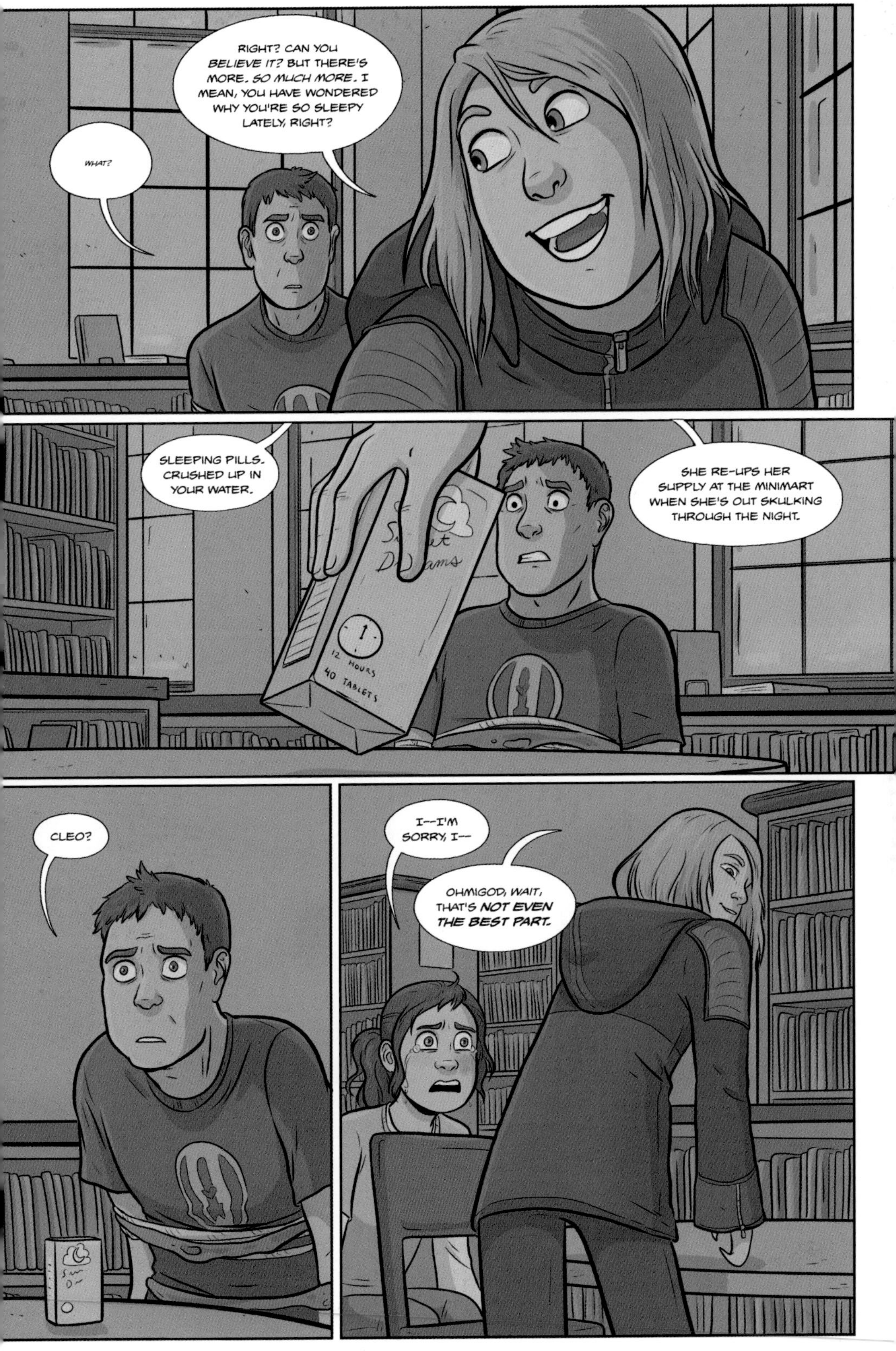
WHAT?
RIGHT? CAN YOU BELIEVE IT? BUT THERE'S MORE. SO MUCH MORE. I MEAN, YOU HAVE WONDERED WHY YOU'RE SO SLEEPY LATELY, RIGHT?
SLEEPING PILLS. CRUSHED UP IN YOUR WATER.
12 HOURS
40 TABLETS
SHE RE-UPS HER SUPPLY AT THE MINIMART WHEN SHE'S OUT SKULKING THROUGH THE NIGHT.
CLEO?
I--I'M SORRY, I--
OHMIGOD, WAIT, THAT'S NOT EVEN THE BEST PART.

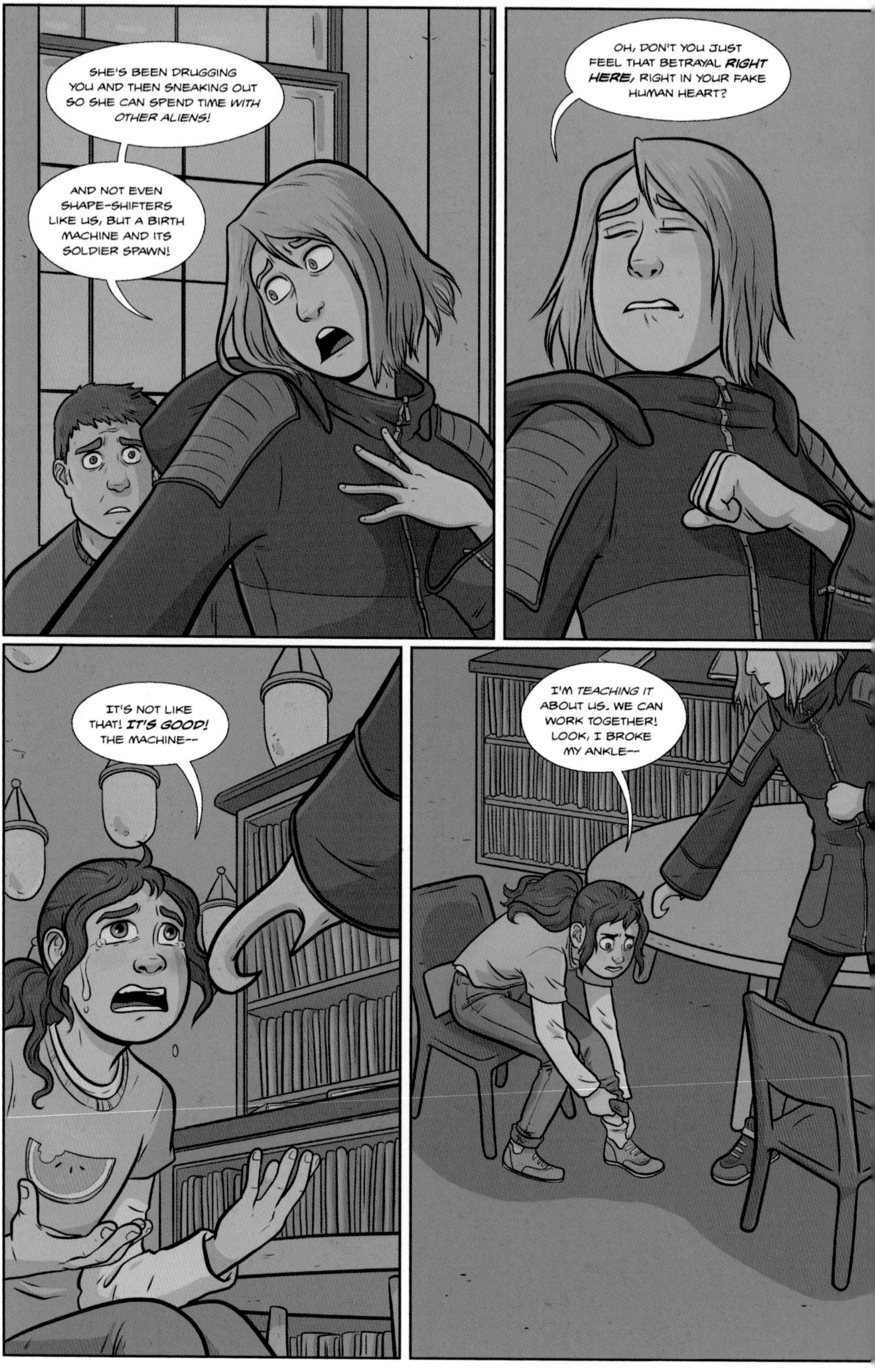
SHE'S BEEN DRUGGING YOU AND THEN SNEAKING OUT SO SHE CAN SPEND TIME *WITH OTHER ALIENS!*
AND NOT EVEN SHAPE-SHIFTERS LIKE US, BUT A BIRTH MACHINE AND ITS SOLDIER SPAWN!
OH, DON'T YOU JUST FEEL THAT BETRAYAL ***RIGHT HERE,*** RIGHT IN YOUR FAKE HUMAN HEART?
IT'S NOT LIKE THAT! ***IT'S GOOD!*** THE MACHINE--
I'M *TEACHING* IT ABOUT US. WE CAN WORK TOGETHER! LOOK, I BROKE MY ANKLE--

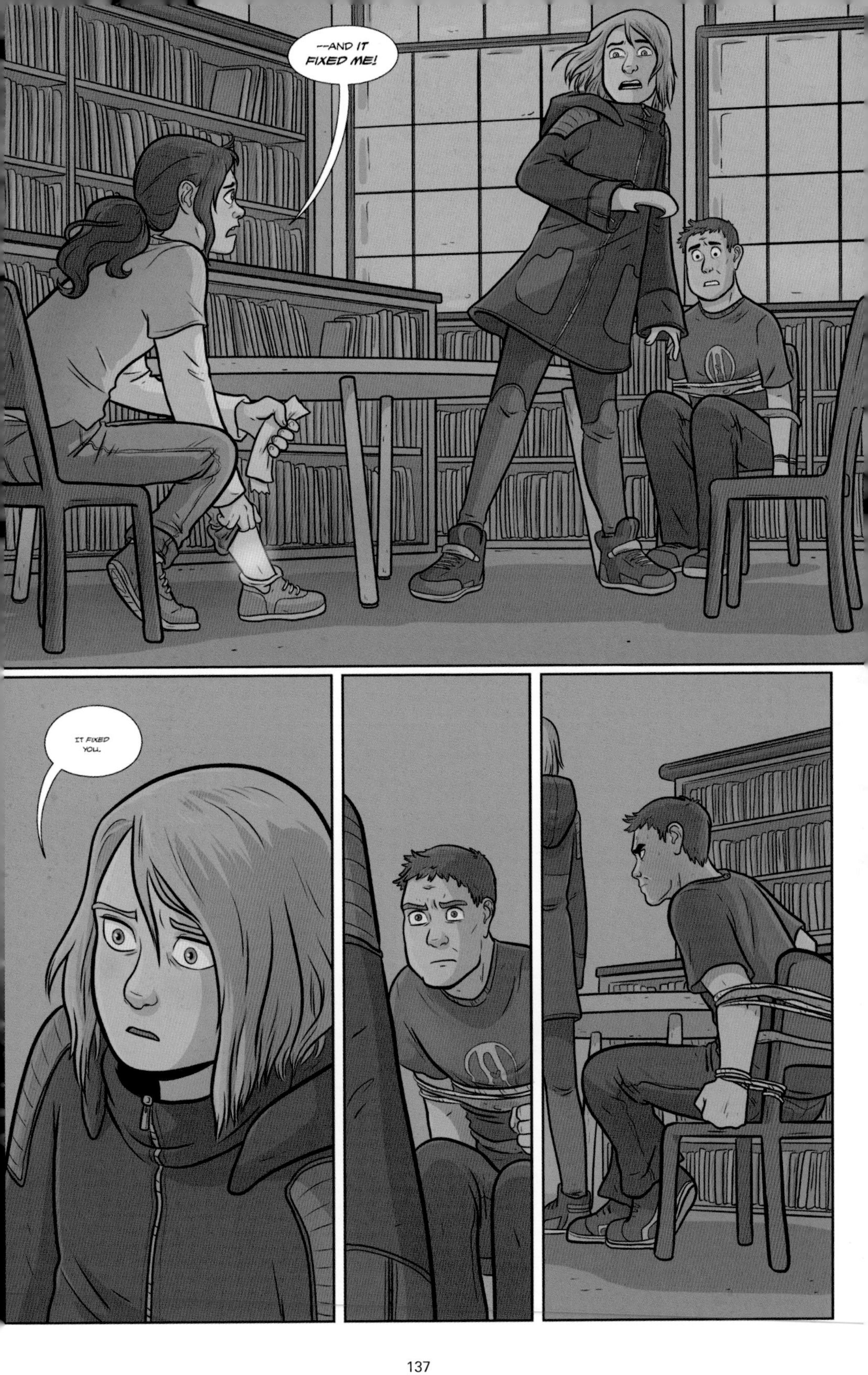
--AND IT FIXED ME!
IT FIXED YOU.

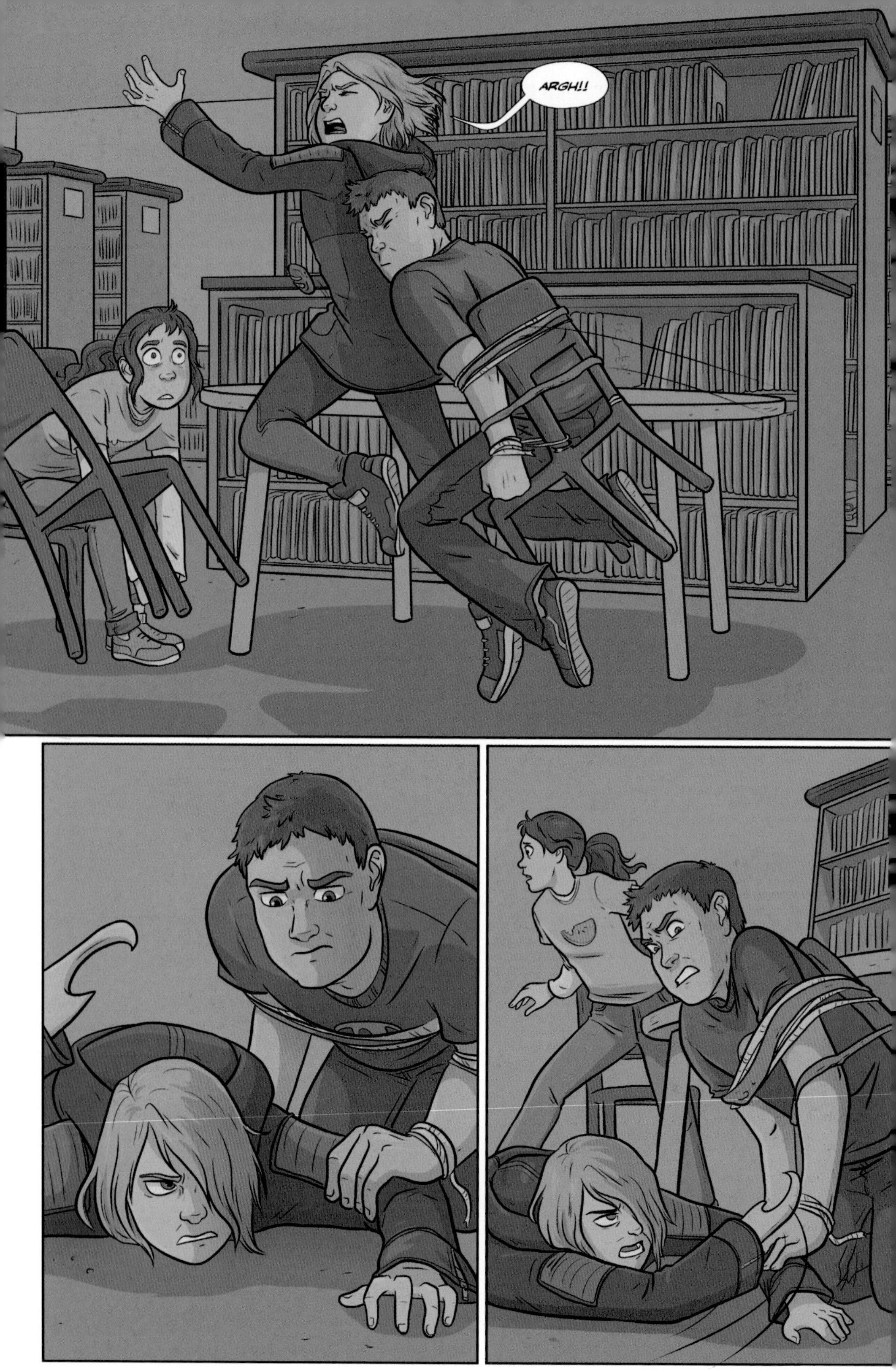
ARGH!!

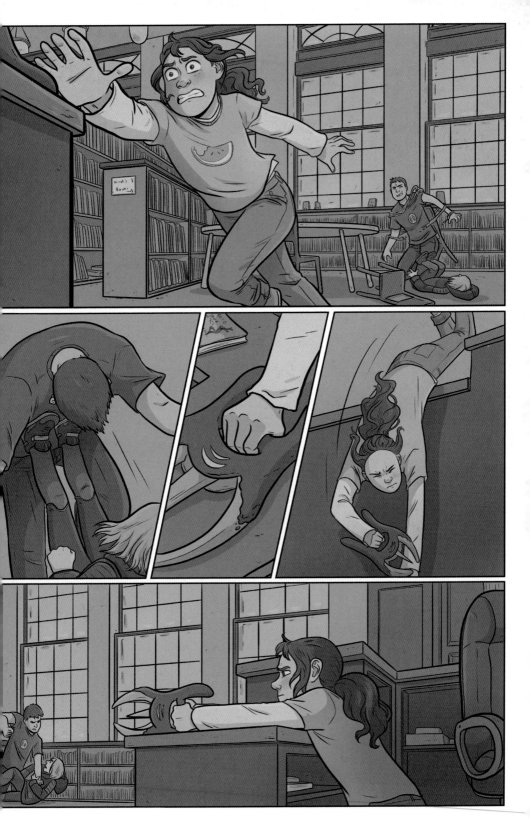

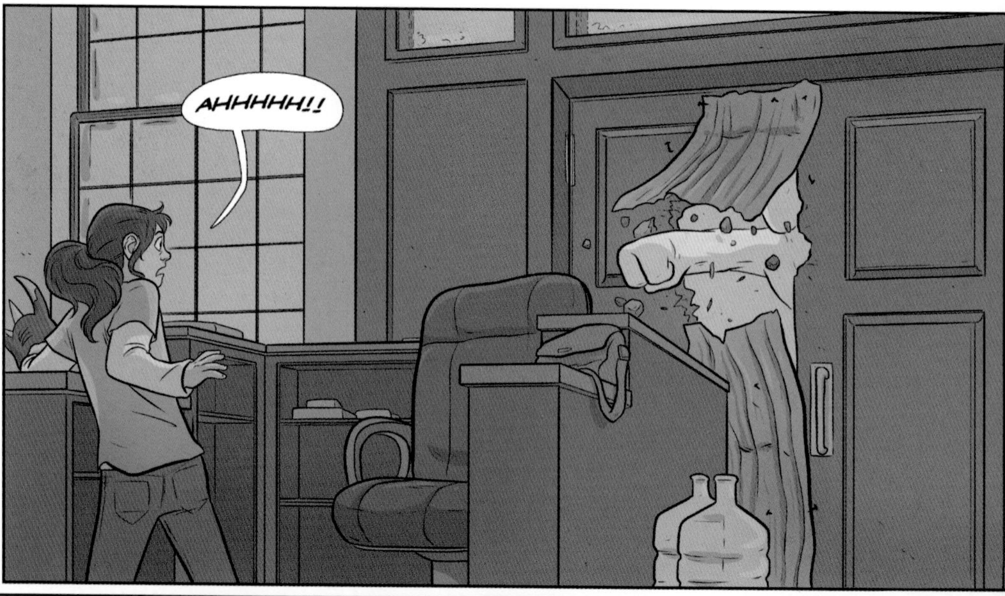
AHHHHH!!

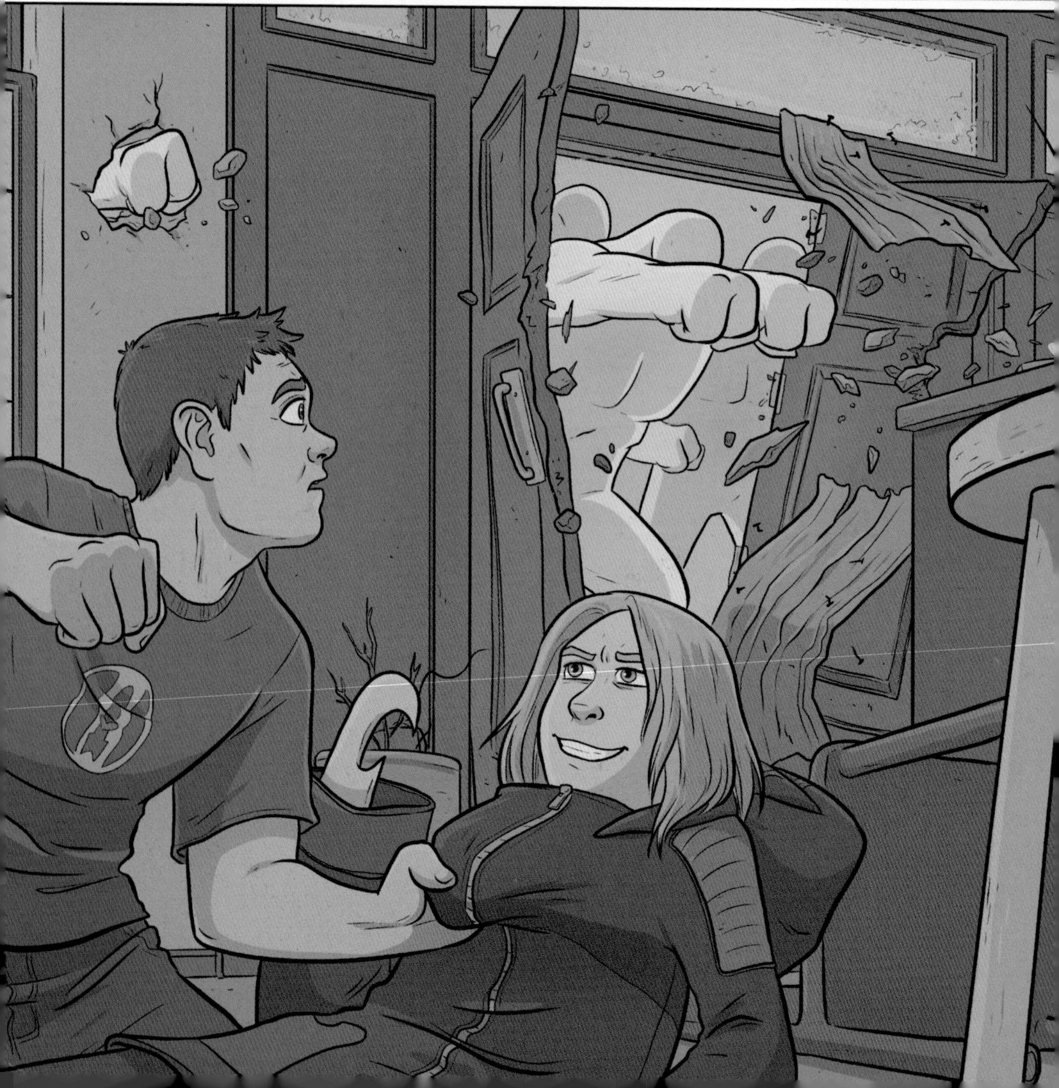

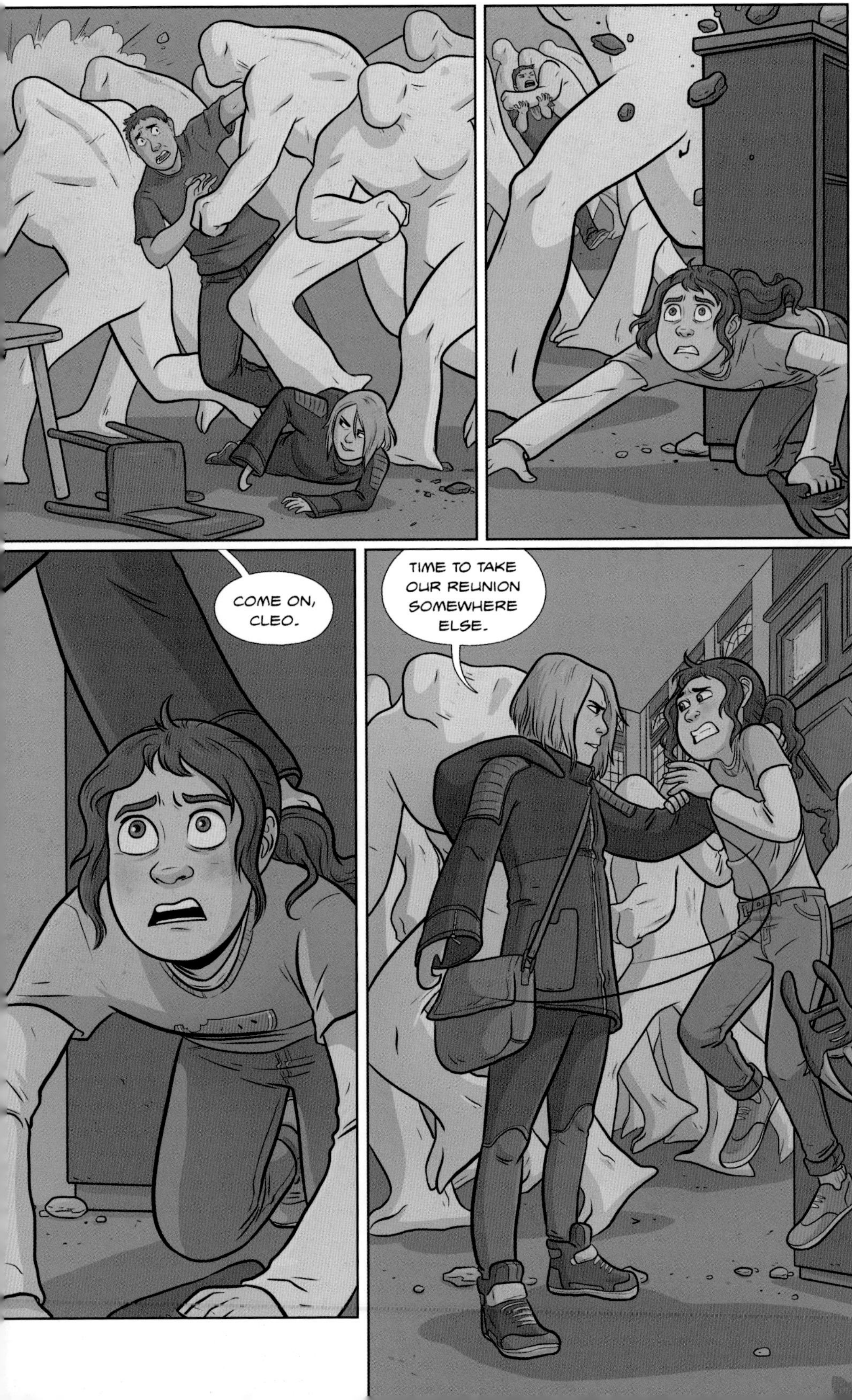
COME ON, CLEO.
TIME TO TAKE OUR REUNION SOMEWHERE ELSE.

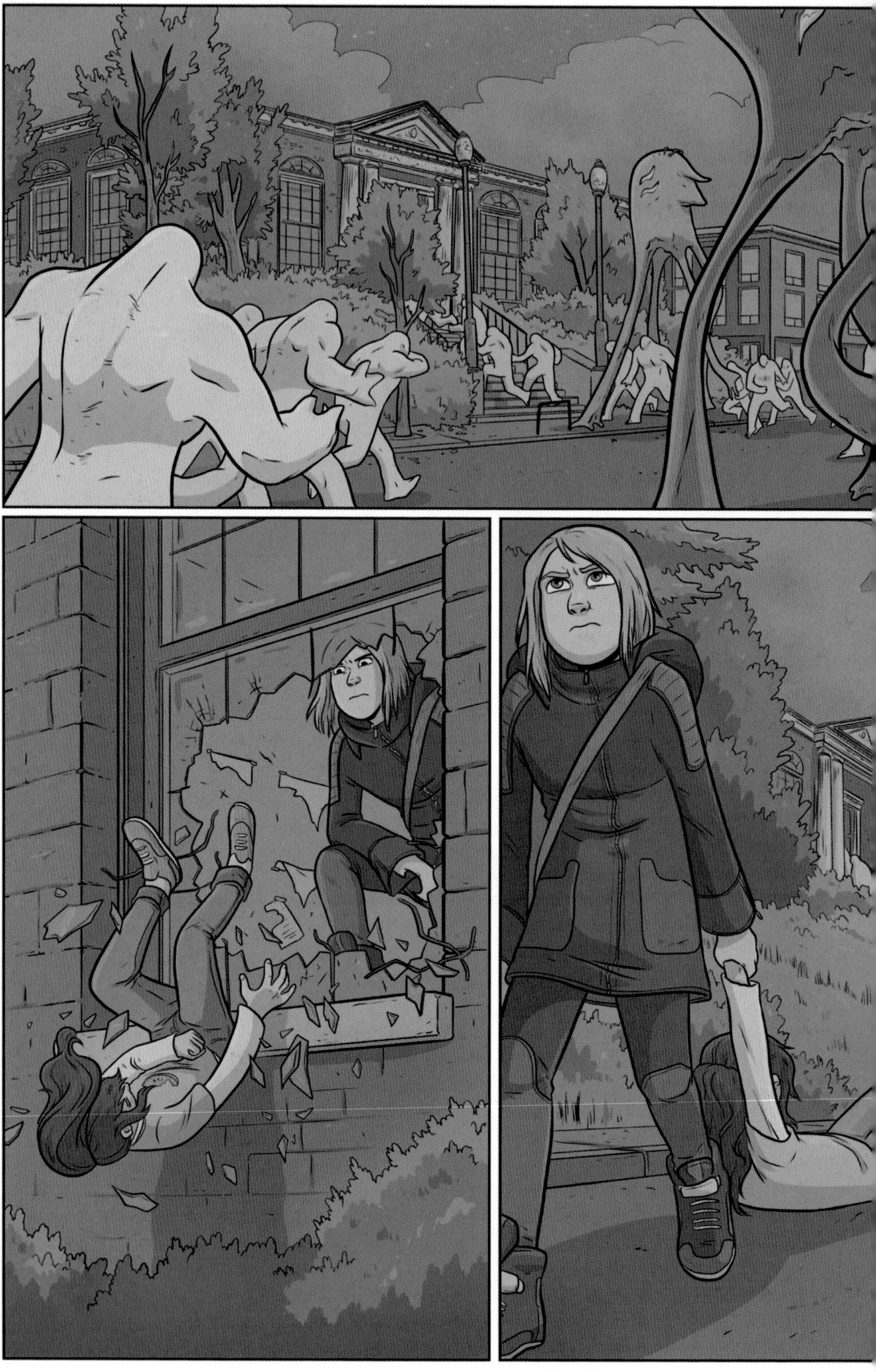

FIVE

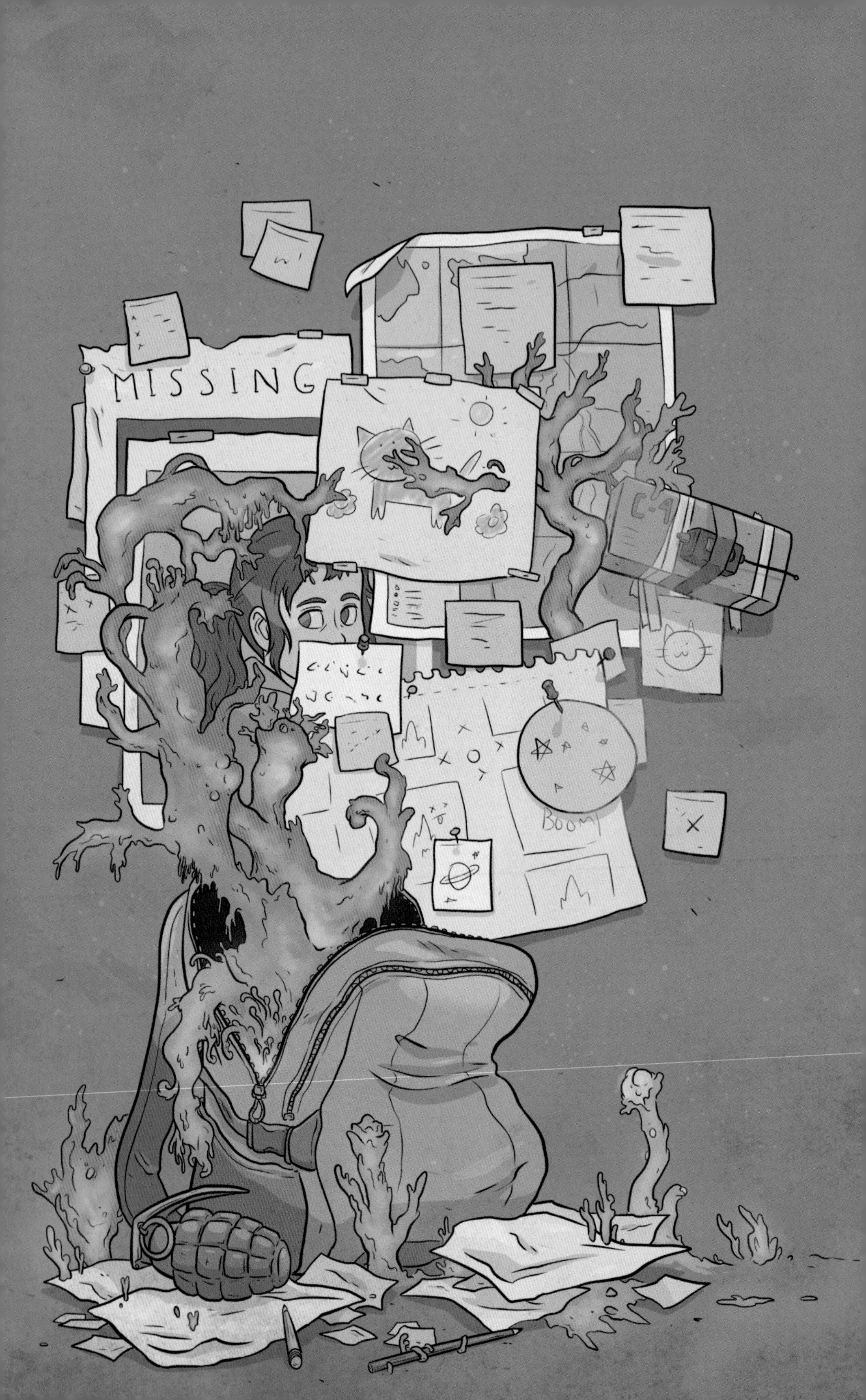
MISSING
C-4
BOOM

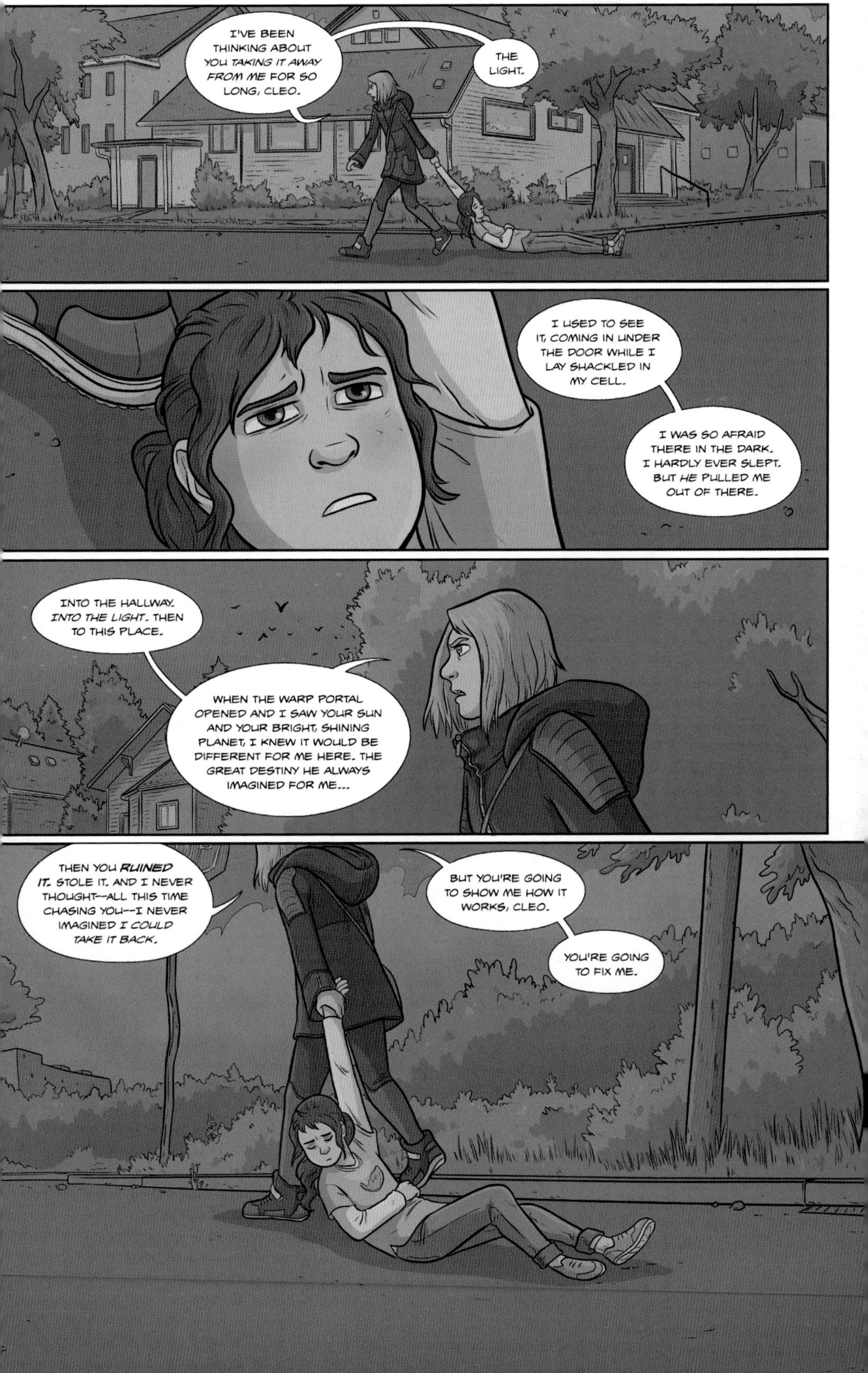
I'VE BEEN THINKING ABOUT YOU TAKING IT AWAY FROM ME FOR SO LONG, CLEO.
THE LIGHT.
I USED TO SEE IT, COMING IN UNDER THE DOOR WHILE I LAY SHACKLED IN MY CELL.
I WAS SO AFRAID THERE IN THE DARK. I HARDLY EVER SLEPT. BUT HE PULLED ME OUT OF THERE.
INTO THE HALLWAY. INTO THE LIGHT. THEN TO THIS PLACE.
WHEN THE WARP PORTAL OPENED AND I SAW YOUR SUN AND YOUR BRIGHT, SHINING PLANET, I KNEW IT WOULD BE DIFFERENT FOR ME HERE. THE GREAT DESTINY HE ALWAYS IMAGINED FOR ME...
THEN YOU RUINED IT. STOLE IT. AND I NEVER THOUGHT--ALL THIS TIME CHASING YOU--I NEVER IMAGINED I COULD TAKE IT BACK.
BUT YOU'RE GOING TO SHOW ME HOW IT WORKS, CLEO.
YOU'RE GOING TO FIX ME.

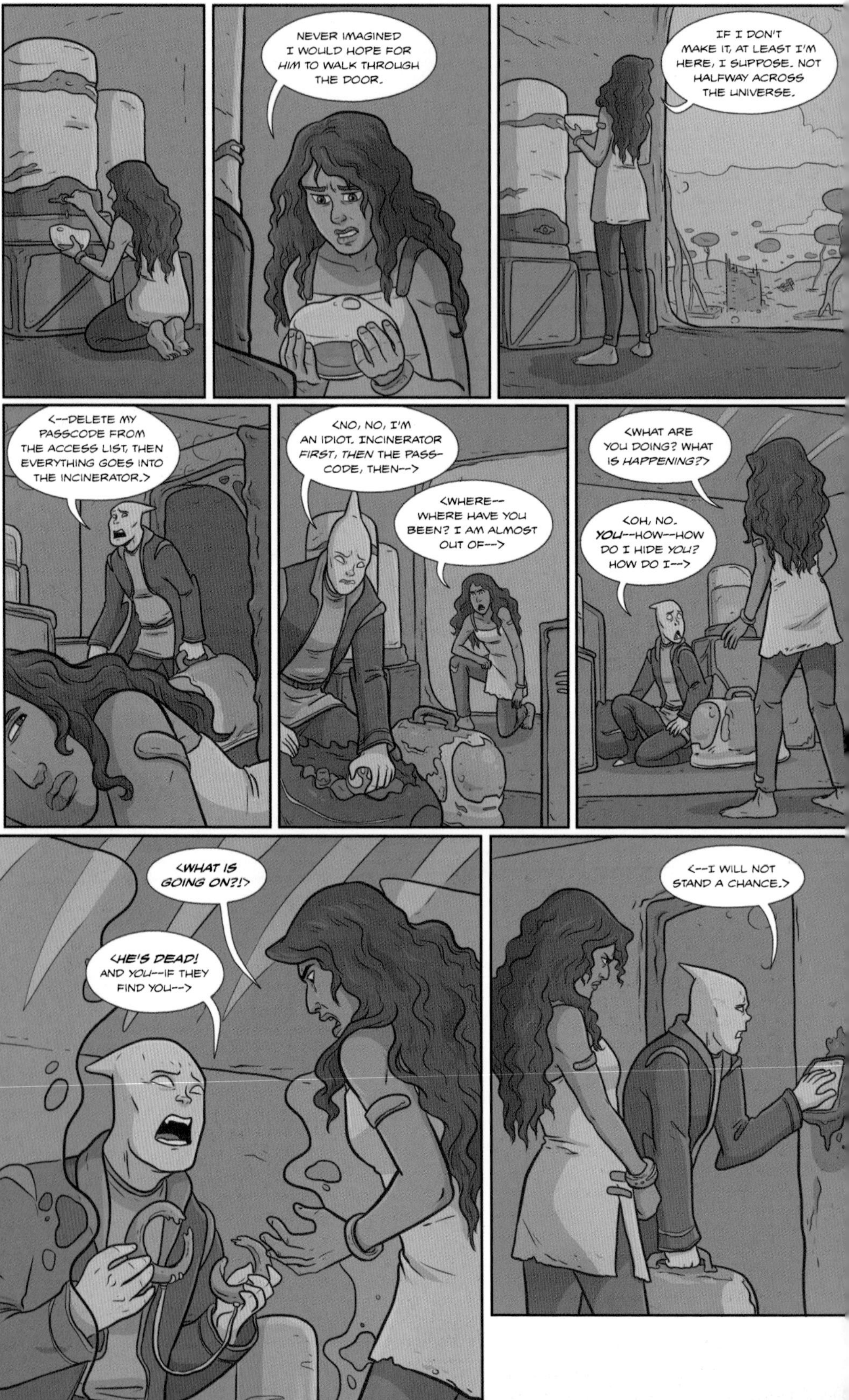
NEVER IMAGINED I WOULD HOPE FOR *HIM* TO WALK THROUGH THE DOOR.
IF I DON'T MAKE IT, AT LEAST I'M HERE, I SUPPOSE. NOT HALFWAY ACROSS THE UNIVERSE.
<--DELETE MY PASSCODE FROM THE ACCESS LIST, THEN EVERYTHING GOES INTO THE INCINERATOR.>
<NO, NO, I'M AN IDIOT. INCINERATOR *FIRST*, THEN THE PASS-CODE, THEN-->
<WHERE--WHERE HAVE YOU BEEN? I AM ALMOST OUT OF-->
<WHAT ARE YOU DOING? WHAT IS *HAPPENING?*>
<OH, NO. ***YOU***--HOW--HOW DO I HIDE *YOU*? HOW DO I-->
<***WHAT IS GOING ON?!***>
<***HE'S DEAD!*** AND *YOU*--IF THEY FIND YOU-->
<--I WILL NOT STAND A CHANCE.>

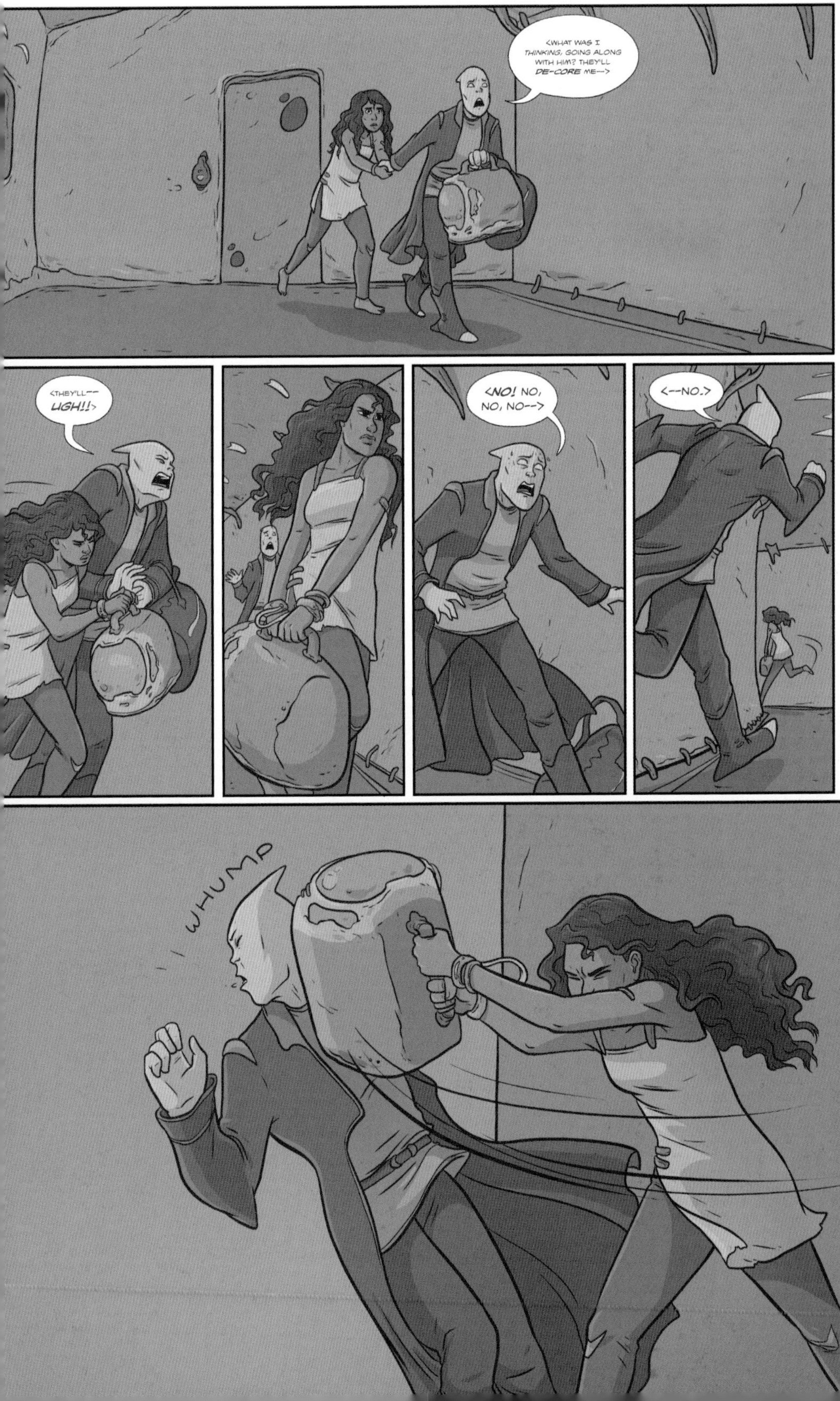
<WHAT WAS I THINKING, GOING ALONG WITH HIM? THEY'LL DE-CORE ME-->
<THEY'LL-- UGH!!>
<NO! NO, NO, NO-->
<--NO.>
WHUMP

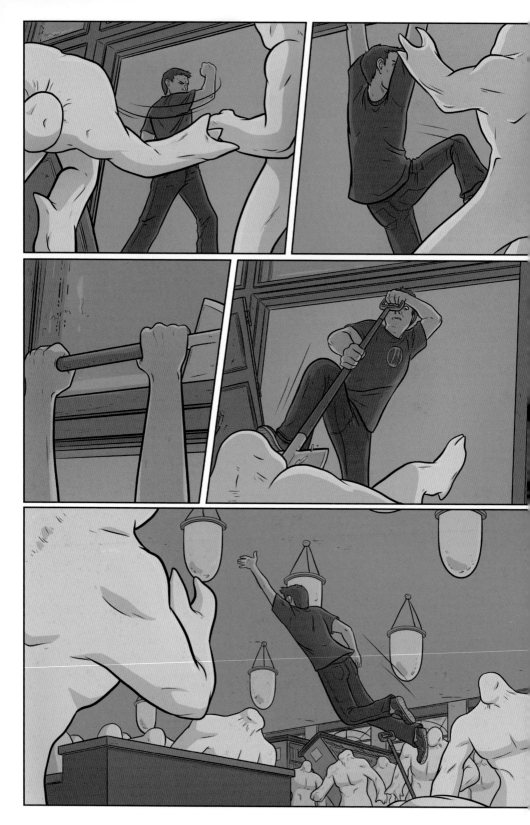

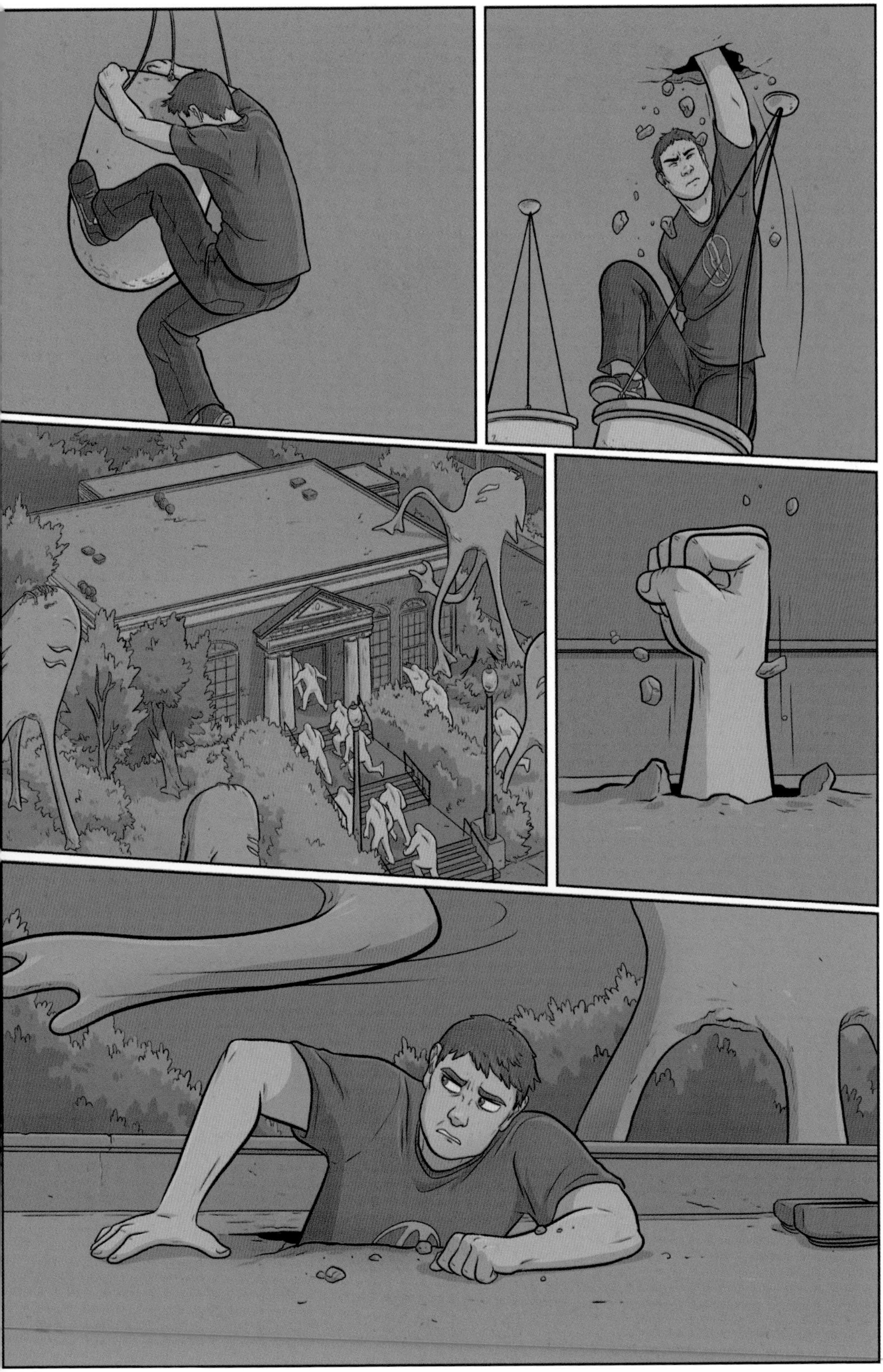

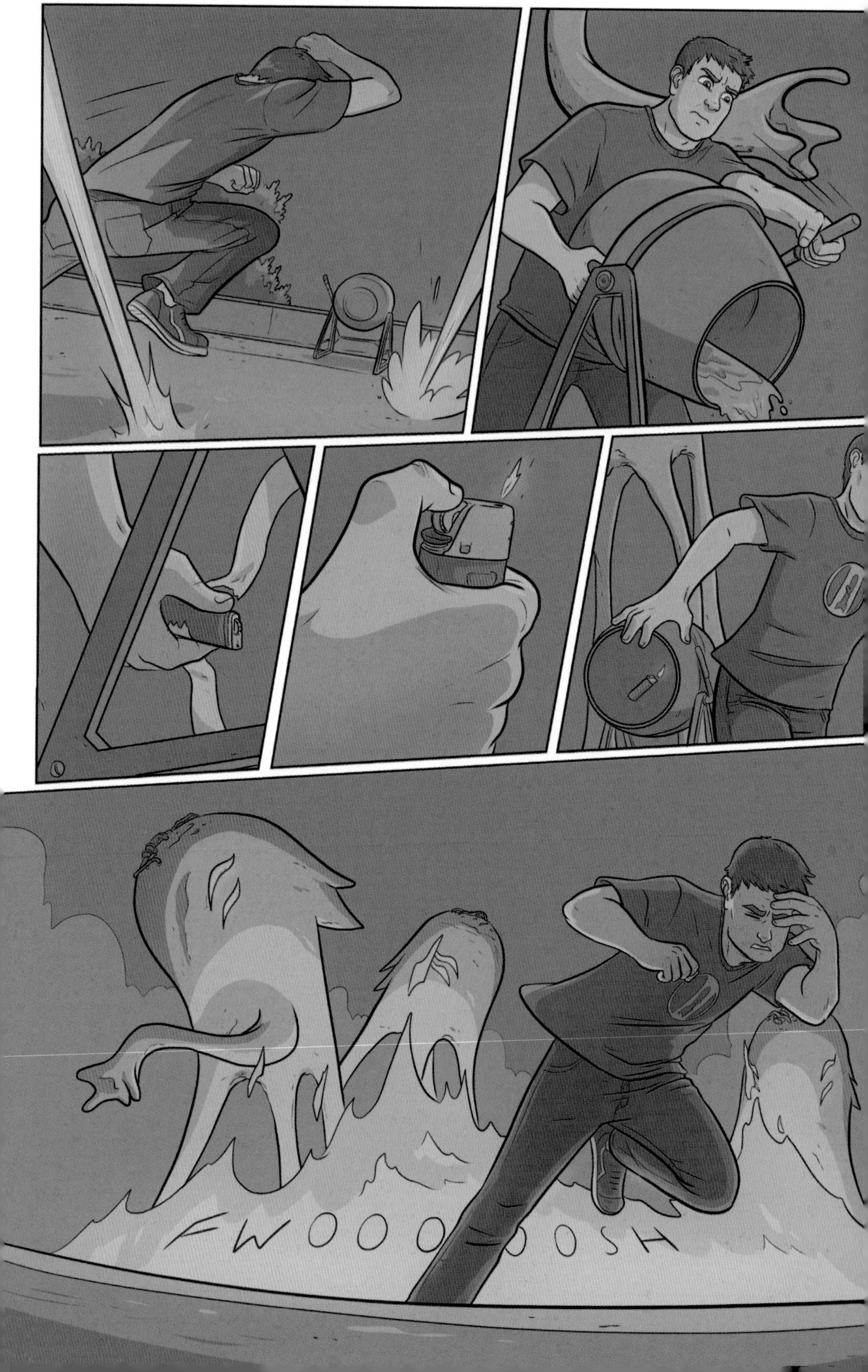
FWOOOOOSH

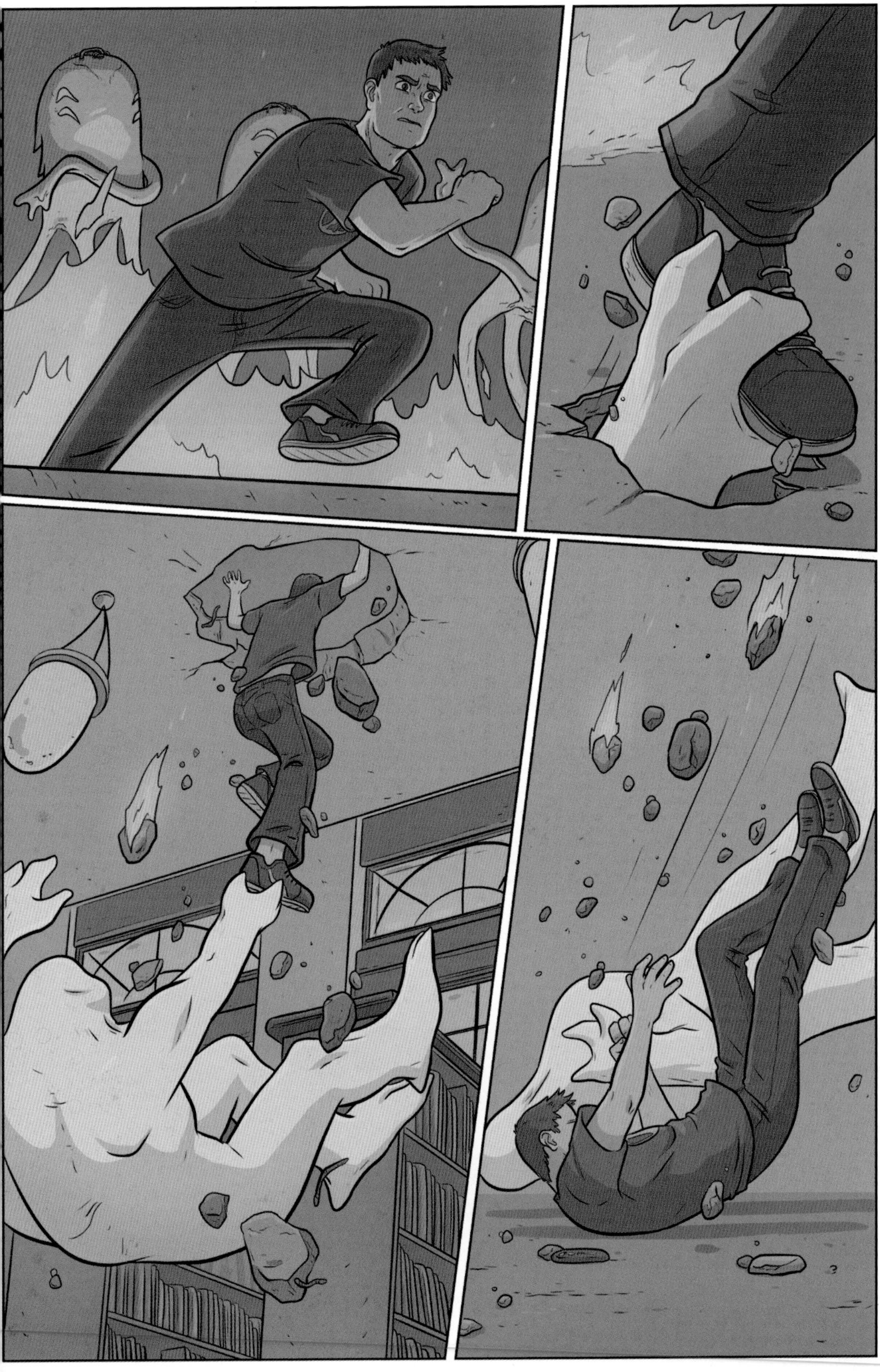

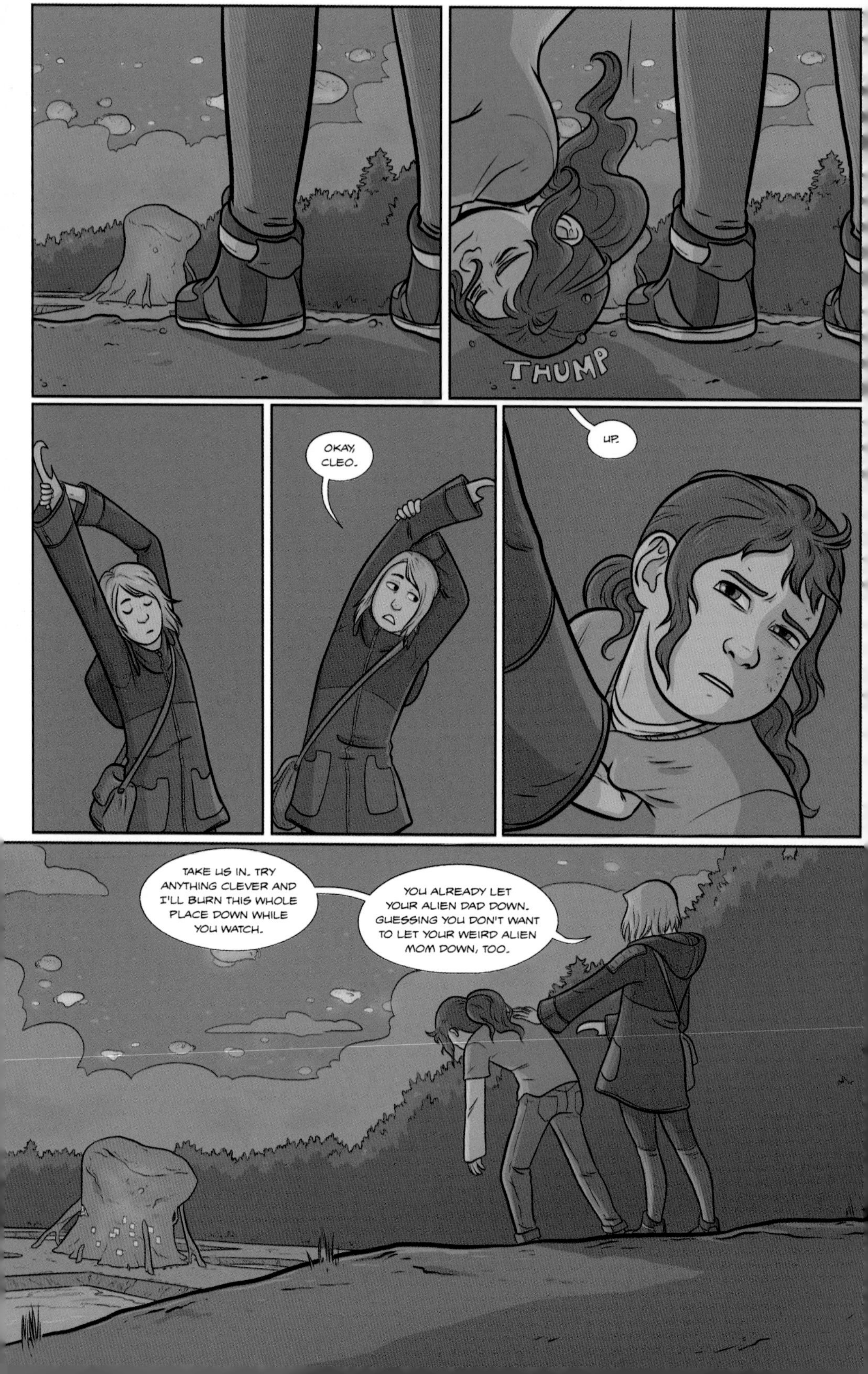
THUMP
OKAY, CLEO.
UP.
TAKE US IN. TRY ANYTHING CLEVER AND I'LL BURN THIS WHOLE PLACE DOWN WHILE YOU WATCH.
YOU ALREADY LET YOUR ALIEN DAD DOWN. GUESSING YOU DON'T WANT TO LET YOUR WEIRD ALIEN MOM DOWN, TOO.

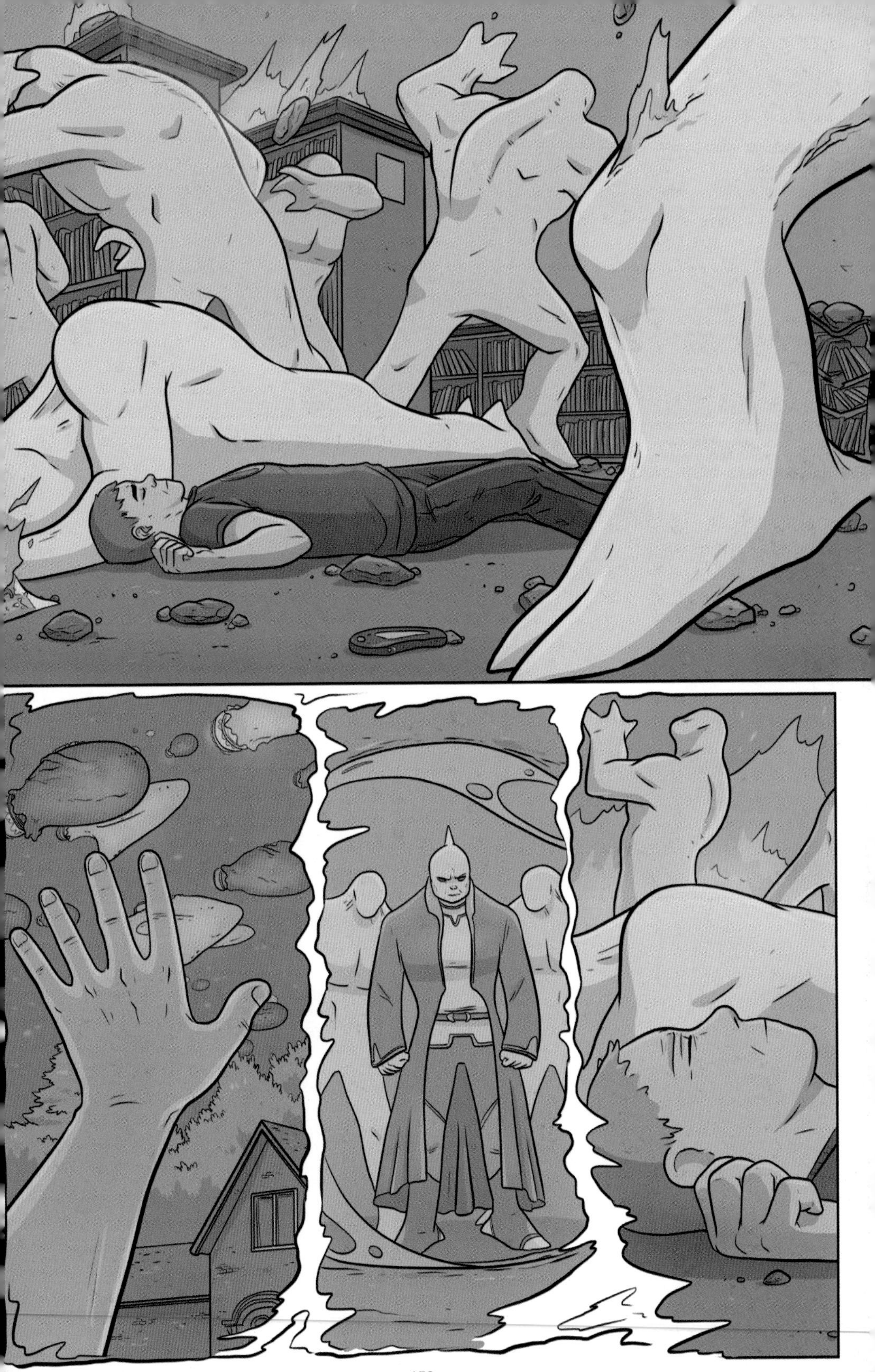

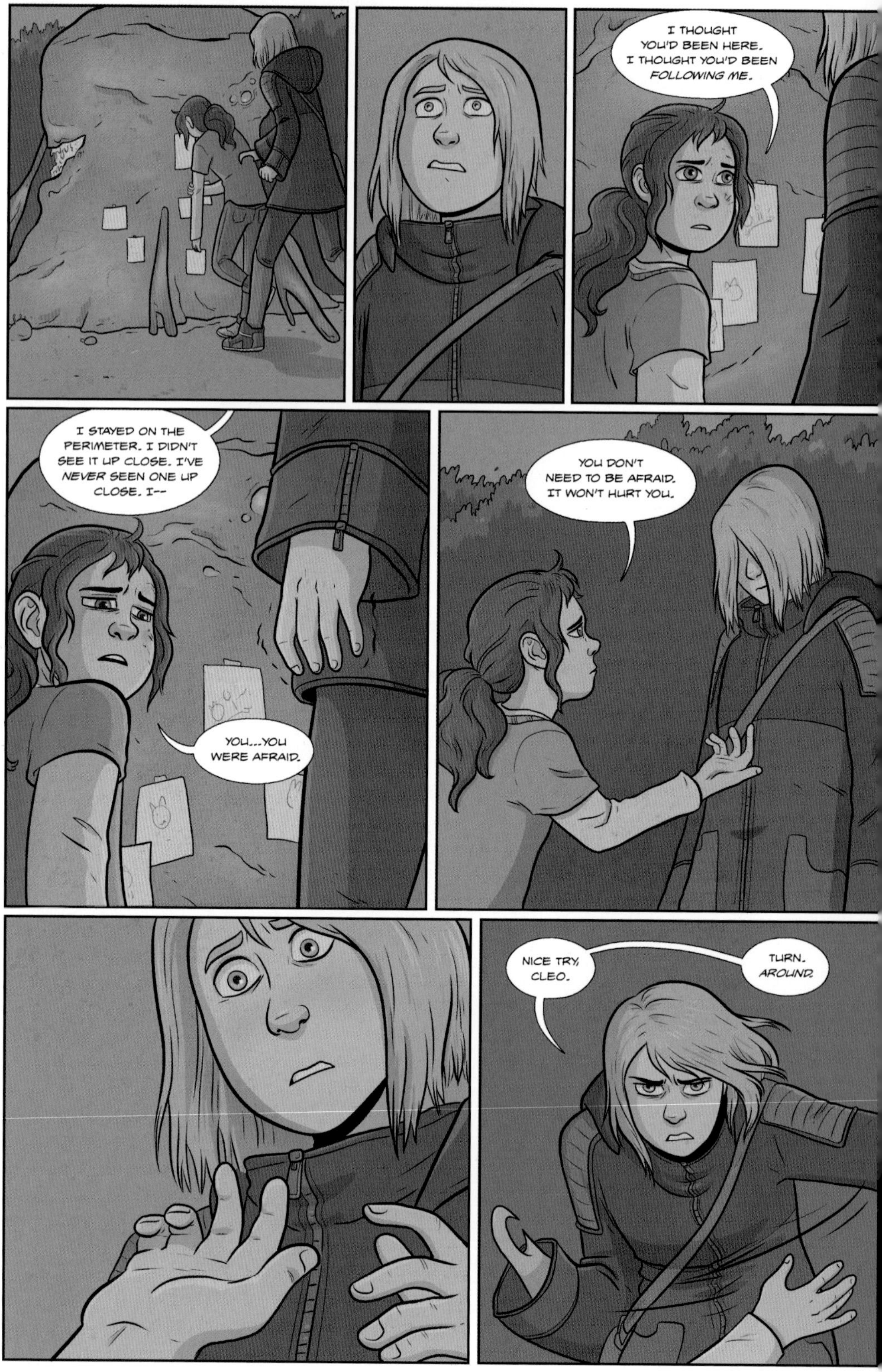
I THOUGHT YOU'D BEEN HERE. I THOUGHT YOU'D BEEN *FOLLOWING ME.*
I STAYED ON THE PERIMETER. I DIDN'T SEE IT UP CLOSE. I'VE *NEVER* SEEN ONE UP CLOSE. I--
YOU...YOU WERE AFRAID.
YOU DON'T NEED TO BE AFRAID. IT WON'T HURT YOU.
NICE TRY, CLEO.
TURN. *AROUND.*

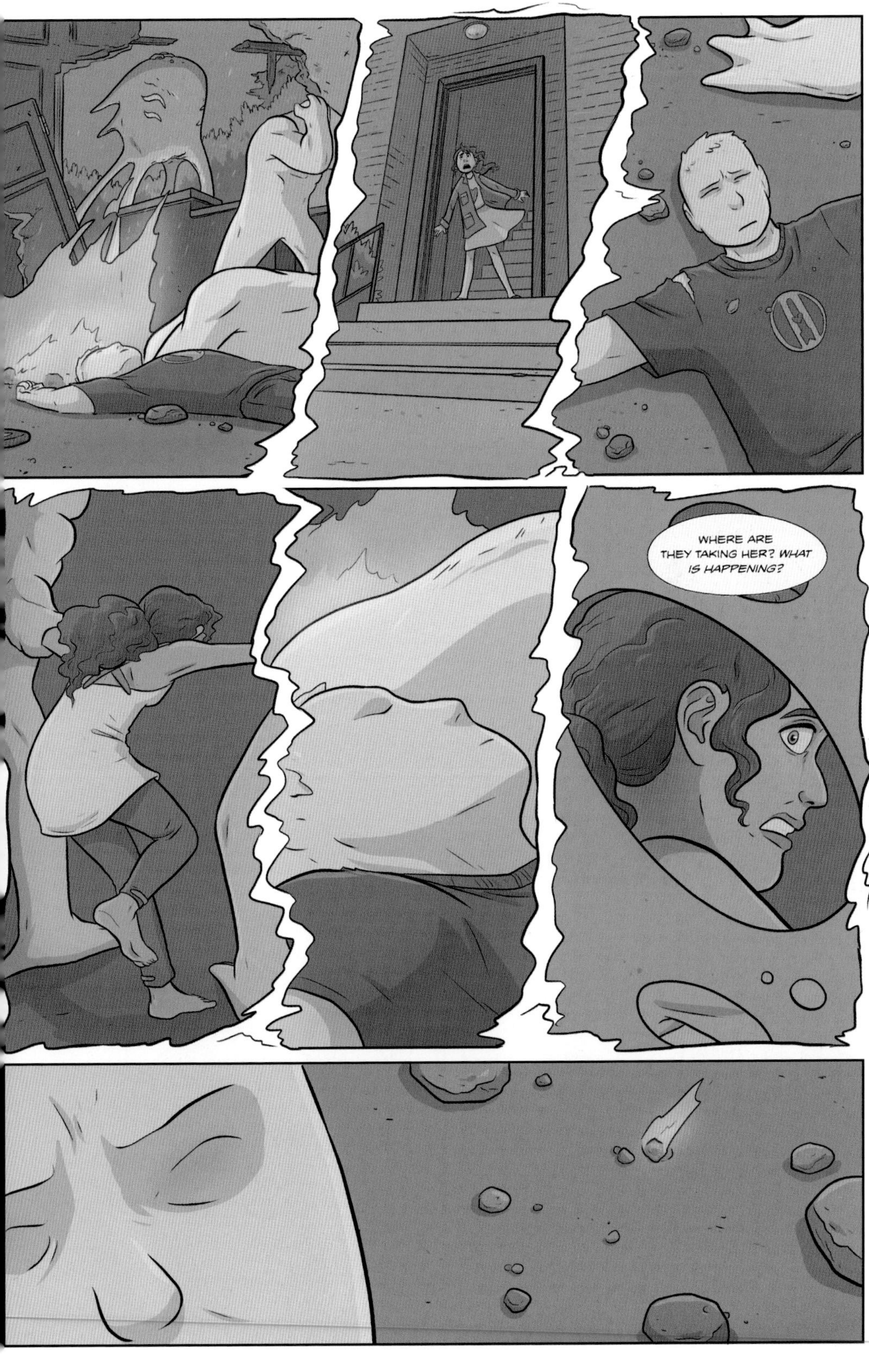
WHERE ARE THEY TAKING HER? *WHAT IS HAPPENING?*

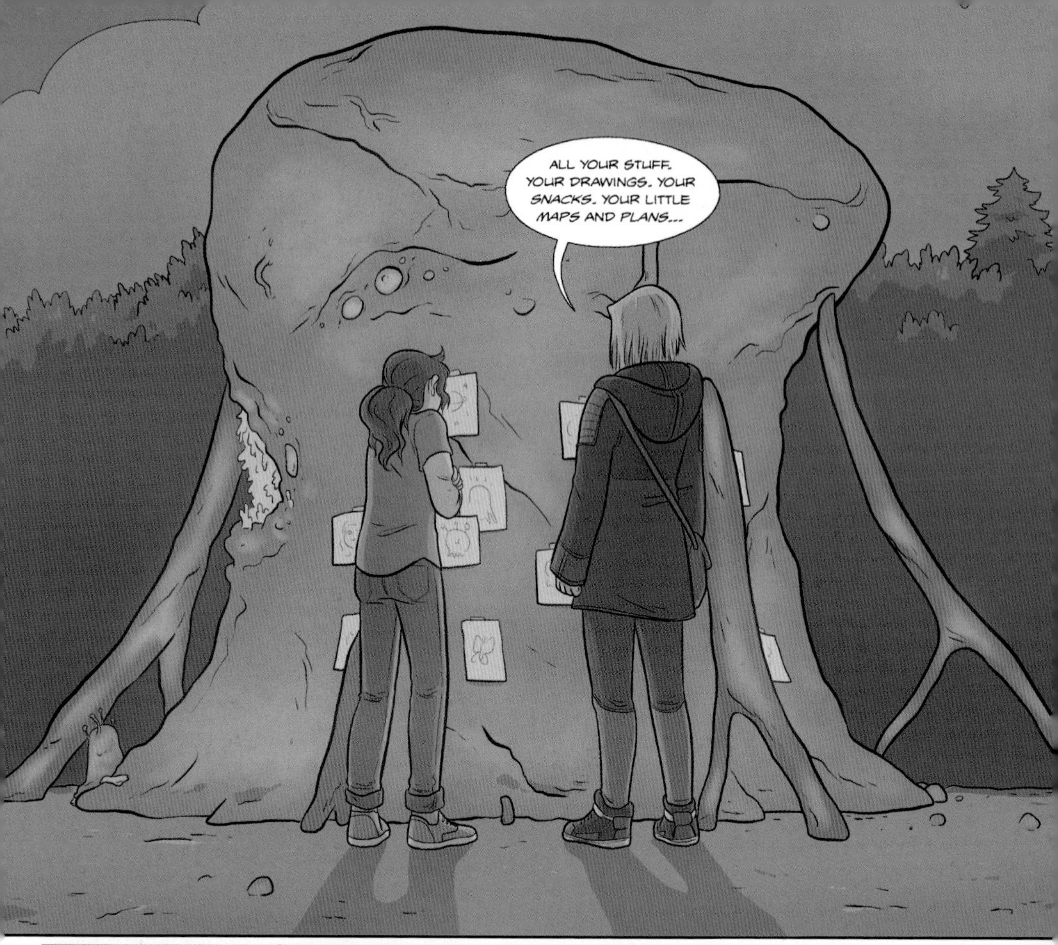
ALL YOUR STUFF. YOUR DRAWINGS. YOUR SNACKS. YOUR LITTLE MAPS AND PLANS...

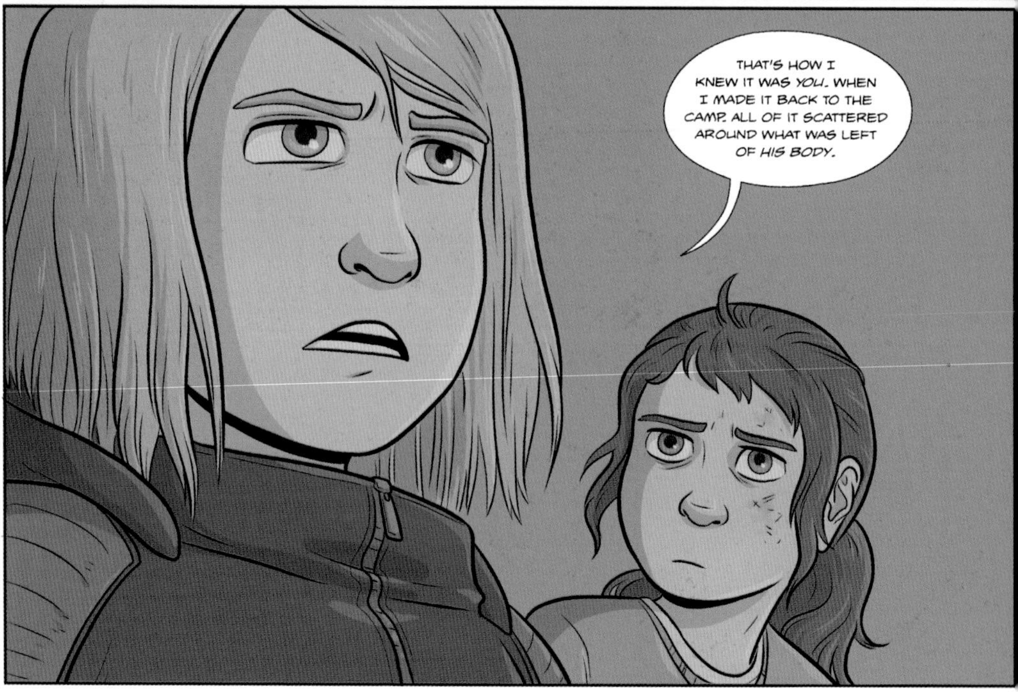
THAT'S HOW I KNEW IT WAS YOU. WHEN I MADE IT BACK TO THE CAMP. ALL OF IT SCATTERED AROUND WHAT WAS LEFT OF HIS BODY.

SUCH A SMALL CREATURE TAKING DOWN SUCH A *GIANT.*

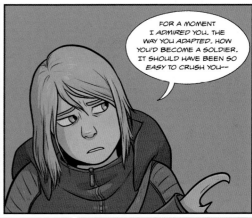

FOR A MOMENT I *ADMIRED* YOU. THE WAY YOU *ADAPTED.* HOW YOU'D BECOME A SOLDIER. IT SHOULD HAVE BEEN SO EASY TO CRUSH YOU--

BUT I...*I NEVER WANTED ANY OF THIS.* I MEAN, ME, A SOLDIER? THAT I'M EVEN *ALIVE*--I JUST GOT LUCKY.

I MEAN, NOT *LUCKY* LUCKY, OBVIOUSLY, BUT, YOU KNOW, HE JUST CRASHED IN FRONT OF MY HOUSE. IT COULD HAVE BEEN ANYONE.

BUT IT WASN'T *ANYONE.* IT WAS *YOU.*

THIS ISN'T ABOUT WHAT WE WANT, CLEO. AND IT'S NOT CHANCE. NOT *LUCK.*

IT'S *DESTINY.* COMING HERE, I--WE THOUGHT WE WERE ITS *MASTERS.* THAT WE WERE GUIDING ITS HAND. SO DELUDED.

WE'RE *PAWNS.* THERE'S NO CONTROL.

WELL, HEY, *MY ONLY FRIENDS* ARE AN ALIEN THAT LOOKS LIKE MY *DEAD DAD* WHO PROBABLY HATES ME NOW AND A *GIANT GOOPY ALIEN BABY MACHINE*--

--AND MY ARMS AND LEGS ARE GLOWING LIKE SPACESHIPS, AND YOU'RE ABOUT TO KILL ME, SO, YOU KNOW, BELIEVE ME--

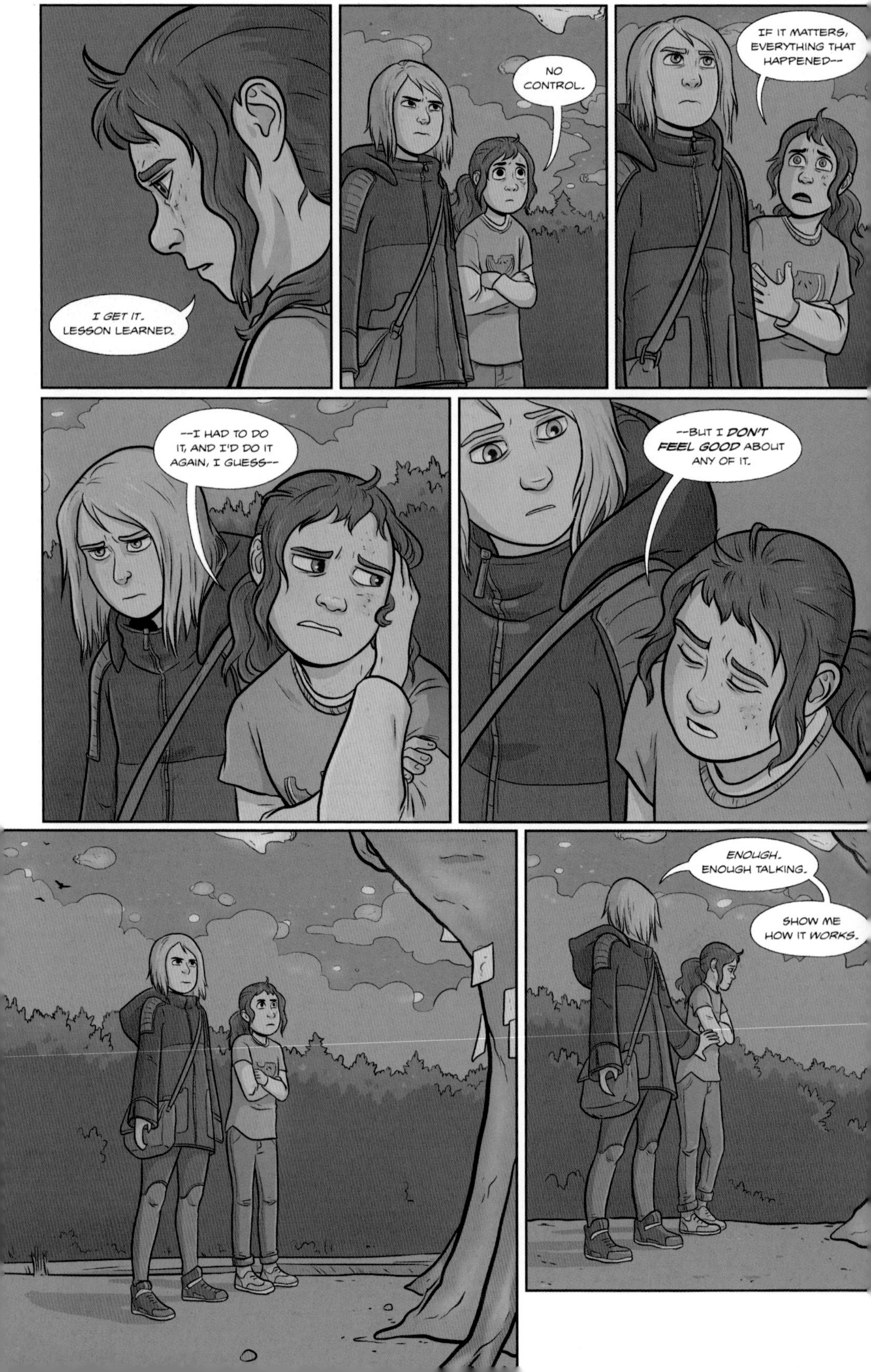
I GET IT. LESSON LEARNED.
NO CONTROL.
IF IT MATTERS, EVERYTHING THAT HAPPENED--
--I HAD TO DO IT, AND I'D DO IT AGAIN, I GUESS--
--BUT I DON'T FEEL GOOD ABOUT ANY OF IT.
ENOUGH. ENOUGH TALKING.
SHOW ME HOW IT WORKS.

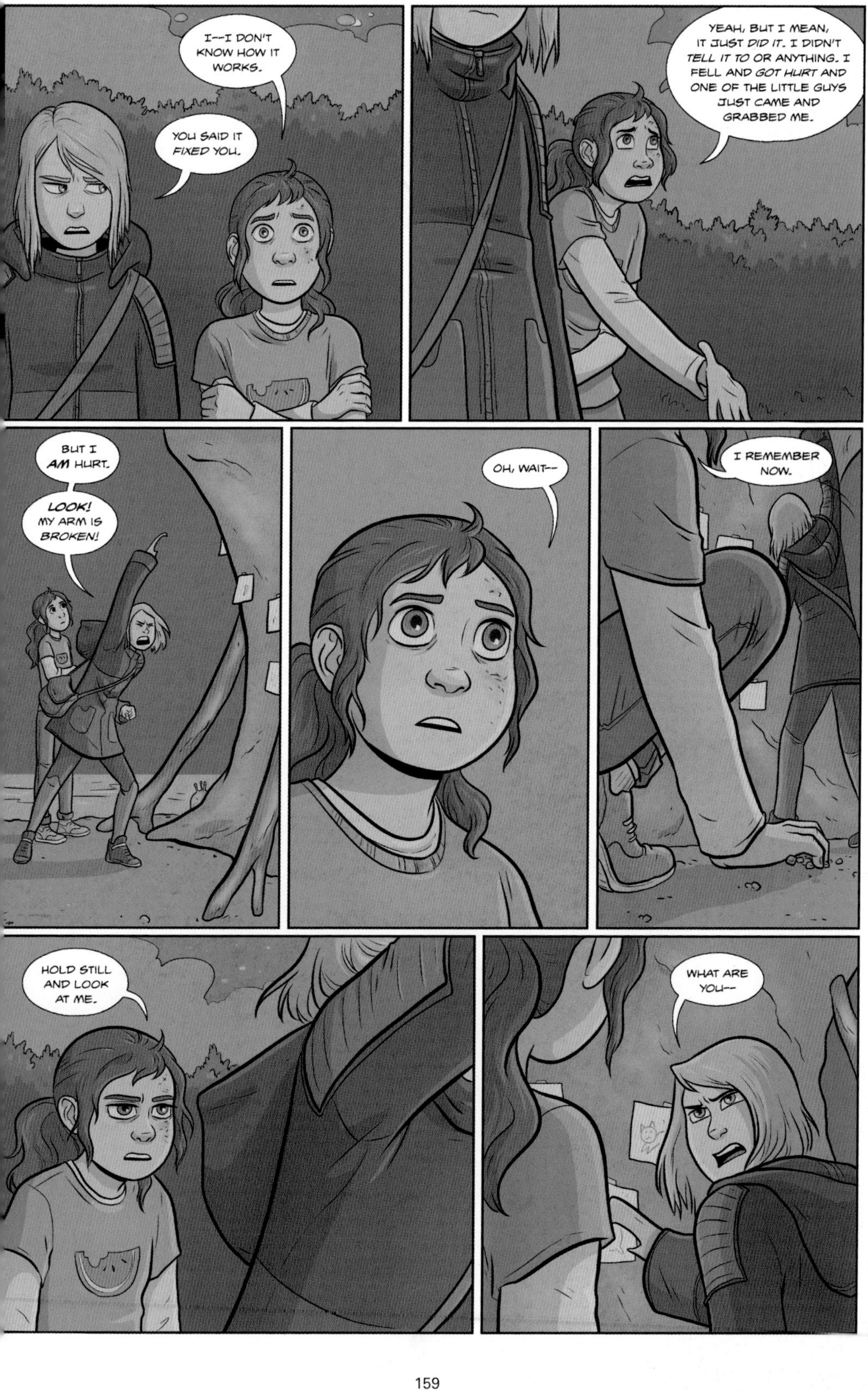

I--I DON'T KNOW HOW IT WORKS.
YOU SAID IT *FIXED* YOU.
YEAH, BUT I MEAN, IT JUST *DID IT*. I DIDN'T *TELL IT TO* OR ANYTHING. I FELL AND *GOT HURT* AND ONE OF THE LITTLE GUYS JUST CAME AND GRABBED ME.
BUT I **AM** HURT.
LOOK! MY ARM IS *BROKEN!*
OH, WAIT--
I REMEMBER NOW.
HOLD STILL AND LOOK AT ME.
WHAT ARE YOU--

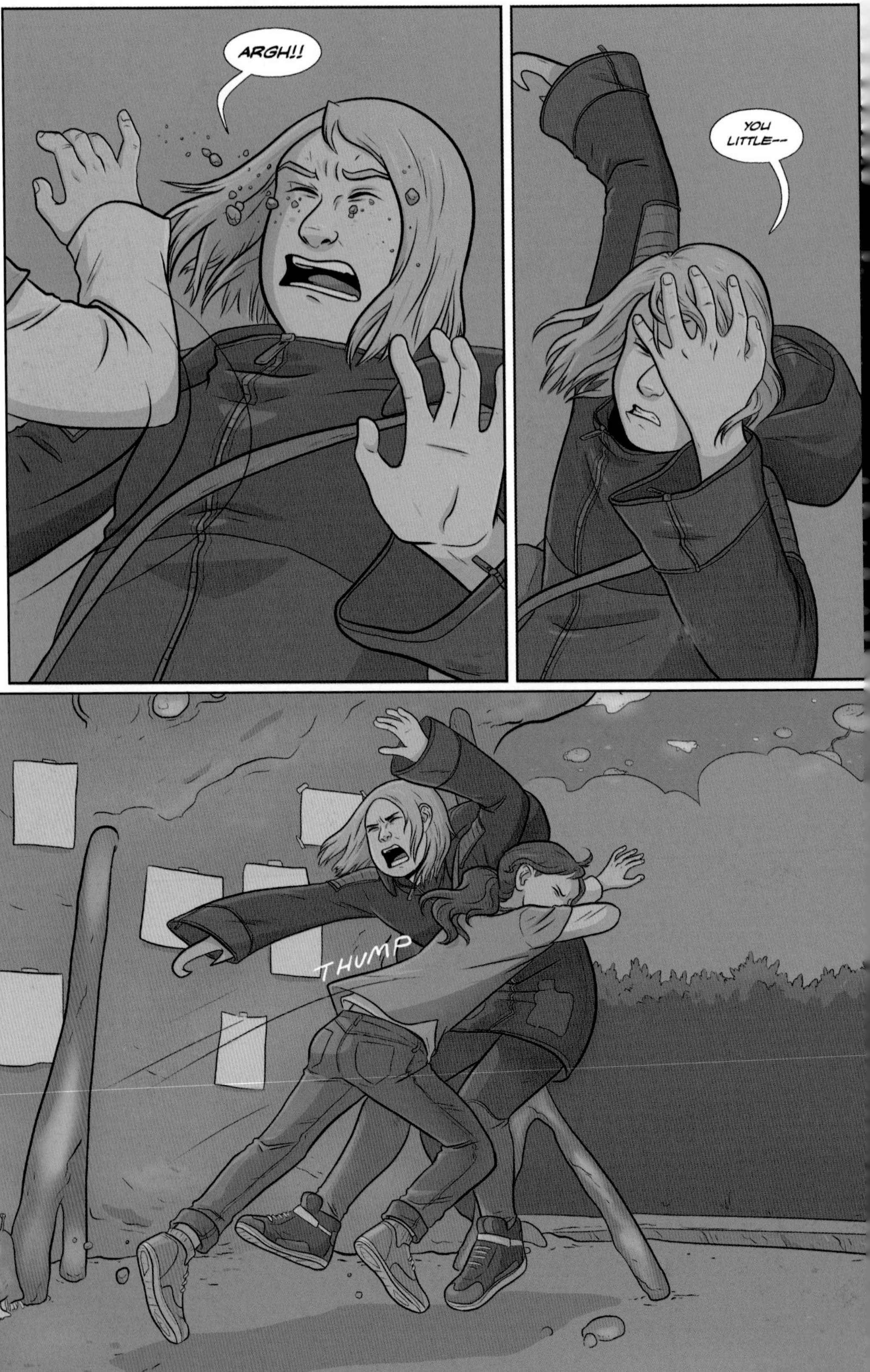
ARGH!!
YOU LITTLE--
THUMP

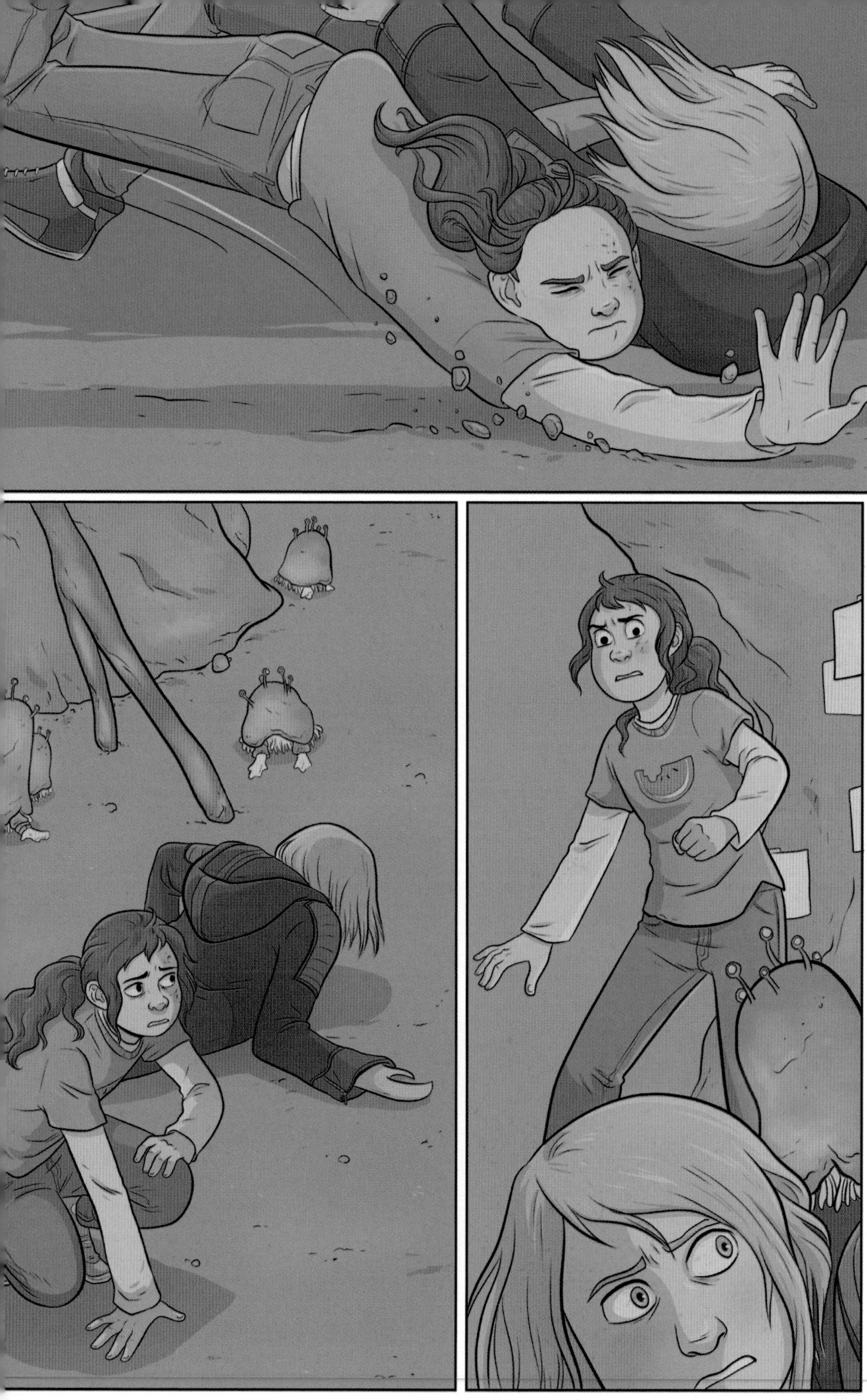

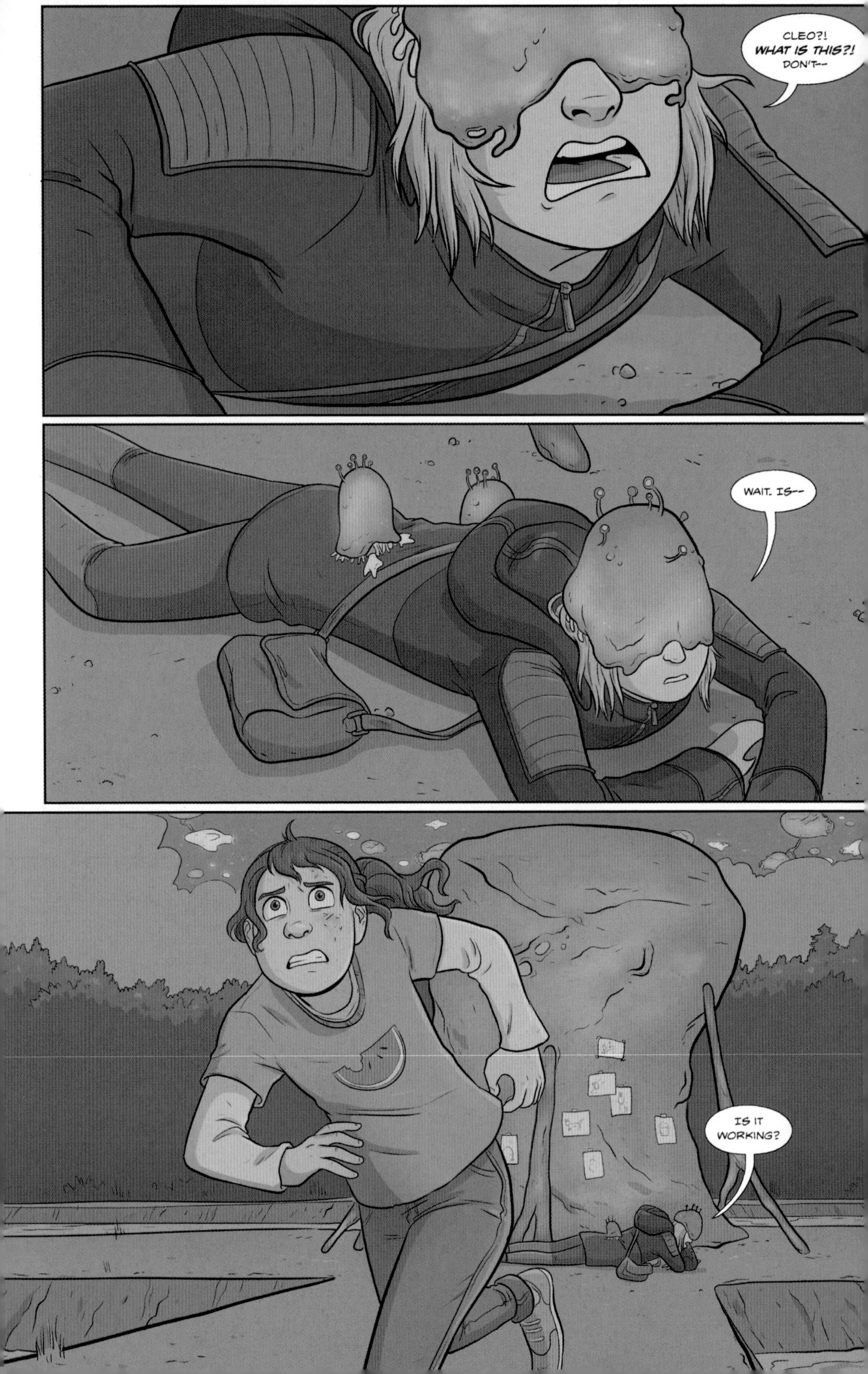
CLEO?! **WHAT IS THIS?!** DON'T--
WAIT. IS--
IS IT WORKING?

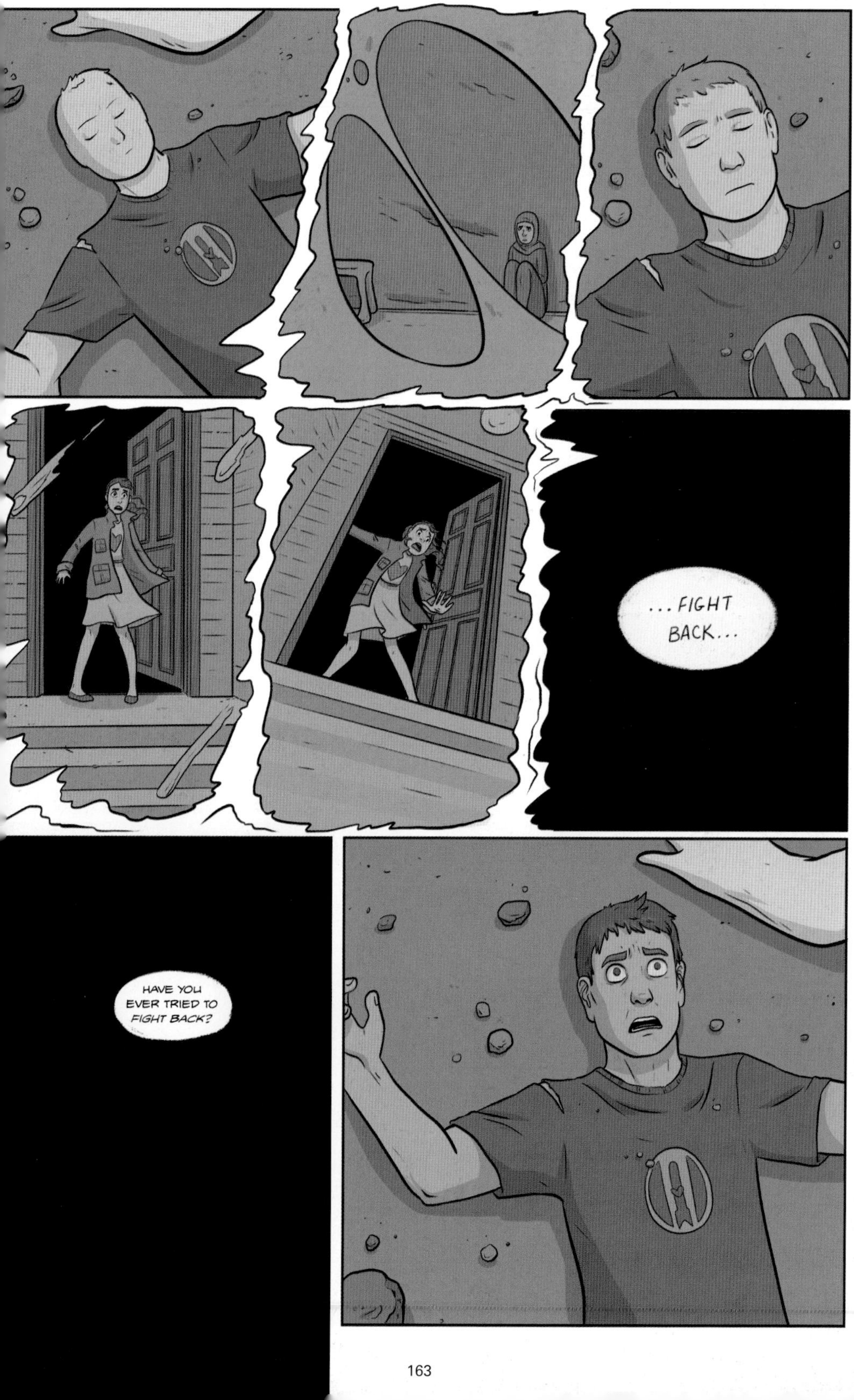
...FIGHT BACK...
HAVE YOU EVER TRIED TO FIGHT BACK?

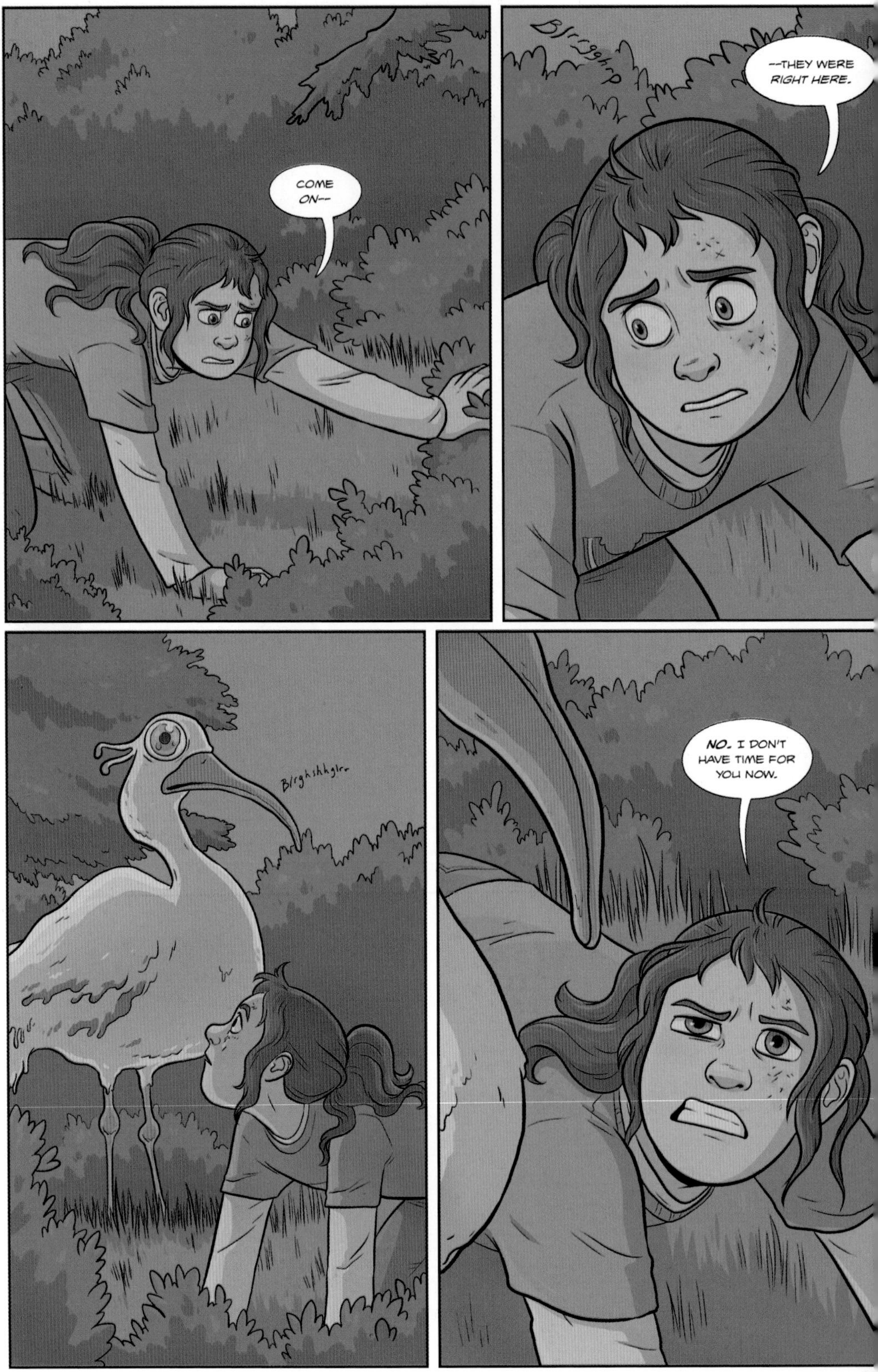
COME ON--
Blrrgghrp
--THEY WERE RIGHT HERE.
Blrghshhglrr
NO. I DON'T HAVE TIME FOR YOU NOW.

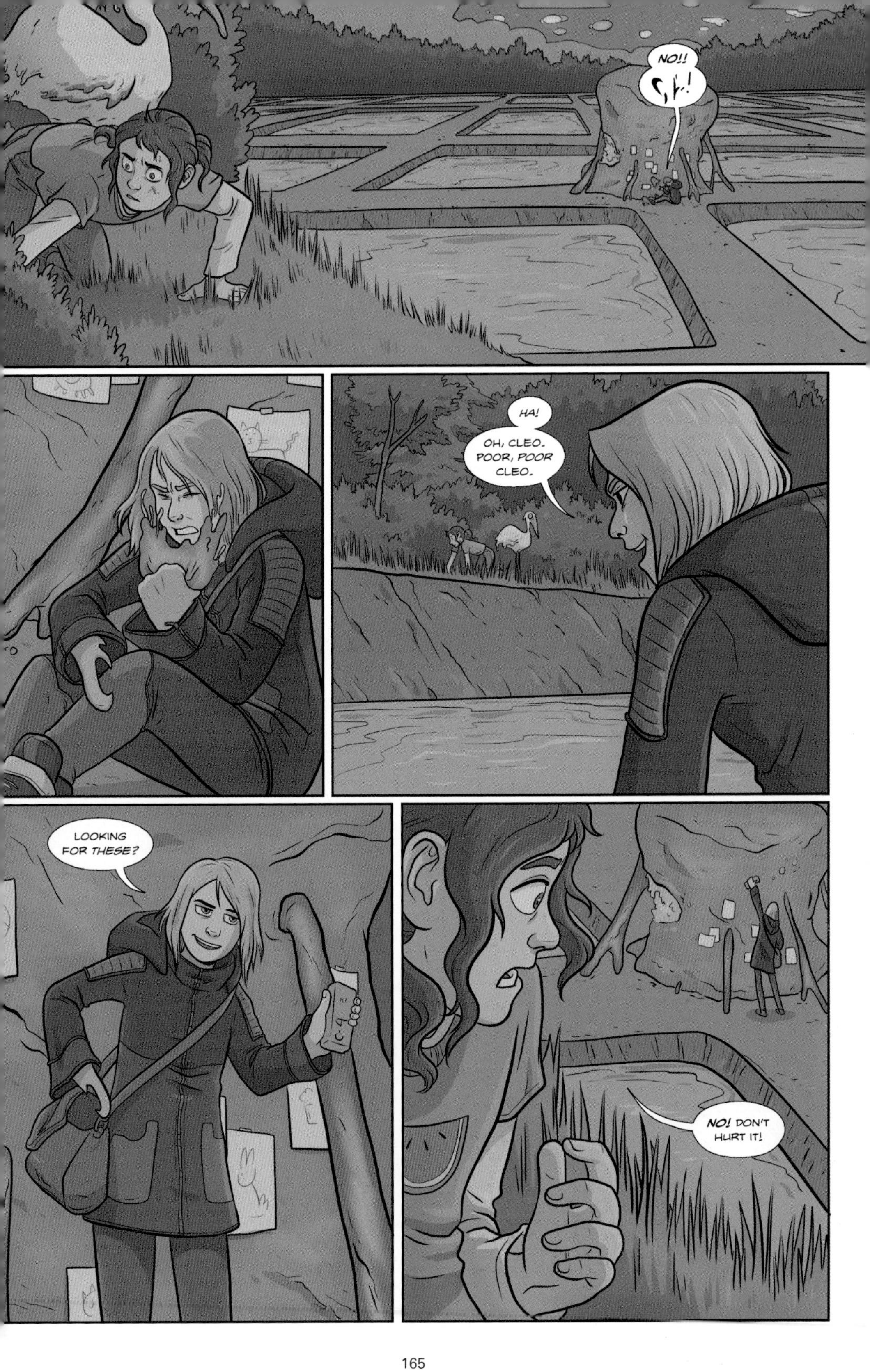
NO!!
HA!
OH, CLEO. POOR, POOR CLEO.
LOOKING FOR THESE?
NO! DON'T HURT IT!

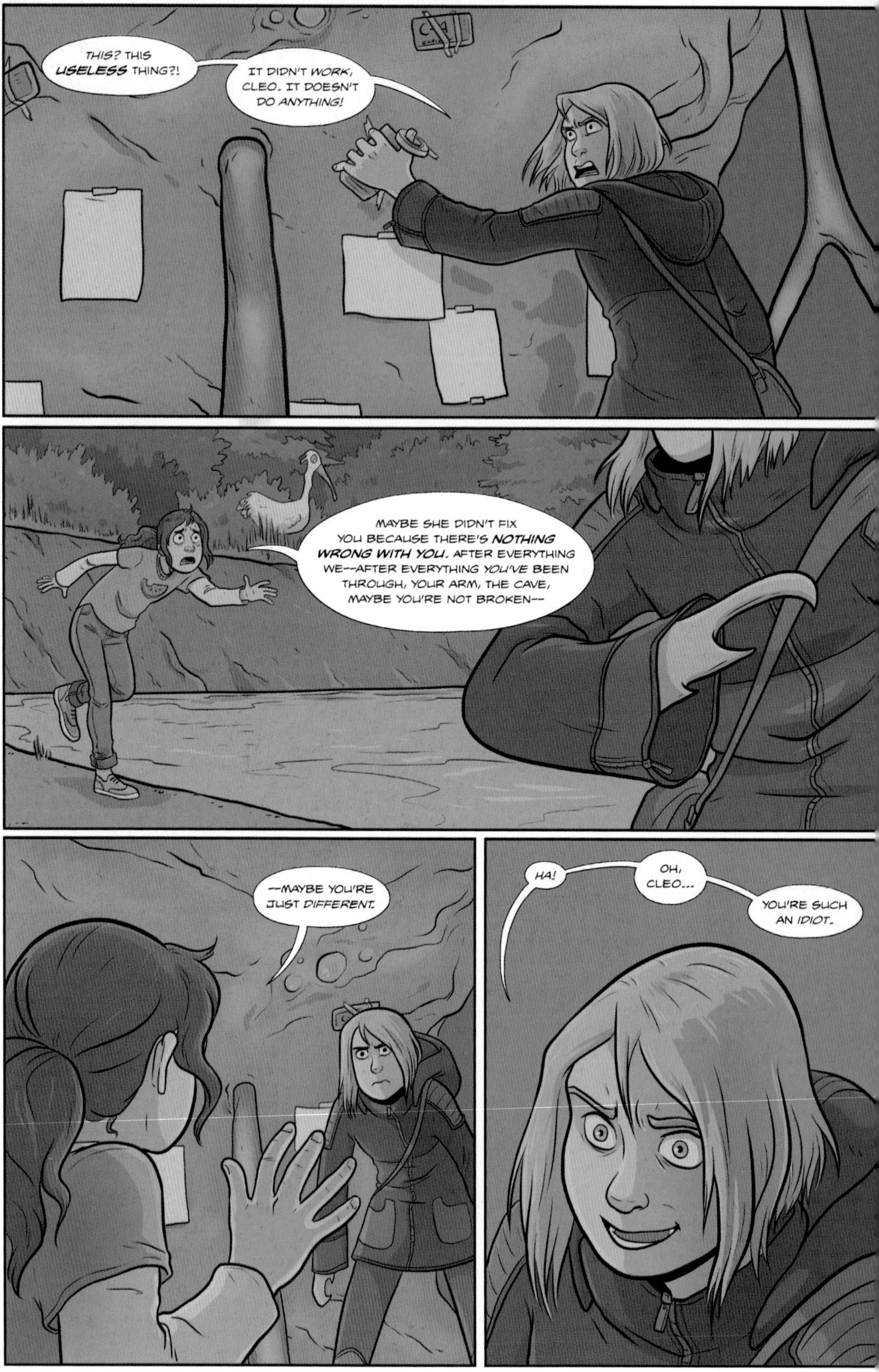
THIS? THIS USELESS THING?!
IT DIDN'T WORK, CLEO. IT DOESN'T DO ANYTHING!
MAYBE SHE DIDN'T FIX YOU BECAUSE THERE'S NOTHING WRONG WITH YOU. AFTER EVERYTHING WE--AFTER EVERYTHING YOU'VE BEEN THROUGH, YOUR ARM, THE CAVE, MAYBE YOU'RE NOT BROKEN--
--MAYBE YOU'RE JUST DIFFERENT.
HA!
OH, CLEO...
YOU'RE SUCH AN IDIOT.

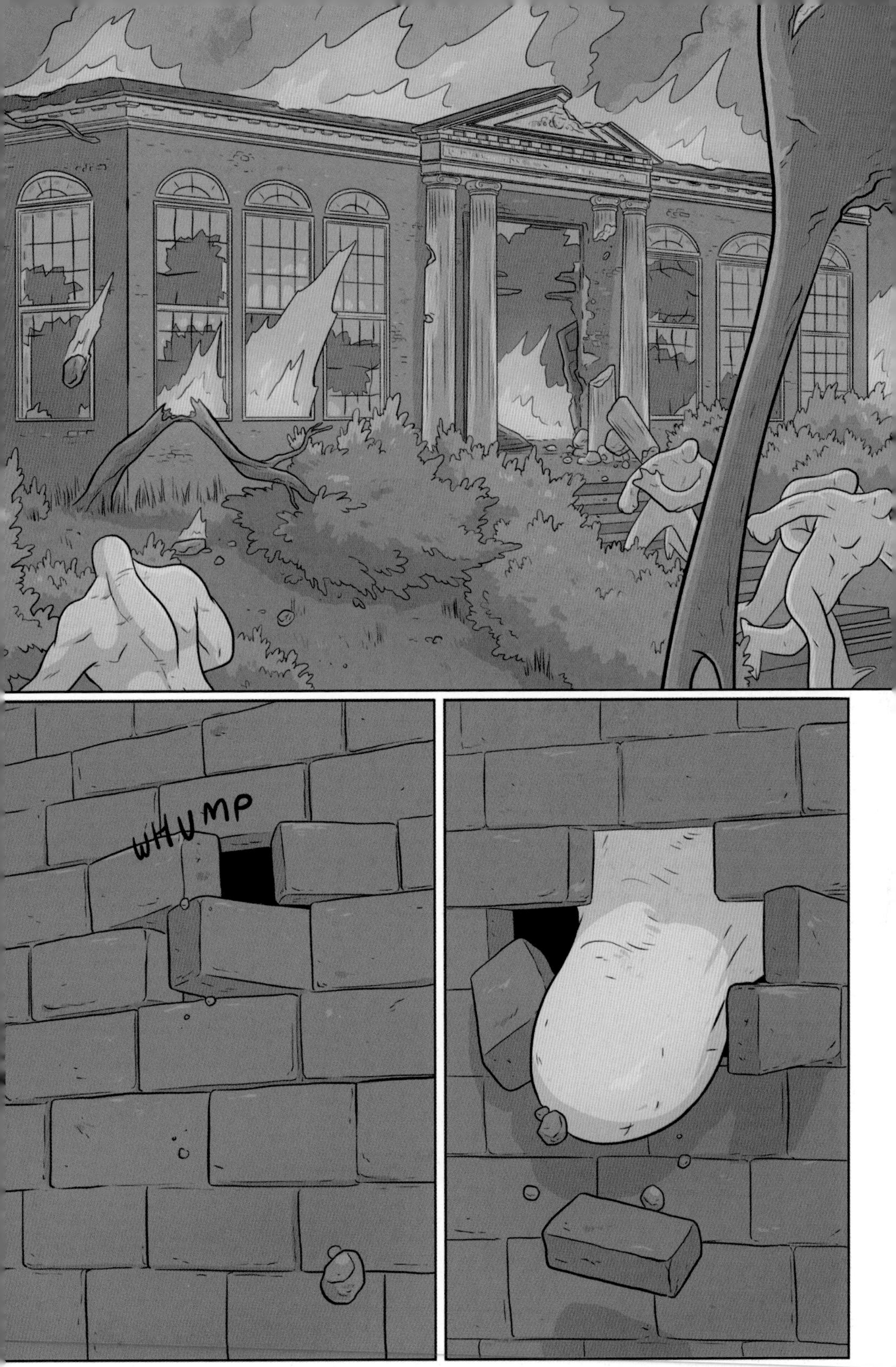
WHUMP

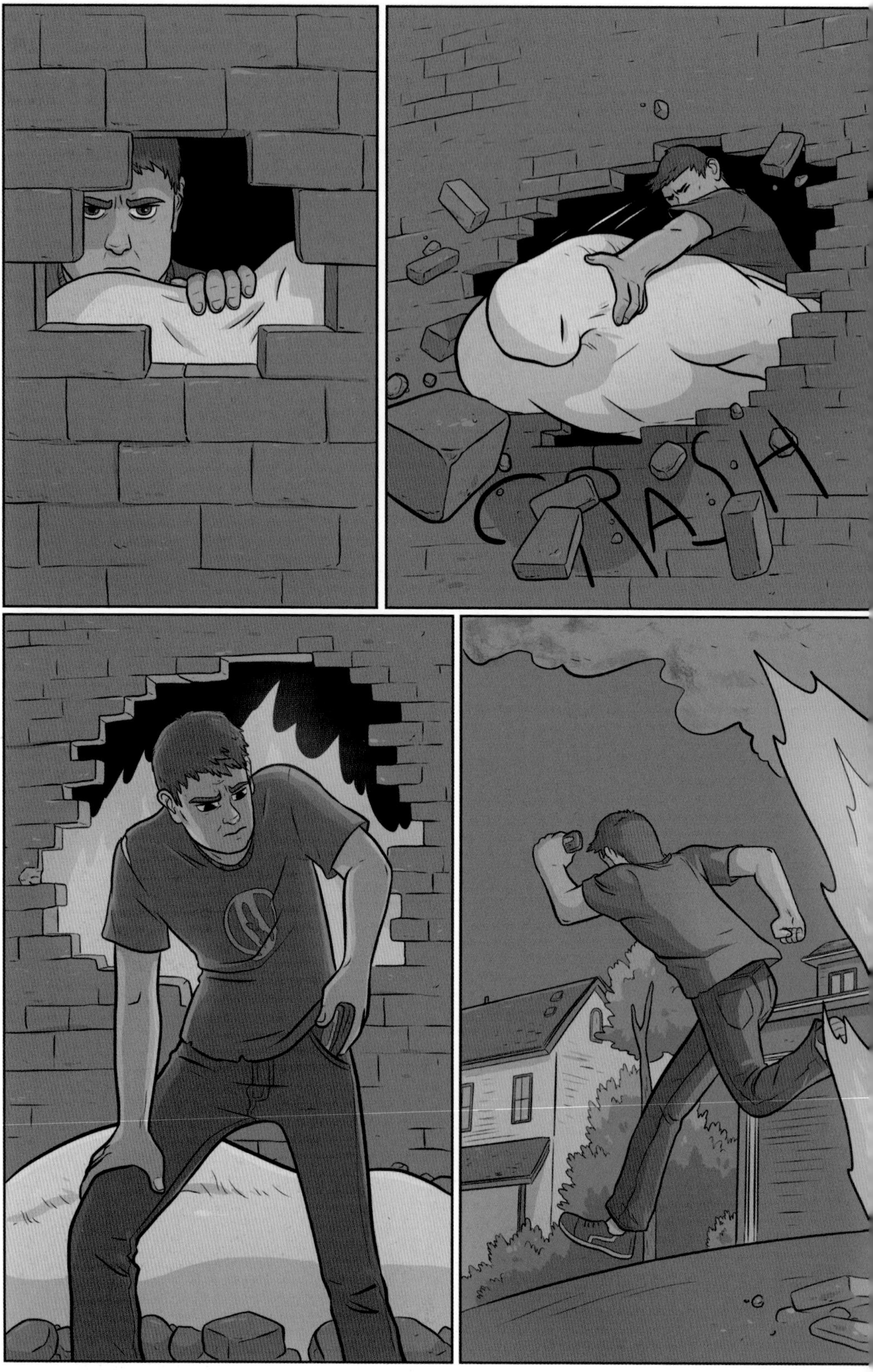
CRASH

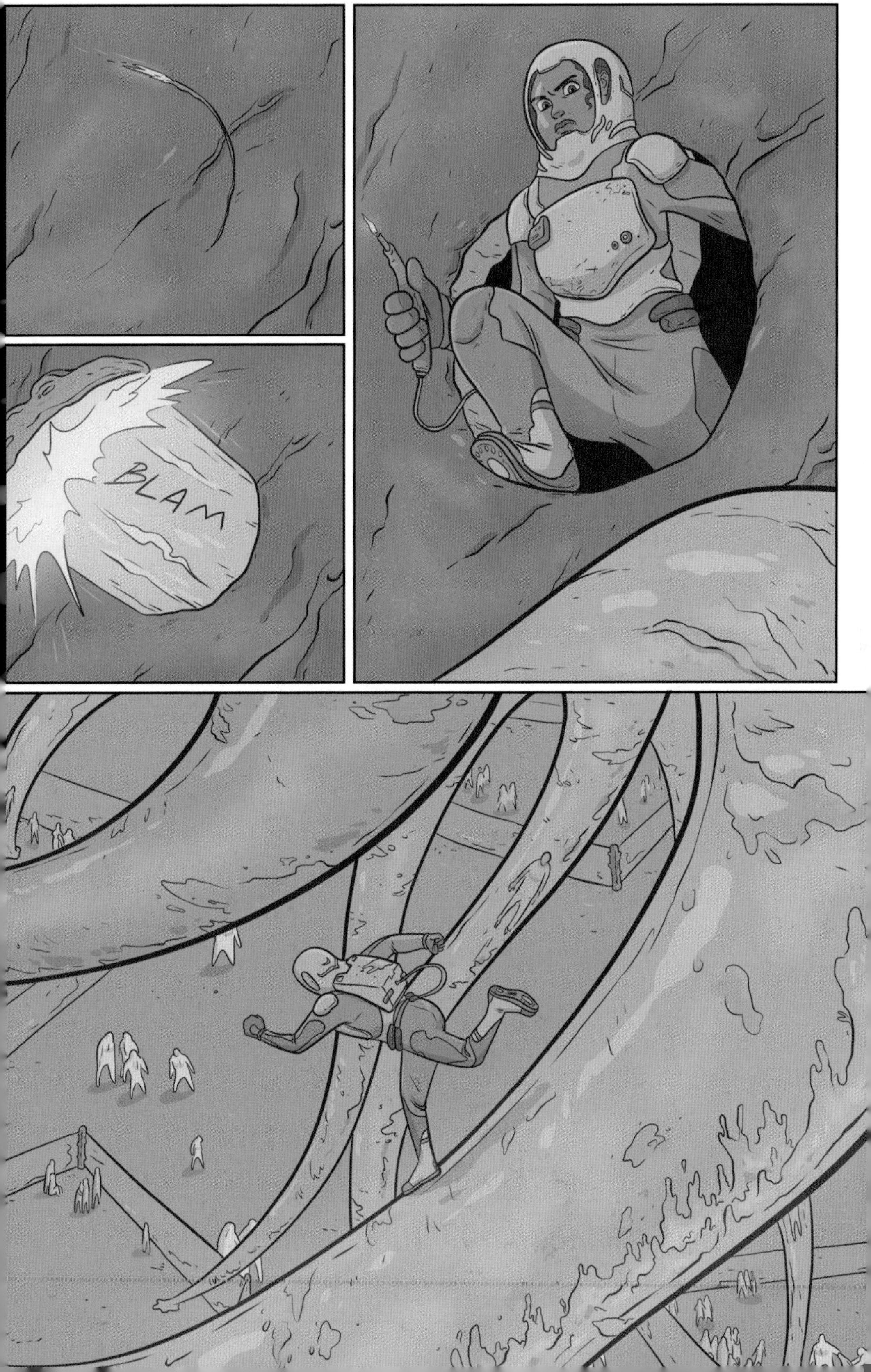
BLAM

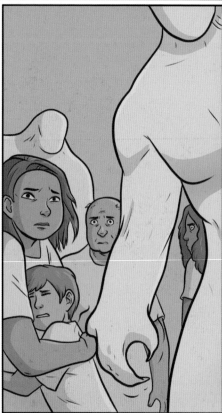

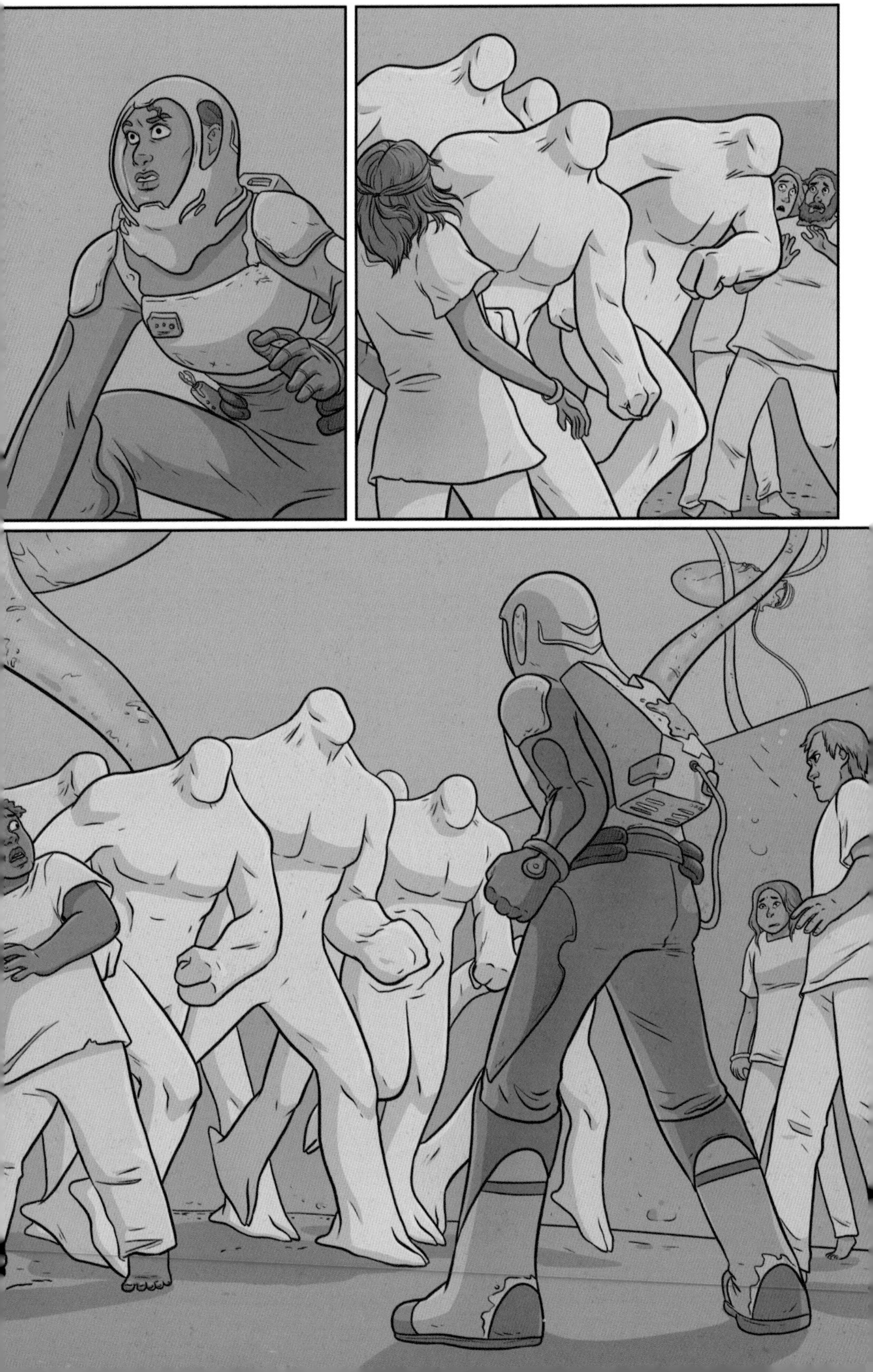

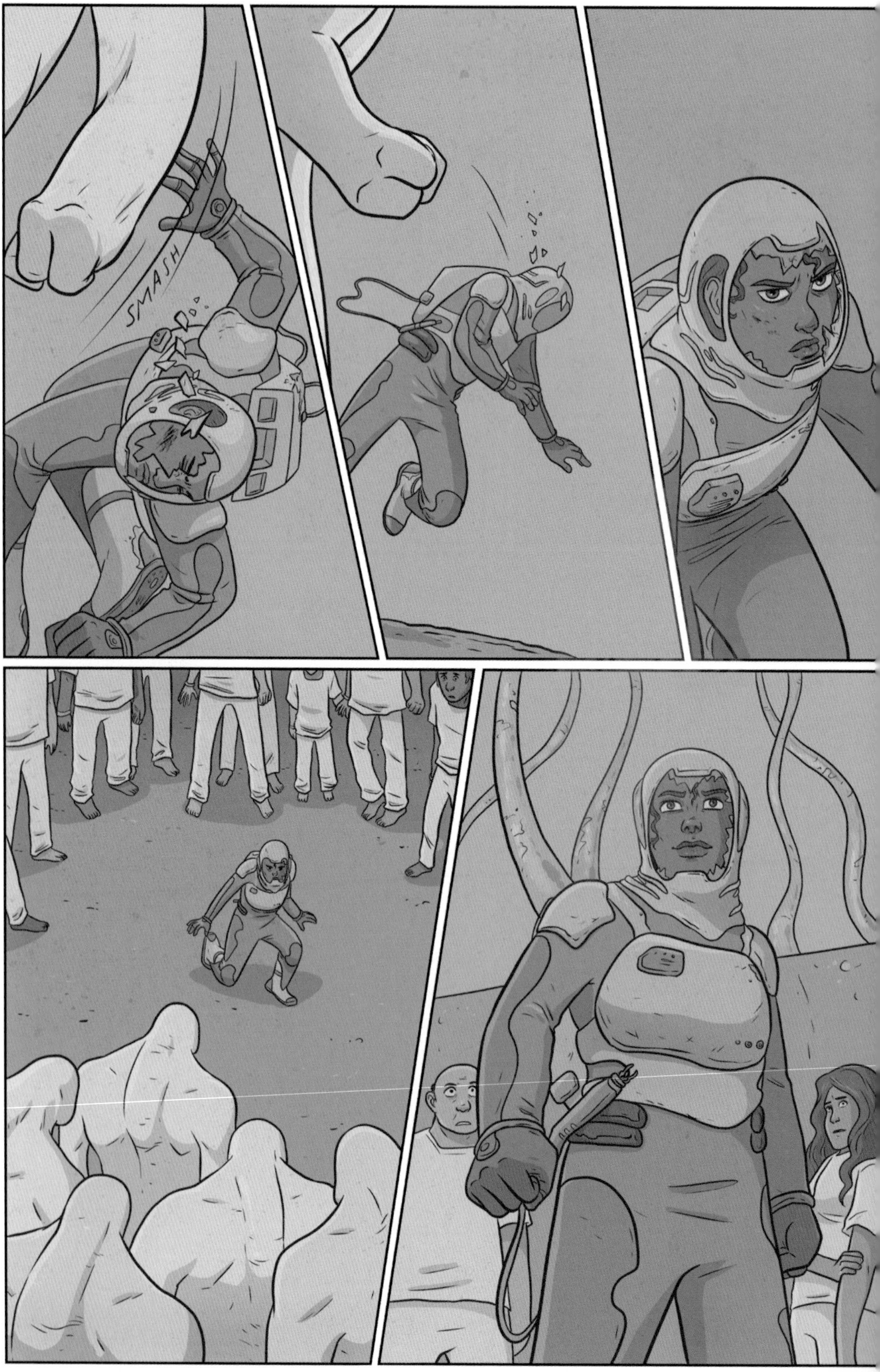
SMASH

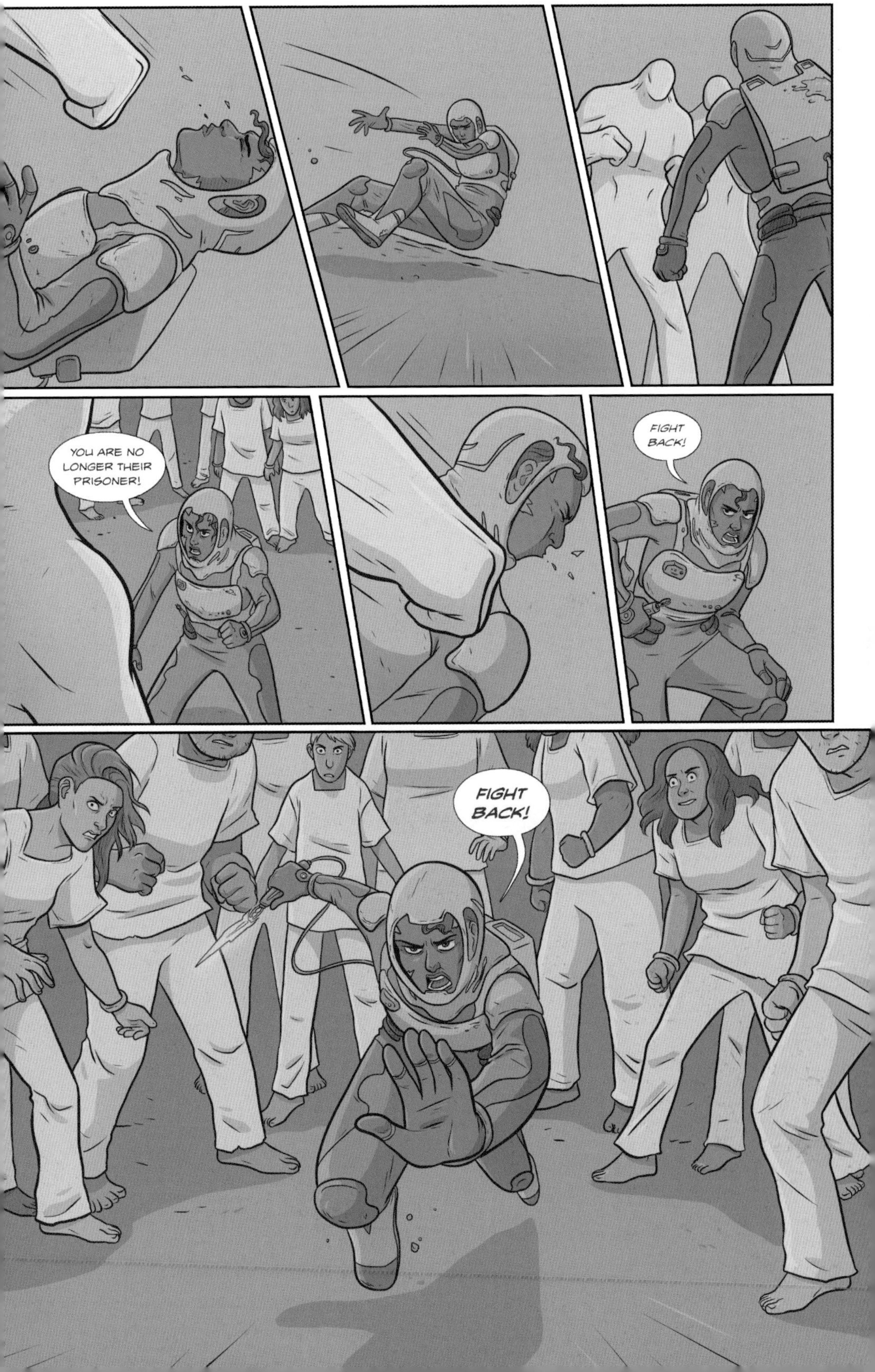
YOU ARE NO LONGER THEIR PRISONER!
FIGHT BACK!
FIGHT BACK!

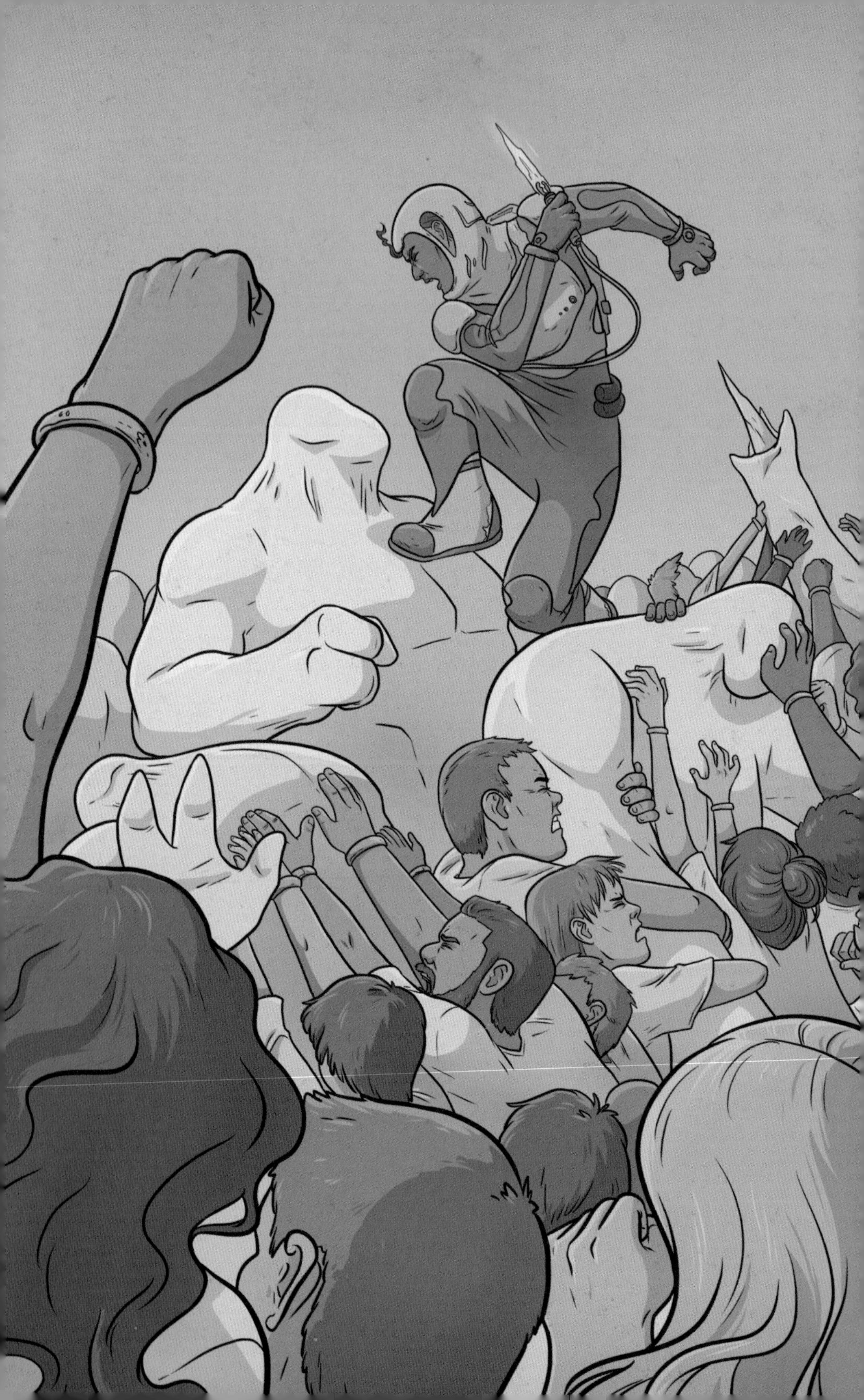

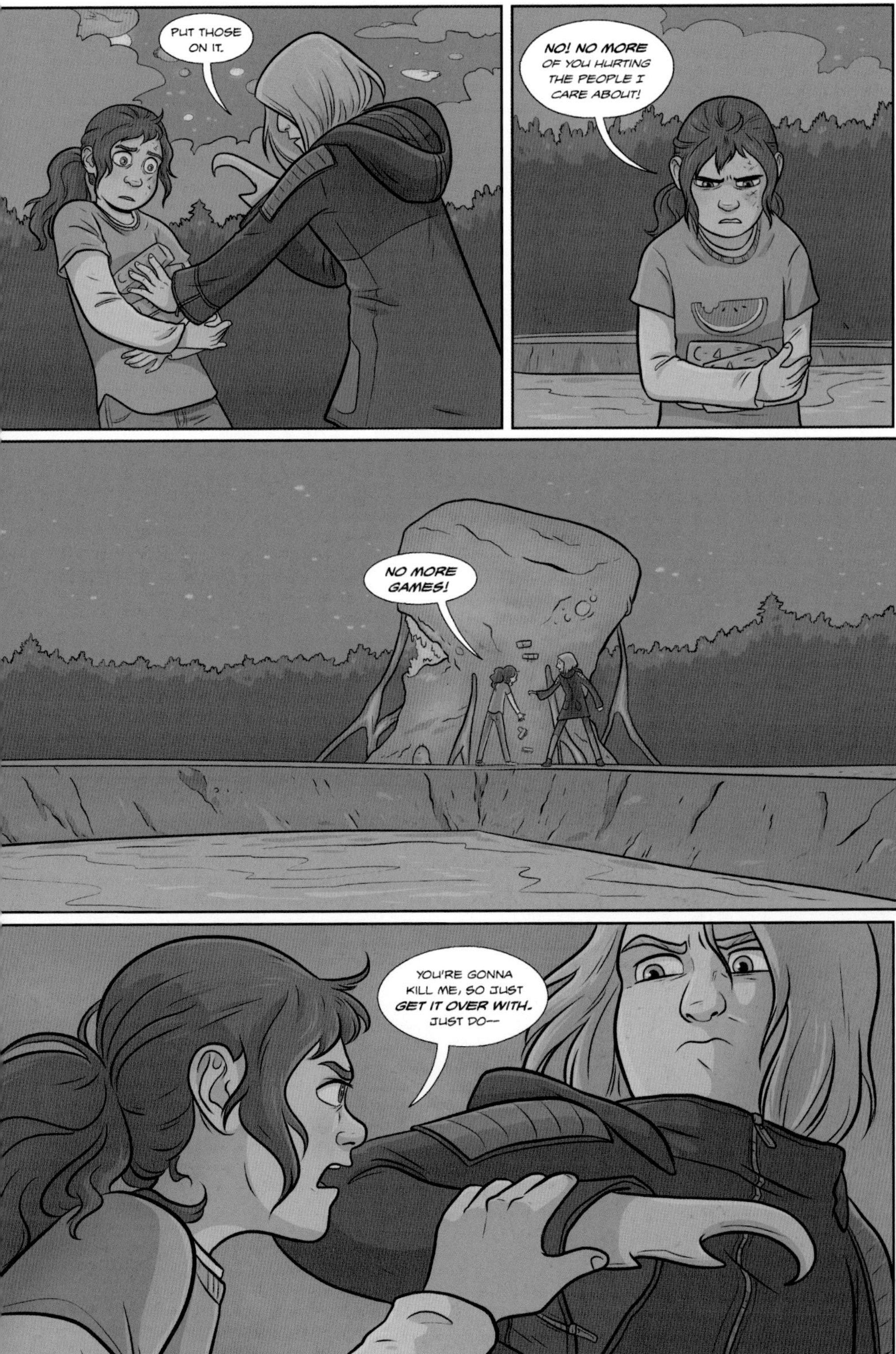
PUT THOSE ON IT.
NO! NO MORE OF YOU HURTING THE PEOPLE I CARE ABOUT!
NO MORE GAMES!
YOU'RE GONNA KILL ME, SO JUST GET IT OVER WITH. JUST DO--

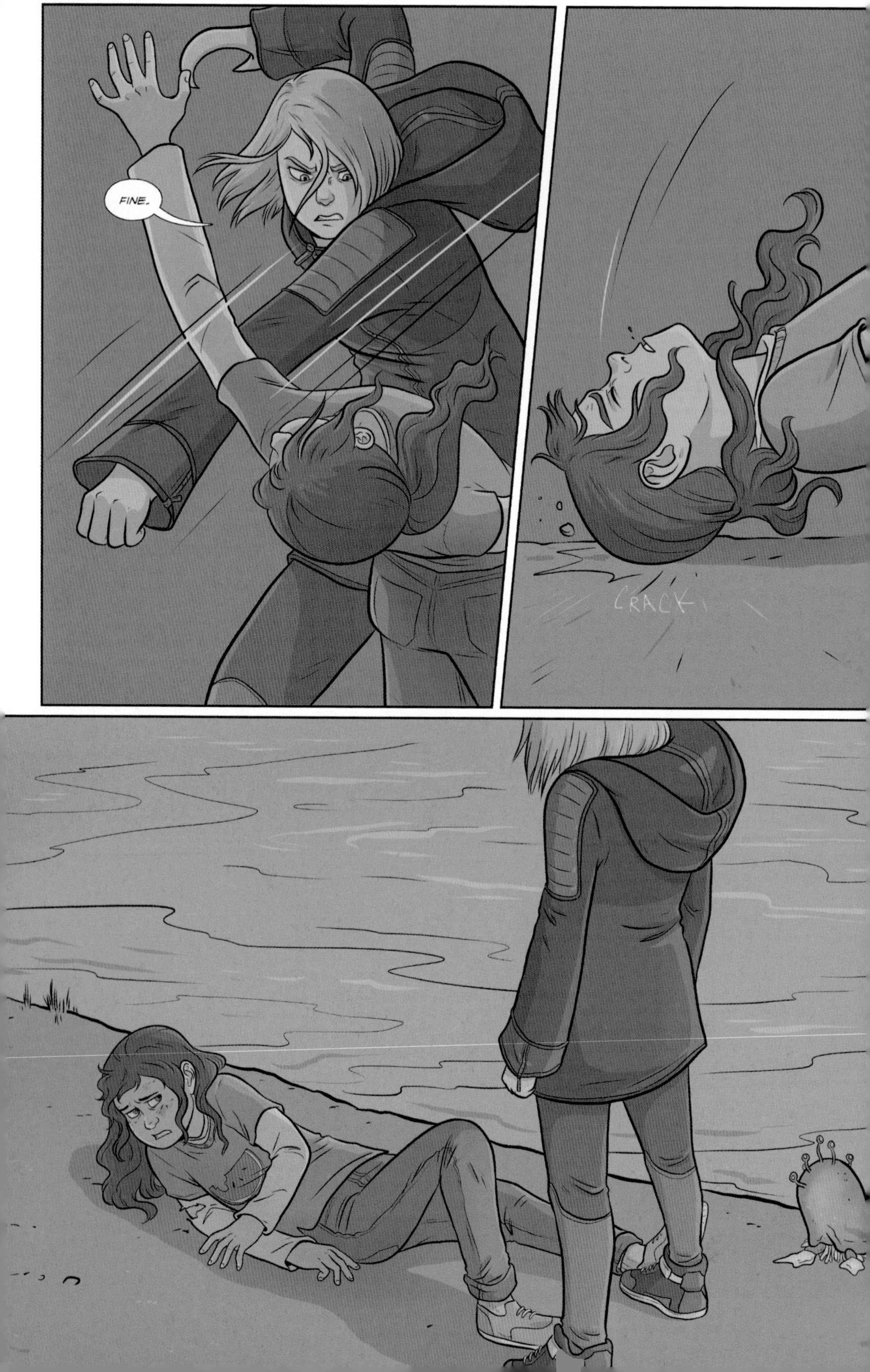
FINE.
CRACK

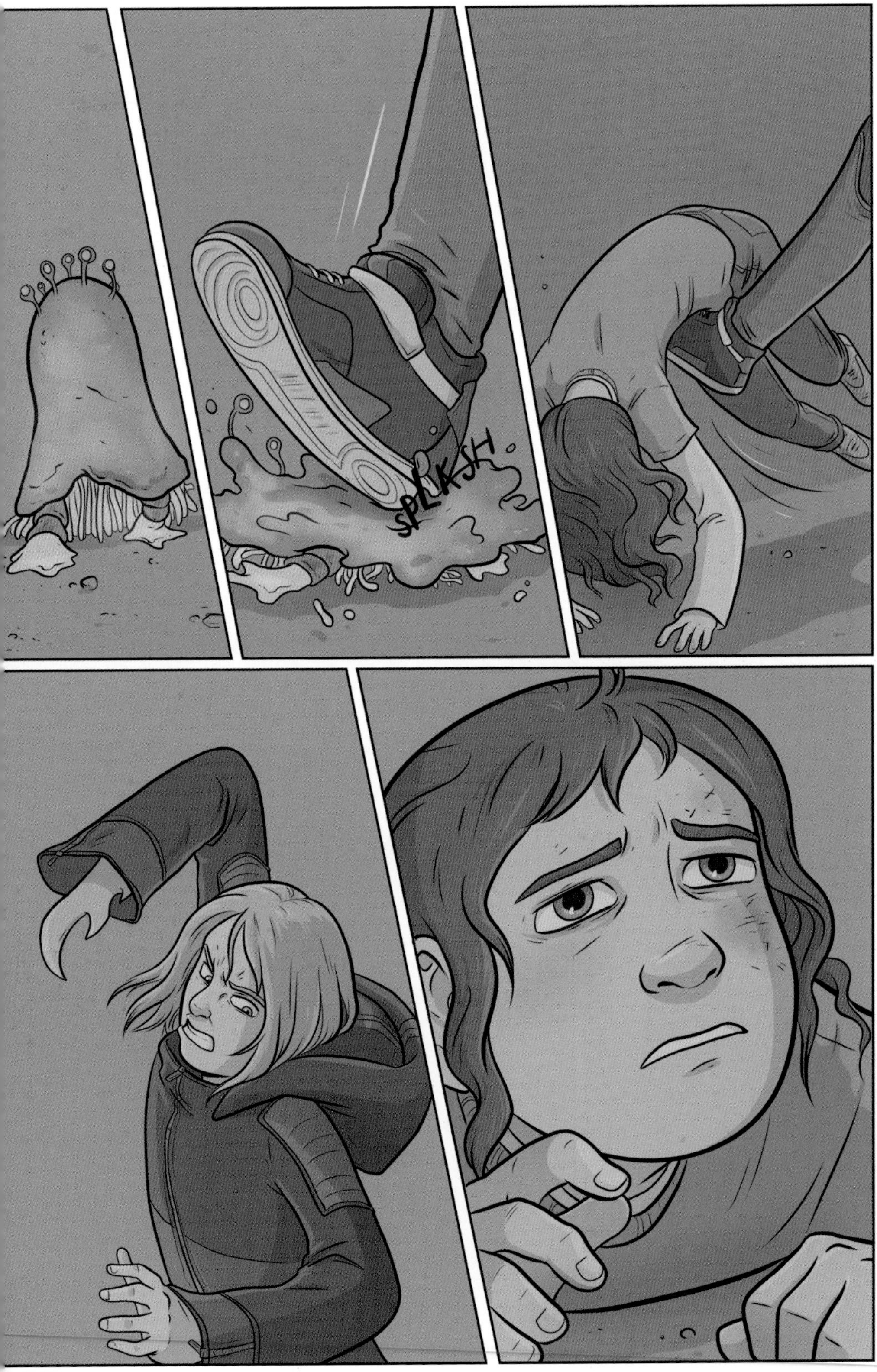
SPLASH

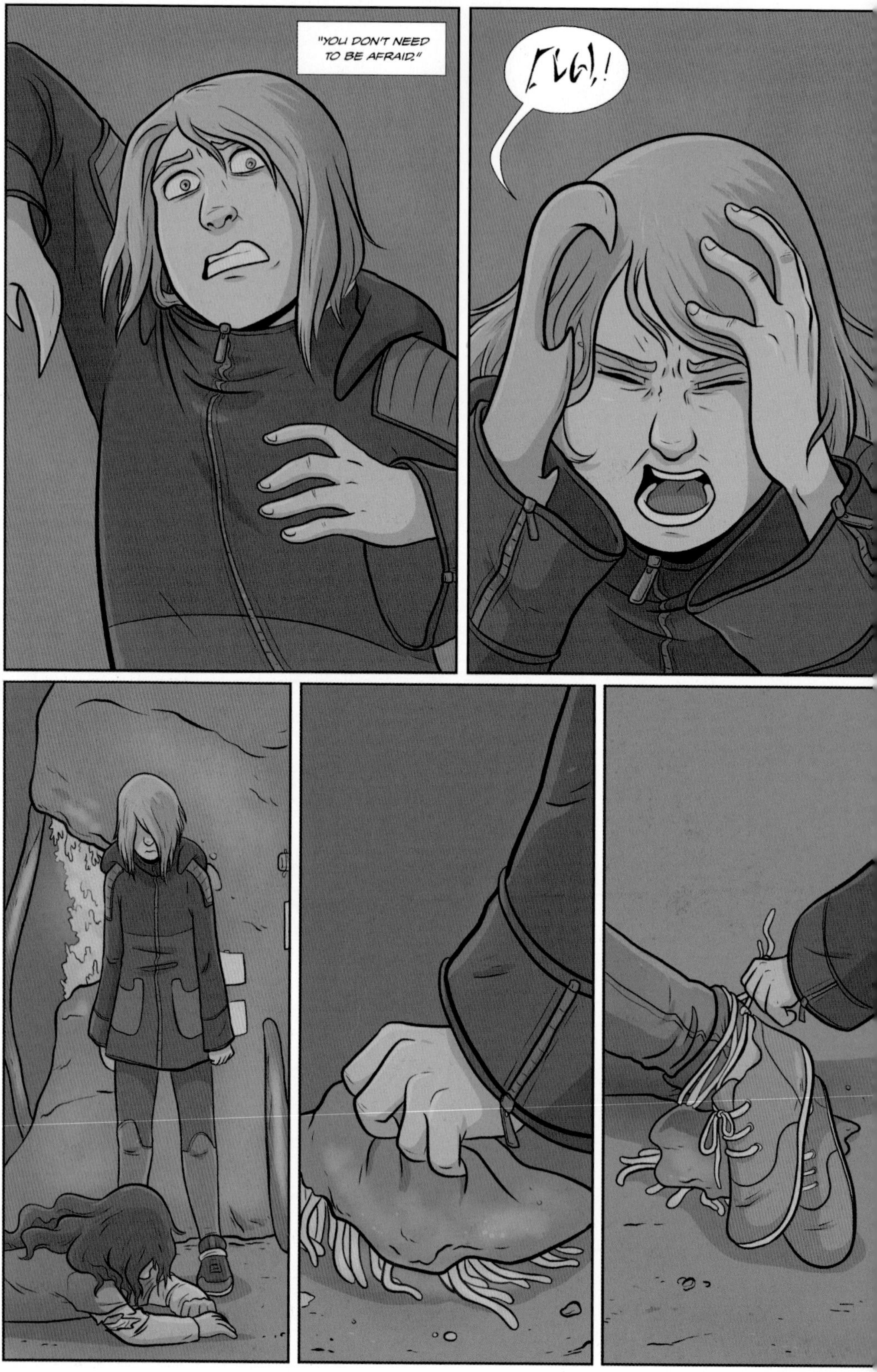
"YOU DON'T NEED TO BE AFRAID."

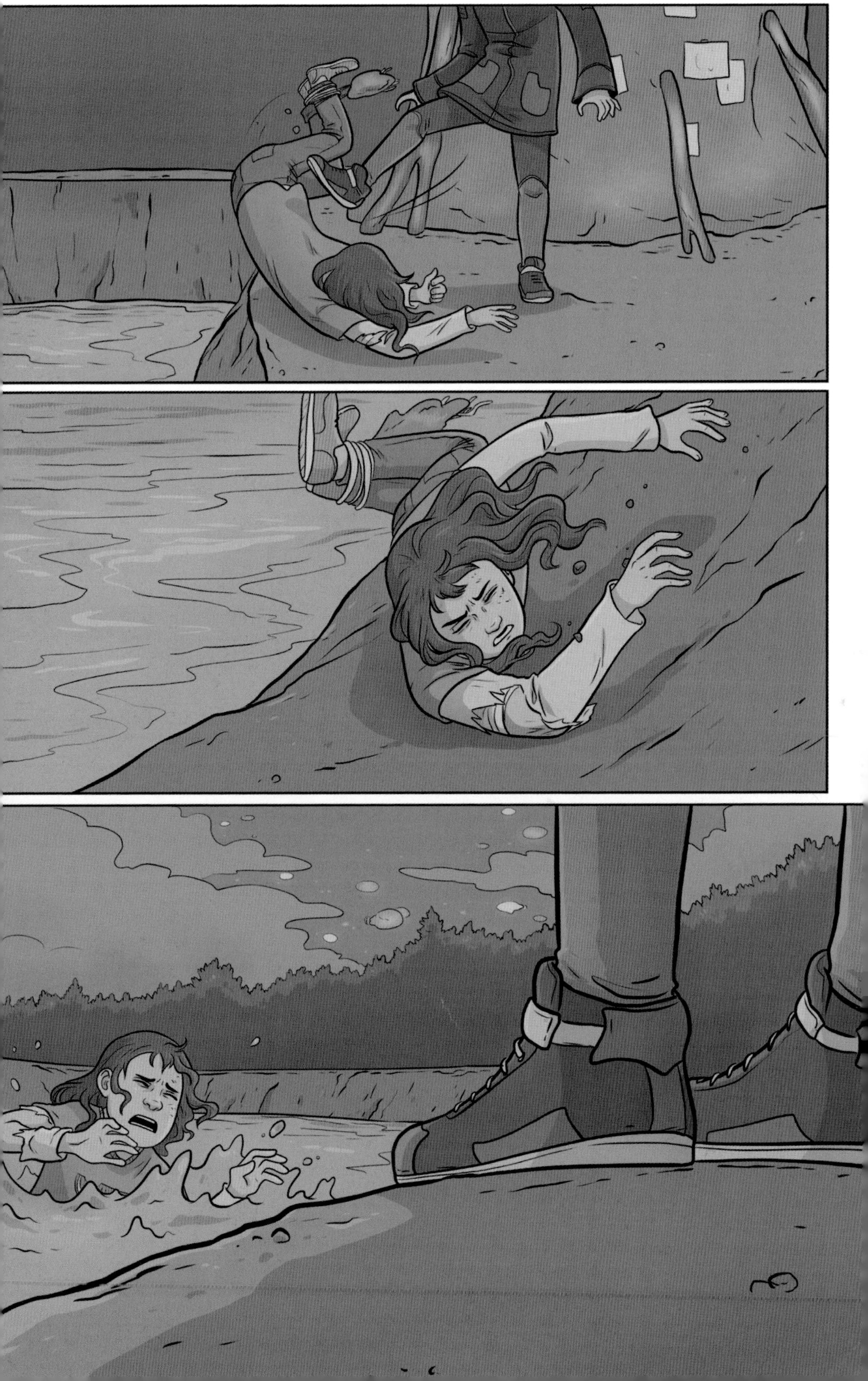

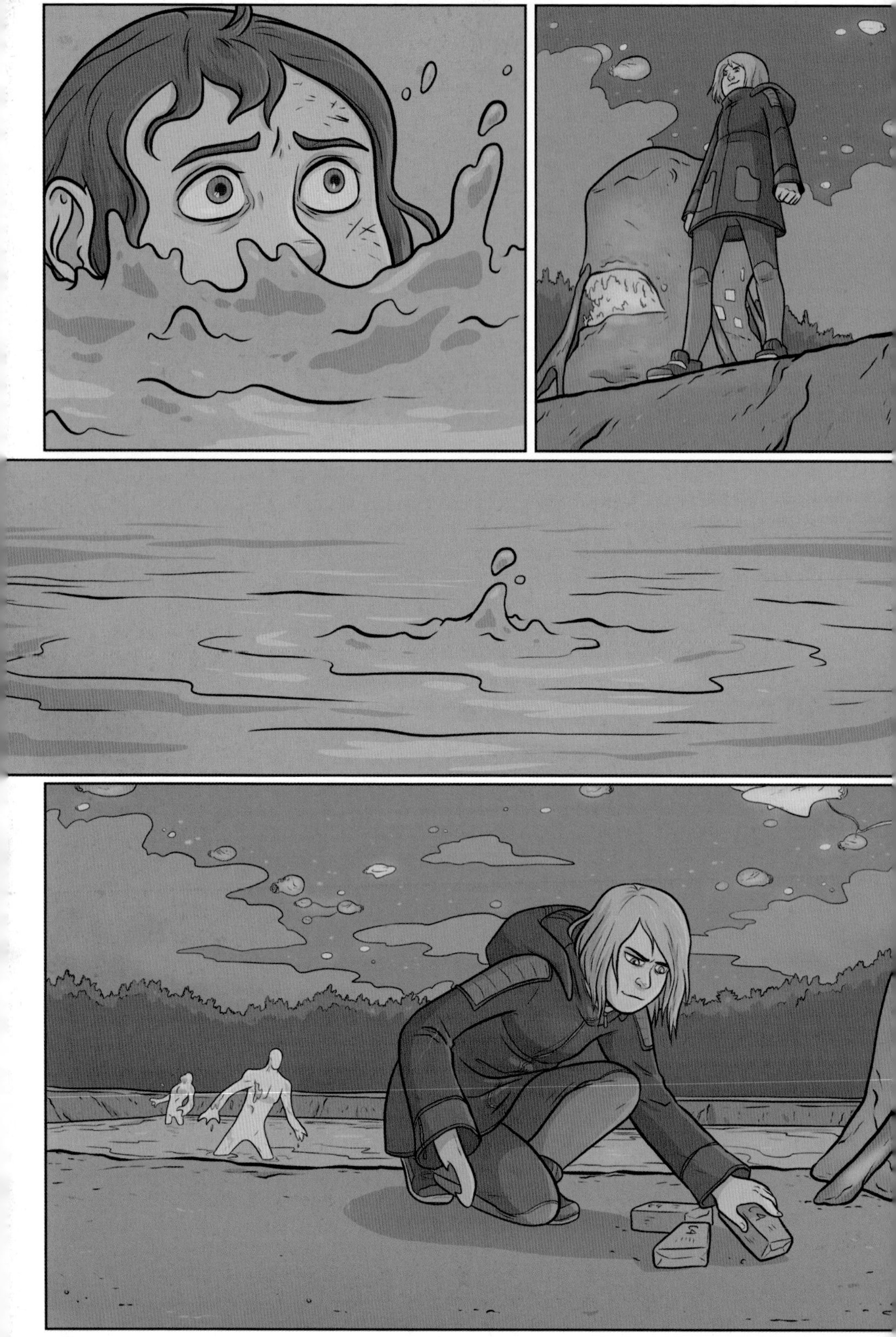

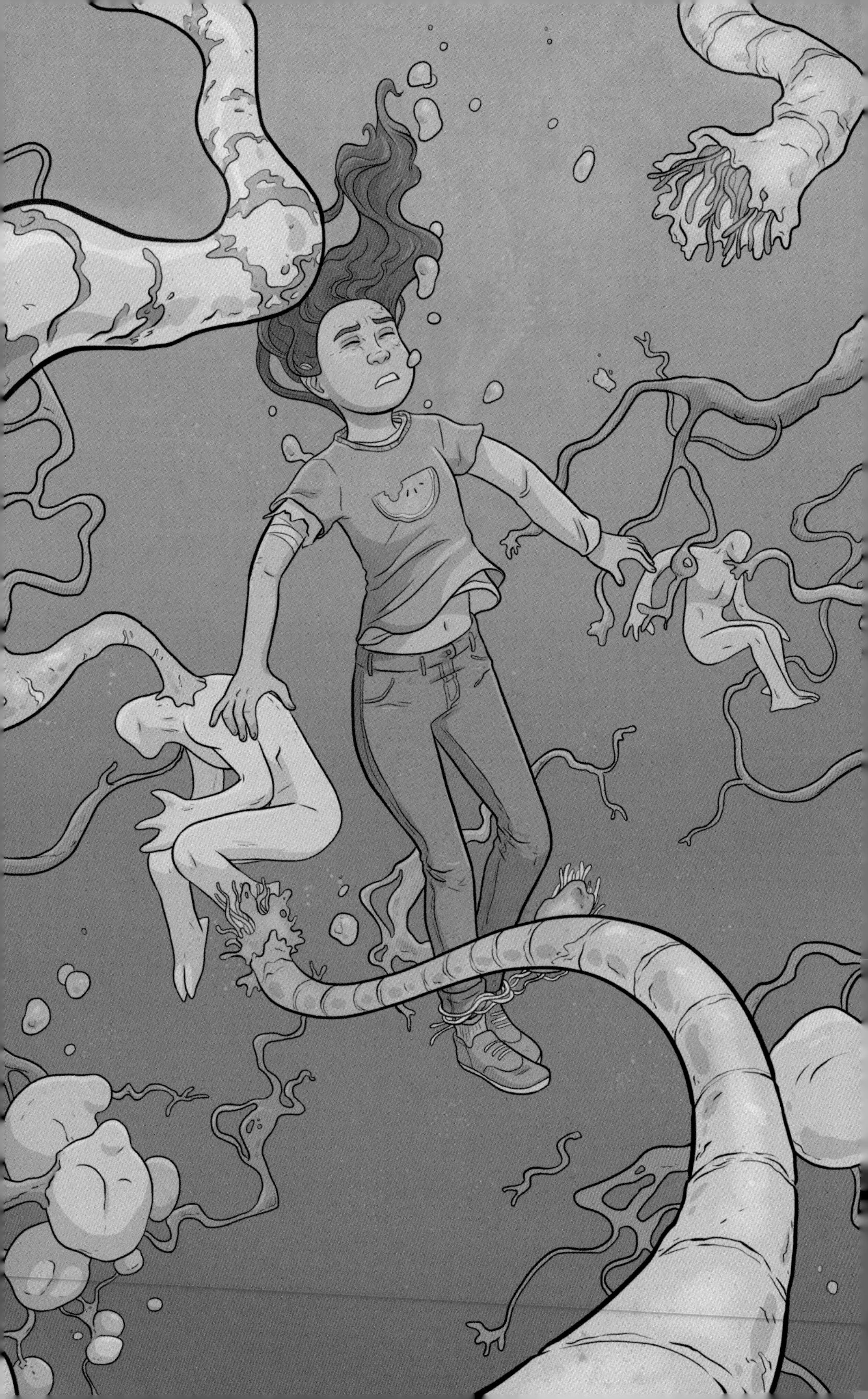

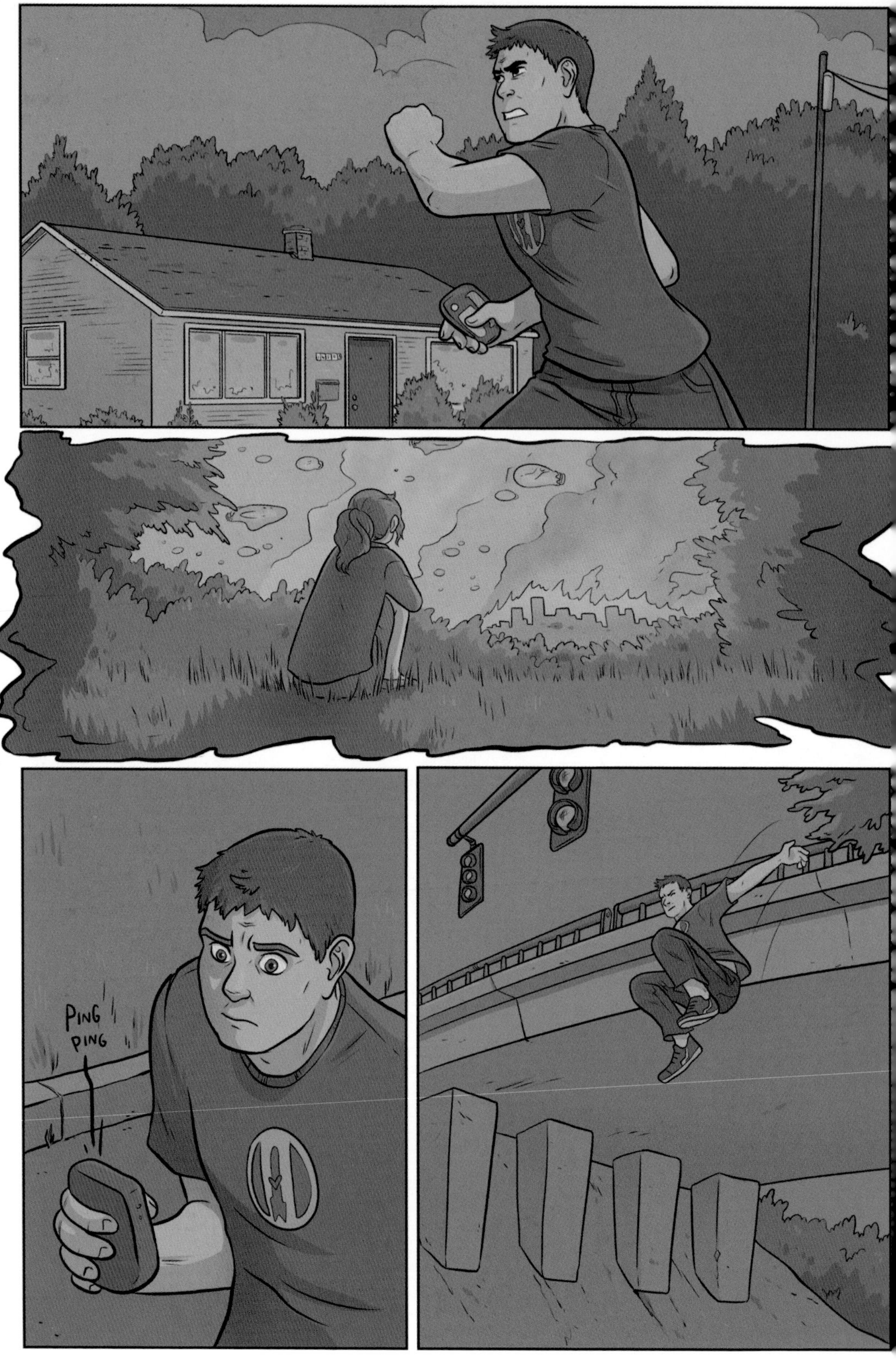
PING
PING

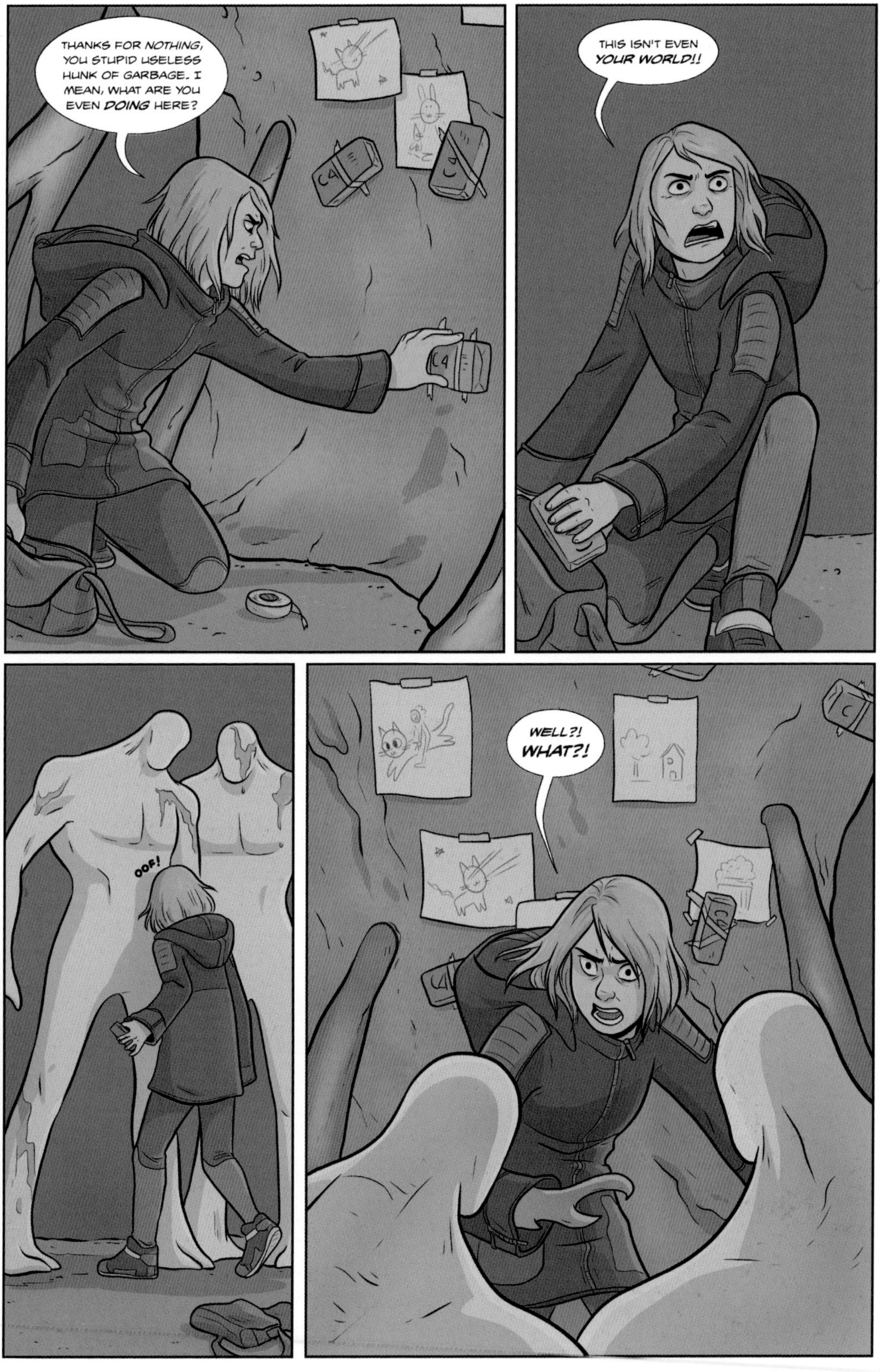
THANKS FOR *NOTHING*, YOU STUPID USELESS HUNK OF GARBAGE. I MEAN, WHAT ARE YOU EVEN ***DOING*** HERE?
C4
C4
THIS ISN'T EVEN ***YOUR WORLD!!***
OOF!
WELL?! **WHAT?!**

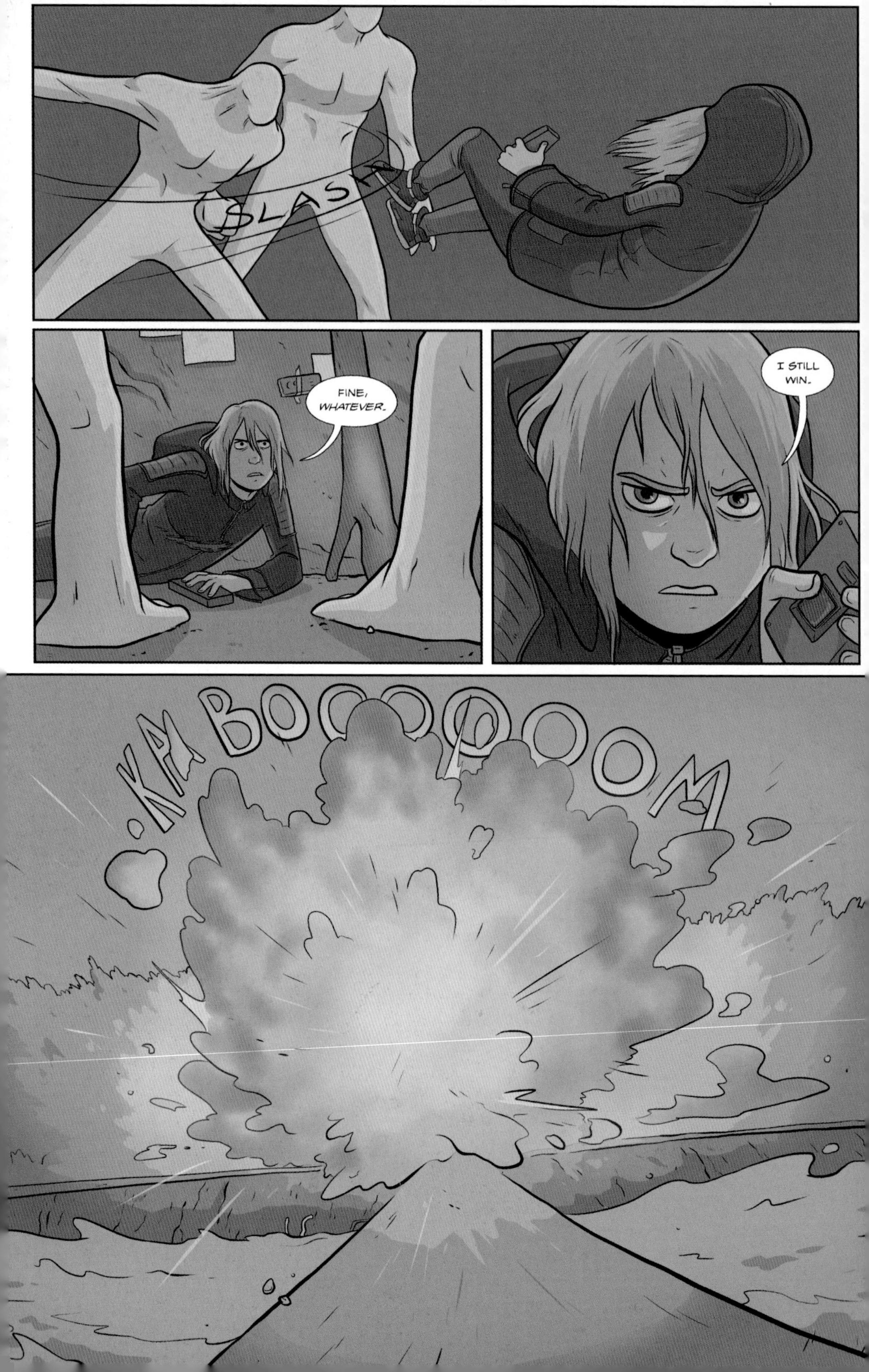
SLASH
FINE, WHATEVER.
I STILL WIN.
KA BOOOOOOM

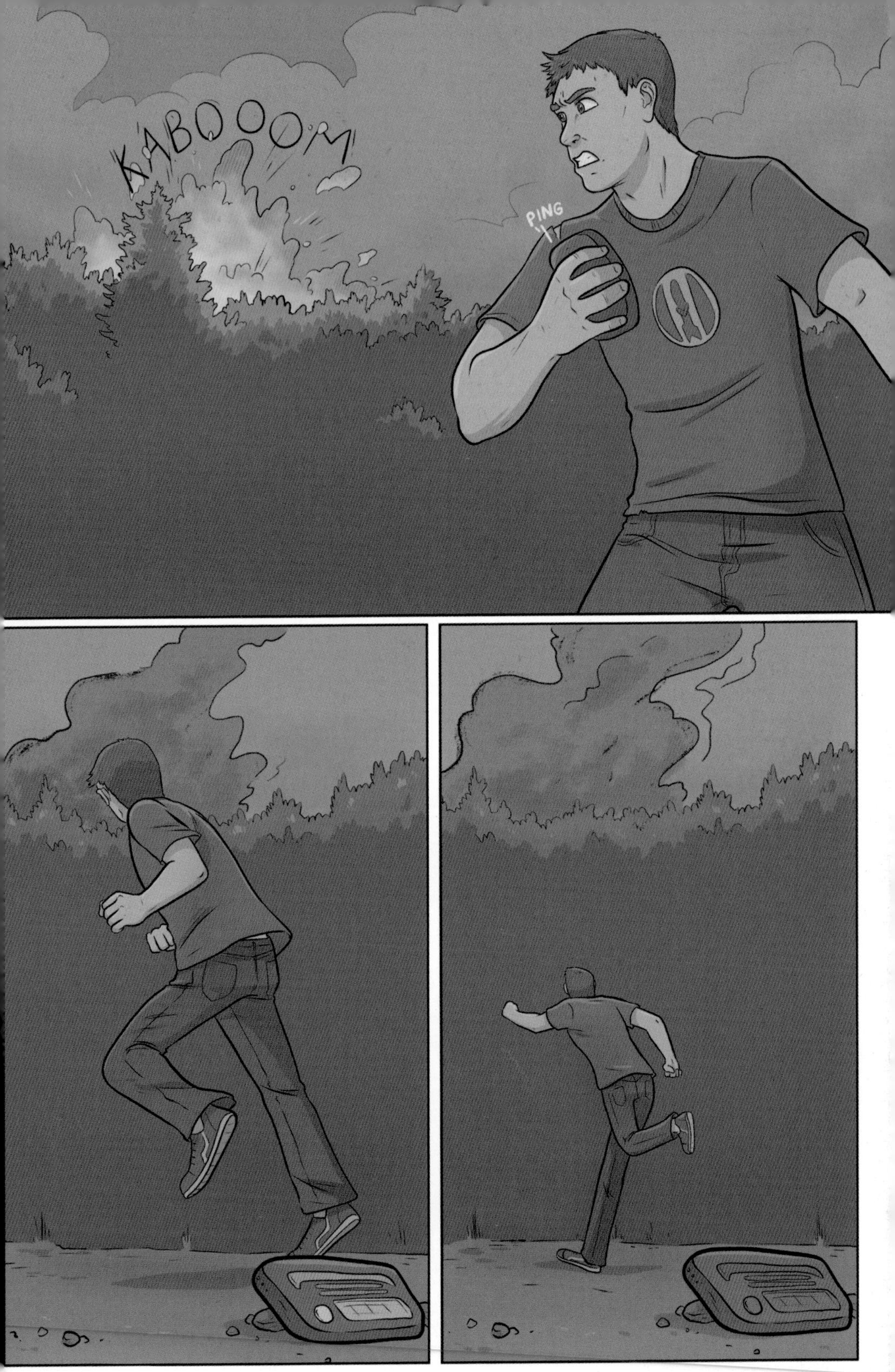
KABOOOM
PING

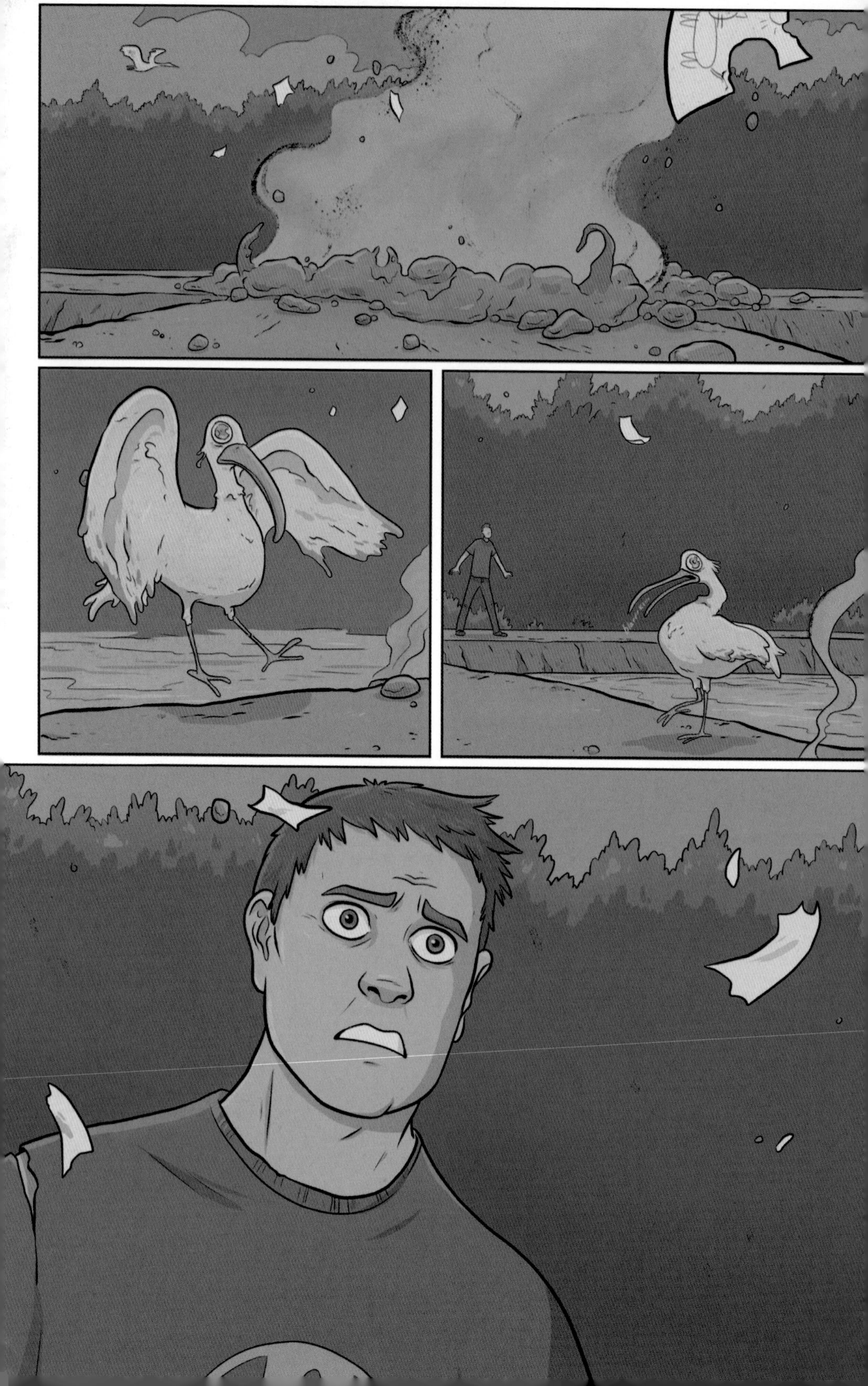

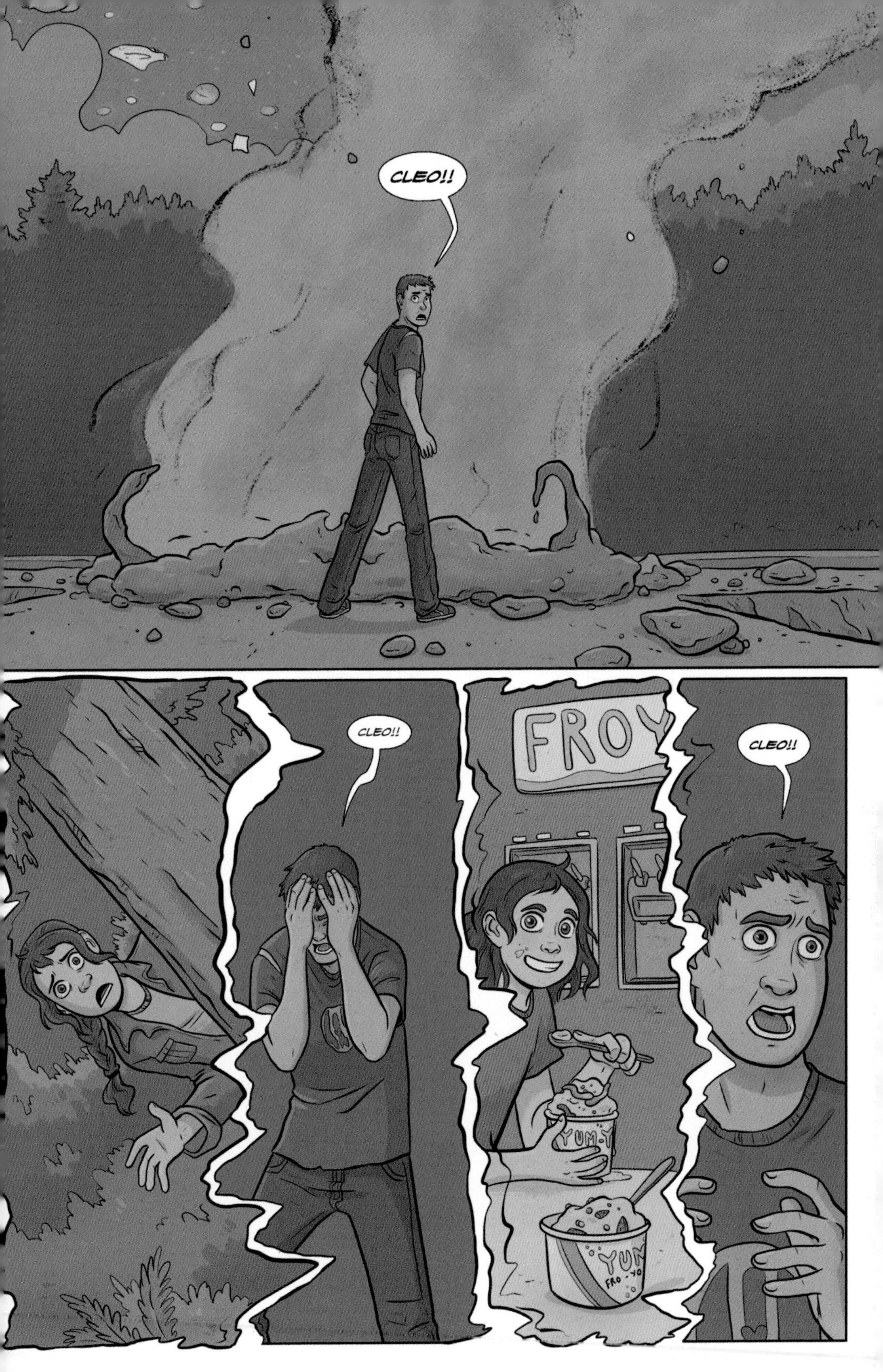
CLEO!!
CLEO!!
FROY
CLEO!!
YUM-Y
YUM
FRO-YO

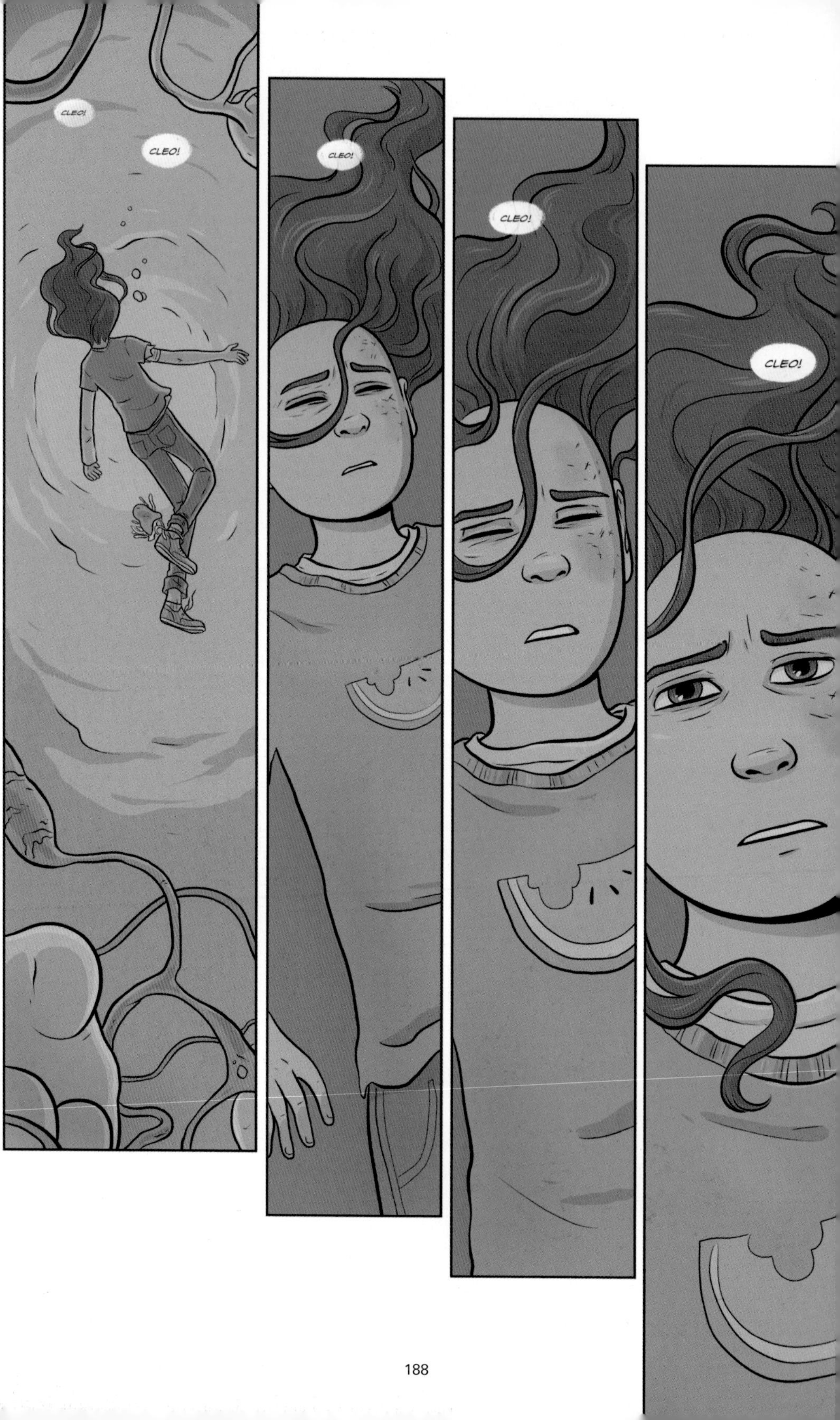
CLEO!
CLEO!
CLEO!
CLEO!
CLEO!

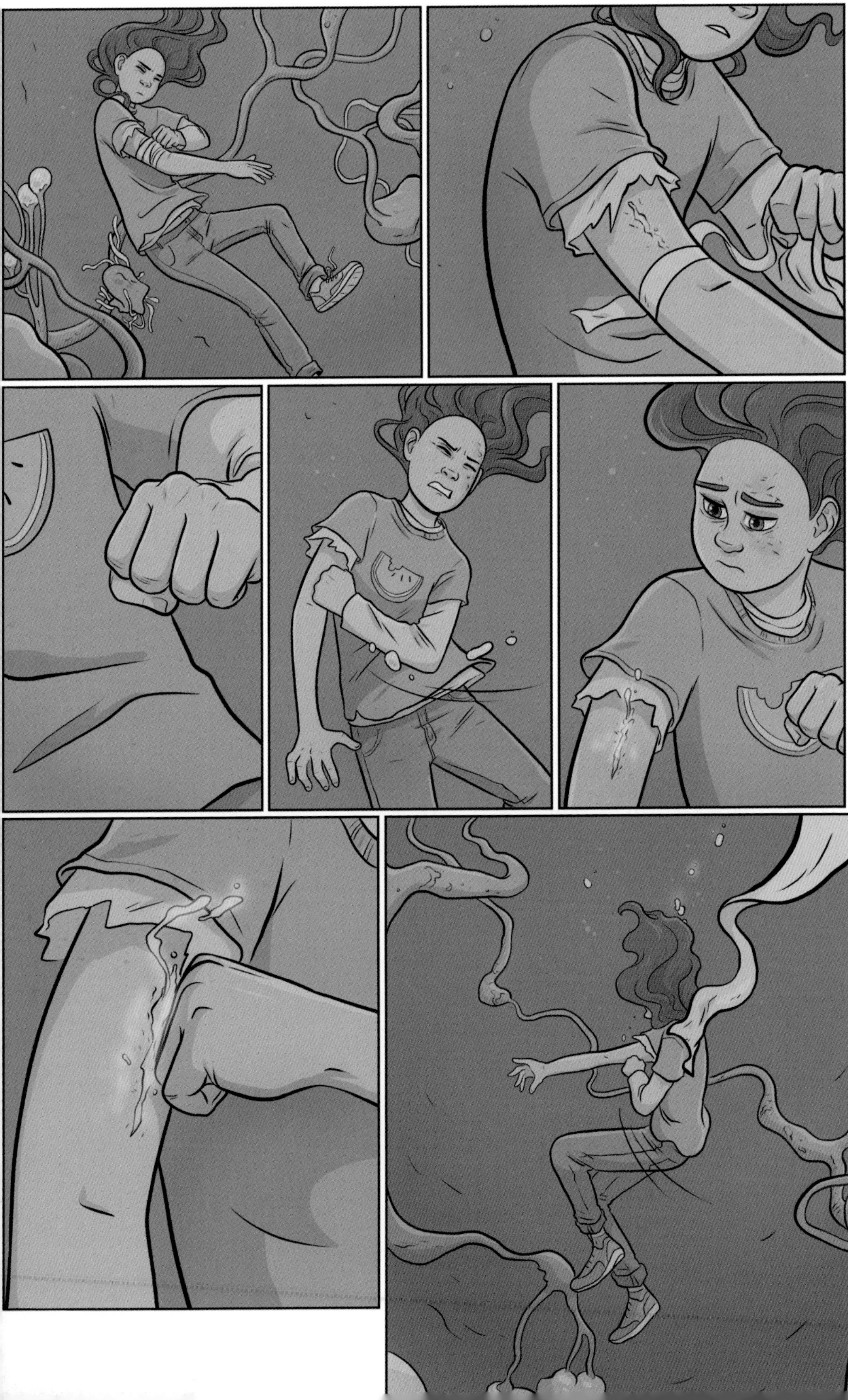

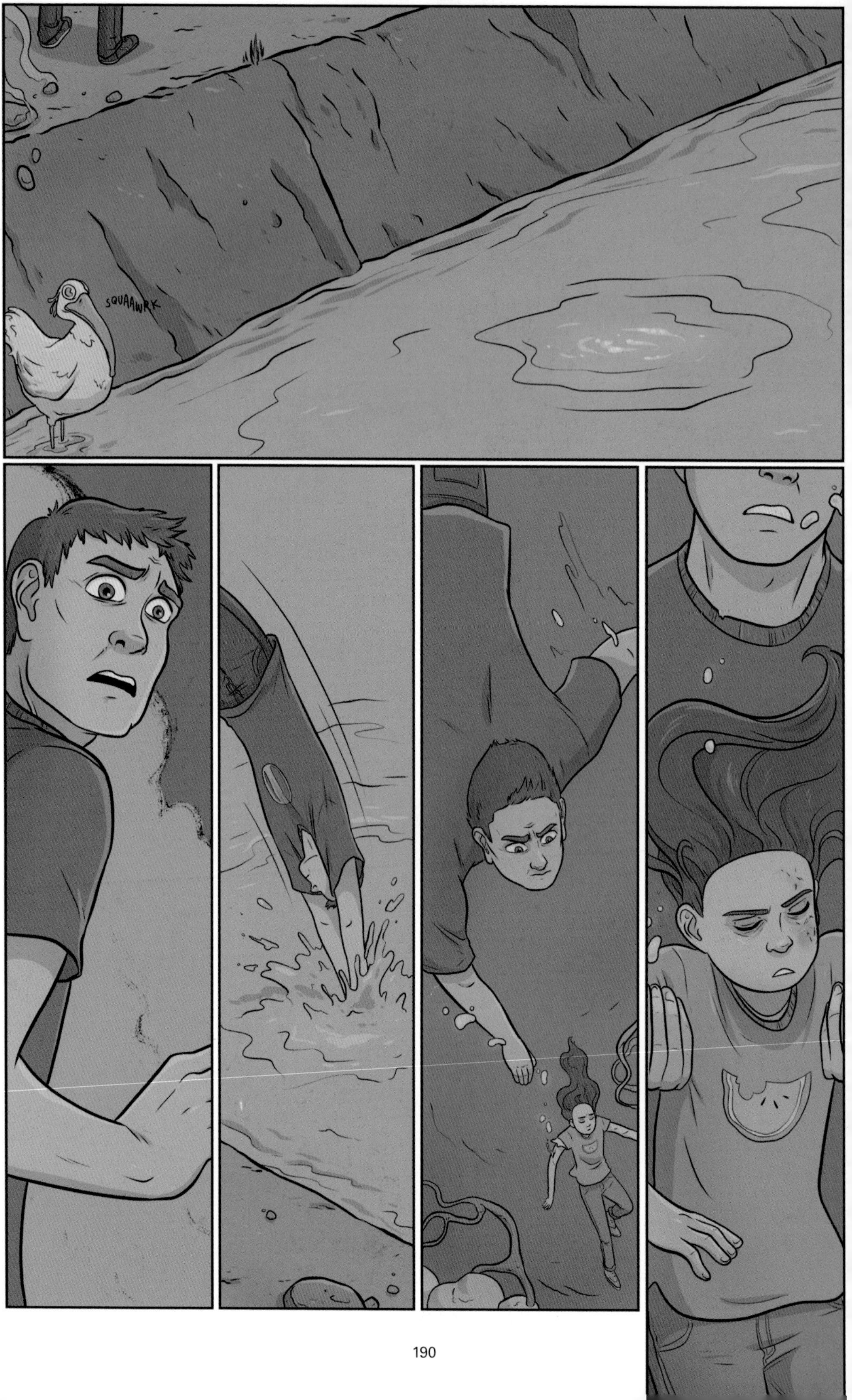
SQUAAWRK

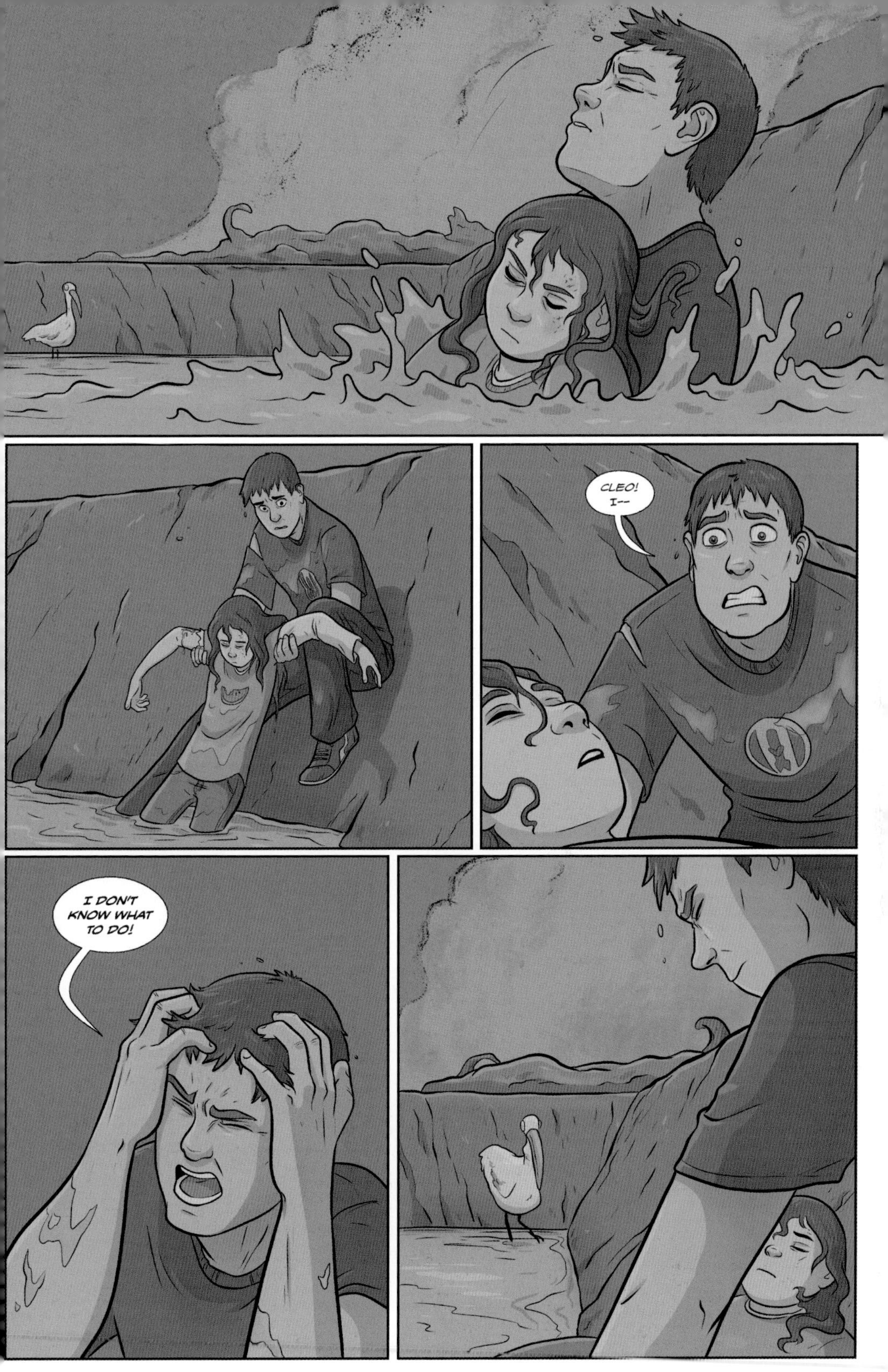
CLEO!
I--
I DON'T KNOW WHAT TO DO!

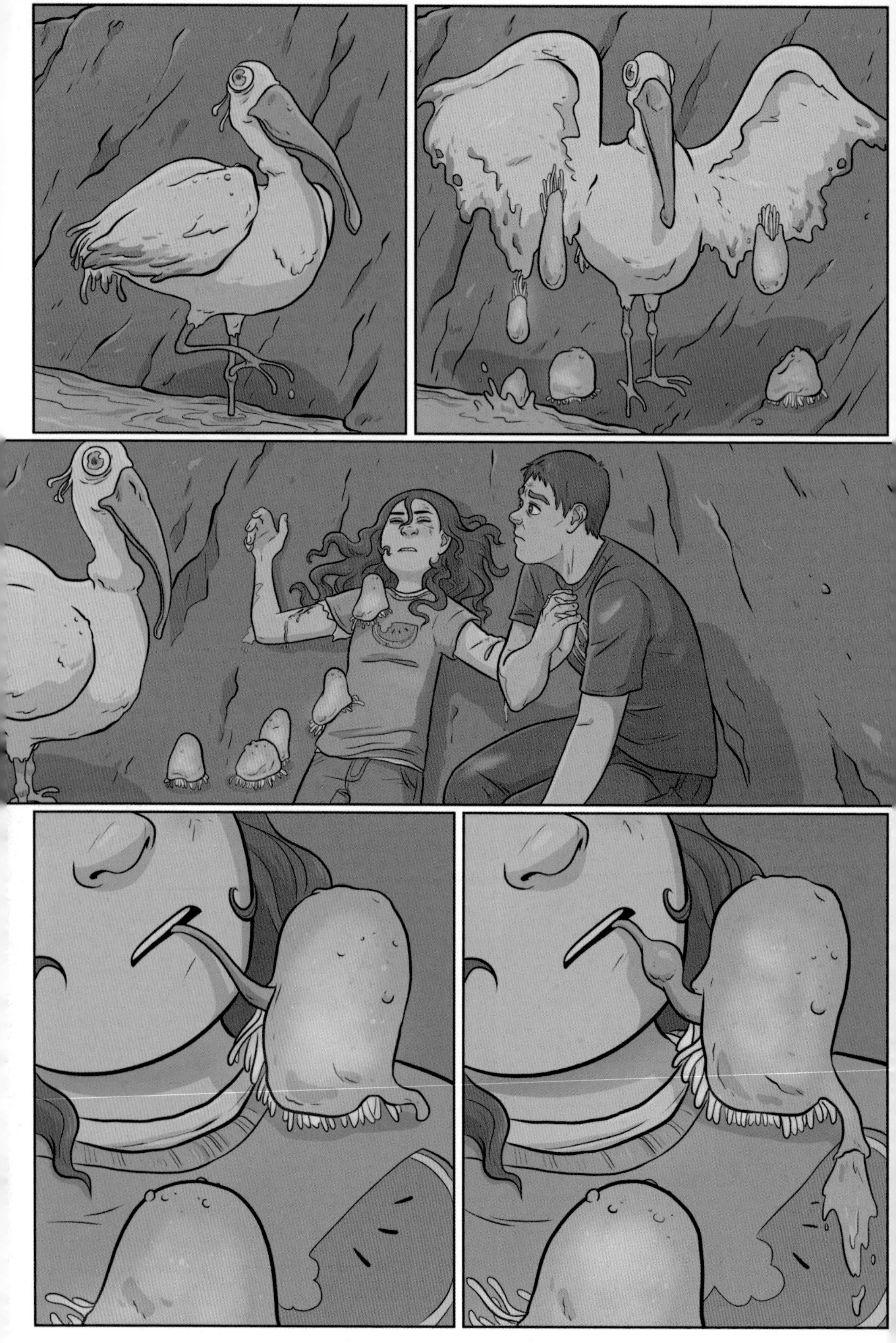

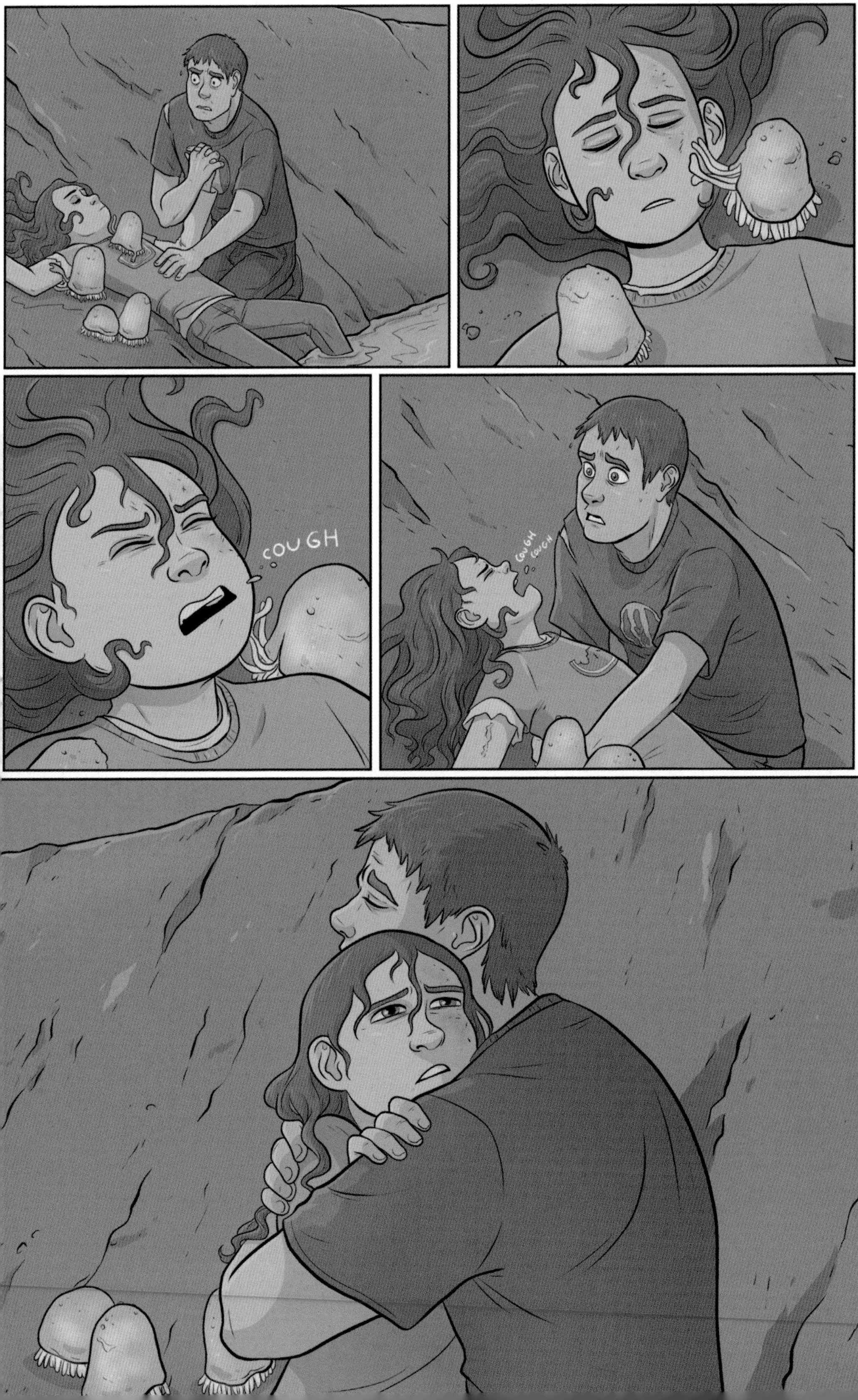
COUGH
COUGH
COUGH

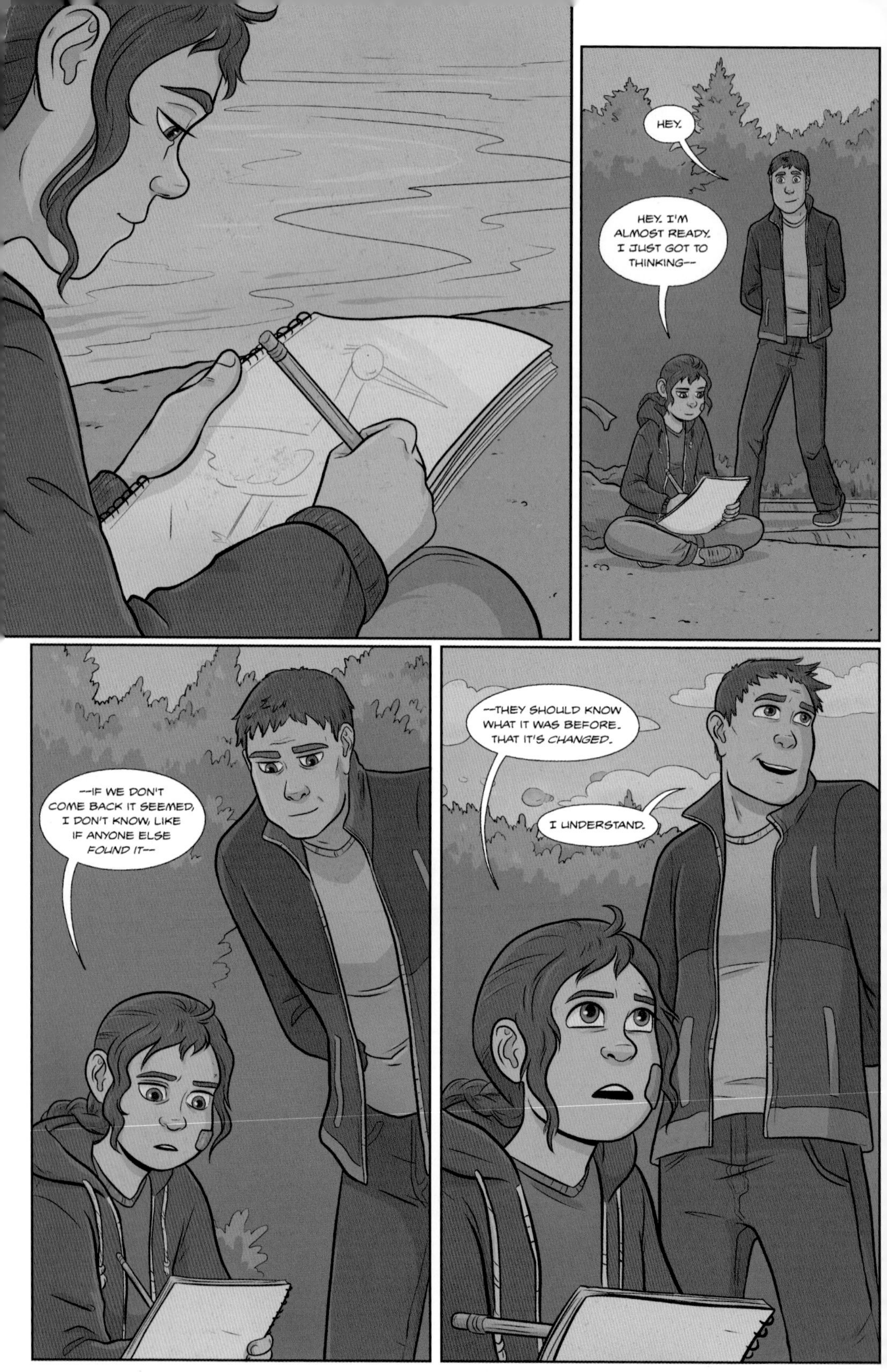
HEY.
HEY. I'M ALMOST READY. I JUST GOT TO THINKING--
--IF WE DON'T COME BACK IT SEEMED, I DON'T KNOW, LIKE IF ANYONE ELSE FOUND IT--
--THEY SHOULD KNOW WHAT IT WAS BEFORE. THAT IT'S *CHANGED*.
I UNDERSTAND.

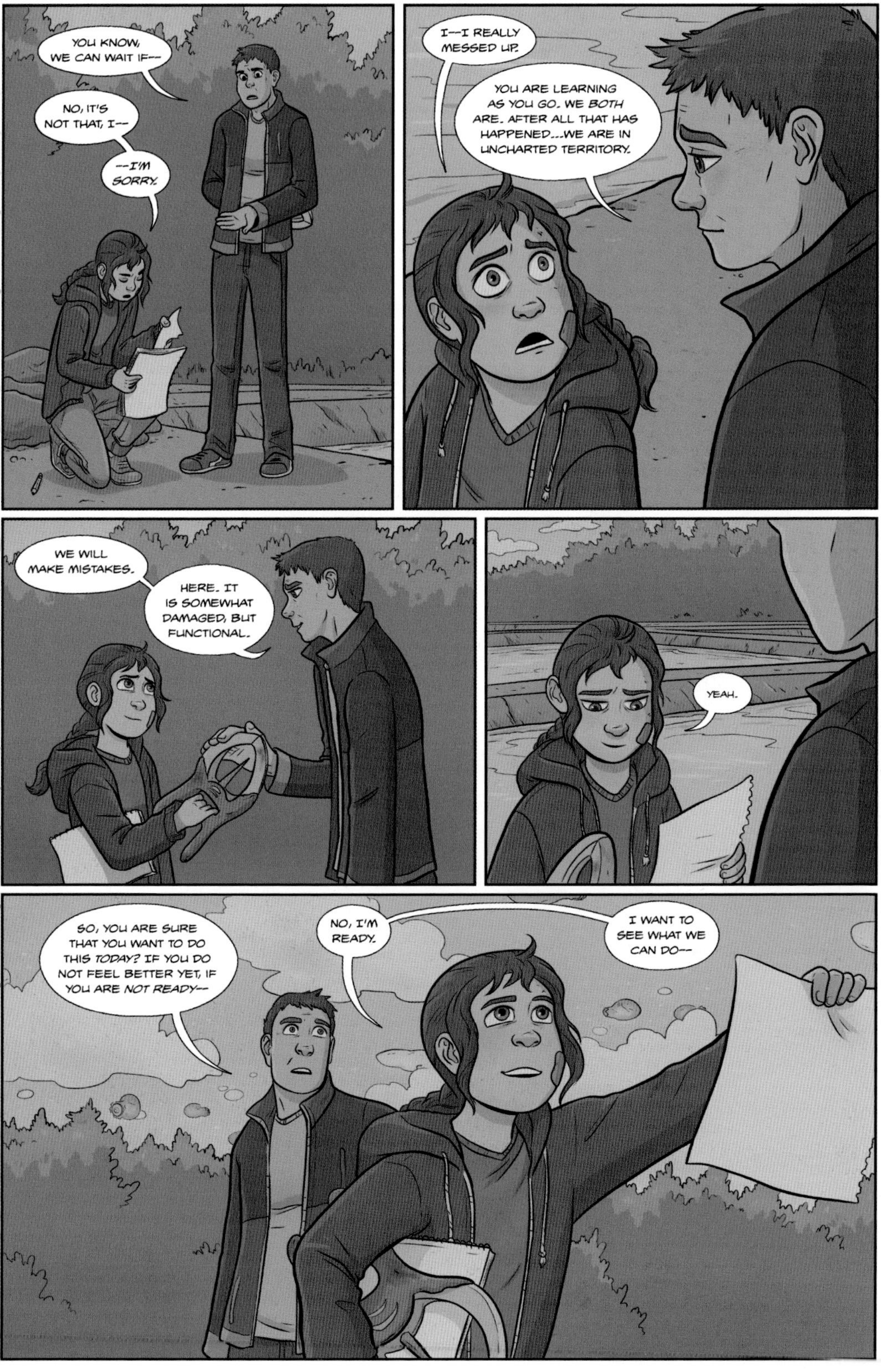
YOU KNOW, WE CAN WAIT IF--
NO, IT'S NOT THAT, I--
--I'M SORRY.
I--I REALLY MESSED UP.
YOU ARE LEARNING AS YOU GO. WE *BOTH* ARE. AFTER ALL THAT HAS HAPPENED...WE ARE IN UNCHARTED TERRITORY.
WE WILL MAKE MISTAKES.
HERE. IT IS SOMEWHAT DAMAGED, BUT FUNCTIONAL.
YEAH.
SO, YOU ARE SURE THAT YOU WANT TO DO THIS *TODAY?* IF YOU DO NOT FEEL BETTER YET, IF YOU ARE *NOT READY*--
NO, I'M READY.
I WANT TO SEE WHAT WE CAN DO--

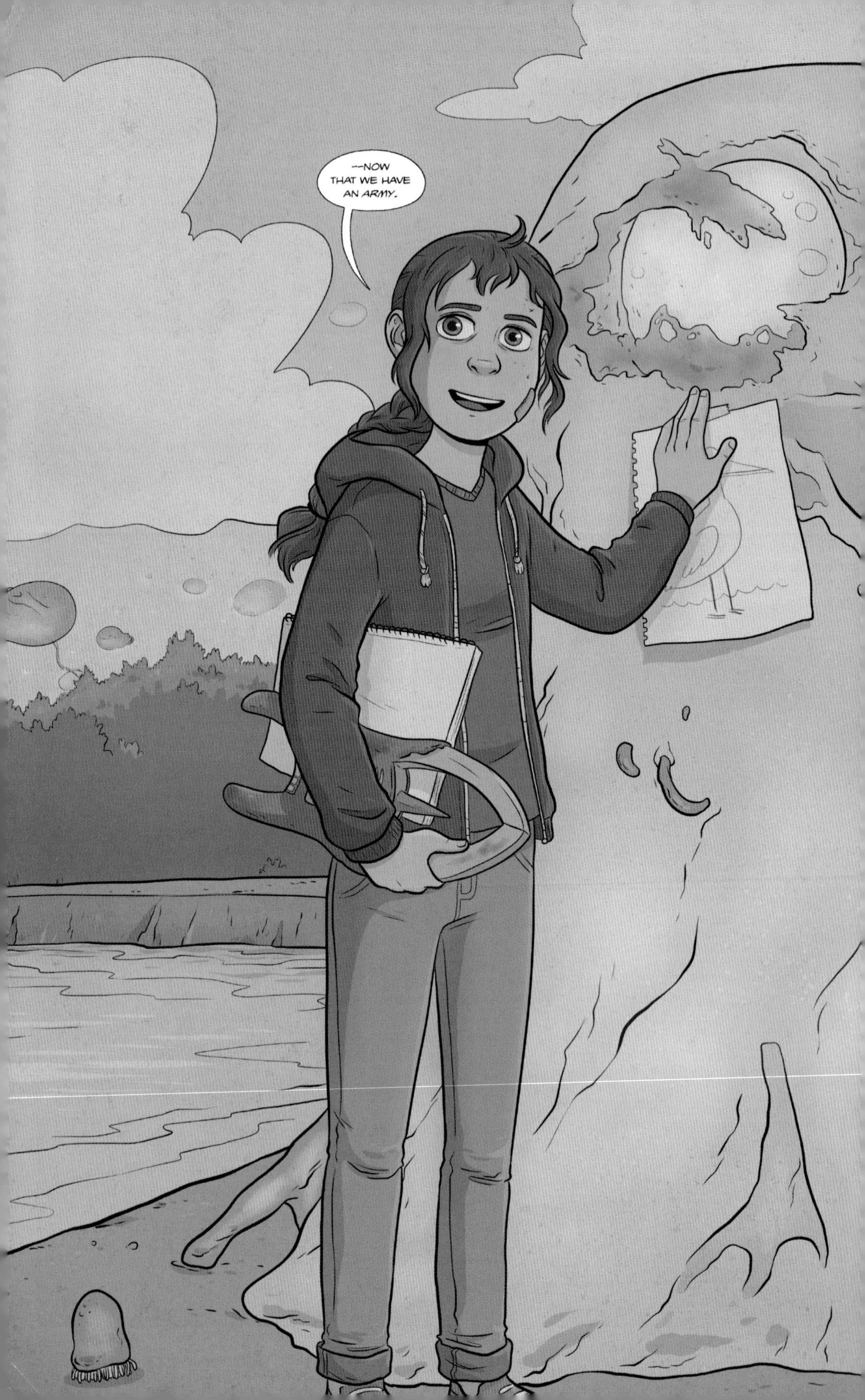
--NOW THAT WE HAVE AN *ARMY*.

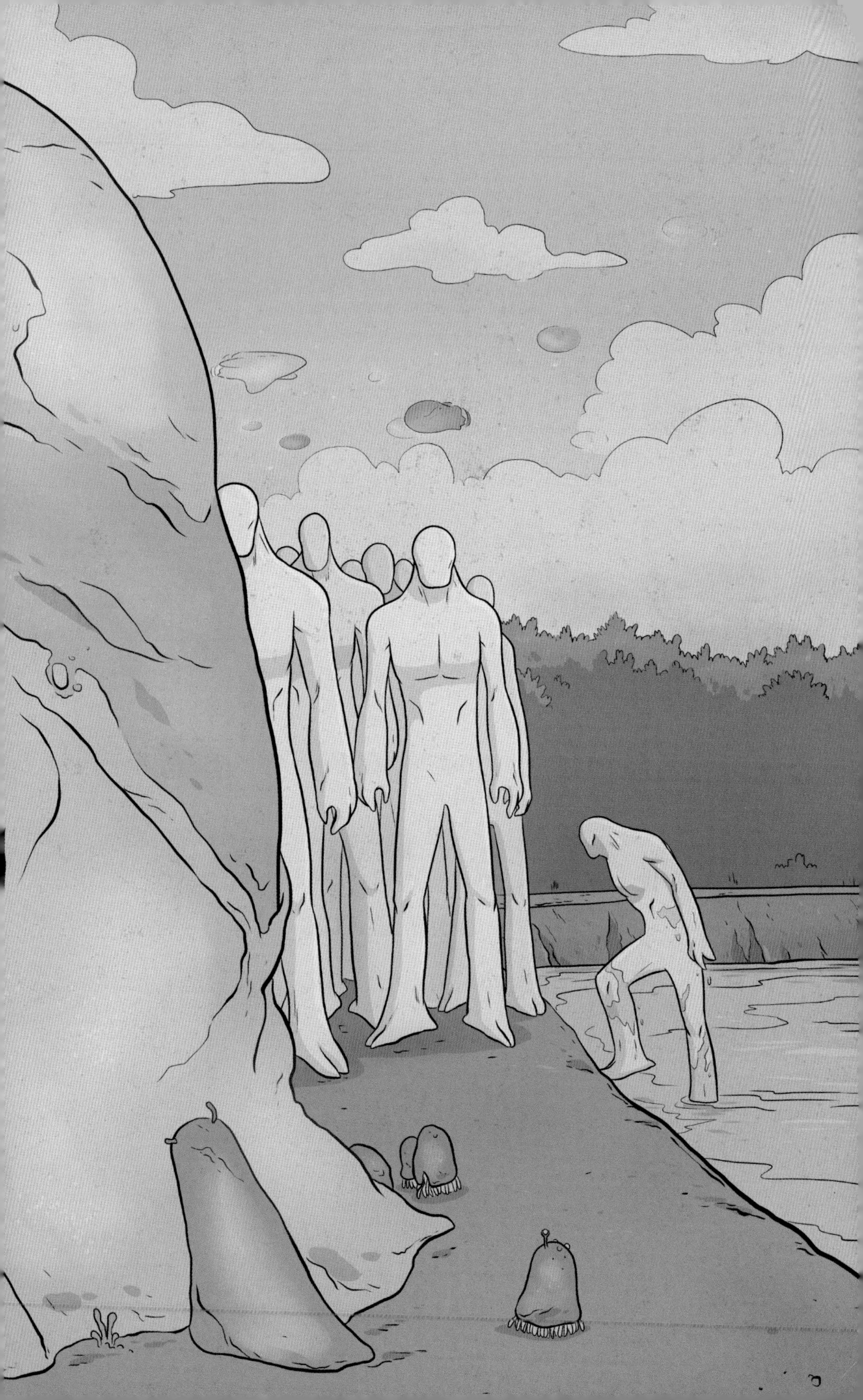

ACKNOWLEDGMENTS

A huge thanks to Rilo Kiley (Jenny Lewis, Blake Sennett, Pierre de Reeder, and Jason Boesel) for their permission to have Cleo sing lines from "Spectacular Views," one of my favorite songs ever from one of my favorite albums ever (*The Execution of All Things*), and to the members of Love and Rockets (Daniel Ash, David J, Kevin Haskins, and manager Darwin Meiners) for permission to use the band's logo. Love and Rockets was formative listening for me as a kid, and continues to be in constant rotation. Being able to incorporate these things I love so much into the world of *Lifeformed* blows my mind.

Many thanks to Sabeeha Rehman for her invaluable guidance in bringing Ayesha's journey to life. You should pick up Sabeeha's wonderful memoir *Threading My Prayer Rug: One Woman's Journey from Pakistani Muslim to American Muslim*. It's a fun, enlightening, and heartwarming read.

Thanks to everyone at Dark Horse for helping us craft and promote *Lifeformed*, especially Rachel, Jenny, Cara, Dustin, and Dave.

To my friends who provide guidance, support and feedback, including Tripp Ritter, Kyle Walters Sheaffer, Matt Howell, Julie Vakoc, Ben Vakoc, Kirsten Ekman, Mike Russell, Paul DeVe, Robert Feeney, Benjamin Skaggs, Scott Dunn, Ryan Burke, Michael Winston, Merrick Monroe and Michael Ring: your willingness to take time out of your lives to read yet another pitch or script and offer your thoughts is greatly appreciated, and I would have stopped long ago without it.

To all the shops and schools that hosted us, to the comic shops, press folks, and fans that got behind *Cleo Makes Contact* and helped spread the word, and to our Patreon patrons: Benjamin Skaggs, AMSedivy, David Mair, Doug O'Laughlin, Dylan Campbell, Jim and Laurie Anderson, Khail Ballard, and Linda Johansson, we are so grateful.

And finally, thanks to my wife Rebecca and my daughters Adeline and Eliza for adapting to and supporting my new comics-making-and-promoting-centric existence.

-MATT MAIR LOWERY

I wholeheartedly thank everyone mentioned above, and also want to thank my friends and family for encouraging me, supporting me, and motivating me with cookies through the whole process. Thank you, Lisa Morris; your friendship is priceless to me. Thank you Mom, Dad, and Reesa for believing in me no matter what. Thank you Naomi, Joe, Henry, and Lola for all the love and laughter. Thanks to my Portland family at Theophilus; you guys ground me and add so much spice to this crazy life. And thank you to our readers who enjoyed the first book enough to make this one possible!

-CASSIE ANDERSON

ABOUT THE WRITER

Matt Mair Lowery, a Portland native, studied journalism and creative writing at the University of Oregon. He maintains (and sometimes tests) his sanity by nerding out with his two daughters, running through North Portland's industrial landscapes, and overanalyzing everything with his wife.

ABOUT THE ARTIST

Cassie Anderson is a freelance artist and the creator behind the graphic novel *Extraordinary: A Story of an Ordinary Princess.* After earning a degree in sequential art (read: comics) from the Savannah College of Art and Design, she moved to Portland, OR, where she currently lives. When she's not drawing comics, she can be found baking tasty treats or exploring the great outdoors.

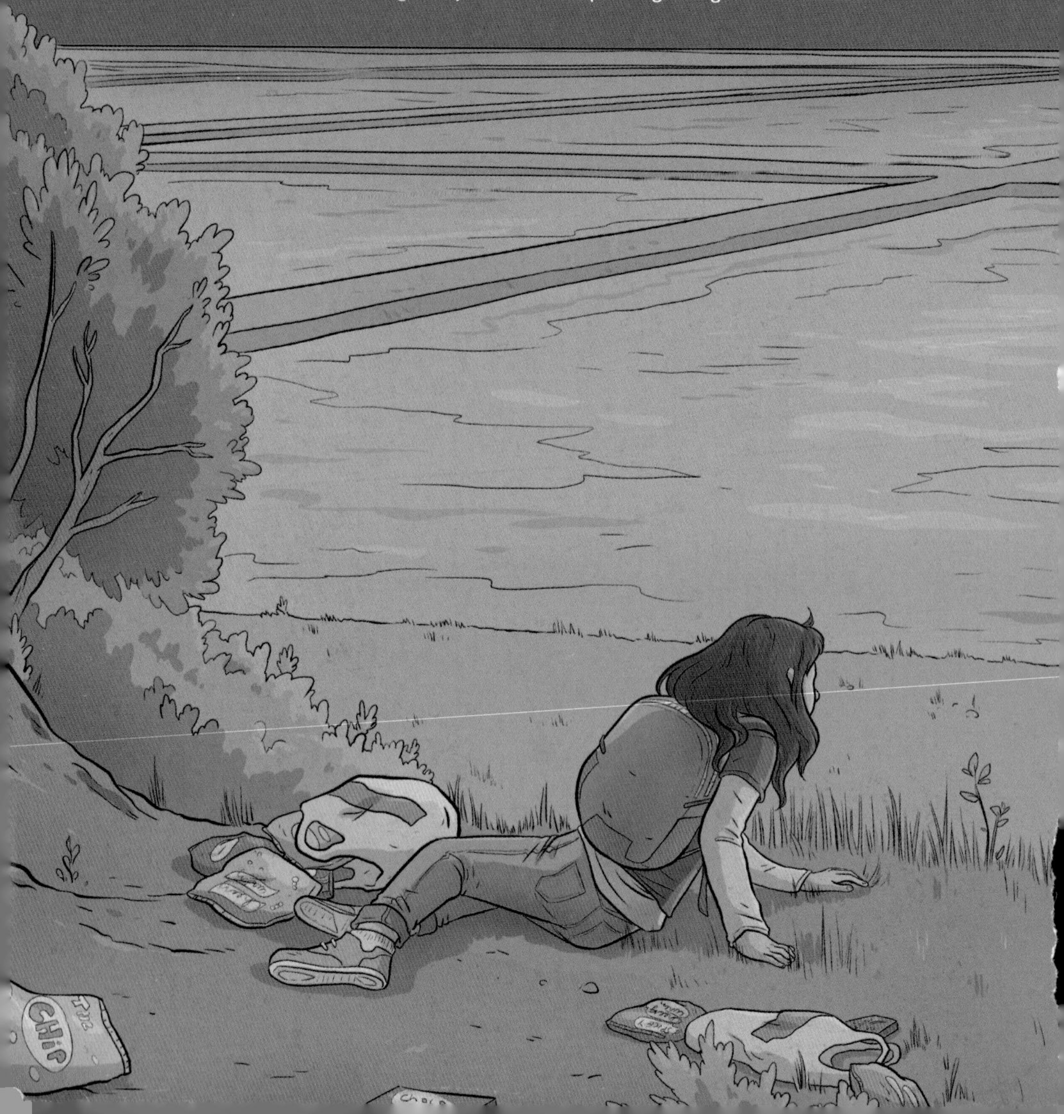
CHIP